MURDER BY SUICIDE

A David Crocket Novel

David Sterago

MURDER BY SUICIDE

ISBN: 978 - 1534966789
ISBN- 13: 1534966781

cover by twinartdesign

Joyce,

Thanks for your support in this my very first novel. I hope you enjoy it!

David Stugo

To my family and friends. This first one's for you.

ACKNOWLEDGMENTS

Sometimes writing the book is the easy part, and then comes everything else that most writers would rather not have to deal with. That's when it pays to have special friends and creative minds to help guide you through that post writing journey. Special thanks to Jeff Harris, Steven Daniels, Mike Nielsen, and Marcia Freiburger for having the patience to sift through the very long and wordy first couple of drafts. Thanks also to Geoffery Lamb and Jerem Schuster for their efforts in helping to make this a better book. Thanks to Cara O'Sullivan and C. Michael Perry for their hard work in editing, and finally to James Jakins for his tireless effort in trying to teach an old dog new computer tricks.

MURDER BY SUICIDE

PROLOGUE

There would be no divorce.

Martin Parker stared at his wife, Sylvia, lying on the bed reading her magazine. Sipping her wine.

So smug.

So sure of herself.

Did she really think that he was so obtuse that he wouldn't find out about her visit to Jakins, Jakins, and Schuster, divorce attorneys?

He had put in thirty-two years and it was time to get his due. Thirty-two years of her upper-crust bearing and subtle, yet endless, reminders of how she had lifted him from his middle-class upbringing to the pinnacles of high society. Years of complaining about his spending habits—digs and reminders that it was her money he had enjoyed all these years. Now she was thinking about throwing him out in the street like some common cabana boy after a fun-filled week in the Bahamas. Not on his life. Just hers.

A smile creased his lips.

He had planned this for over a year. It was foolproof. And even if someone did question her death, with his superior intellect, an IQ of over a hundred and eighty-three, and a charter member of Mensa, no one would be able to figure out how it had been done. Only stupid criminals got caught. He was far from stupid.

For thirty-two years he had tried to tell her family how smart he was, how he was being underutilized in the family corporation. Even when his "sainted" father-in-law and CEO of one of the largest retail companies in the entire country had died and the position became available, had he been invited to New York by the board of directors and given the position as a reward for his decades of dedication and hard work? Had he been shown the respect he deserved? No, his wife had been appointed CEO. Even then, had she decided to move back to New York to run the national empire and take him with her? No, she had decided to run it from Salt Lake City. For weeks he had argued and pleaded with her to move to New York where his business superiority would be appreciated. Still, she had refused, citing the Internet, digital conferences and meetings, their home, friends and Faith, their daughter, whom she couldn't bear to be without.

And what had his reward been? He was promoted to vice-president of sales over all the Utah stores. Vice-president! It was an insult to his years of service.

But he was about to show them all.

Only no one would ever know. How tragic that his greatest accomplishment, committing the perfect murder, was to be unknown and unheralded.

She crinkled her nose at something she had read. In an instant he was reminded of the day they had met. It was Christmas, 1982. He was skating in Central Park when he noticed a young woman being thrown to the ice as exuberant teenage boys whipped past her. Sadly, no one seemed to care.

He skated over and offered her a hand. Embarrassed, she took his hand and as she stood, she had crinkled her nose in such a way that she reminded him of his favorite television actress, Elizabeth Montgomery, from Bewitched. She was blonde and beautiful. He was smitten from the start.

What was he doing?

Was he really thinking of murdering the woman he had lived comfortably with for thirty-two years? Not all of it had been bad. He was living a good life. And she was the mother of his daughter, after all. Faith, of course, was more like her mother than him. She was stubborn and determined to do things her way. And she was sucking his inheritance down the drain with that egregious talent agency of hers. But that was going to stop.

But still, murder? Had it really come to this?

He was beginning to waiver when she looked up and noticed him standing in the doorway. He knew she had gone through a serious bout of insomnia for the past two nights, and was exhausted and stretched thin. But he also knew, from past experience that he would be the brunt of her exhaustion.

"What do you want?" Her voice was cold and distant. His smile disappeared and his brow wrinkled. The image of her arrogant and self-serving sister, Erin Rosenstein Walker, suddenly popped into his head. That afternoon, when he had come home early and overheard their lunch conversation, her nose so far in the air he was surprised it hadn't hit the ceiling.

"Well of course I believe you are doing the right thing," he heard Erin say as he hung his coat on the coat rack in the hallway. Quietly, he had edged closer to the dining room.

"That bore of a husband of yours would bankrupt this company if you left it to him. Look at what he has done with the Salt Lake City store. It's barely making a profit."

She took a bite of her cranberry-orange salad then wiped her mouth with her silk napkin, though there was no food on it.

"If you are seriously considering retiring for this silly plan of yours, then you have no choice but to step down as CEO and appoint someone in your place."

Had his loving wife considered him for the position? Not only had she not considered him, a few months later she announced that she was planning to make her nephew, Jared Walker, CEO of the family business. Adding insult to injury, she changed her will, leaving everything to Faith.

His mouth tightened and his jaw clenched as he thought about that luncheon six months ago. Since then he had planned her demise like NASA planning a space launch. Now it was here. And he was going to enjoy it.

"I brought you something to help you relax dear," he replied, the politeness oozing out of him. "So you can get some sleep tonight."

She put the magazine down on the bed as he approached. "I have all I need," she said motioning to the bottle of red wine on the nightstand.

Martin smiled and gently refilled her glass. "You need your rest, dear. You have done nothing but toss and turn for the last two nights."

"Thank you, but I'll be fine." She lowered her glasses and rubbed her tired eyes.

Parker removed a plastic container of sleeping pills from his pocket and opened the lid. With a smile he sat them on the nightstand. "I insist, dear."

"I said I don't need anything else," she replied exasperated. As she readjusted her reading glasses and picked up the magazine, she noticed the gloves. "Why are you wearing gloves?"

How odd, she thought, but then again this was Martin and he was notorious for doing unusual things.

When Martin turned the bottle of sleeping pills upside

down and poured a handful into his gloved hand, she became nervous. Surely he didn't expect her to take the whole bottle. 'Why that would kill me,' she thought.

He moved next to her, his eyes narrowing and his easy smile disappearing altogether.

"I am afraid you have no choice in the matter, my dear."

He reached for her.

Realizing what was happening, she tried to move but he grabbed a handful of her hair. Pulling back on her hair with such force, Sylvia thought her hair would be ripped out by the roots. She frantically tried to struggle free, but to no avail. His grip was too powerful and so tight that she had no choice but to remain still for fear of breaking her neck.

As she tried to scream, he shoved the pills down her throat.

Angered by her resistance, he slapped her hard with his gloved hand. Her thick hair along the side of her face cushioned most of the blow, but still her head snapped violently around.

As she flayed her hands trying to scratch him, he yanked her head back with even more force until she thought her neck would snap. With her head back, he grabbed the glass of wine and poured it down her throat.

Trying to avoid swallowing the pills she tried to spit them out, only to have Martin's gloved hand clamp over her mouth and nose. Her eyes wide with fright, she had no choice but to swallow the pills.

With a vicious smile, Parker released his grip on his wife. She tried to get up, but he shoved her back onto the bed. As she tried to rise once more, Martin grabbed the pillow from under her head and quickly stuffed it over her face, forcing her back onto the bed. Holding it tight against her, he was careful not to suffocate her only keep her on the bed.

"Relax, Sylvia. Soon it will be over."

He held the pillow against her face until the struggle

began to lessen. Carefully he removed the pillow. Her face was tear stained. He almost felt sorry for her.

Frantically she glanced at the large oil painting of her father, mother, and herself as a child hanging on the wall. He was her hero and had saved her more than once when she was a girl. But now he was gone and couldn't save her.

Noticing her desperate look, Parker laughed. "Your old man cannot help you now. But look on the positive side. You will be back together soon."

Fighting to keep her glazed eyes open, she whispered her protest. "You won't get away with this."

"On the contrary, my dear, I have every intention of getting away with this."

He smiled as he reached down to adjust the glasses on her face. Her breath was becoming fainter as the combination of wine and sleeping pills began to take effect.

"When they find your body, I will be miles away."

His smile turned sour. "You always thought I was too addle-headed to run the company. Well, you were wrong."

Cleaning the wine glass to make sure any finger prints he might have smudged were gone, he then wrapped her fingers around the empty wine glass. Satisfied that her fingerprints would be clear, he placed it back on the night stand. He followed the same procedure with the empty bottle of pills. "I will have the company and all your money."

He carefully positioned the magazine back on her stomach and folded her hands across the magazine. She looked at him with puzzlement. He smiled at the anticipation of proving his brilliance once again.

"You really thought I was too timid to do anything about you a g r e e i n g t o m a k e J a r e d C E O a n d t h e n changing your will and leaving everything to Faith? I warned you about going through with that, remember?"

He lifted the bottle of wine and filled the empty glass about half full. Sitting the bottle back on the table, he positioned the glass as it might be if she had set it on the nightstand. Satisfied, he knocked it over, spilling the wine onto the surface. It was almost perfect, he mused. Taking the bottle of pills he spilled the remaining few onto the nightstand, mingling with the wine. He laid the plastic container on its side, a perfect picture of a depressed woman ending it all.

Removing his gloves, he stared transfixed at the symmetry of the scene. The wine. The pills. It was perfect. He smiled down at his dying wife.

"The only down side to this perfect crime is that no one will ever know that it was orchestrated by me. My greatest moment and it has to remain anonymous." He sighed. "The price of success, I am afraid."

Strolling to the large dresser, he laid his gloves on the corner. He was having trouble keeping the smile off his face. As he started for the door, he stopped to make one more sweep of the scene. Everything had to look normal: the empty bottle of pills, the wine glass with her fingerprints, her comfortable position and the magazine she always read in bed. Success was in the details. And Martin was building his successful murder one detail at a time. There would be no questioning her suicide.

With a satisfied smirk, he moved to the air conditioner and turned it on full blast. By the time his neighbor, whom he planned on calling Sunday morning, discovered her, the room would be cold enough so that the body would still be fresh. Even the most skilled coroner would have no choice but to rule that she had died no earlier than Saturday night. And since he would be away all weekend on his annual September fishing trip to Lake Powell, with plenty of witnesses, who could possibly suspect him? It was perfect. As he neared the door, he glanced back at his wife lying still on the bed, her breath coming in shallow gasps. By the time he loaded the car with his fishing equipment and backed out of the garage, she would be dead.

"You have never looked better, my dear."

Smiling, he turned off the light and closed the bedroom door.

***

At the end of September, when the temperature was beginning to drop in Salt Lake City, Martin and Sylvia would spend a weekend at Lake Powell, one of the premier vacation sites along the Utah/Arizona border, with their friends, the Wingates, enjoying the warm Southern Utah weather. Don Wingate was a Real Estate mogul who lived in South Jordan. Since he loved fishing and spending time on the lake, he had bought a luxurious houseboat, which he docked at the large man-made lake. Unlike Martin and the Wingates who enjoyed fishing and being on the lake, Sylvia was much less enthusiastic and, therefore, she and Martin would show up for the last weekend of the trip. While Martin and Don would spend the hours fishing and boating, Sylvia and Bonnie would spend the time playing cards, talking, shopping, and drinking.

After killing his wife Friday night, Martin Parker paid cash for a cheap motel in Payson, Utah, some fifty miles south of Salt Lake City. With no record of his stop in Payson, a 6:30 am credit card receipt proving he was in Nephi, Utah at that precise moment Saturday morning, was another building block in an air-tight alibi that he believed not even Sherlock Holmes would have been able to crack. He arrived at Lake Powell around 10:00. After apologizing profusely to his hosts, explaining that Sylvia had changed her mind at the last moment, just not feeling up for the trip, they had hit the lake for an afternoon of fishing and boating.

By four-thirty they were back on the houseboat and below deck, out of the hot sun. As Martin, Bonnie and Don Wingate relaxed in the kitchen with beer and snacks,

Martin sat his beer on the kitchen table and smiled at his friends. It was almost five o'clock and time to cement another stone into the block that would be his perfect alibi.

"I want to call Sylvia, if you don't mind?"

Don Wingate grunted. "I thought you came here to fish?"

"I did, but that doesn't mean I don't miss my wife."

"I've never seen anyone so whipped as you, Martin. It hasn't even been a day," Don laughed as he opened another beer. "At least give her some time to miss you."

"What can I say—thirty-two years of true love." Martin picked up his cell phone from the kitchen table.

"You know I don't like being without her."

Don took another swig of his Miller. "Cell phone service here is hit and miss at best, so you might want to use our land line in the bedroom."

"You don't mind?"

"For thirty-two years of true love? Be my guest.""

Martin jumped up and eagerly rushed into the bedroom at the end of the narrow hallway. The phone sat on the table by the bed. Leaving the door open, he picked up the phone and moved to the center of the bed so that everyone in the kitchen could hear and see him. Once he was situated, he rang his home land line. He had made sure to unhook the answering machine so it would simply ring instead of recording the call.

"Hello sweetheart, how are you?" He said cheerfully. "I miss you too," he continued in a loud voice. "No, I didn't catch anything today, but Don caught an eight pound striped bass."

Parker covered the receiver with his hand. "Wasn't it eight pounds, Don?" He yelled towards the kitchen.

After a pause, Wingate yelled back, his voice vibrating throughout the houseboat. "It was nine and a half pounds, my friend, so eat your heart out."

"He's says it was nine and a half pounds, but we all know how he exaggerates," Parker loudly laughed.

"You are just jealous," Wingate boomed again from the kitchen.

"Sylvia says stop exaggerating," Parker replied. Suddenly his voice took on a somber tone. "Have you thought about what I said last night?" There was a pause then Parker raised his voice more fervently. "Sylvia, you cannot just shut yourself away from everyone." Suddenly he yelled into the phone.

"Then I am coming home. You are more important to me than anything else. I can be home in four hours," he said forcefully.

From the kitchen Don and Bonnie tried not to listen, but the temptation was just too much. Without much effort they heard Parker's strong and firm voice. "All right, but you have to promise me you will go see Doctor Bingham first thing Monday morning." Like a teenager with his first crush, his voice became soft and low. "I love you too," he giggled, before warping back into lecture mode. "Sylvia, first thing Monday morning, I mean it. Good-by."

Don and Bonnie tried not to let on that they had heard his conversation. Both were concerned at the way it had gone, so when Martin sat down, looking like a patient who had just been told he only had six months to live, Don gathered up the courage to inquire. "Is something wrong?"

Martin sat quietly for a moment then spoke softly. "I didn't want to say anything, but Sylvia's been depressed and I am afraid it's getting worse."

"Depressed?" Bonnie's eyebrow shot up in surprise. "I would have never pegged her as being depressed."

"She's drinking more and lately she doesn't even want to get out of bed. I didn't want to say anything but that was the reason she didn't want to make the trip."

Don leaned closer to the table. "Surely it's nothing too serious."

"I don't know. She assured me everything was fine but I am not so sure."

"Do you think you should go home?" Bonnie asked gently.

"I am afraid if I did leave, she would feel like it was her fault and that would send her spiraling down even more. I really believe I should stay. I hope you don't mind."

"Of course not," Bonnie answered immediately. "We love having you here."

Before Don Wingate could emphasis his wife's statement their seventeen year old daughter, Chelsea, appeared at the door, impatiently tapping her long colorful blue and red nails on the kitchen door jam.

"Dad, can I take the car over to Big Water to shop and look around? I won't be long."

"Two hours and then I want you back here. We're all going out for dinner tonight."

"Yes, sir."

Chelsea Wingate rushed up the stairs and off the boat, leaving the adults to their boring discussion.

***

Richard West ran to catch his six-year-old, rebelling against his Sunday dress. Jan, his wife of twenty years, was busy dressing their four-year-old daughter, while their eleven-year-old and fifteen-year-old argued about who would ride shotgun. Sunday was supposed to be their day of rest, but trying to get four kids ready for a nine o'clock church service was anything but relaxing.

"You two stop arguing," he barked at his bickering children. "And make sure you have your coats, it's cold outside."

You have to love Utah weather, he mused. All week it

had been in the seventies, and without warning, late Saturday night, a mild cold front had hit, dropping the temperature to about forty-five degrees. Because of the dry air, it didn't seem that cold, but he still wanted his children to wear their coats.

Racing after his outlaw child, he caught him and lifted him into the air. The excited giggles of this little boy whom he loved so much made him smile. He couldn't blame him. Who wanted to get dressed in a stifling suit and tie and go to church? But it was important and that's what they did every Sunday.

He was struggling to straighten the small blue tie on his rambunctious six-year-old when his cell phone rang.

"Hello," he answered briskly.

"Rick?"

He didn't recognize the voice.

"This is Martin Parker."

This caught him by surprise. Why would Parker be calling him? It wasn't like they were the best of friends. In the five years since he and Jan had moved into the neighborhood, Parker had barely acknowledged their existence.

"I need a favor, please." He sounded frantic.

"What can I do?"

"Go check on Sylvia."

"Sylvia?" West replied somewhat confused. "Why, what's wrong?"

"I tried to reach her all last night but she did not answer. I'm worried about her."

"I'm about to leave for church."

"I have called twice this morning and she is still not answering. This is not like her. Is her car in the driveway?"

"Hang on." Lifting his son into his arms, he shuffled to the window. Sitting in his neighbor's drive way was Sylvia's silver BMW. "It's there. Maybe she's in the shower."

"Not for an hour. That is how long I have been trying to

reach her." Parker sighed. "Please, Rick, check for me. She is never away from her phone for this long. There is a spare key in the frog's mouth."

West glanced down at his watch. He figured it wouldn't take too long. They could still get to church on time if they hurried.

"All right, Martin, I'll go have a look."

"Call me as soon as you speak with her." Without another word, Martin disconnected the call.

Somewhat confused, West quickly took his son to Jan.

"That was Martin. He wants me to go over and check on Sylvia."

"Why?"

"He said he's been trying to reach her all last night and all this morning but she hasn't answered."

"That doesn't sound like Sylvia." Jan wet her fingers and smoothed down her daughter's hair.

"That's what he said." He started to hand the boy to his wife, but was stopped cold. "I can't take him now. Let Eric watch him. And hurry or we'll be late."

West dashed off and handed his son to his fifteen-year-old, who was not thrilled with the task.

Holding the spare key and hoping he wouldn't have to use it, West rang the doorbell. There was no answer. He rang again, leaning against the door to make sure it worked. As he heard the bell chime through the house, he waited. Again no answer. He pounded on the door. When no one answered, he pushed the key into the lock and opened the door.

"Sylvia?" he called as loudly as he could. His voice echoed through the perfectly polished entry hall. Still no answer.

Having worked for the past fifteen years as a computer programmer, he was not one to get overly alarmed. In his world of computers and analogues, there was always an answer to whatever the question was. It may take time to find, but it was always there. But this wasn't his computer world. As he made his way up the stairs of his neighbor's house, an eerie feeling was creeping up on him like a shadow on a sunny day. Like some dumb co-ed climbing the stairs in an empty house where eight murders have already occurred, he knew he should turn and run.

Stop it, he chided himself. This isn't a horror movie but Martin and Sylvia's expensive house.

"Sylvia?" he called as he reached the top of the stairs. "Sylvia?"

Only the silence and the hum of the air conditioner coming from the bedroom, greeted him. He wondered why she would have the air conditioner on today. He dismissed the thought and edged to the bedroom door.

"Sylvia?" He knocked on the closed door. When no sound returned, he reached down and opened the door.

The first thing he felt was the blast of cold air. The room felt like a meat locker. Then he noticed the body on the bed.

"Sylvia?"

Sylvia Parker was lying on her back, her glasses still on her face and a magazine lying across her chest. He stood there staring at the lifeless body, not knowing what to do. Should he feel for a pulse? Should he shake her? Should he call the police? What if he called the police and she was just a very sound sleeper? What if he shook her and she woke up and accused him of inappropriate actions? Cautiously, he edged closer to her. She didn't look asleep. She looked dead. His hand shaking, he gently shook her. The magazine fell from her chest. He leaped back almost slamming into the bureau.

Get a hold of yourself, he chastised. Taking a deep breath, he reached down and shook her harder. There was no reaction. She was cold. She wasn't asleep. She was dead.

Having watched numerous police shows on television, he knew he should not touch anything. And he didn't.

Backing out of the room, he glanced around at the surreal scene before him. Never in a million years would he have ever believed something like this would happen in this quiet neighborhood. With a shiver, he instinctively flipped off the air conditioner and reached for his cell phone.

Church was going to have to wait this morning.

One

August 16

Why don't men ever give you daffodils? Why is it always roses or carnations? Don't they know about daffodils, so delicate so fragile. Roses are fine, but everybody gives roses. Maybe that's why men do it—they think you'll like them because women are supposed to like roses. That's what they do in every movie. Why don't they get to know you, then they'd know what you like. Why don't they get to know you???? Is that too much to ask???????

Those were the first words I read from the diary. And four weeks later they still haunted me. Her frailty, her hope to be noticed by someone so as not to disappear into the dark spaces of the universe, drove me like a Mack truck.

The truth is I wanted to protect her, let her know life was

good and worth living, that some men do give daffodils. But most of all I wanted to find her. Who was she? Where was she? Why was her diary filled with such despair?

I know I sound like some love-starved schmuck who can only worship women from afar because he knows he'll never have one. Maybe I am. I've never been able to maintain any kind of normal relationship with a woman for longer than a couple of years. It says more about me than the women. I'm a private investigator. My name is David Crockett.

Yeah, I said David Crockett. Not Dave and NEVER EVER DAVY! I've spent many a night in jail for busting some clown over the head because he thought it was cute to call me Davy and to sing that mind-numbing song after I warned him not to. Nothing against my great-great-great grandfather, Congressman David Crockett, who gave his life in the defense of liberty at the Alamo, but I've had to live with this name for thirty-five years. It's no picnic. Don't parents ever think before they name a kid? My parents and I have had many heated discussions about my name. I won none of them.

It had been three weeks since Jackson Paine opened my office door, hoping to get a favor from me.

I was trying to focus on the morning paper, which for me is difficult since my eyes don't wake up before ten. Yes, I still like to read the newspaper. As convenient as computers are, there is something comfortable about reading the morning paper with a cup of coffee. A two-paragraph story about Richard Harvey, a prominent attorney at one of the major law firms in Salt Lake, who had been in a traffic accident and suffered a concussion, made me smile. Anytime a lawyer can't remember anything for a day or two just seems like a gift from Heaven.

Paine didn't knock. He never knocks. He just barged in like he owned the place. "Here," he said without any fanfare.

"I figured you could use a strong cup of coffee."

He was right.

I know what you're thinking. But you're wrong. Real PIs rarely live swinging lives like fictional PIs. If I got all the hot women Mike Hammer seemed to attract, there'd be no time left for work. No time? There'd be no energy left for work. Or if I drove a flashy red Ferrari like Thomas Magnum, marks would spot me a mile away. So no, I don't stay out all night partying with hot women. Believe me I wish I did, but it's just not in my nature. The truth is, I have insomnia and spend more nights than I care to remember wide awake, reading or working on a case, or just lying in bed staring at the ceiling, so strong hot coffee is always welcomed in the painful mornings.

"Up again last night?"

"Yeah," I mumbled, dropping the paper on the desk. "You going on or coming off?"

I reached for the coffee.

Paine was a detective with the Salt Lake City Police Department. He is the kind of cop you think of when you think of T.V. cops—tall, strong, intimidating, but with a Denzel Washington kind of boyish smile. Make no mistake, he is tough as nails when he has to be, but he would also give you the shirt off his back if he thought it would help you.

We went through the police academy together in San Diego, California. There was instant suspicion, at least on my part, from day one. He was a practicing Mormon who didn't smoke, cuss, drink coffee, tea or alcohol, or chase women. I was a non-practicing Catholic who did all of the above on a regular basis. As far as I was concerned, the pairing was a disaster waiting to happen.

But Jackson Paine surprised me. He was the kind of man I wished I was—well, except for that part about not drinking, smoking, cussing and chasing women.

"Just coming off," he grunted as he plopped down in one

of the two chairs in front of my desk.

"You on nights now?"

"Just for the week. Dick Allen's daughter is getting sealed in the temple this week, so I volunteered to take his night shift so he could get everything done that he needs to do."

I shook my head. "You should change your name to Dudley Do Right, you know that?"

"Would that make you Snidely Whip Lash?" he shot back without missing a beat. That was something else I really liked about him. He never took himself too seriously. He had been taught by a very wonderful mother that a man, no matter what color, or what religion, should do three things: Pray like everything depended on Jesus; work like everything depended on you; keep your eyes open and your mouth shut. Advice I have yet to master, to say the least.

Still half asleep I lifted the coffee to my lips and took a gulp. "Damn, that's hot!" I yelled, nearly burning my tongue off.

"Oh, by the way, the coffee's really hot," he said with a smirk.

"Thanks. I'll remember that," I replied as sarcastically as my fogged over brain could muster. "So what brings you down to the poor side of town?"

He stared at me for a moment then reached into his coat pocket and removed what looked like a book. "I need a favor."

"What kind of favor?"

"Julie gave this to me yesterday."

He leaned forward and dropped it on my desk.

I picked up the small book. "What are you, the police librarian?"

"It's not a book. It's someone's diary."

That was the last thing I was expecting to hear. "I didn't know the Salt Lake City Police Department had a diary patrol," I said in my usual smart-ass way. As I looked up, I suddenly realized there was no humor in his eyes, no smile on his face. That got my attention.

"What's this all about?"

"I think whoever this belongs to might be trying to kill herself."

"What makes you think that?"

"Look at the last entry in the middle of the book."

I opened the book and turned to the last page with any writing on it. It didn't take long to see what he was talking about.

"Any kind of identification inside?"

"There's a name on the inside, but the last name is so smudged I can't read it."

I turned to the first page and stared at the neatly printed name on the inside cover. Jenny J. He was right. Everything after the J was smudged so badly that you couldn't tell what it was.

"What do you want me to do?" I asked.

"Find her."

"What's wrong with you guys?"

"I can just imagine what Captain Sokolowski would say if I asked him to authorize the use of our limited manpower to find the owner of some diary. As far as I know, no crime has been committed."

"But you think she might kill herself?"

"I can't prove it."

"I don't know, Jackson. It's a stretch. Whoever this belongs to could have just had a bad day." I tossed the diary back onto the desk. "Where did you find it?"

"One day each week Julie volunteers at Temple Square. One of the elderly missionaries found it on a bench there."

"When?"

"A week ago." He looked down at the diary. "When the missionary read it she thought it might be important so, after a week when no one came to claim it, she gave it to Julie to give to her policeman husband."

"Temple Square has millions of visitors every year," I reminded him. "She may not even live here."

"She mentions that she likes to go there to sit and think, so unless she has a pilot's license she must live here somewhere."

"Well, that narrows it down to at least eight municipalities."

He stared at me for a moment then added quietly, "I'll pay you if I have to."

"You're serious about this."

He stood. "Read it." He started for the door, then stopped. "When you're finished, if you think I'm crazy, then I'll drop it." Without another word, he left me alone, staring at the small brown diary.

***

I waited for the light to turn green, then turned left on to North Temple. I passed the large Mormon Conference Center on my right and Temple Square on my left. No matter how many times I passed Temple Square I still turned to stare at the Mormon Temple, the center piece of the ten-acre square. It is one of the most impressive buildings I have ever seen. It is a marvelous structure of solid granite, with six large spires, twelve smaller spires, ornate carvings of sunstones, moonstones and stars, and delicate round and oval windows. To think that ordinary people had built it, out of their poverty, over a hundred years ago, without all the giant cranes and equipment that we use today still amazed me. To think that these same people had taken forty years of daily detailed labor to finish it blows my mind. Who has that kind of patience today? I may not know anything about their religion, but I can appreciate the beauty of a great building, and the sacrifice of the ordinary people who built it.

I stayed on North Temple, going over the overpass and away from downtown Salt Lake until I reached Redwood Road. Turning left, I continued past fast food joints and car lots until I came to a small business section. I turned into the parking lot of a large, tan three-story building and stopped.

Turning off the engine I sat in the car for a moment, staring at the large manila envelope lying on the seat next to me. I didn't relish showing some trusting schmuck that his wife of six years had finally gotten bored being left alone while he worked his butt off to make a living, and had decided to do the horizontal mambo with some graphic designer, but that was what he had paid me for. I grabbed the envelope and got out.

James Carson stared at the pictures, his face ashen. "I can't believe it. How could she do such a thing?"

What was there to say? So I sat silently while he continued to stare at the 8x10 color photos of his wife hip hopping her lover.

"I gave her everything, and this is the way she repays me!" He slammed the pictures onto the large cherry desk. "She is the mother of my children!"

"Yeah well, I guess even mothers need love and attention sometimes."

His face shot up, angry and hurt. Okay, it wasn't the smartest thing to say, but I had seen it too many times. Men determined to make a career, spending ten to twelve hours at the office while the wife is left at home with the kids. When they get home, they are too tired to pay more than token attention to her. It must get really boring after six years. It must get boring after two. At least that's what Christine, my second wife, had said the day I caught her with someone else.

"What's that supposed to mean?" Carson asked angrily.

"It means careers can wear you out. Boredom can drive you to do stupid things, and as Jim Morrison once sang, none of us get out alive," I shot back as I picked up the check he had written and left.

I don't know what it meant, and Morrison may or may not have sung it, but it sounded good. And if it made him angry so be it. Anger had sure helped cover up a lot of unbearable hurt once upon a time—and a month-long drinking binge.

It was 12:40 by the time I pulled into the parking lot of my favorite restaurant. Katie Blues Burgers and Fries was owned and run by Kathryn Alice Hendrickson. She was also my best and oldest female friend.

I opened the door and took my usual seat.

Katie smiled, yelled my order, (cheese burger, with pastrami, mayonnaise and mustard, no pickle, extra onions topped off with cilantro, extra crispy fries, and a Dr. Pepper), then moved around the counter to sit with me.

"When are you going to make an honest woman out of me?"

"When are you going to ask?"

"I'm just waiting for you to come to your senses," she smiled.

Yeah, like I had any sense in the first place.

"You look worried. Is everything all right?" she asked.

I never liked discussing my work with anyone because half the time it was depressing, a constant reminder of the deviants I dealt with on a daily basis. And who wants to be reminded of that? But Katie was different. When she asked, I answered. It was an unwritten rule that had developed over the years between us.

We met when I first moved to Salt Lake City during my junior year of high school. We were at a dance, and as I wandered over to the refreshment table, I saw this tall, lanky blonde looking at me. She said 'hi' as if it was the most natural thing in the world. I said 'hi' like it was the most awkward thing in the world. And to me it was. I had already learned the secret to getting along with girls. Stay away from them. The fact that I actually answered was a miracle in and of itself.

It soon became apparent we were both transplants to Salt Lake. She had just moved from Cucamonga, California, and didn't know anyone at the school either. We became fast friends, a friendship which has survived for over twenty years.

She had always loved to cook, so eight years ago, after divorcing her second husband, she moved back to Salt Lake and opened her own burger joint. It quickly became one of the most popular eating establishments in the area.

"Jackson brought me a diary. He thinks the owner might be trying to kill herself."

"What do you think?"

"Her last entry sure leads to that conclusion."

"Anything to go on?"

"Not a lot, I'm afraid. I need to find her before she hurts herself."

"You will. You're the best detective in whole world." She kissed me on the cheek and got up. "Love you, but some of us have to work."

"Glad it's not me," I smiled as she turned and sashayed back to the kitchen. I watched her walk away. Katie wasn't what you would call a typical beauty, at least by the world's standards. She was lanky, with a figure that would make a ninety-eight pound fashion model feel voluptuous. Her dishwater blonde hair, high cheek bones, bright eyes that sparkled even without a lot of makeup, was complimented by a smile that could bring world peace to the Middle East, if anyone had the intelligence to send her over there to negotiate a peace settlement.

Why had we not married? I guess we were both too busy marrying the wrong people. Both of us more than once.

"1962," a voice said, snapping me out of my reverie.

Darlene stood holding my order.

"Piece of cake," I snorted.

"We'll see," she said, her smile disappearing and her aged face becoming serious. "Bobby's Girl."

"At least give me a difficult one, Darlene," I laughed as she stood waiting. "Marcy Blane. It first entered Billboard's top ten November, 1962 and stayed there for six weeks, stalling at number three."

I flashed my victory smile and did my victory dance in my mind, which is where it will always stay so as not to frighten small children. She dropped my plate on the table and rushed off in a huff.

Darlene Rivers had been working for Katie since the beginning. She was sixty-eight-years old, but only in body. Her mind was still twenty-five. She had grown up in Memphis during the birth of rock and roll and knew all the greats. During the Sixties she had worked steadily as a back-up singer for such performers as Jimmie Rogers, Troy Shondell, Little Esther Phillips, Leslie Gore, and Freddy Scott. Music had been her life and she was good at it. In the early seventies she had done some back-up work on two of John Lennon's solo albums, and in 1972 had gone on tour with Elvis, including his triumphant concert at Madison Square Garden.

A year ago I was trying to remember the name of an early rock and roll hit, a favorite of my dad's that I wanted to buy at *Randy's Records,* but was drawing a blank. Not Darlene. All I had to do was hum a few bars and she immediately knew the answer. Since that day we have developed a fierce competition to try and stump each other with little known rock and roll trivia.

It was now my turn. I had the song that would send her crying in shame. I was a professional investigator, after all, and in that capacity had spent many hours at *Randy's* picking his brain for the most obscure songs I could find, songs even a professional singer like Darlene couldn't remember. In the year we had been battling I had yet to stump her. Today Darlene Rivers was going down.

As usual, the burger was a taste bud delight. I don't know what she did, or how she did it (she won't even tell me), but Katie made the best burgers in the entire world. I savored the taste, letting my mind relax, my hands reaching for as many napkins as I could to quell the fountain of juices rushing down my chin.

Darlene returned with my Dr. Pepper and set it on the table.

"Year?" she asked impatiently.

"1955," I said confidently, knowing this song was so obscure that no one in their right mind would remember it.

I made her wait until I could see the anxiety dancing across her face, then announced proudly, "Story Untold."

She started to answer, then stopped, a confused look crossing her brow. I had her. Finally, I was about to emerge victorious. I took a bite of my hamburger, relishing my victory.

She shifted from one foot to the other before a smile began to spread across her worn, but still attractive face. "The Nutmegs, June, 1955, stayed in the top ten for fifteen weeks, reaching as high as number three."

I stared in disbelief. How could she know that? Who in their right mind would know that? I only knew it because I had cheated and asked Randy for the most obscure song he could remember.

"Will that be all?" With a victory smile, she turned and danced towards the kitchen.

Frustrated at being bested again, even if it was by a professional singer, I dipped my extra crispy fries into a small cup of Katie's out-of-this-world fry sauce. Good food was always the best salve for frustration.

I guess I should explain what fry sauce is, since Utah is the only place I have ever seen that serves it. In every other state fry sauce is plain old ketchup. Not in Utah. Someone here decided that ketchup just wasn't good enough for fries, so they added mayonnaise, and who knows what, and came up with a wonderful concoction called fry sauce.

Taking a bite of my fries, dripping with the golden pink liquid, I removed the diary from my coat. There was nothing special about it, just a well-worn, brown-covered diary. I opened it, landing on August 16. It was about half way through the book. The thing that first caught my attention was the handwriting. I don't know what I was expecting, but it still surprised me. It was so neat, so careful, so legible, so beautifully elegant. I stared at it, wondering how anyone could have such beautiful handwriting. My wife, Vickie—the first one—had beautiful handwriting. That was one of the things that had attracted me to her. Sixteen years later, I am still impressed by her handwriting on the occasional Christmas card.

How could anyone with such beautiful handwriting have any kind of problems?

August 16

Why don't men ever give you daffodils? Why is it always roses or carnations? Don't they know about daffodils so delicate so fragile. Roses are fine, but everybody gives roses. Maybe that's why men do it – they think you'll like them because women are supposed to like roses. That's what they do in every movie. Why don't they get to know you, then they'd know what you like. Why don't they get to know you???? Is that too much to ask???????

I'm sure my forehead wrinkled, my eyebrows furrowed, or whatever eyebrows do, when I read that line. *Is that too much to ask???????* Of course it is. Trying to understand women is like a five-year old trying to figure out a Rubik's Cube. As soon as you turn it one way, something different pops up to kick you in the teeth.

I admit my first reaction to the diary was borne from years of frustration trying to understand women. After two failed marriages and scores of unfulfilled relationships, I had finally learned the secret to women. Men are not supposed to understand them. It's the ability to keep you in the dark that they love.

In the battle of the sexes, I had lost the war, surrendered, and been sentenced to Abstinence State Prison in Lonely Land.

Satisfied with my ability to neatly sum up the whole problem between the sexes in one short physiological sound bite, I took a drink of my Dr. Pepper. As I did, I noticed a stocky man in a plaid shirt sitting at the counter. He glanced nervously around, his face soft looking and smooth as if he had never shaved. Everything about him screamed childlike, arrested development. I don't know what caught my attention. Maybe it was his dark eyes that looked like they had been glued wide open and topped by thick and bushy brows that looked like a miniature Beatle hair cut hanging over the eyes. "Beatle Brows" reminded me of the megalomaniac scientist Eugene Levy had played to perfection in Tom Hank's first feature, *Splash*. I could just see this guy out chasing mermaids. The thought made me smile.

Putting him out of my mind, I glanced back down at the diary.

Why don't men ever give you daffodils?

Like a rush of mighty water, all the loneliness I had ever felt in my whole miserable life came flooding into my soul.

Even "Beatle Brows" couldn't make me smile now.

Two

Two hours later, feeling fat and satisfied, I was back at my office. It was a small, cramped, stuffy mess, but it was mine. Situated in a business complex near Ninth and State Street, it was located on the second floor of the southwest corner of the building. It had outside stairs so I could get in without having to go through the lobby where I would be seen, which was useful on occasion. My business neighbor was a talent agency located on the second level next to me. Below us were a tax business and a carpet cleaning and restoration company.

It wasn't the most glamorous of locations but it was away from the bustle of downtown and near *Randy's Records*, one of my favorite oldies record stores, where I could get all the classic rock and roll vinyl I wanted. I enjoy the CDs from my generation such as Boston, Weezer, Train, 3rd Eye Blind and No Doubt, but there was nothing to compare to the crisp, clear vinyl and old 78 records of the past. Even the occasional pops brought back memories of my childhood and a father who was so passionate about the unfettered sound and excitement of classic rock and roll that it rubbed off on m . He also taught me to appreciate such great music as Mozart, Jeannette McDonald, Do Wop, and Billie Holiday. There's nothing wrong with music today, except for the fact that most of it is loud, vulgar, and there's nothing musical about it.

I turned on the ceiling fan and plopped down in my executive leather chair. The rest of the furnishings may be early K-Mart, but my chair is the best Office Max had to offer. I do my best thinking in my comfortable, over-priced, cherry executive chair or my long imitation leather black couch.

As I pulled out the diary and found the page where I had left off, the phone rang.

"Crockett Investigations," I answered automatically.

The sound at the other end made me want to slap my forehead for being so stupid. I have caller ID. Why do I always forget to look at it?

"David, you didn't come over for dinner last night."

"Hi, Mom."

"Your sisters were here."

"Yeah, well I got tied up here at work. Sorry."

I really wasn't.

Don't get me wrong, I love my family but I can only take a weekly gathering about once a month. My mother, bless her little Scottish-Irish heart, has never learned the concept of cutting the apron strings. I'm thirty-five and yet she still wants to know what I am doing, if I'm eating enough, if I'm wearing clean underwear, or when I'm going to quit fooling around with this detective stuff and get a real job. Or at least go back to the police department where I had a steady pay check.

And my sisters! They could star in their own reality

television series.

My oldest sister, Kathryn (I call her Kat just to irritate her) went from the wife of a staunch conservative mayor to a gay liberal environmental/animal rights activist within a year. She divorced her Mayoral husband and moved in with a social studies professor at the University of Utah.

My youngest sister, Jillian, is a new age psychic who has seven spirits, I guess one for each deadly sin, who guide her through her mystical life in Draper, Utah!

Talk about must-see TV.

"I saved you some food," Mom informed me.

"Thanks Mom, but I have plenty to eat." I really did, if you counted left over Chinese food and a six pack of beer.

"Pot roast. I know it's your favorite."

"Mom, I haven't liked pot roast since I was twelve."

"But it was your favorite then. Tonja brought a friend for you to meet. She was so disappointed that you weren't here."

Tonja is my middle sister, who has taken it upon herself to find me a wife. Almost monthly she has a new employee or friend who is perfect for me. None have been, not even close, except Ellen, who was tall, blonde, and very sexy. She cooked dinner for me one night and things seemed to be going along fine until it was time to eat. She then set an extra plate at the table for Maximus, her toy poodle. Call me old-fashioned, but I have always believed that dogs belong on the floor, not at the dinner table. Later, when the "mighty" Maximus joined us on the couch to watch a movie, I came to the conclusion that there would never be anything between us -well, except for that damn annoying little poodle. I never called her back.

"You know how I hate blind dates," I finally answered.

"David Winston Crockett, how do you expect to ever get married again if you don't go out on dates?"

I said nothing, hoping my silence would send her in another direction, namely the rudeness of my silence. It didn't work. It never does.

"I'm right," she continued. "You know I am."

When she used all three of my names I knew the fight was over. "What's for dinner tonight?" I asked meekly.

"Lamb. Be here at 6."

"See you then." Hanging up the phone I closed my eyes. I needed a break. I needed a strong shot of whiskey!

I glanced back down at the diary instead.

> *August 29*
> *Connie has set me up on a blind date. I can't believe I am going on a blind date. Have I reached that point where I can't find my own guy? I'm only 28. Is my life already over?*

Wait until you reach thirty-five and are still being set up on blind dates by your family, I thought as I continued reading her entry.

> *August 30*
> *Last night was miserable. My blind date was a lawyer named Franklin. All ego and attitude. Everything was about him and my breasts, which he stared at like he had never seen a girl before. Why can't men see the heart instead of the breast? I'm a human being. Why can't they see that! I hate being beautiful.*

There was such anguish in her words. And then it happened. I was hooked. Who was this woman? Why such pain? Beautiful women don't have such pain do they?

Setting the diary aside, I reached for the phone book and quickly turn to the Js. Who would have ever guessed that there were so many people in Salt Lake City and the surrounding areas whose last name began with J.

The good news was there were only forty-two people named Jenny, Jennifer, or J. Could she be one of them? Was there a family whose last name began with J out there mourning the loss of their daughter? Picking up the phone, I decided to find out.

Two hours later, suffering from a bad case of cauliflower ear, I finished my last call. I had achieved nothing, except making some parents very nervous by asking them the last time they had heard from their daughter?

Was she even from the area? Maybe she was a graduate student at the University of Utah. I needed more information, so I dragged myself out of the office and headed for downtown Salt Lake. I was about to eat crow. I didn't like the taste.

"Well, well, well. Look what the cat dragged in," Sargent Thomas Clayson frowned as I walked to the desk. "You slumming or looking to get your old job back?"

"I need to see Jackson,"

He stared at me for a moment, trying to decide whether to let me back into the detective's bull pen or not. I had worked here for two years. I had been back at least twice a month since becoming a PI, but he always gave me that look like he wasn't quite sure what I was up to, as if I posed a threat of some kind. "Do I need to get a written note from my mother, Tom, or are you going to buzz me back?"

He hit the door lock and the door opened.

Jackson was sitting at his desk surrounded by—well, actually—nothing. Among his many qualities was that quality that I hated among men like no other. He was the neatest person I had ever seen.

I used to pile all of my paperwork on his desk just to make it looked used. He had a phone, a small organizer for his pens, tape, letter opener, stapler and staple remover, an in-and-out tray, a dead cactus, and three pictures of Julie and the kids. That was it. The in-box had a stack of unsolved case files neatly stacked, while the out-box had a stack of solved case files neatly stacked waiting to be picked up and filed in the closed case files by the filing geeks. It wasn't normal. A man's desk was supposed to be cluttered.

"I see that plant I gave you is still dead," I said as I plopped down in the chair next to his desk.

He smiled at me. "I ignore it every day just like you showed me."

"Hey, CD," I said to Jackson's partner, C.D. Marx, who was sitting at his desk, digging through all the clutter trying to find a report. Marx was a big friendly sort of guy with a ready smile that always made you feel good. I once saw him trying to play "bad cop" like on television. I had to try hard not to laugh. He was one hell of a cop, but no one would ever accuse him of being bad. I always thought he should have been a preacher instead of a detective. I took a small bit of comfort in the fact that his messy desk looked like a cop's desk should look.

I paused for a beat, then swallowed my pride. "I'd like to see the missing person files."

He looked up with a start. I could see it in his eyes; the gloating, the self-assurance from always being right.

"Just get me the files, ok?"

Reaching into his desk drawer, he pulled out a small stack of files. He didn't even have to go to the filing cabinet to get them. He knew I would take the case, and he also knew I would be coming to see him.

"I made copies for you."

"I hate you, Paine, I really do."

"I feel the love, my brother. Want a cup of coffee?"

He dropped the files on his extremely clean desk. They hit with a dull smack, a subtle reminder of my purpose there.

"I thought you might want to take a look at those." Not able to hide the smile starting to creep into the corners of his mouth, he strolled to the coffee pot.

"Anything pop out at you?" I picked up the files and spread them across his clean desk as I began thumbing through them. I take my revenge where I can get it.

"No. Mostly teenage runaways." He sat my coffee on the desk, gathered the files, and neatly placed them in a pile near me. I continued to look them over. He was right. Most of the files concerned runaways.

What about this one?" I asked. "John Anderson reported his wife, Jennifer missing two days ago. She's twenty-eight. The age is right."

Jackson shook his head. "From all indications our Jenny isn't married."

"Here's one about a missing granddaughter."

"The girl's diabetic. Jenny never mentions anything that would lead me to think she was diabetic," he pointed out.

"Paine!"

The voice.

How could I ever forget that irritating voice? We looked up at Captain Jensen Sokolowski standing in his office doorway.

"You and Marx get over to the avenues. Someone's just turned up a stiff." He started back into his office, but suddenly stopped. "And Crockett?" He stared at me through narrow eye slits. "This isn't a hospital. Visiting hours are over!"

Then the slamming of the door. Just like old times.

The Avenues are an older section of Salt Lake City, on the hill near the capital building. Murders don't usually occur in the Avenues.

By the time I arrived, Jackson and Marx were already there and the crime scene had been secured by patrol cops. I got out of my car and stopped to survey the area. Mostly out of habit, I guess. It was a nice upscale area with old houses on each side of narrow streets. Up ahead a blue Chevy Nova was parked on the side of the street with its trunk open. Jackson and Marx stood looking into the trunk.

As I started towards the scene, I recognized Geoff Lamb handling the security. I had known Geoff since he was sixteen. He wasn't sixteen anymore. His slender six foot-three frame had filled out to a bulky two-fifty with a barrel chest and weight-lifting arms. At twenty-six he still had a boyish look about him despite his size and a sandy, beach-colored mustache he was trying to grow.

"Hey, Geoff," I smiled. "What's the story?"

"Mr. Crockett," he said somberly. "A female Caucasian was found in the trunk."

I glanced towards the car. "Who found the body?"

"My partner and I did. We got a call about a car illegally parked for the past two days. As we were checking it out I noticed a foul smell coming from the trunk, so we popped the trunk and found the body."

"Who called the car in?"

He removed his notes from his pocket and stared at them. "Mrs. Josephine Catlin." He pointed to a small gray haired woman her shawl gathered tightly about her, standing on the sidewalk at the front of the small crowd that had gathered. "She noticed the car Tuesday and thought it was strange since she had never seen it before," he continued. "When she saw it was still there today, she called it in." Lamb closed his notebook.

"Let him through!" Jackson yelled from the car.

Lamb moved back and raised the yellow crime scene tape for me to walk under.

When I arrived, Marx was looking through the car while Jackson was busy searching the body. I stopped near the trunk.

"Female. Caucasian," Jackson said as I moved beside him. "Looks like someone slit her throat and dumped her into the trunk."

I felt my stomach tighten. After two tours of duty and seven years as a police officer, I was no stranger to death, but looking at the lifeless bodies of children, teenagers, and young women who should be living, laughing and growing old, still bothered me. Life should be lived, not snuffed out by heartless animals.

"Doesn't look like she was killed here," I answered, looking around the street.

"You're right." Jackson stood and wiped his hands, then removed the thin latex gloves. "There's very little blood in the trunk."

"Any identification?" I asked.

"Nothing," Marx answered, as he moved to the back of the car. "No registration, no purse, driver's license, credit cards, rings, or anything that might identify her."

The police photographer snapped another close up shot of the small blue rose tattoo on her ankle and then turned to Jackson.

"I'm done," he said as he turned and walked away.

I stared down at the young woman, her eyes open in surprised horror. She was naked from the waist up, her blue jeans unzipped and pulled down to her thighs.

"Raped?"

"I don't think so," Jackson replied. "This seems personal."

Marx moved to the left side of the trunk. "I'd say she was posed for effect. Whoever did this wanted to humiliate her."

It was a common practice in murders involving angry spouses or boyfriends.

Jackson shook his head as he turned towards the paramedics waiting to take the body. With a nod to them, he walked away. I followed, trying not to think of this beautiful young girl as someone's daughter, wife, or mother.

And then it hit me.

I felt a chill go down my spine. Could this be Jenny?

All I knew about her was that she was twenty-eight, liked daffodils, and hated blind dates. I sucked in my breath. This Jane Doe looked to be anywhere from 20 to 30.

"You think it's her? Jenny?" I asked.

"Looks like the right age range," Jackson replied grimly, then stopped. "But no. This one was murdered and it looks very personal. We're running the plates now. If we're lucky and it's her car then we'll know who she is."

"Nothing like getting murdered and dumped in your own car," I mumbled. "Ain't life grand?"

"Lieutenant?" Lamb called from his car. "We got the DMV report on the car." He got out of his cruiser and walked toward us. What was taking him so long? Why didn't he just say the name and get it over with? After what seemed like an eternity, Lamb finally ambled up and handed Jackson the DMV report.

After a moment, Jackson shoved it towards me. Eagerly, I grabbed it, my eyes glancing straight to the name at the top. Janet Hickman. Relief washed over me, but only for a second as I realized Janet Hickman was also a person, and now she was dead and lying in the back of her own car with her throat cut. She deserved better and whoever did this to her should have his testicles placed on a chopping block and crushed with a hammer until they were the size of a smashed black-eyed pea.

Handing the report back to Lamb, I turned and walked from the scene. It wasn't my case and unless I was invited to help, I had no authority.

"Hey!" Jackson yelled.

I turned back around.

"Football, Saturday at my house, BBQ and food. Bring your own beer."

I nodded and rushed away, trying not to think about football, BBQ, and dead bodies.

***

Lezann was busy sorting through a stack of paperwork as I approached. She looked up with that 'may-I-help-you' smile. And then it died.

"Well," she said staring at me. Lezann was always a wordsmith. "I don't believe it."

I smiled my best 'I-really-didn't-mean-to-hurt-you-and-it's-been-three-years-so-can-we-just-get-over-it-smile. It didn't work. "You know me, I like to pop up every three or four years," I replied sheepishly.

Lezann worked at the University of Utah library. If anyone could help me find out if Jenny was a graduate student there, she could. But would she? Our past hung like a giant curtain between us. Just out of high school and before my first tour of duty in the Navy, we had been pretty hot and heavy. Everyone thought we would end up married and there was a time I thought so too. I really did like her, but I just wasn't ready to settle down. When I first returned to Salt Lake City and joined the force, we ran into each other again. All the old feelings came rushing back and we tried to rekindle that old spark.

She was ready to settle down.

I had a serious commitment phobia.

A year later she got tired, then mad, and I was history. She was dating someone named Reginald. That wouldn't have been so bad but when I supported her decision instead of begging her to come back, well, hell hath no fury like a woman who feels you just wasted a year of her life and she is now stuck with a bald headed guy named Reginald.

"I need your help."

"And I need my youth back." She was such a kidder.

"I'm looking for someone and I need to know if she is a graduate student here."

She bit the inside of her bottom lip, as she always did when she was thinking about a problem. "Those files are kept at the administration office."

"Yes, but no one in the world knows their way around a computer like you."

"So you just loved me for my computer skills?"

So you just loved me for... no matter the rest of the sentence, was never a question a man should answer. It never turned out good.

"I need to know the names of any graduate student whose last name begins with a J and the first name of Jenny, Jen, and Jennifer," I said ignoring the potential trap.

"Aren't you a little old for graduate students?" she teased.

"She's missing and may be in trouble. I need to find her."

"Oh." Her eyes blinked and she immediately sat at her desk and fired up her computer. The thing about Lezann was that no matter what she may or may not have thought of me, she was the kind of person who liked to help. Sadly, I knew her well enough to exploit her kind nature when necessary. And it was necessary.

"Last name starts with a J," she said more to herself than me, as her fingers worked the keyboard.

Within seconds she had the files. I told you she was good.

"Looks like we have twenty-five students whose last name starts with J," she announced proudly.

"What about the first name of Jennifer?"

"That cuts it to eight. I suppose you want a print out with names, addresses, and phone numbers?"

"If that's no trouble."

"It's no trouble at all, just against university policy."

"This is really important, Lezann."

"I can't help you, David." She stared at me as if waiting for me to leave.

I didn't.

"This girl could be suicidal. I really need to find her."

"And I need to keep my job."

I gave her my best puppy dog look.

She laughed. "That only worked in high school because I was so naive."

"It worked because I was so good at it," I replied with as much modesty as I could.

She shook her head, biting her lip again. "If you'll excuse me, I need to put these books back on the shelves," she said quickly glancing around the room. "Please be gone when I return in ten minutes."

She stood and walked around the counter. "You know that don't-be-a-stranger line?" she asked.

I thought I saw a smile of forgiveness on her face and replied, "Yes."

"Forget it."

So much for the smile of forgiveness. With that she took her cart filled with books and hustled towards the stacks.

I knew she wanted me to quickly hit Print on her computer. Why else would she have left it on?

I can really detect.

Looking around, no one was paying any attention to me as I waited for the page of names, addresses, and phone numbers to print. Once the page printed on the nearby printer, I deleted the page on her screen, grabbed the printout, and headed out the door. Lezann didn't even watch me leave. I wondered how she and Reginald were doing. I should have asked.

Sitting at one of the local eateries on campus, I began calling the names on the list. The first Jennifer answered on the first ring.

"Hello?"

"Is this Jennifer Johnson?"

"Yes."

"Did you lose a diary?"

"I don't keep one. What I think is no one's business."

"I tend to agree. Sorry for bothering you."

The other seven calls followed pretty much the same pattern. None kept a diary or they still had theirs or they wanted to know why I was asking about their diary. Some girls were down right touchy about their diaries.

After leaving the University of Utah, satisfied that Jenny wasn't a graduate student there, I spent the next four hours hitting all the hospitals, morgues, and homeless shelters looking for anyone that might fit her description. Again, I was rewarded with nothing.

Who was this girl and what had happened to her?

It was five forty-five before I finally drove into my garage and entered my house. It was much more of a home than I ever thought I could afford, but when the housing boom crashed, I was able to buy it for almost half its value.

It is a large, four-bedroom rock and stone house, which sits on what we call the benches, level areas up against the mountains. It is south of Parley's Canyon which leads up to Park City where the rich and famous live, vacation and ski and attend the Sundance Film Festival. It backs up against the mountains in an underdeveloped area, which is just fine with me, since I don't like neighbors that close to me. My backyard is fertile ground for deer and cougars that come off the mountain in search for food. I have no problem with them, but Sam has had more than one run-in with one of his larger hungry cousins.

Opening the door, I turned on the light and stepped into the hallway. As I made my way down the hallway to the large kitchen, I heard the scamper of soft feet. Turning on the light, I saw Sam in a mad dash towards his empty bowl.

Sam is the cat that lives with me. Is he my cat? In the strictest sense I would have to say yes, since I am the one who feeds and shelters him, but that is as far as the relationship goes. And I wouldn't have it any other way. I'm not a cat person. Sorry cat lovers, but I prefer a big dog. But I have Sam instead. He is named after Sam Houston, the first president of the Republic of Texas. Houston was strained through the dark tunnels of adversity, coming out the other side a better person. Sam was like that, except for the part about becoming a better cat. We came together one rainy day as I was walking to my car with my latest collection of early Rockabilly records from *Randy's Records*. I noticed a seedy-looking man taking a sack to the dumpster behind a local fast food joint. Normally, I don't care what someone else does, but the fact that the sack was frantically moving caught my attention. When he started to slam it against the side of the large dumpster, I was in full attention mode. My angry yell stopped him cold. Looking at me, he dropped the sack and ran. Had I known what was inside, I would have chased him down and beat him senseless. I'm not a huge animal rights activist, but I do have a healthy respect for living things and anyone purposely treating an animal with cruelty deserves to be tied to a post and whipped.

Watching the sack move, I cautiously opened it. Inside was this mangy-looking, half-starved cat, matted black coat with bald spots all over. It looked to be at death's door. Closing the sack, I laid it in the passenger's seat and headed to the nearest vet. Two weeks later, after tests, shots, and medicine, I was allowed to take him home. I didn't want a cat, had no intentions of ever owning a cat, and now I didn't know what to do it. But if I didn't take it home, its next stop was the pound and a starring role in Humphrey Bogart's classic film *The Big Sleep*. I wasn't about to let that happen, so we became roommates.

If you're thinking we became the best of friends and share a warm cozy relationship then you're reading the wrong book. He doesn't bother me with a clingy need to be petted, stroked, and cuddled, and I don't bother him by forcing him to endure those things. We have a great relationship - I feed him and he tolerates me, although at times he does bring me dead mice and birds. Maybe, secretly, he does like me, but most likely he just likes to mess up my kitchen floor with dead animals. I am, however, the only one that can pet him if that need ever arises. Everyone one else he growls at through his unnatural stare. He leaves me alone, unless he wants something. Then I get that same hypnotic stare, like I'm supposed to know exactly what he wants.

As the light came on, I could see Sam scamper to his empty bowl and wait.

Tossing my key ring on the counter, I removed a can of cat food from the cabinet. "How was your day, Satan?"

He ignored me and moved closer to his bowl.

As he gobbled up the food, I searched for something to eat. Of course there was nothing I wanted. Moving into the living room, I sank on to the couch and closed my eyes. I didn't want to think of unfaithful wives, dead bodies, and missing women.

Sam jumped on his end of the couch, ignoring me as he laid his head down and closed his eyes. It's how we bond. Just as I closed my eyes and began to relax something worse than even Sam's stare hit me.

"Oh crap!" I yelled as I jumped up from the couch and rushed up the stairs. Like a mad man, I washed my face, ran a comb through my hair, grabbed my jacket, and raced back downstairs.

"Twenty extra cans of cat food if you go to my mother's for me." He ignored me. "She's serving lamb."

He opened his eyes, then yawned, laid his head back down and closed his eyes again. His concern was touching.

Thirty minutes later, like a man going to his execution, I opened the door to the house I had called home for eighteen years. It's not that I'm not glad to see my family, but I get all the drama I can handle at work. I don't need any more. Like a reality soap opera, drama is the electricity that runs my family.

"David," my mother greeted me with a hug. "You're late."

"Sorry. Today has been hectic, to say the least."

My worst fear was realized as I entered the dining room. At the table with my sister, Tonja was a pleasant looking woman of forty or so. She looked like a matronly aunt. Very nice, I'm sure, but not my type. If my family was determined to set me up, then at least find someone with the slightest possibility of a mutual attraction. Is that too much to ask? Plastering on the best smile I could, I entered the lion's den.

Not even great lamb was worth this.

THREE

Tossing the mail on my desk, I fell into my chair. After an exhausting night of pretending to be enjoying myself, aimless conversation, not so subtle hints of why I am still single, why this complete stranger would be perfect for me, and why I needed to find a less dangerous job, I was worn out. If they would just listen to me they would know I'm still single because I'm selfish, extremely picky, and haven't found anyone who makes me want to change my life.

I like attractive women instead of matronly looking ones, no matter how nice they are; and as far as my job being dangerous, it is all a myth. I spend most of my time sitting in my very comfortable chair tracking down leads on either my computer or high tech phone. Other times I'm sitting in my car taking photos of rich, overweight men and young gold-diggers. There is absolutely nothing dangerous about that. If the truth be told, most of the time this job is mundane to distraction.

Suddenly my office door disintegrated with an earsplitting crash.

Looking up, I saw the biggest and meanest looking giant I had ever seen, framed in the busted doorway with a baseball bat in his hand. Obviously, he wasn't there for a quick game of pitch and catch. Raising the bat over his head, he stormed towards me. I leaped out of my chair just as the bat came slamming down on my desk. With the force of a hurricane the bat came down again and again, beating my innocent desk to a bloody wooden pulp. When the giant turned to assault my filing cabinet, it was obvious that he was only here to relay a destructive message from someone.

I kept my gun holstered. While I have no desire to have my office become a disaster zone, I also don't kill someone for wanton destruction unless that destruction is directed at me. This wasn't.

Of course, a movie PI would leap the desk, wrestle the bat out of his hand and give him the beating of his life. This wasn't the movies and the bat he was using wasn't foam or plastic. It was a genuine Louisville Slugger that could crush my skull with one swing from Paul Bunyan. I watched, instead, as he pounded dent after dent into my filing cabinet, obliterated my lamps to dust, and knocked my ceiling fan out of the park for a home run. He wasn't even breathing heavily when he stopped to look around the office for something else to destroy. When he glanced over at my framed original, and very expensive 1960 John Wayne's *The Alamo* movie poster hanging on the wall, I cringed. Wayne's version of the battle where my name sake died defending liberty was not necessarily a great movie, but the poster sure was. It was one of my favorite things and had cost a small fortune to have it custom framed.

"Don't even think about it," I warned.

He thought about it. A couple of swings and the movie poster crashed and fell to the floor.

Turning to me cowering in the corner (sometimes cowering is an effective defense), he waved the bat at me.

"You shouldn't go around breaking up happy marriages. The next time you mess with Mr. Duff, I won't be so easy on you."

Making his point clear, he swung the bat at the frosted pane of my office window, shattering the glass. With spit drooling down his pug chin, he hurled the bat against the wall where I was, barely missing my head. He then stepped through the broken glass and crunched his way down the hall with big, heavy steps.

I scanned the damage this mammoth of a man had inflicted upon my office. I guess Duff wasn't such a wimp after all; at least he had the guts to hire muscle. Of course, hired muscle is never employed for their stimulating intellect, and this one was no different. I guess he had never heard of keeping his client's name out of the conversation. His client, Charlie Duff, was a weasel of a man, a very rich weasel, but still a weasel, who had been cheating on his wife with a mousy little brunette half his age. His inability to be faithful had cost him millions in the divorce. And like most arrogant weasels, he had put all the blame on me and none on himself. I was wondering if I should bill him for the damage to my office when a voice started me out of my thoughts.

"Disgruntled client?"

My head snapped up. Standing in my office doorway was an extremely beautiful woman. I tried to smile. "Just toying with a few redecorating ideas." PIs are always witty in the face of danger or embarrassment.

"Maybe you should go in a different direction." She smiled this smile that almost took my breath away, full lips perfect teeth. "Do you have a minute?"

"Sure," I said confidently, trying to hide the prepubescent emotions surging through me.

"I would like to hire your services."

Faith Parker was head of her own talent agency. She moved into the large space down the hall almost four months ago. Though we were neighbors, outside a couple of smiles, and polite nods, we had never officially met. I had seen her leave her office late at night, and a couple of times we rode in a crowded elevator together. Now she was standing in my office.

As she stood there, making the busted doorway look good, I couldn't help but notice her eyes. They were bright and deep blue like the color of sparkling waters off the coast of Aruba. They were eyes that you could get lost in if you weren't careful. Her cheek bones were high like a cover girl. Her outfit was impeccable, consisting of a stylish navy blue skirt, white blouse, matching blue jacket over a slender high-breasted figure that was a fashion designer's best friend. It made me want to join the friendship club. Faith Parker was not the usual kind of client that stood in my doorway.

Tamping down the ungentlemanly thoughts whirling around in my head, I sat back down in my chair. "What can I do for you Ms.—"

Okay, I already knew her name. I had seen it on the agency door numerous times, but it was such a great opportunity to see if the empty ring finger on her left hand actually meant anything. How could a guy pass up information like that? I was a detective after all. It's what I do.

"Parker," she smiled. "Miss Faith Parker." Did she emphasize the 'miss' or was it just my overactive imagination?

I quickly jumped up and moved some of the debris and picked up one of the chairs in front of my newly redesigned smashed-by-Mammoth-Man desk. "Please have a seat."

I tried not to watch her walk to the chair and sit. Never had anyone walked so nicely to that lonely chair. She crossed her long and shapely legs, which I also tried not to notice. Obviously, this wasn't my day for being successful at not noticing things.

"I'm sorry I've been such a distant neighbor, but I just never seem to have the time to be social."

Her voice had a melody to it that made me want to join the choir, and I couldn't sing.

"Nothing to be sorry about, our businesses are not exactly cut from the same material."

I gave her my most professional look. No movie detective here.

"I'm David Crockett, how can I help you?"

"I need you to help put the killer of my mother behind bars."

I tried not to look shocked. I'm sure I failed at that, too. One doesn't think of beautiful talent agents as being involved in a dirty business like murder.

"Wouldn't that be something the police should handle?"

Her body went rigid for a beat before she willed it to relax. "They don't believe me," she replied sharply.

"Why not?"

"Because they believe her death was a suicide." She shifted in the chair. "They've tied it up in a nice and neat bow and are not willing to look beyond the surface."

"Maybe it was a suicide."

"My mother did not commit suicide." The words blasted out of her mouth as she leaned forward. "She would never have done that, never!" Her eyes, her expression was unwavering.

"People sometimes do things we don't see coming, depression, guilt, chemical imbalance. Who knows why people do things."

She jumped up from her chair. "I need someone to believe me." There was a ring of desperation to her voice, then anger. "You sound like the police."

"I'm just trying to get some perspective. What does your father say about it? I have to believe you and he have discussed this."

"No."

"Why not? It's his wife we're talking about isn't it?"

"Yes."

"Does he share your belief that the police were wrong?"

She lowered her head and spoke so softly that I could barely hear her. "No."

Before I could digest the information she looked down at me, her face pained. "He is the one I want you to prove killed her."

I didn't even try to hide my surprise. "You want me to prove your father killed your mother? Why?"

"Because he did. He's arrogant, narcissistic, and believes that he is smart enough to get away with anything."

"Do you have any proof?"

"Not yet, but I know there has to be something. That's why I want to hire you."

"It's not that I don't want the job, but why me? Besides the fact that I'm just down the hall from you?"

She stared at me for a moment, then calmly sat back down.

"Two reasons. One, I like your name, it sounds heroic."

I was far from heroic, but who was I to argue with an attractive potential client. "And the second?"

"Someone I talked to described you as a pit bull. They said once you took a case you gave it your full attention, that you cared more about truth than circumstances or political correctness."

I tended to think of myself as more of a Labrador like Old Yeller, than some stubby pit bull, but that was beside the point. While it seemed unlikely that her father had killed her mother, she seemed to believe it and that was enough to get my attention. Something stirred in my gut; at least I think it was my gut.

I had been trained by one of the best private eyes in the

country. Dale Ebsen retired to Utah after an illustrious career in Los Angeles. After forty years of the same temperature year around, he found the change of season in Utah refreshing.

He had taught me many things about the ins and outs of being a private detective, but the two things he hammered into my head above all were his two golden rules. The first was that only fools think they are invincible, so don't be stupid. There is always someone naturally better than you, so depend on your work ethic and not just your talent. The second was, a good PI should trust their gut and put their trust in character, not circumstances.

"Circumstances constantly change, Crockett," he said over and over again. "But character doesn't." He should know; his character was rock solid until the day he died.

I didn't know this lady from Adam, but something made me want to believe her. She seemed lost and alone in her quest to find her version of the truth. Her penetrating blue eyes and beguiling smile didn't hurt, either, I'm ashamed to say.

"You want to tell me what happened?"

She stared at my dead desk. When she spoke again, her voice was soft and husky. "My father went on a fishing trip last month to Lake Powell. That Saturday night, according to him, he tried to reach Mother at the house but no one answered. The next morning when there was still no answer, he called their neighbor and asked him to go over and see if she was all right. When he went into the bedroom, he found her dead."

"Was there any sign of a struggle?"

"No."

"Was there any sign of a break-in?"

"No." She took a deep breath as if the last bit of information would seal the suicide theory. "The only thing found was an empty bottle of sleeping pills on the nightstand and a spilled wine glass."

"Did the coroner find any indications of foul play?" I asked.

She shook her head, her long, shoulder-length hair flying about like Farrah Fawcett's shaggy mane during her *Charlie's Angels* period. Okay, I admit it, I watched the re-runs on TNT when I was thirteen. Between that and *Baywatch* I led a pretty frustrated teenage existence.

"So the police ruled it a suicide," I stated.

She removed a tissue from her purse to wipe her eyes.

"But you don't believe that?"

"She had no reason to kill herself," she insisted.

"Was your father having an affair?"

This seemed to take her back. "It wouldn't surprise me, but no, not that I'm aware of."

"Then what would be his motive for killing her?"

"I don't know. I just know she didn't commit suicide." She stared at me then leaned forward. "Two months before she died, we were having coffee at one of our favorite restaurants." She paused as if remembering, the pain evident. She continued, her voice cracking slightly. "Out of the blue she says, 'if anything ever happens to me, don't let your father get away with it.' "

"Did she explain what she meant?"

"No. When I pushed her on it she simply repeated not to let him get away with it." Her delicate features hardened as she turned to me. "He killed her and I am going to prove it. Will you help me?"

I wanted to help her, but I had Jenny to think of. The case had already been ruled a suicide and from what she had just told me, there was no evidence to suggest it was anything else. "There's not a lot to go on," I said gently.

"What about her will?" she replied quickly.

"What about it?"

"Mother had always told me she would never leave the business to Father because she didn't think he was capable of running it. Last week when the will was read it had been changed. Everything was left to my father. Even Richard Harvey, our family attorney, was surprised. When I questioned him about it he admitted that he didn't remember her changing it, but that it was his signature at the bottom of the will."

"People change their wills all the time. He was her husband, after all."

"Yes, but she didn't want the family business going to him. She was adamant about that. And she wouldn't have left me with nothing. She wouldn't have."

"It's still not a lot to go on."

Her body stiffened as if she had been down this road again and again. She stood, her disappointment obvious. "Thank you, anyway." She started for the door.

"Miss Parker," I said.

She stopped.

I was out of my mind. This was a clear case of suicide and nothing I could do would change it. But if she really believed it, maybe it wasn't so cut and dried. So I spend a few days looking into something that has already been decided. It would put her mind to rest and I could collect some easy money. Sadly, sometimes I didn't pay attention to what Dale tried so hard to teach me. I guess my character wasn't so rock solid.

"I'll need five hundred up front and two hundred dollars a day for expenses."

"Done," she barked without any hesitation.

"I'll need access to the house, anything and everything you have that might be considered motive."

"Thank you, Mr. Crockett."

"David," I answered then added, out of habit, my standard explanation, "Not Dave, and never, ever Davy."

With a chuckle, she reached into her purse and pulled out a business card. Writing something on the back, she handed it to me. "My private number is on the back." Her eyes twinkled and a mischievous smile crossed her drop-dead, gorgeous face.

"Call me anytime, *Davy.*"

She whispered the name Davy, low and sexy, making it sound like the greatest name in the world. I almost started singing, *Da-vvy, Da-vvy Crockett, King of the Wild Frontier!*

I took the card. She turned and made her way out the door.

I should have looked straight at the card because watching her sway down the hallway in that tight skirt revved up parts of me that I just knew had been killed off by my last wife's attitude towards anything romantic. It wasn't until she disappeared into her office and the door closed that I finally looked at the card. The Parker Talent Agency. Jessica Faith Parker. Agent.

Classy indeed.

FOUR

The only thing that I knew for sure was that Jenny wasn't a graduate student at the U. She wasn't in the morgue—at least I didn't think so. There were three Jane Does that fit her age description, but none were what I would call beautiful, although death does have a way of altering beauty. All three had been fingerprinted but since we had nothing to match them to, it was impossible to know their identities. All of the local hospitals had also proved to be a dead end. Fifteen people by the name of Jenny, with the last name beginning in J, were patients at the various hospitals in the area from Bountiful on the north to Draper at the south end of the Salt Lake Valley. Eight were children, one was a teenage girl, four were fifty-five or older, and two new born infants. I was beginning to think I was searching for that proverbial needle in a haystack. After finishing her diary, the clues I had were extremely scant. She was twenty-eight, beautiful, hated blind dates, and loved to dance. But that's why they pay me the big bucks. Detectives always come up with the right clues at the right time. Well, at least in the movies and on television.

As I drove downtown, I noticed, looming off to my left, the Vivint Smart Home Arena. This is where the Utah Jazz basketball team play their home games. Jazz dancer suddenly popped into my head. She was beautiful and liked to dance. Could she possibly be one of the Jazz dancers? It was a long shot, but then again, what did I have to lose?

I made a quick U-turn and found a parking spot a block away. Getting out of my car, I removed my cell phone and dialed a number I knew by heart. It was answered on the second ring.

"Jazz publicity and promotions."

"I've always wanted to date a Jazz dancer. Can you arrange that?"

There was a pause and then a loud laugh. "I'm sorry they have much better taste."

"I'm wounded."

Laura Fryer was head of Publicity and Promotion for the Jazz organizations. We had dated for a while until she got tired of waiting for a commitment and married a banker. I tend to affect women that way.

"What favor do you need now?" Laura asked.

"You're so cynical," I answered, trying to appear hurt.

"I just know you and you never call unless you want something."

So much for sounding hurt.

"I'd like to talk to the Jazz dancers."

"Why?"

"I'm trying to find a missing girl."

"What makes you think she's a Jazz dancer?"

"She's beautiful and she likes to dance."

"As do hundreds of young women in this town," Laura remarked.

"I know it's not a lot to go on, but it's all I've got. I think she could be in trouble so I really need to find her."

She said she'd leave my name at the gate, then began questioning me about my love life. Some cell phones don't hold a charge very long and die in the middle of a conversation. I hate that.

As I walked towards the arena I realized Jenny being a Jazz Dancer was a shot in the dark, but at this stage I had nothing to lose. So what if questioning beautiful and sexy dancers took time? I was dedicated enough to devote however long it took. Some things you just can't hurry.

I watched as the Jazz dancers went through their routines. What is it about sports and beautiful girls? Is there a rule against average girls being "Laker Girls" or "Jazz Dancers" or "Dallas Cowboys Cheerleaders?" Each one of these girls seemed flawless, from their hair to their body to their irresistible smile.

As the song ended and they gathered to drink water and work on the next dance, I approached the leader. She looked about nineteen, but was most likely twenty-five, was absolutely beautiful with long brown hair, bright green eyes, and a tight body, which her workout outfit didn't even try to hide. She looked at me cautiously as I approached.

"Can I help you sir?"

Sir? Suddenly I felt every day of my thirty-five years.

"Hi." I gave her my best non-threatening smile. It didn't help. "I'm David Crockett, a private investigator, and I was wondering if I could ask you a question."

"You're a real private eye?" Her concern quickly disappeared behind a big smile.

"Yes," I replied, standing a little taller, feeling maybe only thirty.

"I've never met a real PI." She moved closer to me. "Do you drive a hot red Ferrari?" I could see the excitement in her eyes.

"Close," I smiled. "A maroon Honda." The excitement

left and her eyes became a dull shade of green. So much for me and hot women.

"Have any of the dancers failed to show up for work in the last week or so?" I asked.

She looked at me like I was crazy and shook her head.

"I'm looking for a missing girl and I was wondering if she might be a Jazz dancer. Her name is Jenny."

"The only Jenny we have is Jenny Weis, but she's over there." She pointed to a tall blonde with a willowy body. "Do you have a picture?"

"No. I don't know what she looks like or even her last name. According to the description I have she is twenty-eight, beautiful, and likes to dance."

"That could be anyone."

"That's the sad part." I smiled again. "Thanks."

I turned and headed for the door.

"Hey, PI?"

I looked back at the attractive young dancer. "I hope you find her." With that she melded back into the group.

Feeling my age I got back into my car and headed east on the 215 interstate. I drove until I reached Sugarhouse and made a turn on 13th East. I hadn't planned on this side trip but here I was close to the home office of the chain of check cashing and financing stores owned by Harold Duff. Maybe it was the fact that beautiful young Jazz dancers didn't find me irresistible anymore, or maybe I just felt the need to be reimbursed for my office and my John Wayne poster. Or maybe I just wanted to take my frustrations out on a certain giant of a man. Whatever the reason, I parked in a spot near the door of the three-story office building and got out. Removing the bat from my trunk, I marched into Duff's financing empire.

From my time working for him, I knew Duff's office was on the third floor. I took the elevator up and stepped out into the expensively decorated waiting area. I gave Cynthia, the porn star-looking, twenty-five year old, platinum blonde receptionist my nicest smile. She looked sixteen sitting there chewing gum and trolling the Internet; most likely searching all the educational websites to help improve her intellect. When she saw me, a concerned look crossed her face.

"Good to see you too, Cynthia. I'll just be a minute."

She popped the bubble she was blowing and immediately reached for the phone.

I quickly moved past her and made my way down the long hall. Turning left I strolled halfway down the hall to the very large office situated in the middle. I turned into the waiting area where an empty desk sat. Duff's personal secretary, a mousy brunette, usually sat there— that is when she wasn't personally taking care of Duff.

As I burst through the door into his inner sanctum, Duff was sitting at his large desk with his mousy brunette on his lap. Both looked up like they had been caught doing something they shouldn't be doing. Immediately Mousy jumped up like she had been shot off his lap.

"I didn't know personal assistants still did dictation, Harold," I said as I closed the door.

He stared at me nervously, his eyes twitching back and forth as he noticed the bat in my hand. Mousy stood plastered to the wall like a frightened deer caught in high-beamed headlights.

Forcing his anxiety down a notch, Duff snapped at me. "What do you want, Crockett?"

I held up my index finger indicating for him to wait a second. I turned towards the door and waited. Suddenly the door opened and Mr. Muscles came crashing in. When he saw me his eyes narrowed and his jaw clinched. Then he saw the bat in my hand. His eyes went wide as he tried to halt his charge, but he was too late. I swung the bat like I was Babe Ruth in 1929. The sound of the wooden bat hitting his knee wasn't pretty, but it was effective. He crumbled to the floor like a broken accordion.

I tossed the bat onto the floor where Muscles lay writhing in pain. "You left this at my place, dummy."

Stepping over him, I turned to Duff, who backed up in his chair. "If you touch me, Crockett, I'll sue you," he said, gripping his chair.

I advanced towards him, never taking my eyes off his pasty face. I tossed him a receipt I had hastily written. "This should cover the expense of replacing everything your goon broke in my office, including my very expensive movie poster."

"I don't owe you anything." He tried to keep his voice from cracking but wasn't successful. "You can't prove I had anything to do with that."

"So you refuse to pay your debt?"

"I've been here all day," he whined.

Seeing that I wasn't about to attack, he gathered some measure of confidence. "Ask Ms. Cooper." He nodded towards Mousy. "She'll vouch for me."

His smug smile made me want to take the bat to his desk. I didn't.

"I guess you're right," I answered agreeably.

I pulled up a chair and propped my feet on his desk. His face tightened but he remained still. "But that just means we are going to become really good friends from now on."

He looked at me suspiciously. "What do you mean?"

"It means that where ever you go, whatever you do, I'll be watching you," I said. I almost sang the last part but in deference to Sting and the Police I declined.

He shot a nervous glance towards Mousy.

"Just me, you and my camera with a telephoto lens. And, as you know, it takes great shots."

"You can't do that," he stammered nervously. "That's stalking."

"Of course you have nothing to worry about with Mousy. You'd never cheat on her, would you?' I asked innocently.

"Of course not," he replied too quickly before hesitantly glancing at her.

"I'm sure you and Cynthia are just friends. I can see why you hired her. Her secretarial skills must be impeccable," I laughed.

Mousy's face grew tight. Duff shifted uncomfortably in his big black chair. From his reaction, this was a conversation they had had before.

"But hey, since I don't have an office anymore, I can spend all the time I want in my car following your every move, day and night. And you know how patient I can be."

Duff rolled to his desk, opened the drawer, and pulled out his check book. Angrily, he grabbed the receipt.

"No checks," I snapped.

With a frustrated growl, he jumped up and stormed to his wall safe. He quickly counted out the amount. Dumping the money on his desk in front of me, he angrily barked his displeasure. "Take the damn money. Just leave me alone."

I stuffed the money in my coat and turned. I had my money and should have left it alone, but sometimes money just isn't enough. Then again maybe my wife, Christine – the second one - was right, and I received some perverse pleasure in pushing the envelope to the point of exasperation. She was always complaining about that.

I stopped and turned to Mousy.

"He sure handed over six thousand dollars quickly, didn't he?" I asked, giving her my most convincing look of concern. "Makes you wonder what he has to hide, doesn't it?"

Walking around the mammoth, still on the floor clutching his knee, I walked out.

"Are you seeing someone else? Are you cheating on me with that platinum whore?" Her high shrill voice pierced the hallway.

"Lamie pie, of course not."

"If you're cheating on me I'll take a knife and when I'm through you'll never cheat on anyone else again."

I heard objects being tossed and Duff's frantic denials as I turned the corner and continued down the hall.

I tried not to smile. I failed again.

Back on the road, I called a local furniture store I'm familiar with and set an appointment to bring out a new and expensive desk, filing cabinets, ceiling fan, and new client chairs.

That Duff. What a generous guy.

Next I called the restoration company below my office. Joe Leavitt, the owner, and I have an arrangement. I get my office trashed and he cleans it up for below cost. It's a good deal for him, as it seems some angry, disgruntled person caught with their hands in the proverbial cookie jar is always taking out their frustrations on my office. Whatever happened to owing up to your mistakes?

"Joe?"

"Don't tell me, let me guess." I could hear the laughter in his voice. "Someone trashed your office again."

He has a mind-reading business on the side.

"I've got new furniture coming Monday at ten. What can you do for me?"

"Help you get into a new line of work." He also works part-time at the comedy store.

"Why cut off half your business?"

"You've got a point there." He paused for a moment then came back on the line. "Let me see, I'm booked up solid today."

Another pause.

"Any restoration for you this time?" he laughed.

He was referring to the time when Bonnie Curtis, a gold digging wife, who had been having her cake and eating it too, was cut off financially by her husband because of her wandering ways. She believed it was completely my fault and hired two bouncers to come to my office and rearrange my face. They almost succeeded. Fortunately Jackson happened to drop by and, let's just say, we had a spirited workout. While the two muscle bound airheads got what they deserved, my office didn't. It seems muscle bound guys break things when they are thrown violently against desks and chairs. Who knew?

I laughed. "No, this guy was more interested in teaching my desk a lesson."

"If I move my 9:00 I can get in there tomorrow. Are you going to be there?

"Up until the football game at Jackson's house at one-thirty."

"Meet us at your office at nine."

"Thanks, Joe."

At 2800 South I turned west and drove until I reached the Salt Lake City division of the Department of Motor Vehicles.

April Nelson was one of the managers of the Salt Lake DMV and had spent ten years with the Highway Patrol. Eight months ago two local druggies had kidnapped her ten-year-old son, Donnie, thinking they could convince her not to testify against them when their trial came up. She hired me and within three days I had tracked them down and rescued her son. The write-up in the *Deseret News* had spiked business for a while. Of course what I hadn't revealed to the paper was the fact that these Meth-heads were dumber than dirt and an eleven-year-old with a Sherlock Holmes cap could have found them with a little effort. Some secrets shouldn't be revealed. April and I had remained friends.

The place was jam-packed with people paying fines, renewing their licenses, taking their drivers test, and registering their vehicles. Hadn't any of these people heard about the Internet? I moved to the locked security door and showed my ID to the security guard.

"I need to see Lt. Nelson," I said using my best cop voice.
He buzzed me back.

April was sitting at her desk behind a mound of paperwork.
As I walked through she got up and greeted me with a hug.

"You get better looking with age," she said, smiling.

"Don't be taking all my good lines." I countered.
"How's Donnie?"

"Getting as tall as his dad." She sat back at her desk.
"Want some coffee?"

I shook my head then sat opposite her. "I see you still
have nothing to do around here."

She smiled again. It was a smile I had always liked. It
was the kind of smile that made you think Santa Claus was
real and that life was going to get better.

"I need your help."

"Anything I can do, name it."

I removed the diary and tossed it on the desk. "Look at
the last entry about the middle of the book."

She picked it up and quickly turned to the last entry.

September 10th

*How did this happen? Can I go through with
this? Do I have the courage? Do I have the strength?
What will people say? Will they understand? There
is only one thing left to do. Please give me strength
to end this!!!!*

She glanced up at me. "You think she killed herself?"
she asked.

"I don't know. I'm trying to find her but there's not a lot
to go on. I was hoping you might help me."

She immediately turned to her computer. "What's her
name?"

"I wish I knew." I picked up the book. "On the
inside cover is the name Jenny, but the last name, which

begins with a J, is smudged and unreadable."

"I guess I could compile a list of all female license holders whose last name begin with J and then cross reference it with everyone who first name is Jennifer."

"I'd appreciate it."

She typed the information into her computer and hit the Print button. "Donnie asks about you. He wants to know why you haven't come to see him."

"Tell him I'm sorry and I plan to rectify that soon. Does he still like the Utes?"

"The Utes, the Forty-Niners, and the Jazz."

"I've got plans this Saturday, but if he wants to go the following Saturday, I'll get some tickets and we can all meet at Rice-Eccles stadium and watch the Utes play UCLA. The weather shouldn't be too cold for November."

"He'd love that," she smiled. "We all would. I'll bring plenty of hot chocolate just in case the weather decides not to cooperate."

The printer stopped and she handed me the printout. I glanced at the ten pages. I had my work cut out for me, but at least it was a start.

"Thanks, April." I got up.

She jumped up and rushed around the desk. "Don't be a stranger, David Crockett." Her hug was tight and filled with love. What would it be like to find someone like that?

"See you next Saturday."

I sat in my car thinking about April and her family. The friendship felt good, the loneliness not so much. Hey, get a grip, I told myself. You're not alone; you've got Sam to come home to.

We PIs take our victories where we can find them.

FIVE

Living in Salt Lake City you learn two very important things. The first is that the Mormon Church carries a lot of weight. The second is that BYU is the most hated football team in the world. I have seen many rivalries in my lifetime, Texas/Texas A&M, Ohio State/Michigan, USC/UCLA, Army/Navy, but nothing reached the hostility of BYU/University of Utah. State supremacy, conference jealousy, years of BYU success and tradition, Utah's addition to the Pac Twelve without BYU, mixed with a heavy dose of religion and old fashioned bigotry, and you have got some crazy football fans that would move heaven and earth to get the best of the other.

So sitting in Jackson's living room in Salt Lake County watching BYU play football just seemed wrong. But not to Jackson.

He loved his Cougars. He had played tight end during a very successful run for the boys in blue and had beaten Utah three out of the four years he played. That, in and of itself, was an accomplishment as the Utes had had the upper hand before he arrived. Naturally, he considered his play as the difference maker. He met Julie at BYU, fell in love, and had gotten married. So Jackson was true blue through and through.

After the restoration crew had left my office looking like nothing bad had happened, I made the twenty-five minute drive to Jackson's house for the game.

Jackson lives in a modest house in Murray, a suburb of Salt Lake City. It is a two-story, four bedroom house with a stone exterior trimmed with heavy wooden beams, which gives it an expensive look. It would probably cost eight hundred thousand in another state but not in Salt Lake City, which is why so many people come to Utah to retire.

I watched as Julie sat in front of Jackson a plate brimming with food, a large ham and cheese sandwich, chips, salsa, guacamole dip, and a bowl of hot chili, while Jackson wrestled with his two kids, eleven-year-old Andrew and seven-year old Maggie. Watching them made me long for that kind of life. Julie and Jackson had the kind of relationship that everyone should have and few did.

It seemed so effortless, but I knew better. I had seen first-hand how hard they both worked at being there for the other, worked at making the other feel wanted, loved and needed. Many a night while we were working on a case, Jackson had simply left so he could be home for dinner with Julie and the kids, or take her on their weekly date. It was never convenient or easy, but he did it. It was important to him and as much as he loved work and putting away bad guys, Julie and the kids always came first. Maybe that was all it took, being dedicated enough to make them your first priority in life.

I had never been able to do it. But then again I had never met anyone like Julie, at least that's what I keep telling myself when I get in a reflective mood.

Julie laid the law down and the wrestling immediately stopped as the kids scrambled to their chairs to watch the game. Julie sat another plate in front of me and then sat down beside her husband. "If I could only find someone like you, I'd be married tomorrow," I teased her.

"You mean a nice Mormon girl?" Jackson shot back.

"Exactly. Well, except for the nice and Mormon part."

"And that's why you're still single, my friend."

I hated it when he was right.

At half time, with BYU leading Notre Dame 21 to 10, Jackson was in a good mood. It was the perfect time to question him, so I pulled him into the backyard to talk shop.

"Do you remember the Sylvia Parker case?" I asked, popping the top on my can of Heineken.

"The suicide?"

"Yeah."

"She was found dead on her bed with a half filled bottle of wine and an empty bottle of sleeping pills on the night stand. Pretty open and shut. Why?"

I took a swig of beer. "The daughter thinks the father murdered her. She's hired me to investigate."

"What's the motive?"

"Don't know yet. You think I might be able to look at the file?"

Jackson frowned, shaking his head slightly. "That was Harry Reed's case. I'll see if I can get a copy for you. But don't hold your breath. You know what Reed thinks of you."

"That I'm a great detective and wonderful human being?"

"Keep telling yourself that," he smiled. "Anything on our girl?"

"Nothing so far. She's not a student at the U, not in the morgue, although I can't be sure until we find prints on her. I checked out all the local hospitals and so far nothing."

He stared at the lemonade in his hand. I could tell he was feeling the same sense of frustration I was encountering. "I appreciate you trying."

"I got the DMV records of everyone named Jennifer with the last name beginning with a J. Maybe something will pop."

"What about impound records for the past three month? If she is really missing, maybe her car was towed."

"Look at you, going all detective on me," I kidded. "Think you can get them for me?"

He looked at me as if I had asked if he was really a BYU fan. Of course he could get them for me, what was I thinking?

"What about the blind date, the lawyer named Franklin?"

"Mr. All Ego and Attitude? He's next on my list."   I shook my head in disgust. "The trouble is there are more lawyers in this town than cockroaches."

He glanced around his well-manicured backyard, then back to me. "I'll ask around and see if anyone recognizes the name. Who knows, we may get lucky."

"All right," I responded. "I'll check the law registries and the Utah State Bar Association."

"Honey," Julie called from the back door. "The game is about to start again."

With nothing left to say, we headed back inside.

***

I don't know how he did it, but Jackson got me a copy of the Parker file. He was right, there wasn't much in it. According to the police report, Sylvia Parker was found dead on her bed by the neighbor, whom Parker had called when he became worried about his wife. The house had been locked from the inside and, using a key Parker had told him where to find, he entered the premises. The neighbor found Sylvia Parker on the bed. According to the report there was no sign of a struggle or any kind of forced entry. Sylvia Parker's fingerprints were the only ones found on the empty bottle of sleeping pills and on the wine glass on the night stand. All indications led to suicide.

Justin Boudreau, the medical examiner, confirmed that the cause of death was indeed an overdose of sleeping pills. According to the report, Boudreau had put the time of death no earlier than Saturday night, at which time Martin Parker was at Lake Powell in the company of friends. The case was ruled a suicide and closed.

I looked at the photos of Sylvia Parker in death. She looked as if she had just finished reading her magazine and peacefully drifted off to sleep. She was lying on her back, her reading glasses still on, a magazine under her hands, which were folded across her chest, her right wrist resting on her left wrist.

I closed the copy of the file and sat back in my chair. It was pretty cut and dried. But the fact that Faith Parker was so convinced that it was foul play made me curious.

Murders are usually committed for one of three reasons: sex, power, and money. Parker had all the money and the power, which usually allowed for the sex. What could he possibly accomplish by murdering his wife?

I decided to take a walk down the hall to visit my client. I opened the door to the Parker Talent Agency and stepped inside. It was a large office with straight-backed wooden chairs lining each of the walls leading to a desk near the back. The walls were decorated by 8x10 head shots of smiling actors and actresses.

Five girls sat in the various chairs that lined the wall. All young, attractive, and intently studying lines or monologues for their big moment.

At the far end a Latino woman, who looked to be in her mid-forties, sat guarding an office door from all the wanna-be-stars. She had frosted hair, long sharp nails painted a bright red, and too much makeup around the eyes, which made her look more dangerous than she probably was. She looked up as I entered and gave me a pleasant smile. Maybe she had a part for me. Maybe they were looking for a tall, handsome detective to make his cinematic debut in the next Ron Howard or Ridley Scott film. Or maybe she was just making sure I didn't race past her into the inner sanctum of the acting world and be discovered.

I glanced at all the smiling faces staring down at me from the wall of potential success. What made people want to subject themselves to such scrutiny and possible rejection?

One of the girls silently mouthing her lines looked up and smiled. Her smile was warm and bright as she looked at me with dark, brown eyes. Maybe she thought I was a producer looking for a new star.

"May I help you?" the Latino woman called out.

Brown eyes stared intently at me. Maybe I would be able to help her in some way.

"David Crockett to see Miss Parker."

"Do you have an appointment?"

"No, but she'll see me. I'm the private investigator from down the hall."

Disappointed, brown eyes went back to her script.

The woman stood from behind her desk. "Have a seat and I'll tell Faith you're here."

As she disappeared behind the closed door, I sat down and looked for something to read. Old *People* and *US* magazines didn't appeal to me so I glanced up at the wall of p o t e n t i a l stars. Nothing but a collage of perfect teeth, hair, and skin. Did they all really look like that? Were they really that perfect?

As I was pondering such profound questions, a beautiful young girl with a page boy haircut and big dark eyes caught my attention. Roxie Rhodes. Her perfect white smile seemed to be just for me. Then another one also caught my attention, thick, silky hair and sparkling eyes that seemed to burn into my soul making me want to stare at the photo. Jennifer Marie. She, too, seemed to jump off the page. Then Jean Mancil, long blonde hair, cute button nose, and hypnotic eyes. Why did these three girls stand out from all the others? Was this what they called charisma or the "it" factor in Hollywood? Or was I just being manipulated by good lighting and a great photographer?

"Mr. Crockett?"

I tore my eyes from the pictures and turned towards the sound.

"Miss Parker will see you now."

Faith stood as I entered. She smiled that smile that made my heart flutter. Can hearts actually flutter? Maybe *Doctor Who* could tell me.

"Have you found anything?" Her voice was tight and anxious. I hated to disappoint her.

"Nothing yet."

She sat back down, defeated.

"I've looked at the file and so far everything is as the police said it was."

"So you think I'm being overly sensitive about this whole thing?"

"Not necessarily. But I do need to see the crime scene."

"I can arrange that."

"Is it going to be a problem with your father?"

"He doesn't spend much time there. He now lives at the company apartment at the City Creek Center."

My eyes narrowed. "Alone?"

"Is that important?" she asked, her brow wrinkling.

"If he is seeing someone else it could be motive."

"I never thought of that," she sighed. "Do you think you will find anything at the house?"

"It's a long shot, especially if your father has cleaned up."

She shook her head. "I don't think so. He's rarely around, though he does go out there from time to time.

"Let's hope it's not to clean."

"Do you need me to go with you?"

"No. I just need a key and an address."

Removing a set of keys from her desk, she tossed them towards me. After writing the address down, she stood. I followed suit.

"I'm not crazy, David. He killed her. I don't know how he did it, but I know he did."

She was determined. Positive. I wished I was.

I followed State Street to 54th South then turned east and headed towards the mountains. After fifteen minutes I turned on 3200 East, then left into an expensive housing division on the upper bench. Nothing in the neighborhood went for less than a quarter of a million dollars. Someone was making good money. I found the correct address, parked in front, and got out.

The house was a massive two story stone structure. A healthy growth of ivy spread along the side of the house and two monstrous elm trees provided shade for the entire front.

Using the key Faith had given me, I entered the premises. The entry way was bright and well-lit from the two large windows flanking the front door. The floor was wood and highly polished so that you could almost see your reflection in the shine. A marble table stood beside one wall guarded by a large plant. It needed water.

I found my way to the stairs and began my climb. The wide hallway was carpeted in rich, beige carpeting and ran the length of the hallway ending at the door of the master bedroom. Slowly opening the door, I peered into the room. The silence was eerie as I stepped into the dark room. Finding the light switch, I flipped it on.

The room was like a morgue. The large, dark green curtains covering the window were drawn. The bed was still unmade, but everything else looked orderly and in its place. This didn't look promising. If Martin Parker had really killed his wife, he would have surely cleaned up any and all evidence he might have left behind before the crime scene unit arrived. On the other hand, he lived there so anything found could be logically explained. And if his ego was as large as Faith had said, he would have an answer for everything. Now I was motivated.

I opened the curtains, and light poured into the room. The walls were painted a bright peach color that matched the large comforter on the bed. Surprisingly, the walls were empty of expensive art work or family photos. The exception was a large color painting of a very distinguished-looking man, Sylvia Parker, and a young Faith hanging to the left of the bed and above a large oak bureau. They looked like the perfect American family. Opposite the bed, a large entertainment center filled with DVDs stood underneath the fifty-five inch flat screen television hanging on the wall.

I ran my hand over the entertainment center and felt the dust collect on my hand. I glanced around deciding where to start. I decided on the bed. I tried to picture Sylvia Parker there. In the photos she was on the bed with the covers thrown back, a magazine under her hands. Something about the photos bothered me but I didn't know what. I stared at the bed. Nothing jumped out at me. Did I really expect it to? Was I thinking that just by showing up some big red sign would be there pointing to an important clue. That sure would make my job easier.

I leaned down and looked under the bed. Nothing. As I stood back up I noticed one of the pillowcases had been removed from the large pillows at the head of the bed. As I picked it up I saw a faint stain. Looking closer, it appeared to be a wine stain. As I set the pillow back on the bed, I saw what looked like a matching stain on the bottom sheet. I removed my phone and took a close-up picture, then one farther away to show the whole pillow and stain on the bed. I didn't know what was on the pillowcase but it must have been important for CSI to take it.

I stared at the bed hoping to find blood and matted hair, something to show a crime was committed, but nothing. Instinctively, I straightened the top sheet, and then the comforter, examining them for any evidence. Again nothing. Where was that big red sign when I needed it.

If she had killed herself then, as expected, there wouldn't be any evidence to the contrary. But something had caused CSI to take the pillow case. Against my better judgment, I got on my hands and knees and made a careful sweep of the area between the bed and the bureau. I came up empty. Following the same procedure, I searched the area between the bed and the large windows. Near the baseboard under the window, something small and white caught my attention in the afternoon sun. Partially hidden in the plush carpet was what looked like a tiny piece of a pill. A sleeping pill? If Sylvia Parker had taken the pills in an effort to kill herself, why would a piece of one be on the floor under the window? Did this have anything to do with the stain on the pillow? And why hadn't CSI vacuumed the floor and tagged the contents as evidence? But of what? I reminded myself. Most likely it was quickly ruled a suicide and Detective Reed ordered the scene processed with that conclusion in mind. Reed, bless his lazy little heart, was always looking for shortcuts in order to close a case and enjoy the praise from the political hacks in the department for a job well done.

I dropped the small white particle in a baggie I had brought and continued my examination of the carpet floor. My painstaking time was rewarded by three more small bits of pills spread out over the area. My curiosity soared. Gagging and spitting won't send pills flying that far. That kind of flight is only caused by an opposing force of some kind.

After finding nothing else out of place in the bedroom, I moved into the bathroom. It was spotless. Some people really keep their places clean. I looked into the medicine cabinet. Beauty products, cough medicine, arthritic cream, and aspirin. No prescriptions or medicine of any kind. Then what was she doing with sleeping pills?

Closing the cabinet, I re-entered the bedroom and headed for the large walk-in closet. It was bigger than my whole bedroom. Some people. The right side was filled with expensive suits and men's shoes. On the left side, dresses, gowns and coats hung above an entire platform filled with expensive shoes. I searched the coats, hoping to find a receipt for sleeping pills or anything that might shed a light on what went on the night Sylvia Parker died. In one coat I found a folded up receipt for a Vivint Security System, which wasn't unusual for an expensive house of this size. In the last coat, I found a crumpled up business card. It was for the law firm of Jakins, Jakins, and Schuster. Normally, this wouldn't mean much but Jakins, Jakins, and Schuster were the best, and the most exclusive, divorce lawyers in the city. Placing the card in my pocket, I closed the closet door.

On top of the bureau I noticed a pair of men's gloves lying near the edge. I guess someone forgot to put them away. I opened each of the six drawers in the cabinet and rummaged through them. The large three drawers on the left were filled with men's items, socks, underwear, handkerchiefs, belts, and gloves. The right side held female items, bras, panties, slips. Like everything else in the house, the drawers were neat and orderly.

At the night stand I opened the drawer and began shuffling through the papers inside. There were credit card receipts, phone records, and personal cards, but no prescription receipts of any kind. How could she have gotten a prescription for sleeping pills and not have the receipt or doctors instructions that come with all prescriptions?

I was concentrating on this dilemma when a painful blow to my head sent me spiraling towards the floor.

Six

This is really nice carpeting, plush and luxurious.
My head felt like watermelon dropped from a four story building on to a hot pavement, yet all I could think of was the softness of the carpet against my face.

"I said, who are you and what are you doing in my house?" The repeating voice bore into my head like an automatic drill. Opening my eyes, I rolled over and sat up.

"Slowly," the voice demanded.

A man was sitting in a chair above me, holding a gun.

He was well dressed. From my position on the floor I could see his shoes quite well. They were Italian loafers. He was tanned with a wide forehead and a thick head of silver hair. He had Faith's deep blue eyes so I knew I was staring at Martin Parker.

"I'm a private eye." I reached for my card.

"Not so fast."

"I'm just reaching for my card."

"Go ahead."

I pulled a business card from my pocket and handed it to him. He studied it for a moment, then tossed it back on the floor near me. As I picked it up, Parker stood and backed away, keeping the chair between us.

"Get up," he barked.

Using the night stand to steady myself, I obeyed.

"What are you doing in my house?"

"You mean this isn't for sale?"

"Don't get cute with me. Why are you here?"

"I was hired to look into the suicide of your wife."

"My daughter." He spit the words out in anger. "She just won't leave it alone, will she?" He motioned around the room with the gun. "You are not going to find anything so you might as well quit wasting your time."

Normally, I would take the gun away and use it as a rectal thermometer, but my head was still pounding. I decided to buy more time.

"You want to tell me what happened?"

"My wife was distraught and she committed suicide. That's all there is to it."

"Why was she distraught?"

"Someone I loved very much died needlessly and it is still a very painful subject. I would rather not discuss it, especially with you."

"Were you having marital problems?"

"Go to hell."

He was starting to get angry. Maybe if I made him angry enough he would blurt out the truth like all those poor saps in the *Perry Mason* re-runs. "Maybe you found out she was going to divorce you. Is that why you killed her?"

"I did not kill her. I loved her."

"Mr. Parker?"

I turned to see two officers standing in the door way. One was fresh shaven with a boyish face that didn't appear to be more than twenty-five. Most likely just out of the police academy. The other was about thirty and the senior partner. Parker moved back and turned to the officers. "This is the burglar, officers."

"Burglar? I'm not a burglar. I'm a private eye who was hired to take a look at the crime scene." I handed the senior officer my card.

"There is no crime scene!" Parker's voice raised an octave. "I want him arrested for trespassing."

"I have a gun, right side, shoulder holster," I informed the rookie moving towards me. He stopped and immediately reached for his gun.

"If I was going to shoot, you'd already be dead," I said. It didn't ease his anxiety. "Put your hands on your head," he commanded.

As I followed his instructions, he removed my gun while the second officer cuffed me.

"Let's go, sir."

Jail is not my favorite place to be, but sometimes that is the price of doing business. I knew they couldn't hold me for long since I had permission from the daughter and was given a key to enter the premises. Sometimes cops just like to teach you a lesson, let you stew a little. I never did like stew.

"Open the door."

I heard a familiar voice entering the holding area. The deputy immediately rushed to the cell and unlocked it.

"What took you so long?" I asked petulantly.

Jackson ambled to the cell. "I had to finish my cup of hot chocolate," he said with a shrug.

I rushed out of the cell and Jackson and I left the holding area. Making our way up the back stairs to the detective station, two floor up, we settled in at his desk. Marx gave me a 'what's up' and went back to his endless paperwork.

"I got your personal belongings for you," Jackson said as he motioned to my wallet, keys, and plastic evidence bag lying on his desk. He held up the evidence bag. "You want to explain this?"

"I found them in the Parker bedroom," I stuffed my wallet into my back pocket and my keys into my coat then sat down. "If I'm right those are part of the sleeping pills found in Sylvia Parker's system."

"So? We know she took sleeping pills and washed them down with wine."

"Who takes sleeping pills and then spills bits and pieces of them over by the baseboard? Something doesn't add up, Jackson."

"Maybe, but the husband was at Lake Powell when she died. His alibi is rock solid. We've been over this. There is no way he could have killed her."

"I also found this." I pulled the card from my inside coat pocket. "It's a business card for Jakins, Jakins, and Schuster, divorce attorneys."

"You think she was divorcing him?"

"You don't go to see that firm unless you have money and are serious about divorce. And if she was thinking of divorcing him that could be motive."

"Except he couldn't have done it," Jackson answered slowly, as if I was an eight-year old who just didn't understand.

"He could have hired someone," I replied defending my position.

"There was no sign of forced entry or struggle. David, the evidence just doesn't support anything you're saying."

He was right and maybe it never would, but my gut was telling me there was something more to this case and I was determined to find out what.

"Anything else on Jenny?"

"I haven't had a chance to go through the DMV records. That's number one on the list when I get back to the office."

He reached into his desk and pulled out an 8x10 envelope. "Here's the impound records on anyone named Jennifer J in the past two months."

I took the envelope and stood. "I'll keep you informed." With a nod to Marx, I turned to leave.

"Hey," Jackson smiled, "try to stay out of my jail."

"The service is lousy," I answered.

"I'll work on that."

We both knew he wouldn't.

An hour later I walked into Justin Boudreau's office. Boudreau was the Salt Lake City Medical Examiner and one of the most cantankerous men you would ever want to meet. He was in his late sixties, and, after a life of working with dead bodies, would much rather spend his time with the dead than the living, whom he called useless piles of wasted protoplasm.

For all his personality quirks, and there were many, Boudreau was great at what he did. Many a case would have slipped through the cracks if not for his amazing skill and perception. We had become friends, as far as you can with Justin, when the local politicians decided he was past his prime and tried to replace him with a younger, but inexperienced political appointee. They had forced the young coroner on him in the middle of a very public murder case.

When evidence surfaced that a critical mistake had been made that almost cost the prosecutor the case, the blame went directly to Justin and he was fired, opening the door for the favored political son. As a favor to Jackson, I got involved and proved the mistake was not Justin's but the appointee. The Mayor had no choice but to reinstate him. At a substantial pay raise to boot. After that he tolerated me better than most.

Since his worthless assistant, Wesley Wyler, was not at his command post, I wandered straight into the morgue.

Boudreau was in the process of removing the skull cap

of a female cadaver as I entered. On the table beside him sat an extra-large meatball sandwich, the rich marinara sauce dripping over onto the metal tray. This was not surprising as Boudreau's heritage was planted deep in the food-loving Cajun soil of New Orleans. He was not only a great medical examiner, but a fair to middling cook, and was famous for bringing all kinds of exotic dishes to work. He glanced up at me as I moved towards him.

"Let me show you something," he grinned as he pulled the skull back. "Talk about a marvelous compartment. Look at the way the brain fits into this space and all the bone and skull around it to protect it."

"Can't get that kind of compartment at Walmart," I joked.

He frowned and continued working. Jokes about the marvelous intricacies of the human body were not appreciated in his domain.

I took advantage of the quiet. "Two months ago you worked on the death of a Sylvia Parker. Do you remember that?"

"Of course I remember, I remember all my cases. I'm old, not stupid." He took a large bite of a meatball sub sandwich. "What about her?" he asked, his mouth full.

"You ruled her death a suicide."

He glanced at me like I was an ignorant student. "Her prints were the only ones on the wine glass and empty bottle of sleeping pills. She had a stomach full of said pills and wine and there were no other marks to indicate anything different, so duh?"

"What if you were wrong?"

His head snapped around and his nostrils flared. "How could I be wrong, you protoplasmic pie hole?" He wiped some sauce from his mouth. "I followed the evidence."

I removed the plastic bag from my coat. "I found these in Sylvia Parker's bedroom."

He took the bag and gazed at the white particles inside.

"Let me guess," he muttered. "You found these particles and are now convinced she was murdered?"

Nothing like taking all the excitement out of my discovery. "I found them by the baseboard under the large window," I replied defensively. "If they are from the same batch that killed her, then what were they doing so far from the bed? There was also a stain on the pillow like she had tried to spit out the wine and pills."

"That's consistent with a stain and white particles on the silk pillowcase," he said irritably. "Most likely they were produced when she began choking and coughed out some of the pills and wine."

"That wouldn't explain how these particles got so far from the bed?" I countered.

He sighed as if preparing himself for my off-base explanation. I continued. "What if she was hit by someone causing the pills to fly out of her mouth?"

"I don't do shoddy work, Crockett," he snapped. "Except for a very slight discoloration on her left cheek, which looked like a mild rash, I didn't find any evidence of bruising."

"Isn't it possible the discoloration could have been caused by a hit?"

"If someone had hit her as hard as you seem to think, the hand would have left a pronounced mark. This mark was barely visible."

"Could they have used some kind of buffer, like a towel or pillow or something?" I asked, pursuing my point.

"That kind of buffer wouldn't have left any mark."

"Gloves," I mumbled almost to myself.

"Gloves?" he replied abruptly.

"I saw a pair of gloves on the bureau. Could a gloved hand have produced such a mark?"

"It might."

"Could you take another look and see if you might have missed something?"

"Crockett, I have enough work down here to keep me busy without being your personal investigator."

"All I'm asking is to send these particles up to SLID and see if they can match it with what you found in her stomach, to see if there is any of her DNA on them."

"That's it, huh?" he snapped sarcastically.

"And take another look at the autopsy photos to see if the discoloration might have been caused by a slap. That's all."

"You don't ask for much, do you?"

"This is important, Justin."

"With you it's always important." He stared at me for a moment. "Get out of my office. I've got work to do."

"One more question," I persisted.

His glare told me he'd had enough of my questions. And this was one he was not going to like. "How come your boys didn't find these particles when they processed the room?"

I could see the veins in his neck bulging as he controlled his temper. I had hit a sore spot.

"Don't you think I would have found them if I had been looking for them?" he snapped. "It was ruled a suicide from the get go by that idiot Reed. We took the glass, the empty bottle of wine and pills, and the body. I noticed the wine stains on the pillow case and took that also. Reed and his partner had already made up their minds so we were forced to do a quick process and get the hell out of there." He took another bite of his meatball sandwich. "Turns out he was right. Now get the hell out of my office."

"I appreciate this, Justin."

"I didn't say I'd do anything, so save your gratitude for someone who gives a crap," he snarled.

I thought I saw a flicker of a smile, but then again, it could have been gas from the extra-large meatball sandwich.

***

Jakins, Jakins, and Schuster was located in the Wells Fargo

Building downtown Salt Lake City. They weren't your average divorce lawyers. They also weren't the kind of divorce lawyers you went to just for exploration. If you were seeing them, you were serious.

I parked and made my way towards the large glass doors.

An older looking gentleman with a handful of paperwork was coming out the door. I held it open for him then started inside.

"Mr. Crockett?"

I turned to see the older man staring at me.

"Yes?"

"Enuizo Marcelo."

He looked familiar but at the moment I couldn't place him.

"I run the sporting goods store across the street from Katie Blues."

"Mr. Marcelo, yes. How are you?"

"Much better now thanks to you. I can't tell you how much I appreciate what you did for us."

Four years ago when I was still with the force, a sixty-three-year old man named Karl Stallings showed up at the strip mall across from Katie's in a wheelchair. He demanded that all the businesses put in wheel chair ramps so he could enter. He protested outside for a week, getting the media involved. At the height of the media storm, he went to the owners and said he would settle for two thousand dollars cash from each owner. Four of the five stores paid him off. Mr. Marcelo didn't.

The pressure increased. Soon fifty or so handicapped individuals were protesting in front of the stores, and the public began to boycott the entire strip mall.

When Stallings hit Katie up for the same money, she came to me. If he really believed in what he was doing, why settle for chump change? Something didn't add up so I decided to watch him.

On my off hours, I watched as he went into his doctor's office, Gold's Gym, The Salad Bar, and other public places using his wheelchair. He looked legit.

After filing an injunction against the store owners, he showed up in court in his wheelchair. He made a very convincing argument. Even I believed him.

He also played the media for all he was worth, which helped sway the public into his corner against the evil business owners. The court ruled in his favor and Katie and the other businesses were ordered to pay two-hundred and fifty thousand dollars apiece for his struggles.

He was extremely careful, and, had it not been for the greatest snow on earth, I would have never caught him.

In early November of that year, I had gone to visit friends in Provo, Utah, about forty-five miles south of Salt Lake. Darrell and Gina were avid skiers, so we had drive up Provo Canyon to the Sundance Ski Resort for a day of skiing and good food.

As we got off the tram and moved towards the sloping mountain edge to begin our run, I noticed an older gentleman with a deep tan and silver hair standing and putting his goggles on.

What caught my attention was the fact that he wasn't bundled from head to toe in expensive ski clothes. Instead, he had on sweat pants and a tank top. In Utah this isn't unusual since it can snow in the morning and in the afternoon the sun can come out, making it feel like spring. That he looked to be in his seventies, and in such good shape, made me look twice. His body was toned, muscular, and firm. It looked like the body of a thirty-year-old athlete.

Upon closer inspection, I recognized Karl Stallings.

Using my phone video I followed him down the hill. At the bottom, I waited until he removed his goggles, then had Gina call his name. Two things trip up a con artist every time, being in a place where they believe no one knows them, and the lure of an attractive woman. This was a case of both. Being so far from Salt Lake and seeing a beautiful woman waving at him was something he couldn't resist. He smiled and waved back.

He was convicted of extortion and welfare fraud and sentenced to five years in jail. As he left the court room he turned and yelled at me, the judge, and his own attorney that one day he would get even with us for messing up his life. Like I haven't heard that before.

"What brings you downtown?" I asked Mr. Marcelo.

He motioned to the stack of paper in his arms. "I just had to see my accountant. I swear the government is trying to bleed me dry in taxes."

"I hear you," I commiserated.

"Anytime you need any sporting equipment you come to me. I'll treat you right."

"I know you will, Mr. Marcelo. I appreciate that." I turned to go. "You take care, sir."

I left him struggling with his mound of paperwork and entered the building.

Getting off the elevator on the tenth floor, I moved through the large oak doors into the reception room of Jakins, Jakins and Schuster. I felt my pocketbook get smaller just by walking into the place. Instinctively, I reached for my wallet to see if it was still there. It was. After two divorces some habits are hard to break.

The reception area was large and well furnished with expensive chairs, end tables, and lots of beautiful green plants. The receptionist sat behind a large, curved mahogany panel. She was about fifty, with slightly graying hair and large tasteful ear rings.

"May I help you?" She smiled as I approached.

"I'd like to see Mr. Jakins?"

"Which one, James or Jared?"

"Which one's the best?"

"Do you have an appointment?"

"No appointment, just an angry wife who is determined to take me to the cleaners." I leaned across the panel. "And between me and you I don't want to lose any of my fifty-million-dollar estate."

She glared at me as if wondering how someone dressed as casually as I was could have fifty-million dollars. In the end, the possibility of money always does the trick. She picked up the phone. "Whom shall I say is waiting?"

"Jason Huntsman."

"Mr. Jakins? Jason Huntsman would like to see you about his divorce."

She listened then cupped the phone with her hand and smiled at me. "Are you a member of the Huntsman family?"

I gave her my best offended look. She immediately drew her own conclusion.

"Yes sir, he is. Yes, sir." She hung up the phone. "Mr. Jakins will be right with you."

I waited about ten minutes when a tall, pleasant-looking man in a two-thousand-dollar Armani suit, gold cufflinks, and Italian shoes approached.

"Mr. Huntsman? I'm Mr. Jakins." He offered his hand and we shook. His handshake was firm and confident. I could see why they were so successful.

"Janice, bring some mineral water and fruit to the office." His tone was sharp and to the point. He was used to giving orders and having them obeyed.

His face was lean and tight, his eyes brown behind gold horn-rimmed glasses that gave him the look of an educated college professor. He had a well-trimmed beard surrounding a smile that must have cost thousands. His teeth were bright and perfect in every way.

"This way, Mr. Huntsman."

I followed him down the long hall to his plush office.

It was large and filled with ornate furnishings. Numerous

diplomas dotted the light green walls. There were so many I wondered if he had started collecting them in grade school. His desk was shiny white oak with gold strips decorating the legs. His chair was Mahogany-colored leather that put my imitation chair to shame. I guess he didn't shop at Office Max.

On the wall behind him was a large framed family photo with Jakins, his wife, and six perfectly dressed kids standing from the shortest to the tallest.

He offered me a seat then moved gracefully behind his desk. As he sat down he stared at me as if trying to decide if I really was a Huntsman. Needless to say my attire wasn't anything a Huntsman would be caught dead in.

"I thought I knew all of the Huntsman children. Where do you fit into the picture?"

"I'm the one on the far left."

He stared at me with unblinking eyes. No sense of humor, I guess.

"And your father is Jon Huntsman?"

One thing about the Huntsman family is they didn't get divorced very often, so the odds were on my side that he had never met all of the children. No doubt he was fishing to see if I had the kind of money I was implying.

"You know my father?" I asked, again letting him draw his own conclusion.

He shifted in his chair. "Not personally, but the name is well respected around here."

"Well if you did you would know that some of his children are not exactly cut from the same mold."

"Of course." He cleared his throat. It was time to move on. "How did you hear about us, if I may ask?"

"A dear friend recommended you to me."

"And who might that be?"

I shifted uncomfortably in my chair and glanced around the room. The detective playing the caring friend. Maybe

I could get my picture on Faith's wall of potential success after all.

"I'm hesitant to say due to the unfortunate circumstances of her death."

"You mean Sylvia?" He looked at me with suspicious eyes.

"I still can't believe what happened. She was such a dear woman," I said with as much sadness I could muster.

"It was so unlike her." He sat back in his chair giving me his best pensive and thoughtful look. The caring attorney.

"My thought exactly." I nodded with a sigh. I wasn't about to let him out-care me. "Of course, the divorce must have been weighing heavily on her."

"Divorce?" he replied, playing his cards close to the vest.

"I'm sorry," I said as penitently as I could. "I forgot Sylvia didn't want anyone to know." I leaned in closer to his desk. "I hope no one let it slip to Martin. We both know how that would have turned out."

"What do you mean?" He sat up and studied me with penetrating eyes. Nothing worse than a cautious attorney. He wasn't as gullible as I had hoped. Of course with what he charged an hour, I was crazy to even think it. It was time to change tactics, to go on the offensive. I knew he wasn't about to leak any privileged client information but if I played it right, he might give me some insight into the actual state of the Parker marriage and Martin Parker's personality. Did he have a temper? Was he violent? Did he have it in him to kill his wife?

I leaned into to him and gave him my most serious look. "With all due respect, Mr. Jakins, you know exactly what I mean."

He sighed and interlocked his fingers across his expansive chest. "Sadly, I do."

"You don't think he would have actually harmed her do you, just for coming to see you about the divorce?"

"Well, I can't say if there was a divorce." He smiled his professional attorney smile. "Privileged information, you understand?"

Most attorneys like to talk if you let them. They enjoy sharing information if they can, since most of the time they can't, so the trick is to just let them go where they want to go. "But do you think he was capable of harming her?" I repeated.

His face was unreadable as he stared at me. "You know Martin?"

"Sadly, yes," I agreed.

"He was arrogant, hostile, and walked around with a chip on his shoulder," he said hotly.

"I don't know why Sylvia put up with him as long as she did."

He nodded in agreement. "Sometimes it takes a person a while to see the forest for the trees," he replied thoughtfully.

Bingo. In my court room that was as good as an admission. Confident he could get my business he smiled and leaned forward across his large desk. "Now what can I do for you?" The door opened and Janice entered with the water and fruit. Since I had no intentions of getting divorced or writing a retainer check that would pay for a new BMW, or getting caught passing myself off as a Huntsman, I needed to get out of there. Without betraying any client/ attorney privilege, Jakins had as much as confirmed that Sylvia Parker was divorcing Martin Parker. That would leave him without the golden calf, and for an arrogant man with a chip on his shoulder, a pretty solid motive for murder.

I glanced at the large, expensive grandfather clock standing by the door. "Is that clock right?"

"Of course." He seemed slightly offended that I would question such a prized clock.

I jumped up. "I'm so sorry but I didn't realize the time." I reached out to shake his hand. "I have a meeting at the

Huntsman Cancer Center that I can't miss. I'm sorry, I'll reschedule as soon as possible." I left them standing there in stunned silence. I guess no one ever walked out on Jakins, Jakins, and Schuster.

As I rushed down the hall and out the door I realized that Faith's description of her father had been accurate. Add that to the fact that Sylvia was planning a divorce and a motive began peeking out from under their beige carpet.

Now I just had to prove it.

SEVEN

I shifted uncomfortably in the seat. One of the things they don't tell you in private eye school, is that long periods of sitting makes your butt hurt. Some things only come with experience. I had been following Martin Parker for two days without anything suspicious, until now. He had moved out of this house right after the murder so why was he back, especially two days after he had caught me snooping around? Was he looking for evidence he might have missed? Was he cleaning up and destroying anything he might have left behind?

I sat up as the door opened and Parker exited. He was carrying a box of something. Maybe it was only his toiletries. He moved to the side of the house and when he returned he was pushing a large trash can. I noticed other trash cans waiting patiently in the street like rows of soldiers guarding the houses.

The box was gone. So much for toiletries.

After setting the can in place he walked to his car and drove away. I lowered my binoculars and left my hiding place down the street.

Since the trash can was on the street, which was public property, I had every legal right to dig through it and recover whatever was inside. I took my camera and snapped a close up of the number spray painted on the side, and then opened the large brown lid. On top of the pile of trash were the gloves I had seen on his dresser two days ago. I snapped another picture, and, taking a plastic bag from my evidence bag I keep in my car, I slid the gloves inside. Why was he getting rid of a perfectly good pair of gloves? I removed the trash bag from the can, tied it with a twist tie from my evidence kit, tossed it in the trunk and drove off.

I arrived back at my office in time to see my new furniture being unloaded.

Two giant Polynesians were standing by the back of the moving truck looking at the address. One was about six two and must have weighed 300 pounds. The other was about six feet and 310. From the look of them they must have been former University of Utah football players, which reminds me of a joke, which, of course, no one in his right mind would share with these two giants.

How do you get a University of Utah graduate off your porch? Pay for the pizza. Okay, one more.

Everybody knows about BYU's strict honor code. But the University of Utah has its own honor code. "Yes, your honor, I'm sorry your honor, I'll never do it again your honor."

And there are just as many BYU jokes floating around. How do you keep a BYU football player out of your yard? Put up a goalpost.

What's the difference between a B YU coed and an elephant? About ten pounds.

During rivalry week these jokes fly back and forth. They

are corny and they irritate each school but each fan base really enjoys irritating the other. That, and good football, is what makes a good rivalry.

I quickly approached the two giants. "Hey guys, I hope that is for me."

The larger of the two looked at the name on the form. "David Crockett?"

"Yes. My office is up the stairs and down the hall. You need any help?"

They looked at me like I was crazy. "Nah, bro we got it," one of them replied nonchalantly.

I watched as they carried my new desk up the stairs, down the hallway, and into my office. It was solid cherry wood and must have weighed a ton, but you'd never know it. They carried it as if it were a piece of cardboard.

After instructing them as to where each piece of new furniture went, I signed their receipt and watched them waddle down the back stairs, smiling as they went. I had already picked up my re-framed Alamo poster and hung it back in its original place. Now my office was back the way it had once looked, only with much more expensive furniture.

I needed to get back to business. I sat down at my new cherry wood desk, pulled the DMV files that April had given me from my briefcase, and sat them on my new cherry-wood desk. I did say it was new, and cherry wood, didn't I?

I began the painstaking task of reviewing all the records. After looking at the pages of DMV records only four crossed with the impound records, matching name and age.

Jennifer Jocoby, twenty-eight, lived in Sandy, drove a 2012 blue Toyota Celica, no driving infractions or tickets. Her car had been impounded after a drunk driver had hit it while she was parked at a McDonalds.

Jennifer Jessup, twenty-eight, lived in Draper, drove a 2010 silver Chevy Belair, two parking tickets, but no accidents. Her car had been impounded after it was recovered by the police from thieves who had stolen it from the Southgate Mall parking lot.

Jennifer Justice, twenty-eight, drove a black 2002 Honda Civic; lived in an apartment near Westminster College on 13th East, no tickets or accidents. Her car was impounded after being left in the parking lot of the High Class Motel in Midvale for more than a week.

And the last was Jennifer Jardine, twenty-eight and her 2013 Silver Isuzu had been found in the parking lot of a Seven Eleven near Fifth West and Fifth South after two days. According to the report, no one had claimed the car in the two weeks since it had been impounded.

Sad to say there is usually only one reason someone leaves their car unattended for that long a period, and it isn't good. Did one of these cars belong to our Jenny J? As I began studying the files for anything unusual my phone rang.

This time I looked. It was Tonja. I hesitated. I wasn't in the mood for lectures or blind dates.

I let it ring.

On the third ring I felt bad. "Hi, sis."

"David." Her voice seemed strained and angry.

"What's the matter? Is Chris all right?" Chris Robertson was her husband serving in the army in Afghanistan. He had been there for over a year and was scheduled to come home in a month. That is usually the time those unwanted, and dreaded calls come. "No, he's fine. It's Joseph."

Joseph was their six-year-old. He was a handful. He had the heart of a lion and the imagination of a six-year-old. He could be Superman fighting against evil one minute, a cowboy fighting against aliens the next, or anything else his mind could dream up. He was all boy. I liked that about him.

"He's been suspended."

"Suspended? He's in the first grade. What can they possibly suspend him for? Coloring outside the lines?"

"He was eating breakfast, and, according to the school, chewed his pastry into the shape of a gun. A teacher noticed and took him to the principal. She suspended him."

"Are you kidding me? He got suspended for that?"
"With the way schools are run today, that's enough," she sighed.

"You want me to go talk to the principal?"

"Heavens no!" The words shot out of her mouth like I had asked her if she wanted me to kill someone for her.

"I'm stuck here at work and there is no way I can get away at the moment. Would you be able to go pick him up, please?"

"Sure. Who do I ask for?"

"Madeline Cook. She's the principal."

"All right. I'm on my way."

"David." She paused. When she finally spoke her voice was low and harsh. "Just pick him up from her. The last thing I need is you antagonizing Joseph's principal."

"Me, antagonize someone? Perish the thought."

"I mean it, David."

"Come on, sis, you know me."

"Please don't make things difficult for me."

I hung up the phone and rushed out the door.

As I reached the spot where I park my car, I hesitated. There was a note stuck under the windshield wiper. Thinking someone had hit my car, I made a quick inspection. There was no visible damage. My next thought was that it must be a love note, because I get so many of them. Right. I pulled the note from the wiper and opened it.

Crockett, you're going to Die. And SOON. Enjoy the short time that you have left.

It wasn't a love note.

I stared at the note, mentally running through all of

David Sterago

the people I might have really pissed off. While the list was long, I couldn't think of anyone angry enough to actually want to kill me. But someone was. My eyes swept the immediate area, hoping to see someone or something that would explain this. At Bayless's Deli down the street a few people were standing outside smoking. Was my note-writing friend one of them? Was he hiding somewhere close-by watching to see my reaction? Was part of the thrill hoping to see me scared? He was out of luck, then. I wasn't about to show him anything, at least not now. I had another problem to solve.

I turned into the parking lot at the Clinton Elementary School. Daniel John Clinton had been a long time principal and school board member during the Eighties. He had started a lot of the no-tolerance policies that were still being used with brute force in the school. While I agreed with some of them in principle, the extent at which they had morphed into a blob-like policy monster that ate everything in its path, bothered the hell out of me. I had a giant burr-under-my-saddle when it came to the subject.

In the Navy I had seen first-hand the danger of such politically correct thinking. While serving in Afghanistan, I became aware of a very dangerous man who had wormed his way, through political means, into the good graces of our military leaders. He was a captain of the Afghanistan police and worked closely with our unit. One day, through a reliable source, I was made aware of a plot this captain was part of. He was to lead one of our top units into an area where Afghanistan terrorists were waiting to ambush them. With no time to go through the chain of command or classified channels, I immediately emailed the information to one of the captains of that particular unit. Because I had levied unsubstantiated charges against a political ally, which politically wasn't a good thing to do, caused damage to his person (I hit the traitor when he laughed at my accusations) and because I had also done so through unclassified channels, I was brought up on charges. Never mind that the information proved to be accurate. Even though this unit was indeed attacked and eight of the twenty men were killed, two by this very Afghan policeman before he was shot dead, I was still put through the judicial wringer.

I was found guilty by a panel of political military appointees of putting our unit in danger by going through unclassified channels and striking a political ally. Because I had been right about the attack, however, they were forced to give me an honorable discharge.

It turned out that the person responsible for putting this policeman in with this unit was the son of a high-ranking politician, the very captain I had emailed. Someone had to take the fall and it wasn't the politician's son.

Digging up painful memories, a threatening note and an educational moron who had suspended my nephew for being, what I perceived as a normal, creative six-year old, had revved me into a combative state of mind. I should have called Mother or Jillian to pick up Joseph, but instead, I got out of my car and headed into the school.

Opening the door under the sign that said Principal's Office, I glanced around the large room. Cook's office was set back on the left with the vice-principal's office on the right. They were both protected by a large counter at the front of the room where a gregarious, heavyset receptionist sat, screening, like the best TSA screener, all persons trying to see the principal.

Along one wall, sat a row of chairs for the students unfortunate enough to have been sent there. It brought back a rush of high school memories, none of them good.

Tough private detective.

I approached the counter. "I'm David Crockett and I'm here to see Principal Cook."

The coco-colored receptionist smiled at me. I liked her

smile right away. She had large earrings, a ring on each finger, and glitter on her eyes, but it was her smile that attracted me. I felt better. Maybe the glitter helped the small kids sent to the principal's office to feel better. Or maybe she just marched to her own drummer and liked glitter.

"Please sign in," she smiled as she motioned towards the registration book on the counter in front of her.

I did as instructed.

"Thank you, Mr. Crockett. Now if you will be so kind as to have a seat, I'll let Ms. Cook know you're here."

I noticed Joseph in one of the chairs that lined the wall near the principal's office. He looked so frail and small sitting there in the adult chairs. I sat between him and another nervous-looking young boy.

"Hey, buddy."

With a confused, and frightened look, he leaned over, clinging tightly to me.

"Are you okay?"

The smell of urine reached my nose.

"They said I was bad and made me come here," he whispered.

"They didn't explain anything to you?"

He shook his head. "I was just eating and the teacher came over and took my pop tart away. She said I was being bad so she brought me here."

He shifted uncomfortably in his chair. As he did I noticed the wet stain on his jeans. I forced my anger down.

"Do you have to go to the bathroom?"

He stared up at me with his innocent big brown eyes. Tears of embarrassment started flowing down his cheeks.

"I tried to tell them but they wouldn't let me go. I didn't mean to, honest."

"Who did you tell?" My blood pressure was rising with each moment.

"Mrs. Lyrock. She brought me in here and wouldn't let me go to the bathroom."

"You've done nothing wrong, buddy."

He tried to smile, but I could tell he wasn't so sure. He had been taught to respect authority and now that authority had come crushing down on him.

"I'm going to straighten this out right now. Look at me." I knelt in front of him so we were eye to eye. "You did nothing wrong. You have nothing to be ashamed of. Do you understand me?"

He nodded. "Come on, let's get you cleaned up." He took my hand and we walked down the hall to the boy's bathroom. He cleaned himself as best he could and dried his pants using the hand dryer. As we walked back to the office, I wondered how supposedly intelligent people could act like such fools.

As we sat back down, Joseph seemed to relax. I glanced at the kid on the other side of me. He looked to be about seven. The knee of his pants was torn and his hair was a mess.

"Get in a fight?" I smiled.

He looked at me, satisfaction in his eyes and nodded.

"Sometimes I guess you just can't avoid it, can you?" I said.

"He pulled my girlfriend's hair," he sniffled.

"You have a girlfriend?"

He proudly nodded. I gave him a high five. I guess I really was the only one in the world without a girlfriend. Now even the glitter didn't help.

"Mr. Crockett?" I looked up. Madeline Cook was a sour-looking woman with dark eyes and weathered skin. Her posture was ram-rod straight and I was positive she was holding a ruler in her hand. She wasn't. Even more high school memories came flooding back.

David Sterago

She stood in her office door waiting for me to make the trip to her. Like a good servant I obeyed. I stood and made my way towards her.

When I reached her, she held out her hand. "I'm Principal Cook." Her grip was firm and manly.

I followed her into her office. She shut the door and then moved behind her desk and took her seat. I took a chair directly in front of her large desk.

"Are you the boy's father?" she asked curtly, making it clear by her tone that she had little tolerance for anyone associated with teaching a child anything about guns.

"No. Joseph's father is overseas in the military. I'm the pissed-off uncle."

Her superior tone easily slid into offended. "There is no need for that kind of language, Mr. Crockett."

I stared at her and didn't waver. She cleared her throat then continued. "Do you know why Joseph has been suspended?"

Just pick him up from her. The last thing I need is you antagonizing Joseph's principal. Tonja's words came rushing into my head.

I ignored them, my righteous indignation burning hot.

"The sheer stupidity of the progressive educational system?"

"Mr. Crockett you may allow your nephew to act like a hooligan, but here at Daniel John Clinton Elementary School, we do not. We take any kind of threat with a gun serious."

"As you should," I quickly agreed. "I shudder to think of all the little kids who could have been killed or injured if Joseph had had time to chew little pastry bullets, load his little pop tart gun, and actually use it." I shook my head in disbelief. "All that pastry devastation."

Her face took on an even sourer look. "With the number of mass shootings today, his actions could have terrified the entire school."

She got up, straightening the jacket to her dark brown pants suit. "Since you refuse to take this seriously, I think we're done here."

I stayed seated.

"How many?" I quickly inquired.

She looked at me confused. "How many what?"

"You said his actions could have terrified the whole school. So just how many kids sitting next to him came to your teachers terrified because of the shape of his pastry?"

"None, thanks to the appropriate action of Mrs. Lyrock."

"Then if no child felt threatened, why the hysteria on your part?"

Reluctantly, she sat back down. "Mr. Crockett, I hope we can agree that we cannot have our children being taught the use of guns, pretend or otherwise. I would think as a parent you would appreciate the seriousness of this."

"And I would think as an educator you would know the difference between a real threat and death by pastry."

Her mouth tightened and I swear she huffed out loud.

I continued. "No one is denying the seriousness of a real gun and the violence it can inflict, but to treat a child eating in the cafeteria like he was John Dillinger is the height of stupidity."

"We're done here," she said, her eyes boring into me. "Since you think this is such a joke, Joseph is expelled, not only for tomorrow but for the rest of the week. You may take him home." Her victory smile made me cringe.

She stood again, effectively dismissing me. She had rendered her verdict and I was to accept it without question.

Fat chance.

"No way," I said calmly as I smiled at her from my chair.

She blinked at me through shocked little girl eyes. "What do you mean, no way?"

"If you don't go out there and apologize for your overzealous behavior and revoke his suspension, I will sue this school and you personally for everything you've got."

"Are you threatening me?" she asked.

"You denied my nephew his breakfast, forcibly taking away his pastry. Your thugs remove him from the cafeteria, in front of the whole school, like a common criminal. You refused to let him go to the bathroom, causing him to wet his pants. You terrified him by making him sit outside your office for an act he didn't understand. And lastly, you embarrassed him in front of the whole school, potentially doing irreparable harm to his fragile little six-year-old psyche. You expect me to ignore that?"

Her eyes were indignant. "It didn't happen that way."

"That's exactly how it happened and you know it," I shot back as I leaned across the table. "I'll file one nuisance suit after another tying up every ounce of your useless time."

"I don't take kindly to being blackmailed," she whispered coldly.

"And I don't take kindly to hysterical teachers bullying their students. We both have our crosses to bear."

Her mouth tightened around the edges, her eyes narrowed into closed slits and she fell back into her chair. It took her a minute to gather her thoughts. When she spoke, her voice was low and angry.

"Very well," she finally said quietly. "Joseph may stay in school." Her face hardened, and her chin shot skyward. "But I will not apologize."

I tamped my anger down and replied as evenly as I could. "That little boy thinks he's been bad and is scared to death. So yes, you will go out there and apologize to him and assure him that it was all a mistake brought on by your over-zealous agenda."

She stiffened in her righteous indignation. "He broke school policy. I will not apologize to him for that."

She seemed more concerned with her sacrosanct rules than the feelings of a small frightened boy. Rules were one thing, institutional bullying was another.

"Lady, I'm a private investigator and I have no problem spending the next six months talking to every one of your neighbors, all of your colleagues, looking at every receipt you've ever turned in, every item you bought for yourself or your family, every particle of food, every pencil every vacation until I find just how many times you've broken school policy. You will apologize, you pompous pedantic."

There was no doubt in my mind that she had broken her fair share of rules. We all do from time to time, but people in power do because they know they can. Very few will ever challenge them. It was a fact I was banking on.

Finally she stood and straightened her stylish, and expensive pants suit jacket. Her head high, she brushed past me and out of the office.

I exited the office behind her. She marched to Joseph and spoke to him. I couldn't hear what they were saying but I saw him smile, jump up, and race off to class. Cook turned, marched past me into her office, and slammed the door. I hoped there wasn't a Mister Cook who would have to bear the brunt of her wrath when she got home.

As I made my way back around the counter to sign out, a woman eagerly approached the receptionist, planting herself directly in front of the sign-out book. I waited. She was attractive in an understated way, with very little make-up and a long brown dress that hung almost to her ankles. She wasn't very stylish, and seemed out of place.

"I need a substitute for the Thanksgiving holidays," she said softly. "Can you call Patty for me?"

"She'll be on her honeymoon around that time," the receptionist replied without looking up.

"What about Brenda? The kids seem to like her," the teacher asked hopefully.

The receptionist opened a large planning book on the counter and flipped through it. "She is scheduled to sub for Mrs. Swanson for those days." She turned the pages until she landed on someone she thought might be available. "I can try JJ again."

The young teacher stared at the open page as if trying to make up her mind. "I need someone I can depend on," she finally responded softly. "She is wonderful, but she just hasn't been responsive for over two weeks. That makes me nervous."

The receptionist shook her head as she continued to look through her book of substitutes. "That's so unlike her. She's usually so dependable, always telling me how much she loves teaching the kids."

"Please find me someone soon." She turned and left the office.

As I watched her rush down the hallway and into one of the classroom, an idea stuck me. Maybe Jenny J was a dance teacher? She never gave any indication of what she did for a living.

"Excuse me," I turned back to the receptionist, giving her my best professional detective look. "I'm a private detective and I am trying to find the owner of this diary."

I removed the diary from my jacket and laid it on the counter. "I think she might be in trouble, so it's important that I find her."

The receptionist picked up the diary and gave it a quick scan. "Is she a teacher here?"

"I don't know. I'm just asking everywhere I go, hoping to get lucky. Her first name is Jenny and her last name begins with a J. Do you have any teachers here, or maybe anyone you know in any of the other schools, that might fit that description?"

"We don't have any teachers by the name of Jenny or Jennifer. We used to have one named Jennifer Moss but she moved. Sorry."

I knew it was a long shot but I had to try. "Thanks, I

appreciate your time." I signed out and turned to leave.

"What about a substitute?"

"A substitute?" I asked surprised, and embarrassed that I hadn't thought of it.

"We have various substitute teachers that we use when one of our teachers is sick or has other commitments."

"Are there any substitutes with the name Jennifer?"

"JJ," she said with concern. "You think it might be her?"

"I don't know."

She looked down at the book and then smiled up at me. "Her full name is Jennifer Justice."

A shiver shot through my spine. Jennifer Justice was one of the four names on the impound records.

"Can you tell me anything about her?" I inquired.

"I don't know them as well as the teachers do. Ruth might be able to help you. JJ substitutes a lot for her."

"Ruth?"

"Ruth Mosley, the teacher that was just in here."

"Thanks."

I made my way down the hall and to the class room I had seen Ruth Mosley enter. As I opened the door, she glanced up from the chalkboard she was cleaning. Her features were delicate, her eyes brown with specks of green, her complexion clear.

"Yes, may I help you?"

"I'm sorry to bother you, but could I speak to you for a moment?"

"Is this about a child that goes here?"

"My name is David Crockett. I'm a private investigator." I removed a card and handed it to her.

She put the eraser in the tray and studied my card. Suddenly her concern intensified. "Has something happened to one of the students?"

"Nothing like that," I tried to reassure her.

"What's this about?"

ʊ ᵛ

. am trying to find a missing woman. The receptionist ₋aid you might be able to tell me about one of the substitute teachers named Jennifer Justice."

Her eyes blinked rapidly and she bit her bottom lip. "Is she in some kind of trouble?"

"I hope not, but I really would like to find her and make sure she's all right. I could really use your help."

"Of course, whatever I can do, but l don't know her very well."

"Is there anything you can tell me about her?"

"The kids seem to like her, but that's about all I can tell you. I haven't seen her in a while."

"Do you know where I can get in touch with her?"

She leaned against the edge of her desk. "No. Whenever I need her I just tell Lakeisha and she calls her for me."

"Lakeisha? Is she the receptionist you were talking to?"

"Yes. I wish I could help you but, I'm ashamed to say, I have never actually sat down and spent any time with JJ."

"JJ?" I inquired.

"That's what she told us to call her. We all do."

"When she substitutes, don't you go over the lesson plan with her?"

"No, I leave it on the desk for her, or whoever is taking my class."

She tried to smile but it faded behind her apology. She moved around the desk and began gathering her lesson material. "I'm sorry, I wish I could be more helpful, but I'm late for an appointment."

"One more thing."

Picking up her large book bag and slinging it over her left shoulder, she waited impatiently.

"You said she hasn't been responsive for over two weeks. What did you mean by that?"

She looked at me nervously. "I don't want to get her in trouble. She really has been a good substitute."

"But?"

"It's just that I've requested her twice in the past two weeks to fill in for me next month when I am planning a vacation and she hasn't responded at all."

"Is that unusual?"

"She has always been very dependable, which is why most of the teachers ask for her first. Please forgive me, but I really do have to go."

She started off then stopped at the open door. "I hope you find her. From the little interaction I've had with her, she seems like a very nice person."

With a half-smile, she rushed out the door and down the hallway.

I walked back into the office and approached the receptionist with the big smile and eye glitter.

"Back already?"

"It's got to be the glitter," I smiled.

She gave a deep belly laugh. "I hear that." I liked her even more. She just had an infectious personality.

"Did you find out anything helpful?" she asked.

"No. Mrs. Mosley said she hasn't been in touch with her for over two weeks. Has anybody called or checked out her home?"

"I've called, but haven't gotten any response."

"Maybe I could go to her place and check it out." I gave her my best private detective smile, the kind that always got Thomas Magnum the information he needed to keep the show moving. "Is there any way I could get an address for her?"

She glanced around the room then lowered her voice. "We are not supposed to give out addresses, but if this really is important."

Now, I really liked her. "It is," I assured her.

She opened her substitute book and flipped through it, landing on the right page. She smiled up at me. "Here we go."

"Lakeisha!" Cook's voice cut through the room.

My new best friend, Lakeisha, turned to see Cook standing in her office doorway. The sour look was still on her face. Maybe it was me causing it.

"Mr. Crockett is through here. Please quit detaining him."

Lakeisha glanced at me with an apologetic look. As she turned back towards Cook, she rotated the substitute book my direction.

"I will take care of it right now, Madeline." She turned back to me and raised her voice. "Thank you for coming today, sir, but I must ask you to leave."

Quickly burning the address and phone number in my brain, I glanced up at Cook, raised my index finger and thumb in the air in the shape of a gun. Taking extra care not to directly point it at her, I simply put it in my pretend holster. Sometime my inner child gets the best of me.

Like an ancient volcano, an explosion began bubbling up inside her. Her face went white with anger, her hands clinched at her side. She turned and stormed into her office, slamming the door behind her. To work on my suspension papers, I supposed.

I winked at Lakeisha. "No sense of humor."

"I hear that."

Back in my car I wrote down the address and phone number for Jennifer Justice. I dialed the number. It went straight to voicemail.

"Hi. This is Jennifer. Sorry I missed your call but you know what to do."

It beeped. Her voice was light and pleasant and filled with hope. It made me feel like she really wanted to speak with me.

I hung up.

I dialed again. Tonja answered on the second ring,

desperation in her voice. "How is he?"

"He's fine."

She breathed a sigh of relief. "You can bring him by the office if you want."

"No need. You can pick him up at the usual time at school," I said, ever so casually.

"What do you mean? Joseph's not with you?" Tonja asked, suspicion creeping into her voice.

"No, he's in school where he belongs."

"But I thought he was suspended."

"Let's just say Principal Cook had a change of heart."

"Oh no," Tonja said fearfully. "I told you not to say anything to her. Do you know how bad she can make it for Joseph?"

"Get a grip, sis. You have to quit letting these bullies make you feel guilty for living."

"I'm trying to protect my son."

"Then stand up for him, and quit buying into their ridiculous premise that he did anything wrong, because he didn't."

I hung up.

Back at my office my anger was still chewing up my insides when the office door opened and Jackson entered. He plopped down in one of my chairs and sighed. It was his I-can't-believe-you-did-that sigh. I had heard it enough over the years.

"What did I do now?" I asked.

He tried to be serious but the corners of his mouth betrayed him.

"You actually threatened Madeline Cook with your finger? He shook his head laughing. "She called Captain Sokolowski, fit to be tied. She wanted you arrested and prosecuted for threatening her."

"Is there such a statute as threat by finger?"

"According to her there is. She swore that because of

your violent actions she was so shaken up she was going to have to take the rest of the day off."

"Pretend guns can do that to some people," I said, dead panned. "What did Sokolowski say?"

"He tried to reason with her but when she continued to insist that he should arrest you, he finally yelled that unlike the school system, he wasn't about to use public resources to arrest someone for threatening her with a finger. And the wrong finger at that!"

"Wow, Sokolowski actually standing up for me. There's a shock"

"Don't get too big-headed. I think he was more irritated at the insistence of Cook. She threatened to go over him to the commissioner, the mayor, and even the governor if necessary."

"Nothing like getting my license yanked for an unregistered finger."

I started to tell him about the note but stopped. Most likely it was just some prank. And even if it wasn't, it was my problem, not his.

"I may have something on Jenny," I said instead.

He leaned forward in his chair. "What?"

"I compared DMV records to the impound records and two names popped up that seem to be more than just traffic infractions. It seems one of them is a substitute teacher at Daniel John Clinton Elementary School and has been out of touch for over two weeks. According to the school it's not like this person."

"Did you get a name?"

"Jennifer Justice. I was about to go to her apartment and look around. Want to come?" I asked.

"Not if you're planning on breaking in."

"Come on Jackson, I never plan on breaking in." I grinned at him. "It just happens."

EIGHT

We drove in separate cars to Jennifer Justice's apartment. She lived in a small four-plex on 21st South, three blocks from Westminster College. It was an older, well-kept building that sat back off the street on a grassy rise. The lawn was green and the sidewalks clean. A sign on the lower-left apartment said 'Manager.' The curtain in the lower-left window was slightly parted and I could see an older woman intently watching us as we came up the sidewalk.

I rang the bell.

A woman in her late sixties answered. She peered out at us from behind her chain-locked door. Her face was rectangular and contoured; her nose small but straight. Her eyes were hidden behind thick black glasses and her gray hair was bound tightly to her head. Though her skin sagged, you could tell she had once been very attractive.

"Yes?" she asked.

David Sterago

"Are you the manager?"

"Who wants to know?"

"David Crockett," I answered

She squinted through the crack. "I thought Walt killed you in the last episode," she joked.

I ignored her obvious reference to Disney's 1955 classic, *Davy Crockett King of the Wild Frontier.*

"And this is Detective Jackson Paine."

"Let me see some ID." Her attitude said she had not always lived in Utah. She was cautious of people showing up unannounced at her door. I immediately thought of Los Angeles or New York.

Jackson and I looked at each other, then pulled out our identification. She stared at them carefully, glanced from the identification to each of us, then back at the identification. She chuckled as she stared at my photo. "You might want to change that picture, son."

Nowadays everyone's a critic.

"Are you the manager?" Jackson asked as he placed his identification back in his coat pocket.

"Yes. I'm Earlene Templeton," she said suspiciously. "What is this about?"

"I'm a private investigator. We need to ask you a few questions about one of your tenants."

She stared at us for a moment then closed the door. I could hear the chain being removed and the door reopened.

She moved to let us in. "I bet it's those two college boys," she said with a snort.

"What makes you say that?" Jackson asked.

"They are always playing their music too loud and always yelling and arguing with their girlfriends. Are you here to arrest them?"

"No, ma'am."

"No sense standing on ceremony. Sit." She motioned to the black leather couch cutting the room in half, then scurried to a comfortable chair opposite it.

We sat.

Her apartment was a time machine to the Seventies. The carpet was brown shag, the appliances harvest gold, and the walls a dingy white. The drapes were dark brown, thick and hung to the floor, giving the room a dark, closed-in feeling. Maybe she liked keeping the world out. On the coffee table were a variety of entertainment magazines. The only really new item in the room was a giant entertainment center setting against the back wall. Hundreds of VHS tapes and DVDs framed a large 32-inch television screen. She liked movies.

"We'd like to speak to you about Jennifer Justice," Jackson said softly so as not to alarm her.

"Jennifer? I can't say anything about Jennifer. She's the best tenant I have." She folded her arms as if daring us to ask her something about her best tenant. "I make it a policy to not say anything about my tenants to strangers."

"Except the two college boys, of course," I laughed.

"I do make exceptions for pinheads."

Score one for Bill O'Rielly.

I picked up one of the magazines. "That's quite a movie collection you have there."

"I was an actress once," she stated proudly.

"Here in Utah?"

She frowned as if I had insulted her intelligence.

"In Hollywood," she said with more than a hint of pride.

She got out of her chair and creaked to the desk and returned with a photo album.

"I had a bit part in *Easy Rider.* Oh, that Peter Fonda was something, such a bad boy."

She opened the book and showed us yellowed photos of her acting career: pictures with Peter Fonda, Dennis Hopper, a very young Jack Nicholson, Richard Chamberlin, Vincent Price, and Barbara Stanwyck. Flipping the pages, she landed on a color photo of two beautiful actresses standing with their arms around Elvis Presley as if they were not about to let him get away.

"That's me on the left," she announced proudly. "In 1964 I was in *Roustabout* with Elvis." Her face lit up as the memories came flooding back.

"This picture was taken the day Raquel and I did our scene with him. That's Raquel." She pointed to the other actress.

"Raquel?" I politely inquired.

"Raquel Welch. It was her very first part. We use to giggle like school girls when Elvis walked by. We just couldn't help ourselves."

"I guess a king can do that," I remarked.

"He was the biggest star in Hollywood at the time."

She ran her hand over the 8x10 photo of her and Elvis.

"Talk about drop-dead gorgeous. And sexy. These movie guys today, Brad Pitt, George Clooney, Leonardo DiCaprio, pshaw." She waved her hand at us. "They're nice looking but when it comes to just plain sexy they can't hold a candle to Elvis. Let me tell you, the first time he walked by and smiled at me I almost had an—" the word died in her throat.

She smiled at us sheepishly, though the twinkle never left her eyes. Something told me Earlene Templeton may have had a wild side once upon a time in a land far, far away called Hollywood.

"Let's just say he was one of the sexiest men I have ever seen. And such a gentleman even to us bit players and dancers."

"Isn't Jennifer a dancer?" I inquired, bringing the subject back full circle, before she took off on the exploits of the youthful Peter Fonda or Jack Nicholson.

"She's not in trouble, is she? I won't say anything to get her in trouble," she frowned.

"That's what we're trying to find out. She may be

missing," Jackson said.

"Now that you mention it, I haven't seen her for a while."

Jackson leaned forward. "And you didn't find that odd?"

"I just assumed she was out of town on a dancing gig. She does that, you know," she said hotly, as if defending herself.

"What can you tell us about her?" I inquired.
"The nicest girl you would ever want to meet. She's always saying hi and smiling. I've never had a moment's trouble from her, and she always pays her rent on the first of the month."

Jackson took out his notebook and pen. "Does she have any family around that you know of?"

"No. She was always here during the holidays. I asked her this past Christmas if she would be spending Christmas with her parents. She said they had died two years ago."

"Did she ever talk about any boyfriends or anybody she was dating?" I asked.

"She was always hanging around with one of the actors from her agency, but I don't think they were actually dating. He didn't seem her type, though nowadays one can never tell."

"Do you remember his name?" Jackson asked.

"I think she introduced him as—" she paused as if staring into space would help her remember. "It was the same name as that folk singer in the Sixties, the one who sang Mellow Yellow."

"Donovan?" I volunteered.

"That's it. Donovan something. You know your classic rock and roll."

I nodded in agreement then asked, "Did you ever see any guys come around or anyone that seemed suspicious?"

"Not really, but then again I don't spend my hours watching what is going on in the other apartments. I do have a life you know."

"There's no doubt you're not the interfering kind of landlady," Jackson quickly interjected. "But sometimes we see things that make us wonder, you know like one day if you just happened to be looking at the beautiful sunset and something odd caught your eye, something that seemed out of place."

"Well now that you mention it, one day I saw her leaving with a much older gentleman."

"Older?"

"You know," she frowned, "the sugar-daddy type. I remember because it wasn't like Jennifer to be dating someone like that. I thought maybe he was a producer or something."

"Did you ask her about it?"

"I saw her the following day. She said he had told her that he could help her with her dancing career and they should have dinner. When I asked what happened, she said he had lied to her, and she didn't want to talk about it."

I thought back to her diary where she had written: *Lies, lies, lies. Mr. 'I can help you with your career' was not interested in my career but my body. Is that all I am to men? Has my face and mind somehow magically disappeared and there is nothing left but my figure? Why do men lie? Because we still believe them? I wish I could just dance away with someone that's honest and real? Does he even exist in today's world?*

Jackson stopped writing. "She never said who he was?"

"No. Maybe that was why she didn't date much, which I thought was strange because she was so beautiful. I think she was embarrassed by her looks and the attention people paid to her."

"Would it be possible to see her apartment?" I asked.

"I make it a habit on not invading my tenants' space."

"It would be very helpful," I said. "It might give us some clues as to what happened to her and where she might be."

"If you really think it will help."

She got up and moved to the door where she removed a ring of keys hanging on the molding. We climbed the stairs to the apartment directly above hers and she let us in.

"Thank you," I smiled. "We can take it from here." She still didn't trust us and didn't want to leave, but when we left her standing on the landing she turned and hobbled back down the stairs.

Jennifer Justice's apartment was laid out similarly to Templeton's, and just as old. It was, however, extremely neat and organized. Though sparsely decorated, what was there was nice. A light brown love seat, a large throw chair, a coffee table, a dresser drawer, and a television sitting on a large black decorative block from IKEA filled the living room. Two book cases stood on either side of the television/DVD player. One was filled with books and the other with DVDs. The books were mostly biographies of dancers, political biographies, religious books, various volumes of basic child psychology, and a few suspense and romance novels, which seemed out of place for some reason. Her DVD collection was nothing but pure entertainment from Hollywood classics to every dance movie ever made. Against the far wall leading to the kitchen was a small desk. A telephone bill, cable bill, power bill, and gas bill lay in a neat stack beside a small lamp. I took a photo of her last phone bill then placed it back on the stack of unpaid bills.

As Jackson checked the bathroom I rifled through the desk and came up with nothing unusual: writing paper, letters, class schedules, and dancing classes. Closing the drawer, I wandered into the kitchen. With the exception of a bowl and glass in the sink, the place was spotless.

Then I saw it.

Hanging on the wall by the refrigerator was a shopping list, reminding her to pick up eggs, milk, lettuce, tomatoes, peas, chicken, and Oreo cookies. I had seen that impeccable handwriting before. I took out the diary and compared the two. There was no doubt about it. Jennifer Justice was the owner of the diary. We had found Jenny J.

I left the kitchen and walked to the bathroom where Jackson was busy looking through the medicine cabinets and drawers searching for anything that might give us a clue as to who she was and what might have happened to her.

"It's her," I announced as I glanced around the bathroom.

"Are you sure?"

"She left a shopping list by the refrigerator. The handwriting is the same as the diary. Jennifer Justice is Jenny J."

He looked at me with a sense of relief, but it was short-lived.

"Now we know who, but we still don't know where or what happened to her."

"Anything here?"

"Nothing out of the ordinary. No prescription drugs or anything illegal if that's what you're thinking."

"Why would I think that?" I gave him offended. "Everyone knows marijuana and roach clips are kept in the bedroom under your underwear so your mother won't find it."

He looked at me, shook his head, and tried not to smile. "Maybe her bedroom will tell us something useful," he said glancing at me.

I gave him hurt. He ignored it.

Like the kitchen, everything in the bedroom was in its place and well organized. The twin bed, covered by a beautiful multi-colored comforter, was made. The large oak trunk at the foot of the bed was closed. With the exception of a comfortable looking pair of UGG house shoes sitting neatly by the bed, there were no clothes, paper, or anything else littering the floor. On the wall near the bed was a large framed poster of a ballerina's well-worn dancing shoes lying on the dance floor. The large dresser was dusty as if it had not been cleaned in a week or so. A small tray filled with various cosmetics and perfume sat in the middle of the desk. I sprayed the perfume thinking it might give me a sense of the girl. It was light, fruity, and very captivating. It must have smelled wonderful on her. Jackson glanced at me. I just shrugged. At least I wasn't trying on her dresses. The only thing besides the cosmetics and the dust on the top of the dresser was a framed photo of a young Jenny (maybe ten), with her parents. On the night stand was a stack of 8x10 black-and-white stills which actors and dancers take to casting calls or dance auditions. It was one of the head shots that had instantly caught my attention on Faith's wall of hopefuls; young, beautiful and charismatic, only the name was Jennifer Marie instead of Jennifer Justice.

"I know her agent. She has the office down the hall from me."

Nothing looked out of place and there was no sign of a struggle. I opened the dresser drawers and rummaged through the neatly folded clothes. They smelled of faint perfume, the way a girl's clothes should smell. No hidden clues or notes saying 'I've been kidnapped by so and so.' "Maybe she cleaned up knowing she wasn't coming back."

Jackson closed the lid of the oak trunk and frowned. "If a woman is going kill herself, normally they do it in a comfortable setting like home? The old adage that women who kill their mates do it in the kitchen, where as women who kill themselves do it in the bedroom almost always holds true. This doesn't feel right."

I moved to the nightstand beside the bed. A Bible and a Book of Mormon lay on top, both with markers indicating the last pages read. I opened the drawer. More photos and resumes, which made me think of the older man who took her out. "Maybe the older gentleman decided not to take no for an answer," I said.

Jackson glanced at her head shot on the nightstand. "She was beautiful. He could have become obsessive."

I rummaged through the drawers but found nothing more. "I'll go back to the office and drop in on her agent to see if she can help me reconstruct Jennifer's activities for the past couple of weeks."

"See if you can get an address for 'Mellow Yellow.' An old boyfriend is always a good place to start," Jackson said. His phone rang and after looking at the number he answered. "Paine." He listened, his face remaining passive. "I'll be right there." He hung up and turned to me. "Speaking of boyfriends, they just returned Janet Hickman's missing boyfriend to Salt Lake."

"The dead girl in the trunk?"

"Yeah. He was picked up in Reno yesterday. He still had the knife in his pick-up."

"Criminals are notorious for being stupid."

"It sure helps," he laughed as he turned to go. "They extradited him this morning. He's at the jail waiting to be interviewed. Let me know what you find out."

"You want to be there when I question Mellow Yellow?"

"I trust you." He left without a backwards glance.

Something was gnawing at me as I walked towards the living room. But what? What was I missing? Then it dawned on me. There was no computer in the apartment. Everyone has a computer, so where was Jennifer's? Of course she could have had a laptop and it had disappeared when she did. Was there something on her laptop that could tell us what was going on in her life? Emails from someone special? From someone dangerous?

NINE

I kept my promise to April and got tickets to the University of Utah football game against UCLA for her, Donnie, and her husband, Dillon.

When it comes to the weather, November football games in Utah are a crapshoot. One Saturday it will be beautiful, sunny, and warm, and the next Saturday you will be sitting under a blanket of snow. This was one of those in-between Saturdays. It was clear but cold. The sun was shining but the wind was blowing, dropping the fifty-degree temperature even further down the thermometer.

Even so, football is football. Whether it is beautiful or cold, it is always a fun experience.

Utah pulled out a victory in the last two minutes. I thought young Donnie would burst with excitement. Needless to say, he and his dad, Dillon, a Utah fanatic, were very happy.

After the game we decided to finish the day at the Spicy Thai Restaurant. As usual after Saturday afternoon football

games in Salt Lake City, most restaurants are crowded with
college kids and Utah fans making a triple sweep of football,
fun, and food.

As Katie and I pushed our way through the crowd to the
desk to place our names on the waiting list, I saw Jackson
and Julie waiting amid the mob of hungry diners.

I wasn't surprised to see them since this was one of their
favorite places to eat. It was also one of their date nights.

After putting our names on the forty-five minute waiting
list, we swam through the sea of people toward them. Julie
gave a surprised smile when she noticed Katie and me
shoving our way towards them.

"Who forced you to eat here this time?" Julie laughed as
she hugged me. It was a good-natured jab at my inability to
try new things willingly. The first time she had suggested
that we eat at Spicy Thai, I had thrown a major tantrum.
Having grown up on hamburgers, Mexican food, sea food,
steak and potatoes, I had always considered anything else
not worth trying. I knew what I liked and I considered it a
waste of my culinary time to spend money on anything I
hadn't tried. Thai food was something I was clueless about.
But it was one of Julie's favorite places to eat.

I begrudgingly went along, but not alone. Whenever I
didn't have a date or was being forced to try something I
didn't care for, I dragged Katie with me. She was my food
monitor. If she said it was okay then I would try it, and
since she loved Thai food as much as Julie, I was stuck.

It was a Thursday night and Jackson and I had lobbied
heavily for a quick trip to Sizzler and then back home to watch
the Thursday night football game between the Cowboys
and the Bears. Julie and Katie wanted Spicy Thai and a
night at the theater. We were now at the unwanted
restaurant and there would be no football later on. Whoever
said there was a war on women must have been single.

"Curry?" I had said with as much disgust in my voice

as possible when the choice of restaurants had been raised. "Why would I ever want to eat something called curry? Everybody knows real food comes from a cow, not a spice."

I sagged in the chair and looked at Jackson for help. He had been married for ten years. He knew the secret: A happy wife, a happy life. He just smiled weakly at me.

"I'm not going to get steak tonight am I?" I sighed.

"Cheer up, David. You'll like it," Katie smiled.

"Does it taste like steak, fried shrimp, hamburgers, or Mexican food?"

"It tastes like something hot enough to burn any remaining taste buds that you haven't already burned off your tongue with jalapeños peppers and salsa," Katie said, knowing the way around my protests.

I learned a valuable lesson that night: never question Katie's judgment when it comes to food. Spicy Thai is now one of my favorite restaurants.

Jackson gave April a hug and shook Donnie's hand. "You've grown at least a foot since the last time I saw you, kid."

"I'm almost twelve now," Donnie said proudly.

"Cosmo," Dillon laughed, calling Jackson the name of the BYU mascot, as he shook his hand.

"Swoop," Jackson responded with the name of the University of Utah mascot. Friends were still rivals when it came to the two universities.

When food is as good as it is at the Spicy Thai, waiting twenty five minutes for a table is the norm. We lucked out and were seated within fifteen.

Looking at the menu was a waste of time since I only order one thing, chicken massaman.

The first time we had eaten here, Katie had suggested it. Explaining that it was pieces of chicken cooked in coconut milk with potatoes, onions and carrot topped with cashews, she said it could be eaten alone or served over rice. It still wasn't steak but it didn't sound half bad. Reluctantly, I ordered it.

Now it is the only Thai dish I am willing to order.

In the middle of our catching up with each other and enjoying the food and company, Jackson's phone rang. Julie glanced at him. He was off the clock. He answered anyway.

He listened. His eyes darted to Julie then back down at the table.

"I'm in the middle of date night with my wife."

He listened some more. "The party isn't going anywhere. I'll be there in an hour." He clicked off his phone. "I'm sorry honey. Detective Allen was supposed to take my calls but he's tied up with a jumper downtown."

"187?" I inquired. That was the code for murder. It seemed like the more appropriate phrase to say at dinner than asking if someone just got whacked?

"Looks accidental. It'll wait."

It did.

After dinner Jackson asked if I wanted to go with him. With apologies to all, and Julie promising to take Katie home, we left and made our way to a rundown apartment complex in West Salt Lake. The first thing that hit you as you stepped off the elevator onto the third floor was the smell. The hallway reeked with death.

The victim lived alone in a dingy one-bedroom apartment. The living room was bare except for a couch and small television.

Jackson handed me a pair of latex gloves and paper booties to cover our shoes and hands in order to protect the integrity of the crime scene.

The kitchen area had a week's worth of dishes in the sink and what looked like a half a pot of oatmeal still on the stove.

Putting a handkerchief over my nose, I followed Jackson into the bedroom.

The deceased was lying on the floor between the wall and the small iron-frame bed, which was covered with nothing but a sheet and blanket. He was gaunt with a receding hair line. He looked like a junkie. Of course, the needle sticking in his arm might have colored my opinion.

Justin Boudreau was leaning over the body, poking, prodding, and taking his temperature. He glanced up as we entered, grunted and continued working.

"What do you have, Justin?" Jackson asked as he moved towards the victim.

"A dead junkie," he grumbled and removed his meat thermometer from the body. "He's been dead for at least seventy-two hours, which accounts for the rotting smell."

Jackson stared at the body then shook his head.

"You know him?" I quickly inquired.

"His name is Johnny Lee Baker," Jackson said as he leaned over the body. "He was a small-time hood. I sent him to Point of the Mountain Prison three years ago."

"What for?"

"Breaking and entering." Jackson stood.

I could tell he was bothered by something. He glanced around the room then back at the body.

"What's wrong?"

"This doesn't make sense. He was a thief and a forger, but as long as I knew him he was never into drugs."

"People change."

"I guess." Jackson continued to look around the dingy room. He frowned, then said, "Something else though."

"What?"

"You see any drugs or drug paraphernalia anywhere?" he asked.

"You've got the needle," I pointed out.

"But nothing else, no drugs, no plastic bags, no tie-offs, nothing associated with a drug addict." He shook his head. "It doesn't add up."

"Like I said, people change."

Jackson stared at the body as if it would magically tell him what had happened. Suddenly, he got the answer he was looking for. "No, he was murdered," he said.

"How do you know?" I asked.

"Look at the needle."

I glanced down at the needle sticking into his left arm. "So?"

"Baker was left-handed. If he had shot up, the needle would be in his right arm. "Someone overpowered him and then shot him up with drugs."

"You may be right," Boudreau interrupted. He turned Baker's head to the right side, giving us a clear view of the back of his head. "Looks like someone hit him with something."

Jackson turned to Officer Samuel Chumley, who was first on the scene. "Did you find anything that looked like it could have been used as a weapon?"

"No, sir," Chumley replied.

"Maybe they took it with them," I said as I looked over and noticed the bump on the back of his head.

"Makes you wonder what he was silenced for," Jackson muttered out loud.

While Jackson and the other detectives processed the crime scene, I wandered around the room. There wasn't much there. The small bed and a tiny three-drawer, pressed-wood dresser were the only furniture in the room.

The small closet was bare, with the exception of two shirts, one pair of tan slacks, and a sports coat hanging there. He didn't have a lot to show for his thirty-five years.

I opened the top dresser drawer. A pencil rolled from the top to the bottom of the drawer where a small pad of paper lay. Other than that the drawer was empty. Two pairs of tighty whities and two pairs of socks were the only items in the second drawer. The third drawer was empty. The man traveled light to say the least.

I picked up the pad in the top drawer. There was a faint imprint on the pad. "Jackson."

Walking over, he stared at the pad. "Looks like he wrote something down, then tore it off," he said as he took the pad and laid it on the dresser. Removing a pencil, Jackson began coloring over the imprint. Soon the address 284 North State Street was visible. It was familiar to me, but I couldn't place it.

"I've seen that address somewhere recently."

"Chumley, bag and tag this." Jackson yelled as I quickly wrote the address in my notebook.

"It's in the high-rise district downtown," he continued. "The offices there are filled with banks, hedge fund offices, insurance corporations, and high-priced lawyers."

Officer Chumley brought an evidence bag over, dropped the scribbled pad into it, and then moved away.

"You think he hit one of the banks?" I asked.

"Not without someone reporting it."

"Maybe he hadn't yet pulled it off."

"Then why kill him?"

Why indeed? Why had a low-level breaking and entering artist written down the address of a downtown high-rise building unless he was planning on hitting it? None of this made any sense.

Then something on the floor between the dresser and the wall caught my attention. I leaned down and reached back to retrieve a small, white object. It was a card.

"What is it?" Jackson inquired as I stared at the small white object.

I handed it to him. "A business card."

"Discreet Party Services. Looks like a card for an escort company."

"I've never heard of it."

"I guess that's why they call it Discreet." He stared at me

and smiled. "Feel like planning a party?"

***

I tossed the card on my kitchen counter and pulled out a can of cat food for Sam. He must have had a good day, sleeping and pooping—what else do cats do all day long—because he seemed somewhat friendly. He moved around my leg until I looked down at him and then he quickly moved away and towards his bowl as if to say 'just testing you fool.' I wonder if cats actually think that way at times. Do they make humans do stupid things just so they can laugh at them and meow behind their backs?

I lifted his bowl to the counter and filled it with chicken delight. As I set it down, Sam eagerly gobbled it up.

I took a Heineken from the refrigerator and plopped down on the couch. Opening it, I took a long swig and lay my head on the back of the couch. I was bone-tired but I knew sleep was impossible. My mind was racing. What was I doing? I had a missing girl I couldn't find. I had no leads and was running out of options.

Had she run out of time? Was she already dead? If she was still alive, why hadn't she returned home or to work? Why hadn't any of her friends heard from her? It was a conclusion I really didn't want to think about. I took another drink, then another. It didn't help. My gut tightened as images of her lying dead in some seedy motel, alley way, or trunk of some car popped unwontedly into my head. What more could I do?

And Martin Parker? A feeling way down inside told me he was guilty as sin. He seemed arrogant enough to think he could get away with murder. Maybe he was, because I had come up empty on every occasion. I didn't want to let Faith down, but at this juncture that seemed to be my M.O. Faith. Jenny. I seemed to be letting everyone down.

Stop it! I berated myself. Holding a pity party wasn't

going to accomplish anything. Someone out there knew something. I just had to find them.

I took another swig of beer and sat up. There are times when you have to jump in with both feet, to take extraordinary measures. This was one of those times.

I reached for my phone.

Thirty minutes later I was engaged in a mighty duel with a large steaming meat lover's pizza with extra cheese, sausage, and onions.

Sometimes I do my best detecting over pizza and beer.

Jumping up on his end of the couch, Sam watched me stuff the hot, cheesy pie into my mouth. Then I got the stare. He had just eaten, but watching me enjoy myself, and not include him, was just too much for his satanic little ego. We were a team, if by team you mean he gets to enjoy everything I have and my job is to make sure he gets it.

I tore the lid from the pizza box, tossed a slice of pizza into it and laid it on the floor. He stared at me for a moment as if I were crazy to suggest such a thing, then he stretched and lazily jumped off the couch as if he had nothing better to do. Once he was on the floor, he sniffed the pizza, moved around the lid once, and then devoured a piece of sausage like he hadn't eaten in three days.

I felt all warm inside at his appreciation.

I was into a full pizza coma when the phone rang.

"What's up?" I answered when I saw Jackson's name on the screen.

"That address we found at Baker's?"

"Yeah?"

"One of the law firms in the building is Richard Harvey's."

It took me a moment to place the name. Then it hit me like an NFL linebacker running over a seventh grader. "That's Sylvia Parker's family attorney!"

"I thought you might find that interesting."

"But what would a small-time thief like Baker have to

David Sterago

do with Richard Harvey or anyone else in that building?" I asked.

"I don't know. I just thought you would want to know."

He hung up.

I stared at the pizza then took my last swig of beer. I was beginning to feel like Alice down the rabbit hole. Only the mad hatter and the Queen of Hearts made much more sense. After the pizza and three beers, I struggled to my feet and headed for the bedroom. Removing my shoulder holster, I laid my Sig on the night stand.

I had gotten used to the Sig Sauer P226R 9mm while in the Navy. It fit my hand and I liked its weight. Also, I really liked the engraved anchor on the left side of the slide.

I kicked off my shoes and fell onto the bed. I would undress later, I told myself. It never happened.

I woke up and glanced around. It took me a few minutes to clear my head. I hadn't slept like that in months. After a hot shower, I dressed in my finest casual wear, which is pretty much the only wear I have, and headed for the kitchen.

I expected Sam to be waiting in his usual spot but he was nowhere to be found. He must have gotten tired of waiting for me and slipped out the doggie door to go hunting. He's like that sometimes. I guess he wants to keep his hunting skills sharp in case I ever run out of tuna fish or canned liver and chicken.

I put the coffee on and turned to the cabinet to take out a bowl in which to scramble a couple of eggs. As I reached towards the cabinet I saw it. Lying on the floor near the end of the counter. It was a dead bird. Sam's gift. Who said you couldn't bond over pizza?

I removed a plastic bag and, using a paper towel, placed the bird inside, zipped it up and tossed it into the trash can, then replaced the lid tightly. I didn't want to hurt his feelings.

After a breakfast of sausage, hash browns, hot cakes, and

soft scrambled eggs, I locked the door, climbed in my car, and pulled out of my garage.

It was a crisp, clear November day. The snow on the mountain tops looked virgin white as the sun reflected off the peaks. There was a nip in the air but not enough to make it too cold. It was one of those perfect days, I thought as I drove down the canyon towards Highway 80. It was a perfect day to plan a discreet party. I didn't know how this cover for an escort service fit into the grand scheme of things, but I was curious to find out.

Then my phone rang, and everything changed in an instant.

TEN

I stared at the unknown number as it rang again.

I was on my way to Discreet Party Service and really didn't want to get sidetracked. I decided not to answer. If it was important they could leave a message. After the fourth ring, a voice in the back of my head whispered, then shouted, that I should answer. Maybe it was Martin Parker calling to say I was the greatest detective in the world, that he really did kill his wife, and could I come and arrest him.

On the fifth ring I pushed the button on my headset

"Crockett Detective Agency."

There was a slight pause then a woman began speaking. It wasn't Parker.

"Mr. Crockett?" She sounded tentative and unsure.

"Yes."

"This is Roxanna Lewis from St. Mark's Hospital."

"Yes, Ms. Lewis, what can I do for you?"

"You left me your card when you were here two weeks

ago asking about patients with the first name of Jennifer."

"I remember."

"I didn't think about it at the time but there is a Jane Doe that might fit your description. She's about the right age."

"And her name is Jennifer?"

"I don't know. There was no identification on her when she was brought in."

"She hasn't told you her name or anything about herself?"

She paused. "She can't speak."

"Why not?"

"She's in a coma."

"A coma?"

"She was beaten almost to death. She was left at the front of the hospital by an unknown person."

"How is that possible?"

"Sadly, it happens more times than it should. Someone finds an injured person and wants to help, but doesn't want to get involved, so they leave the body by the emergency door."

"Could I come by and see this person?"

"Of course. I can be available whenever you have the time."

"Is now too soon?"

"That would be fine. Ask for me when you get here." I thanked her and hung up.

Thinking of Jennifer Justice's head shot on Faith's wall, smiling with twinkling eyes ready to take on the world, I felt my stomach tighten with the same kind of anxiety bubbling up inside of me that I had felt while looking at the body of Janet Hickman. I wanted to pound someone's head against a concrete wall until they told me why they had done such an unspeakable thing.

My mind filled with questions as I raced to St. Mark's

Hospital. Why had this woman been beaten so badly and by whom? Whoever did this was angry and wanted to hurt her, even kill her. But then, why had they taken her to the hospital? And if they hadn't, who had and where had she been found?

I still had no answers as I pulled into the parking lot of the large five-story, full-service hospital.

I made my way to the front desk and asked for Roxanna Lewis.

"I'm Roxanna," a pleasant-looking women in her late thirties said, smiling as she looked up at me. Her face was angular with a wide forehead and large green eyes. Her hair was coal black and she had a slight overbite, which did nothing to distract from her looks.

"I'm David Crockett."
"Cecilia," she said to one of the nurses," Could you fill in for me for a minute."

She moved around the circular counter to greet me. "I'm sorry I didn't think of her before, but this morning as I went into her room, it dawned on me that she was the right age. So I took a chance and called you."

"No problem. We don't always connect the dots immediately. I'm just grateful you decided to call."

I have never been real comfortable in hospitals and felt even more uneasy as we passed through the *Kay Sargent Memorial Wing* dedicated to curing children with cancer. Children in pain always gets to me, so I was glad when we reached the elevator banks. The door closed and she pushed the button for the basement.

As we stepped off the elevator, the depression hit me like a blanket of wet moss. The hallway was dimly lit and there seemed to be no one around. Formaldehyde stung my nose as we passed the closed doors of the morgue.

What a lonely place to be.

We moved past the morgue, around the corner to where the various testing labs were located. Two doors down and across the hall from the blood testing lab, Roxanna stopped at a closed door. Opening it, she moved back to let me pass.

As I entered the room I wasn't sure what to expect. I wasn't prepared for what I saw. It was a large empty room that looked more like a storage room than a hospital room. In the middle of the room was a bed and even in the dim lighting I could see a body on the bed.

"Could we turn some lights on in here? This is depressing," I said.

Roxanna flipped a switch and more light filtered into the room. It didn't do much to relieve the depression. I moved over to the bed for a closer look.

A young female lay there, her blondish brown hair cut and her head wrapped in a white, sterile bandage. Her face was battered and slightly swollen with fading yellowish purple bruises covering most of it. Her breathing was shallow, but consistent. Even though she was on the upside of recovery, the damage was still frightful. If she still looked this bad after a couple of weeks, I couldn't imagine what she must have looked like when they found her dumped like a pile of garbage on the sidewalk outside the hospital. Her left eye was swollen shut, her lip still cracked from the deep cuts. I swallowed the fast rising anger, but not the hate. I hated whoever had done this. I hated them with white hot passion.

Because of all the bruising, I couldn't be a hundred percent, but I was pretty sure I had found Jenny J.

"How long has she been like this?"

Lewis picked up her medical chart and stared at it. "Four weeks. According to this, she was found near the emergency room doors at about 10:42 p.m. on the fifteenth of last month."

October 15, a week before Jackson had given me the diary.

"And no one saw who dumped her?"

"No. As you can imagine the staff was busy taking care of patients. A family member of one of the patients discovered the body as he was leaving. He immediately got a nurse."

"Were the police called?"

"Yes, but there wasn't much we could tell them. They took a report and that was the last I heard about it."

"No follow-up visits or questions?"

"No. They did say to keep them informed of her condition." She stared at Jennifer, a sadness clouding her eyes. "Who would do such a thing?"

I wish I knew. "Has she been fully examined?"

She looked at me with a blank look. "What do you mean?"

"I mean, has she had a CAT-scan for brain damage, has a neurologist checked her for nerve damage? Has she been checked by a radiologist, a cardiologist a nephrologists, a rapeologist and any other kind of 'ologist' you have around here?" I found my voice rising and the anger exploding out of me. Someone had left this girl to die and I wanted to make sure she had been given the best treatment in the world.

I took a deep breath and tried to relax. It wasn't Roxanna Lewis's fault. "I'm sorry, I didn't mean to get carried away," I said quietly.

"It's all right. I know how you feel."

She studied the chart again. "There was some right hemisphere cerebral swelling due to bleeding. The doctors had to drain the blood to relieve the pressure on the brain stem. If the RAS—"

I stared blankly at her.

"I'm sorry," she blushed. "That means Reticular

Activation System, which is the part of the brain responsible for arousal and awareness. If that has been damaged then her chances are slim."

The news hit me in the gut like drinking the water in Mexico."

"Do we know how much damage has been done?" "We won't be able to tell until the swelling goes completely down."

"And if it's damaged beyond repair?"

"Let's hope that's not the case."

"And if it is?" I asked.

"The right brain controls the left side functions. If there is serious enough damage then she could have severe left side dysfunction, maybe even be paralyzed." She glanced back down at the chart. "Her heart and lungs are strong and there doesn't seem to be any acute nerve damage."

"So if she comes out of the coma, she could be fine?"

"If she comes out of the coma."

"You don't think she has a chance do you?"

She hesitated, and then glanced down as she slid the chart back into the bed slot. "I wish I could give you some assurances, but it doesn't look good. Survival rates are 50 percent or less, and for those who do come out of it, less than 10 percent completely recover from it. It's a miracle she's not dead, considering the beating she was given." She shook her head gently.

"But there is a chance?" I asked hopefully.

"Like I said, when the swelling goes completely down and her body heals, who knows. We all pray for miracles."

"Did the police take her personal effects?"

"No. There were none except for her clothes."

"Could I see them?"

"They are in storage, but I'll get someone to bring them to you."

"Thank you. That would be helpful."

She turned to leave. "Oh, Ms. Lewis?"

She turned back around. "Could you bring me a pair of latex gloves also?" I asked. With a nod, she left the room.

I stared at the beautiful young girl lying so still on the bed. No friends, no family, no one to care about her. No one deserved this.

I took out my phone and called Jackson.

"I think I found her."

He paused, as if afraid to utter the next words, I knew he was wondering about.

"She's alive," I said, sparing him. "But just barely."

"What do you mean?"

"She has been beaten almost to death. She is in a coma at St. Mark's Hospital. There is a lot of swelling and bruising, but I'm pretty sure it's her. Whoever did this did a bang up job."

"I'll pick up Earlene Templeton and see if she can positively identify her," Jackson said.

"I appreciate that." An uneasy silence hung thickly in the air. Finally Jackson answered for both of us. "We'll find who did this. That's a promise."

"The Midvale police came out and filed a report, but that is as far as it went," I informed him. "They didn't even take her clothes to analyze."

"Sounds like someone decided it wasn't a high priority." His voice tightened and I could tell he was swallowing his anger. "I'll make some calls and see what I can find out," he continued.

"I'm going to have a look at her personal items, though according to the nurse there are only her clothes."

"Maybe they will tell us something."

"I hope so. I'll call you later." I started to hang up when his voice stopped me. "David."

"Yeah?"

"Thanks."

He hung up.

Roxanna re-entered the room and came to the bedside as I placed my phone back in my pocket.

"Is this the young woman you were looking for?" She asked, handing me the latex gloves.

"Yes." I could barely get the words out. And to paraphrase Scarlet O'Hara, with God as my witness, I was determined to find out who did this and make them pay.

"I appreciate your help. May I stay awhile?"

"Stay as long as you like," she smiled. "Hospital protocol, however, dictates that I stay with the items. I hope you don't mind?"

"I have no problem with that."

An attendant came into the room with a large plastic bag. He gave it to Roxanna and left without a word.

"Not much here. I hope it helps."

Putting on the gloves, I reached into the bag and pulled out her clothes.

The night she had been beaten she was wearing blue jeans, a white blouse, a tan jacket, bra, panties, socks and running shoes. The jacket and blouse were covered in dry, crusted blood as were the blue jeans. They didn't look to be anything more than casual clothes from the Gap or Marshals. There were no high-end tags or markings, not that I expected any. From everything I had read in her diary, Jenny wasn't a high maintenance type of girl, no rings, expensive jewelry, or purse. That struck me as odd. What woman goes out without her purse? There was also no laptop or cell phone.

I wasn't sure what I was looking for but I kept hoping something would give me a clue as to where she had been and who had inflicted such brutality upon her.

I reached into her jacket pockets and found a piece of paper. It was a crumpled up receipt for dinner at La Caille, a very expensive French restaurant up in Little Cottonwood

Canyon in Sandy. It was a restaurant that a teacher could ill afford. It was a restaurant that I could ill afford.

I laid the receipt on the tray, straightened it out as best I could then took a close up picture with my cell phone. It was dated exactly one week before she was dumped at St. Mark's.

"What is it?" Lewis asked, her eyes widening with excitement.

"A receipt for dinner."

"Does it mean anything?"

"It means she liked to eat well."

"Oh." Her face fell as if she had just received a dunce cap.

"If nothing else it gives me a place to start. This is not a receipt from your average Salt Lake City restaurant. This is high class all the way."

"How does that help?"

"People who go there stand out. Maybe someone will remember her and who she was with."

This brought her out of her doldrums, causing her to smile as if she had been part of the discovery that would solve the case. That's me, always trying to uplift the spirits of the downtrodden.

As I continued to study her clothes, the depression of the place began to bear down on me. I hated that she was being kept in such a location.

"How come she is down here and not in a hospital room?" I asked.

"Sadly, this is what you might call Potter's field. It is for unknown and uninsured patients," Roxanne explained.

"Would it be possible to move her to a more cheerful location?"

"Someone would have to pay for it, and, since she has no relatives or family, I'm afraid it's out of the question."

"Find a room. I'll pay for it."

"I don't know, Mr. Crockett. You're not family."

"No, but my money looks just like family money. Find her a bright and comfortable room. I'll check in on her tomorrow."

I hadn't been able to prevent what had happened to her, but I could make sure that she was in a bright and cheery room with everything she might need to help her recovery.

Someone had to care. She deserved at least that much.

The only lead I had was the receipt, so I took a drive up Little Cottonwood Canyon to sample the hospitality of a very expensive French restaurant.

Le Caille was one of Utah's premier and luxurious dining experiences. It was situated on twenty acres of beautiful, lush vineyards, manicured gardens and Old World-styled brick sidewalks nestled near the mountains of Little Cottonwood Canyon.

The restaurant was housed in an eighteenth century French-style château hidden back among a thicket of trees, giving it the feel of a secret monastery. Guests could dine in their choice of three unique dining rooms, or, when the weather permitted, one of their three spectacular patios.

It was definitely a five-star restaurant, or at least that's what their website claimed, and if it's on the Internet it must be true.

I felt out of place just opening the door. About as high-class as I care to get is Katie Blues where the food is great, the prices reasonable and the atmosphere casual and relaxed.

The hostess automatically smiled as I entered. "May I help you?" she asked.

She was tall, well-proportioned, wearing a tight fitting dark blue gown that fell to just above her ankles. She was wearing black high heels that made her even taller. She had shoulder-length dark hair with bangs cut just above pale green eyes, light brown eye shadow, and long lashes.

"I have a question for you," I said.

"Deliveries are around the back," she said. "You just need to go outside down the stairs and drive to the far end of the complex and head south to our delivery area," she said helpfully.

I guess I looked like a delivery man in my blue jeans, tee-shirt, brown Corduroy sports jacket and well-worn boots.

I removed my card and handed it to her. "I'm a private investigator and I'm hoping you can help me."

"A real private investigator, like on television?" she asked.

I guess even up-scale hostesses are easily impressed. "And no, I don't drive a red Ferrari," I quipped.

She gave me her best sexy look. "But I bet you get the girls."

"Only the beautiful ones," I grinned. The private eye getting the subject on his side, so he can squeeze information out of her.

"This is so exciting. How can I help?"

I removed the 8x10 head shot of Jennifer Marie and showed it to her. "Do you recall this girl coming in here about two weeks ago? It would have been a Monday night."

"Oh yes."

Her confidence surprised me. "She came in with Mr. Parker."

"Parker?"

"Yes, Martin Parker. He's a regular here."

My imaginary spider senses began to tingle and the hair on the back of my neck stood up at the mention of Parker.

"Are you sure?"

"Yes. I remember because Rebecca and I, she's the other hostess, were shocked that he was with someone other than Abigail."

"Abigail?"

"Abigail Collingsworth. She is a socialite who Mr. Parker usually brings in here. They dine here at least twice a month."

"And how long has this been going on?"

"About six months."

"Do they come on a regular night?"

"No. I never know when they will show up."

"You have my card. The next time they show up would you give me a call?"

She looked down at the card in her hand. "I guess so." "And if we could keep this between the two of us I'd appreciate it."

She still didn't seem too convinced so I added the private eye bonus. "You know, every private eye needs a reliable secret source to feed him information so that he can solve his cases."

Nothing gets free information like ego building.

"You could really help me out, Ms..."

"Regina Wooten."

"What do you say, Regina?"

"Okay."

"Like I said, let's just keep this between you and me."

"Okay."

I left before she could change her mind. Sometimes the ploy worked and they called with information, but most of the time they forget about you as soon as the door hit you on the way out.

Sylvia Parker had died a little over a month ago, which meant Parker had been cheating on her even before her death. Divorce, an affair, ego, money, all the usual motive suspects were falling into place. My gut told me Martin Parker had killed his wife. But had he also beaten Jenny? Was he a man with a dark side who used women until he was finished with them and then tossed them away?

I called Faith Parker and asked her to meet me in my

office.

Investigations are not as complicated as they seem. Boiled down to its basic component, it involves following the path of a person's life and finding out where they intersect with someone else and why. Jenny's path now intersected with two people, Martin Parker and the school teacher, Ruth Mosley.

All I needed to know now was why?

According to the police records, her car had been towed from the parking lot of a small motel at Forty Ninth South and Eighth East. That was about two miles from St. Mark's Hospital. That seemed like the place to start. Maybe someone had seen something.

***

The High Class motel was anything but. It was a one-story complex in the shape of an extended L with the office in the crook of the L. It had only twelve units that looked like they hadn't been painted since World War II. There was no grass, only a large paved parking lot that ran from the four back units on top of the L to the four units at the front and the four near the office. Even Mr. Rogers would have found this place depressing.

I parked in front of the office and went in. It was small, with two chairs along the window side of the wall with a wooden counter stretching the length of the room, topped by bulletproof glass. To the right was a heavy wooden door that would take a tank to break through. Cameras were hanging from every corner of the office. The office was separated from the living quarters by a dingy brown curtain. Management might want to think about renaming the place.

I rang the bell and waited. Soon a craggy-faced, middle-aged man with bad complexion and thinning hair wearing a University of Utah sweatshirt appeared from behind the curtain. He smiled like we were the best of friends.

"Looking for a room?"

"Just information."

The smile disappeared. I guess we were no longer best friends.

"Have you ever seen this girl?" I removed the 8x10 of Jennifer and laid it in the slot underneath the thick glass. He picked it up and stared at it for a moment, gently nodding his head like he was about to make an important discovery. He turned it slightly as if that would make her more recognizable then straightened it back up.

"She's a lesbian, right?"

The question took me by surprise. "Why would you ask that?"

"She came in here last month with another woman. I'm not judging, of course, but we don't get too much of that sort of thing here."

"What did this woman look like?"

"She was attractive, not as hot as this one, but still attractive. It made me wonder about relationships, you know?"

"In what way?"

"This one was hot and dressed like it, you know stylish. The other one was cute but in a plain way. She was dressed like she belonged in another era, if you know what I mean."

"Enlighten me."

"Her dress wasn't very stylish. She wasn't wearing a lot of make-up and no jewelry that I can recall. They just didn't fit together, you know? I remember wondering what the hot one saw in her. Why is it that the plain ones always get the smoking hot ones?" He shook his head in disbelief. "I guess that's why I remember her."

"Did they rent a room?"

"Yes, but just for the night."

"What makes you think they were lesbians?"

"Because they rented a room together. I asked if they wanted a large single bed or double beds. The hot one said a single would be fine."

"Can I see the room?"

"I don't know, man."

I removed a twenty-dollar bill and slid it towards him. "Would this help you decide?" He glanced at the bill and quickly slid it into his pocket.

"Room 12."

He reached for the key and came around the corner and opened the heavy door. While everything looked low brow, security seemed high tech and solid. That meant they would have a video record of the night Jenny and her companion rented the room. It also meant I would be able to see who she had been with.

I followed him out the door and down the walkway to the corner. A man in his early forties, unkempt hair that looked like he had just survived an electrical shock, wearing tan trousers, a rumpled light blue shirt, and carrying an ice bucket, opened the door to his room and almost ran into me as he weaved his way down the sidewalk.

I glanced into the open door of his room. It was as depressing as the office. The walls were dingy. The bed, with its dark brown bedspread, was a mess. The carpet looked like it hadn't been changed since 1972.

Class had come and gone from the High Class motel!

We rounded the corner and made our way to the back of the motel and Room 12. It was the last room, and far away from the office and prying eyes.

He inserted the key into the door and opened it. I moved past him into the dark room. Turning the light on, I scanned the small room. The room was exactly as the room I had just glanced into. The dark brown carpet was crushed and worn, yet surprisingly clean. A small lamp sat on the nightstand; a dresser bureau sat against the wall opposite the queen-size bed. A small table and one straight-back chair sat near the bureau. A small television hung above the bureau. The room was clean, the walls freshly painted, which was about all I could say for it.

Why would Jennifer Justice need a motel room? If this was indeed a lover, why not just go back to her apartment? Was she afraid a neighbor might see? One of her students? Was she worried that Earlene Templeton would raise a ruckus and evict her?

Was she leading a secret life? Was she hiding her sexuality from the rest of the city? Did someone close to her find out and make her pay for her sexual choice?

I stood staring at the room. Something wasn't right. Then it dawned on me. "How often do you paint your rooms?"

"When they need it."

"That room we just passed needed it and yet the walls were dingy. Why this room?" I stared at the bed and its light brown bedspread. "And a new bedspread."

I walked over to the bed and pulled back the spread. The sheets were clean and semi-white.

"Hey," he protested as he took a step towards me.

I turned to face him. He stopped. Holding his hands up as if to fend me off, he quickly backed up against the wall.

With one giant tug, I heaved the mattress off the bed spring. It landed upside down against the wall near the bathroom. The bottom was stained a dark reddish brown.

The man's eyes went wide with fear as I grabbed him and hurled him back against the wall. His head bounced off the fresh paint.

"I want to know what happened here!"

"I don't know, I swear, I don't." Beads of perspiration dotted his forehead and bits of saliva gathered around his mouth.

"The next morning when the maid went to clean up she found all the blood."

"And you didn't call the cops?"

"I thought it was just a cat fight, you know, a lovers' quarrel. It was none of my business."

"And you didn't see or hear anything?"

"Nothing, I swear."

I tightened my grip on his shirt and bounced his head off the wall to make sure he wasn't leaving anything out.

He was.

"Okay, okay, I heard what sounded like a truck at about ten thirty. I peeked out my apartment window and saw a large black truck."

"What kind?"

"A Dodge Ram, I think. Yeah, I remember the ram horns on the back."

"Did you see who was driving?"

"A big dude with short hair. The other woman was sitting in the truck with him."

"Anyone else?" I pressed my arm against his throat for emphasis. His memory got better.

"There were two other big guys in the extended cab. I swear. That's all I saw."

"What about her purse and computer? What did you do with them?"

His head fell back against the wall. "She was gone and there was no way to get it to her." His voice rose and cracked.

I had played a hunch and it had paid off.

"Let's go get them."

I let go of him and he nearly fell down. Quickly, he regained his balance and rushed out the door. I followed.

Inside the office he produced the purse and laptop.

Opening the purse, I fished out her driver's license, which read: Jennifer Justice. Now, I was certain Jennifer Justice was Jenny J. I wrapped the laptop in a plastic trash bag the nervous manager provided, then took the purse.

"Now I want to see the tape."

"What tape?"

I motioned to the camera high in both corners of the office. "The security tapes for the night they came in."

"I don't have them. I swear."

He began talking fast as if that would convince me. "The company that owns this dump is cheap as they come. They rarely spring for anything we need here. As far as security tapes go, we tape over them each week."

"If you're lying to me—"

"I'm not, I swear."

I had gotten about as much out of him as I could.

"The police are going to be here to look at that room. Stay out of it until they get here."

Taking her laptop and purse, I left him frantically nodding his head.

I called Jackson. I told him to forget about picking up Earlene Templeton and then filled him in. He promised to send a CSI unit out to process the scene.

Driving back to my office I tried to piece together what I knew, which wasn't a lot. Jennifer Justice had rented a room in a sleazy motel with another woman. Were they lovers? Were they running from someone so they could be together? Had the husband or boyfriend tracked them down and taken his revenge? Was this nothing more than homophobic jealousy? It didn't feel right, but that was the only thing that made sense.

I needed to talk to "Mellow Yellow" after all. I dialed Faith's number.

It didn't take her long to give me the lowdown on Donovan Barnet. A twenty-six-year-old graduate student at the U majoring in dance, he was an excellent dancer and a hard worker. He volunteered at the local schools to help teach kids to dance. He was an all-around good guy. Wasn't everyone in her agency?

She had no knowledge of Jennifer and Donovan dating. When I pressed the issue she said it was highly unlikely.

"Why is that?" I inquired.

She gave me a chuckle. "David, he's a serious dancer."

"So?" The only thing I knew about the dancing world was old movies of Gene Kelly, Fred Astaire, and John Travolta.

"When you find him, have him call me. I've been worried about him. I haven't heard from him in two weeks."

"Is that unusual?"

"In this business the talent should check in with their agent two or three times a week. You never know when a job will come up and we need to get a hold of them."

Donovan Barnet lived six blocks over from Jennifer.

Like her apartment complex and most of the others surrounding Westminster College, his apartment complex was old but well maintained. It was a large four plex with gray stucco offset by black wood trim. His apartment was on the top left.

I knocked on the door. There was no response. I knocked louder and then rang the bell. Finally, a shaggy haired kid of about twenty-five answered. His eyes were half closed. He looked like I had just awakened him.

"Donovan Barnet?"

"No."

"Is he here?"

"No."

"Do you know where he is?"

"No."

"I really need to talk to him."

He yawned then wiped his eyes with his hands. "What's this about?"

"It's important. Do you know if he is in school or working?"

"He teaches dance."

"Where?"

He told me.

As I rushed back to my car I had a bad feeling. In my line of work there are no such things as coincidences. When lives intersect in the middle of a freeway, there is usually an accident.

Three lives had just intersected at one major intersection.

ELEVEN

I parked in one of the visitor's parking spaces and rushed towards the building I had already become familiar with, the Daniel John Clinton Elementary School.

Jennifer Justice was a substitute teacher here, Ruth Mosley taught here, and now Donovan Barnet volunteered teaching dance to sixth graders. Even a private eye like me knew something was going on here. But what? What was the connection between these three people?

It wouldn't have surprised me to learn that Principal Cook was an alien, known to the Men in Black, and was using alien mind control to force everyone to work free for the state. That would explain a lot.

Lakeisha smiled when she saw me. "Still on the case, Mr. PI?"

"Still on the case, and I still need your help, Lakeisha."

She laughed. "Maybe I should get my own license and give you some competition?"

"Choosing between me and a sexy thing like you, I'm afraid I'd lose every time."

"Ain't it the truth? What do you need, sugar?"

"Is Donovan Barnet teaching today?"

She quickly checked the schedule and nodded. "He's in Room 23, down the hall and to the left."

Principal Cook exited her office, making her way to the copy machine, a half smile on her face. Seeing me her face froze. I smiled my best smile. She turned, stormed back into her office and slammed the door.

"That woman has got to quit flirting with me. It'll go to my head."

"All warm and fuzzy that one," Lakeisha said in a low tone, then laughed again.

"I don't want to get you in trouble, so if she asks I was just asking about my nephew."

"It don't matter," she sniffed. "I got a cousin that works in the mayor's office. She can only push me so far."

"Maybe you should open up your own private investigator's office. You're as tough as they come."

"I hear that, sugar," she chuckled. "Now you best be getting on out of here before I come across this counter and show you my sweet side."

I winked at her and left before she could get that much woman across the counter and show me her sweet side. That would be a lot of sugar.

It was three o'clock. As I reached Room 23 the bell rang.

Like water over a dam, excited and happy kids began pouring out of classes. I stood back against the wall hoping not to get crushed in the avalanche of rabid kids rushing to get home to midday snacks and playgrounds.

Donovan Barnet was standing at the lone desk in the empty room. He was tall and lanky with a toned body. He had a boyish face, black hair, dark eyes, and big ears protruding from his pear-shaped head. He was wearing dancing leotards.

He noticed me and looked up. "Can I help you?"

"Are you Donovan Barnet?"

"Yes," he answered suspiciously.

"I'm David Crockett. I'm a private eye and I'd like to ask you a few questions."

"About what?"

"Jennifer Justice."

Animation suddenly engulfed him and he floated towards me.

"Have you found her?"

His voice rang with anxiety. "Please tell me you have found her. Is she all right?"

"Do you know her well?"

"Of course," he answered definitely. " She's my best friend. I have been worried sick about her."

His voice rose higher and his speech became fast. "She hasn't answered her phone forever. I've called the police, the fire department, the mayor's office, the White House."

"The White House?"

"That had nothing to do with Jen. I just think the President is the cutest thing and wanted to talk to him."

He smiled and I suddenly I knew why Faith had laughed when I pressed her on the possibility of them dating.

The smile quickly vanished. "Please tell me she's okay. If anything ever happened to her I don't know what I would do." He waited anxiously for me to speak.

"I found her. She's alive."

"If someone hurt her I'll rip their 'you know what's' out and stuff them in their mouth and stomp them with my feet!" His tough talking belied his slender frame. But he had passion and that counted for something.

"Maybe you ought to sit down, Donovan."

He swayed back to the desk and sank into the chair, steeling himself for the worst. His passion and anger made me like him a lot. If someone hurt Katie, I would feel the same.

"Someone beat her nearly to death and left her at St. Mark's Hospital."

He gasped and covered his mouth. "Oh my goodness." The tears rolled down his cheeks. "I need to go to her. She needs me."

He jumped up and tried to rush past me. I stopped him.

"She's in a coma."

He crumpled to the floor and stared into space. Then he began beating the back of his head against the wall.

"Who would hurt her? Who could do such a thing?"

I lowered myself to the floor and rested my head against the wall. "I was hoping you could tell me."

"All she wanted to do was dance. She loved dancing and making people happy."

"Did she have any enemies?"

"Enemies?" He looked at me, shocked that I could ask such a question. "No one could hate her. Jenny was my definition of an angel. If you needed help, she was there, no matter what. She would be dead tired and still stay and help me with a dance move I was struggling with. Even Principal Cook liked her and that's saying a lot."

"What about the other teachers?"

"What do you mean?"

"Did anyone seem to resent her?"

He shook his head. "No, of course not, at least none that I'm aware of. I only volunteer here two days a week, but she never mentioned anything like that to me."

"Did she hang around with any of them?"

"I don't think so, not socially at least."

He paused as if trying to remember anything that might help. "She did say, one day, that she was concerned about one of the teachers here."

"Did she give you a name?"

"No, she just said she was worried and wanted to help them."

"In what way?"

"I don't know. I just assumed it was with class or a student. She was always worried about this or that student." He forced a laugh. "Believe me they can get to you with their innocent eyes and their mischievous personalities."

"Anything else you can remember?"

He beat his head on his knees as if trying to pound thoughts and memories out of his brain. It must have worked.

"She said something really strange one day." He sat up and turned to me, excited. "We were finishing lunch and out of the blue she said that she just didn't understand how such a smart woman could be so deceived."

"What do you think she meant by that?"

"I don't know. When I asked her, she just shrugged it off and said it was time to dance."

I got up and helped Donovan to his feet.

"One more question; a very personal question."

He stared at me then gave me a half smile. "Sure, why not?"

"Were you two lovers?"

His blank look said it all before he broke out in laughter.

"I love her more than life itself, but not in the way you think. I'm gay."

I felt foolish asking my next question, but I had to know.

"Was she?"

"Gay?" This surprised him. "Of course not, but we still loved each other."

"She was beaten at a motel where she had checked in with another woman. Do you have any idea why she would check into a motel with another woman?"

"No, but I can promise you it wasn't for the reason you are hinting at."

"How can you be so sure?"

"Because I know her. That wasn't Jennifer."

His confidence in her when facts pointed in the opposite direction impressed me. That was what friends did. They believed in the person, not the situation. All of us need someone like that in our lives. I was glad I had Katie.

His stern face melted and he looked at me with the saddest eyes I had ever seen. "Please. I have to see her. She needs me even if she can't see me."

"She's in Room 236 at St. Mark's Hospital. Ask for Roxanna Lewis and tell her you're a friend of mine."

"When you find out who did this, please don't tell me. If you do I will kill them." His face hardened and I knew he meant it.

I admired his devotion and understood his passion.

"You're going to have to wait in line, my friend."

He rushed out and down the hall. I was glad Jenny had a friend like him.

As I exited the room I saw Ruth Mosley closing the door to her classroom. She headed my way. Was she the teacher Jennifer was trying to help?

When she saw me she slowed down then stopped as if she had forgotten something, then quickly turned and rushed back towards her room.

Maybe I was just being paranoid, but had she really forgotten something or was she trying to avoid me?

In Afghanistan when you stumbled upon a possible terrorist cave, you tossed in a few hand grenades and waited to see who or what came out. I decided to toss a few verbal grenades at Ruth Mosley and find out just what she knew.

I made a big deal out of stomping down the hall and out the front door. If I was right, she wouldn't be far behind.

Hiding behind my car I watched as she dashed out of the

building and ran to her car. She opened the door and tossed her book bag into the car.

"You knew she couldn't come in for you, didn't you?" I said.

She jumped like a scared rabbit at the sound of my voice.

"I want to know what happened to her."

When she turned and saw me approaching, her whole body stiffened. "I don't know what you're talking about."

She tried to sound calm, but was failing miserably. Was she just the nervous type or was she hiding something?

"Please leave before I call security."

"I'm not going to stop until I know what happened to Jennifer,"

"I don't know anything. Please believe me."

The desperation in her voice told me I was on the right track. Now it was time to go fishing.

"Jennifer was trying to help you. Were you in some kind of trouble?"

"I don't know what you are talking about. Jennifer was my substitute teacher and that's as far as it went. We didn't hang out, and she wasn't trying to help me with anything."

I could see her trembling, even with her back to me. She started to climb into her car.

"I have Jennifer's diary."

She froze.

"Diary?" she asked as casually as her quaking voice could.

"Yes, she kept a diary and I have it."

I pulled the diary from my coat pocket and held it up for her to see. She tried not to be interested but curiosity got the best of her. She glanced at it then instantly turned back to her car. It was obvious her mind was racing, calculating the things that Jennifer might have said about her in the diary. I decided to push her further.

"It is a very interesting read. And you'll never guess who

is mentioned more than once in it."

"Why should I care who's in it?"

But she did.

She stared at her car for a long moment then slowly turned toward me. "Please leave me alone. I had nothing to do with what happened to her."

"How do you know something happened to her?"

She looked at me like a frightened doe, her eyes falling to the ground. "Because you said you wanted to know what happened to her."

I remained silent, waiting to see what she would say. Sometimes a nervous person will blurt out things just to interrupt the quiet.

She nervously fumbled with her hands. When the frustration got the best of her she shook her head and jumped into her light brown Toyota Celica and fired up the engine. Without looking at me, she quickly drove away.

Ruth Mosley was hiding something. I decided to find out what.

TWELVE

She turned on Twenty-Seventh West and made her way to State Street. State Street runs the entire length of Salt Lake City and the surrounding municipalities from Murray to Draper. It makes following someone extremely easy because it goes so far, and unless they turn you are just heading home like they are. It also makes it hard to detect a tail for the same reason.

She stayed on State Street until she reached a Hundred and Sixth South then turned left towards the eastern mountains. I followed her at a distance until she turned into a high-class gated community in the Cottonwood Heights area.

There was a guard booth behind the gate but I didn't see anyone there. Maybe I had lucked out and it was their coffee break or it was empty during the day when tenants could use their gate pass.

Using her card, Ruth opened the gate and dashed through.

I gunned my car and barely made it past as the large

gate slowly closed.

This was not your typical gated community. Each home sat on a half a lot and was spacious and elegant with well-manicured front yards and fenced-in backyards.

She passed a large park surrounded by trees, nestled against a large, ten-foot concrete wall, which surrounded the entire community. Talk about privacy.

She turned left, then right. Halfway down the block she pulled into the drive of a large home and parked beside a truck. Jumping out of her car, she rushed inside.

The house was an expansive two-story stone house with no fewer than five gables supporting two windows each. It had a large, open front porch with two white swings on each side. Two large trees were conveniently spaced in the green and gently sloping front yard.

I parked two houses down, turned off my engine and waited, wondering how a public school teacher could afford such an expensive home.

The truck she had parked beside immediately caught my attention. It was large and black. It was also a Dodge Ram. Had Ruth been involved in Jenny's beating? Had she set her up?

While this gated community seemed like any other well-kept neighborhood in Salt Lake City from the outside, the inside was nothing but unique. The houses were well spaced with what looked like large gardens in the back. A large recreational center sat by itself at the end of the block. Behind it lay a community park.

What struck me most was the quiet. In most neighborhoods the sounds of children laughing, dogs barking, men working on cars, or women talking with each other would fill the air. None of that was going on. Not even at the park. This was the quietest neighborhood I had ever seen. Then something even odder caught my eye.

Standing beside the two large columns surrounding

the porch of the giant mansion across from the house Ruth Mosley had disappeared into, were two giants with no necks. These men, who looked like Arnold Schwarzenegger in his prime, were standing guard. They had military-type haircuts, wore dark suits, and, from the bulge underneath the coat of one of them, I knew they were armed. Why did a mansion in a gated community need bodyguards? And why was this house the only one on the block to have such a unique amenity? As I was pondering these questions I noticed that I wasn't the only one paying attention to the surroundings. They had also spotted me.

I quickly grabbed a city map from my glove compartment and franticly began looking at it. I ignored the first tap on my window, pretending to be engrossed in the map. The second tap was harder. And serious. I looked up, gave them confused, then rolled down the window.

"Hi," I said quickly before they could stop me. "Can you tell me which house Sarah Palin lives in?"

The no-neck giant staring down at me from my side of the car gave no hint of recognition at the name.

He glared at me as he spoke. "This is private property. You have to leave."

I'm sure it was my overactive imagination, but I could swear this muscle-bound gorilla sounded just like Schwarzenegger?

"I'm sure this is the address she gave me."

"She doesn't live anywhere in this community."

"I'm supposed to be picking her up for a date."

The no-neck reached into the car and grabbed me by the shirt. "I said she doesn't live here. Now leave."

"Thanks for your help."

I knew I shouldn't have, but I just couldn't resist. I looked up at the muscle bound no neck, and, in my best Arnold I deadpanned, "I'll be back."

He leaned in close enough that I could smell his foul breath. Pastrami and pickles. "No, you won't. Now leave before something happens to you."

I guess he wasn't a big fan of the movies.

"Can one of you nice gentleman open the gate for me."

"It's open. Now get out," pastrami breath said forcefully.

I drove eight blocks to a local hamburger place and ordered some food, then parked a block down the street facing the closed gates.

I ate in silence, wondering why such a normal looking community from the outside needed locked gates and bodyguards on the inside. What was so secret that no-neck goons were willing to throw you out just for getting lost?

It was going to be a long night. I made myself as comfortable as possible and settled in to wait.

THIRTEEN

Ruth Carson Mosley was the fourth wife of Joshua Mosley. She had met him at Cottonwood High School, where they both taught. She was twenty-two. He was tall, handsome, and very knowledgeable when it came to politics, history, and science. He was also very religious, not afraid to stand up for what he believed. She had admired his courage.

For a year he had told her about his beliefs which, in some ways, were not a lot different from the way she had been raised. By then she was madly in love with him and was willing to do anything to be with him, even becoming wife number four.

When she was given to him by Allen Peterson, the self-proclaimed prophet of their church, she considered herself the luckiest woman in the world. He was everything she wanted in a husband, He was smart and fun, and, most of all, a man who followed God in everything. A man whom she believed saw and talked to

David Sterago

angels.

Having been raised Mormon, she was familiar with polygamy. She had been taught how it had been ordained by God until it had been rescinded by the Church. Through Joshua, she had learned that it had been stopped strictly because of political pressure, which, according to him, was evidence that the Mormon Church had fallen into apostasy and was no longer God's church on the earth. That distinction now belonged to "The Eternal and True Church of Christ in the Last Days", founded by Allen Peterson in 1974 and now headed by his son, Rulon Peterson.

Joshua also instructed her that Allen Peterson talked with God and had been given the sacred priesthood by angels. He also had been personally told by Jesus that the Mormon Church was now a cancer among his people, and that Peterson, had been chosen to lead the new Church, the only one with all the restored ordinances including polygamy. It was only through Peterson's revelations, and strict obedience to the husband, that families would be able to reach the highest glory in heaven together.

While the outside world scoffed at such things, Ruth knew they were true. She had felt the happiness this lifestyle had brought her, the camaraderie with her fellow sister wives, and the love she had for their children. She had seen the spiritual growth in her life as she learned spiritual truths from her husband, Joshua and from their prophet.

Her biggest problem had been forcing herself to curb her excitement, to not shout her happiness to the world. Even with all the shows on television about polygamist wives, and with all the various court rulings supporting polygamy, she had still been afraid she would lose her teaching job. It was one thing for parents to accept a polygamist lifestyle. It was another to allow a polygamist to actually teach their children. It was a secret she had guarded with extreme diligence, especially in Utah. To everyone at the school she was the only wife of Joshua Mosley, though it was getting harder to keep their secret.

It had been three years and six months since Ruth had joined The Eternal and True Church of Christ in the Last Days. Three years, and six months of marital bliss and spiritual renewal.

Was it now slipping away, she wondered.

Ruth sat at the large table with her husband and his three other wives, staring at the bounteous spread of food before them. She should be grateful for everything she had. So why was she struggling so much? Why were seeds of doubt and fear growing in her brain?

Joshua Mosley smiled at everyone gathered around the long wooden table in the middle of the dining room, then held out his hands. With the exception of the eleven wooden chairs surrounding it, there was no other furniture in the room.

Carol and Eve, both flanking Mosley, immediately grabbed his hand. As they did, they each held out their other hand for Sarah, Ruth, and the six children.

All but Ruth took their neighbors hand and silently bowed their heads. Sarah nudged Ruth out of her reverie. Quickly, she glanced at Joshua who was staring at her. Forcing a smile, she took Sara's hand and bowed her head. All eyes were shut as Joshua blessed the food. At the end all echoed his amen and patiently waited for him to nod his approval. With a smile he nodded and the meal began.

Ruth looked at her husband, then lowered her eyes towards the table. "Someone came to the school today asking about Jenny," she said softly.

Joshua's head snapped up, but he immediately gained control.

"Who?" he asked, keeping his voice low and casual.

No one else in the family paid any attention.

Carol, Joshua's first wife, with a wide face and narrow eyes, began filling his plate. She dumped a large helping of mashed potatoes onto his plate then reached for the green beans and carrots. Finally, as the rest of the table silently watched, she removed a large chicken breast from the serving plate and gave it to her husband. Once his plate was filled, she dumped a helping of mashed potatoes on the plates of the six children. Eve, the second wife, six years younger than Carol, with brown hair, brown eyes and somewhat plump, followed with green beans and carrots. Sarah, the youngest of all the wives at twenty, was the only blonde of the wives, with blue eyes and short hair. She was attractive even in her plain cloth dress and no make-up. She placed a piece of chicken on their plates.

"A private detective," Ruth replied softly.

"What did he want?" Joshua asked sternly.

"He was asking about my relationship with Jennifer."

"Did he say anything about the church or your lifestyle?"

"No."

"As long as he doesn't pry into our affairs then all is well." Joshua took a bite of meat, then smiled at Carol. "This is very good, dear."

Carol, basking in his approval, nodded.

Ruth spoke again. "He said he had her diary."

"Diary?" Joshua sat his fork down and turned to Ruth. "Did you know she had a diary?"

"No she never mentioned it to me."

He stared at the far wall, contemplating the complications such news meant. "This could prove a problem."

"Why?" Ruth stared at her husband of three years, the patriarch of their family and the right-hand man to their spiritual leader.

"Ruth," he began patiently as though she was a child. "Given the anti-polygamist attitudes that prevail in this state, it could hurt us if people find out we are proselytizing young women. Do you remember how your parents reacted when you told them of your plans to marry me?"

"They threatened to call the police and have us arrested."

"We are being told today that all is well, but we can't let our guard down," Joshua said grimly.

"There is nothing wrong with trying to teach someone the truth, or inviting them to share in our happiness," Carol interjected between bites of chicken.

"Listen, my family." Joshua paused until all eyes were on him. Then he spoke in a soft but firm voice. "We must never forget that the devil is real and that he uses everything in his power to destroy us." He went from one wife to the other making sure they understood him. "He has turned this city, this state, and even this country against us. We stand alone in the principles of God's true ways."

The wives and children were nodding as he pushed his chair back from the table. "They want to destroy this family, but we will not let them." He rose, folded his napkin and laid it on the table. "We need guidance from the prophet."

Carol glanced up at him with concern. "Can't it wait until after you have finished your dinner?"

"No, it can't," Joshua said firmly then looked at Ruth. "Ruth, come with me."

Minutes later, one of the guards knocked on the large front door of the home of Rulon Peterson and immediately opened it for Joshua and Ruth. They were greeted warmly by Elizabeth Peterson.

"We need to see Rulon, please," Joshua pleaded as he quickly entered the residence. "It's most urgent."

"Of course. He is in his study," Elizabeth answered with a friendly smile. They followed her to the study and entered. Rulon Peterson was a thin, almost gaunt man with a long face and deep set eyes. At sixty-three, his skin was pale and sagged on his face, his hair white and thinning. He was not handsome by any means.

He stood up to greet them. Thanking Elizabeth, he nodded. She closed the door behind her.

"Joshua, Ruth, what a nice surprise. Please have a seat."

He waited until they were both seated before speaking again.

"What brings you here?" he asked gently.

"Ruth had a visit today from a private detective," Joshua replied.

Rulon nodded his head. "Yes, I know," he said.

"You know?" Ruth seemed surprised.

"My dear, God tells me many things," Rulon smiled kindly, not about to let on that his no-neck, prophet squad also kept him informed.

He stared at her for a long time, making her feel uncomfortable. Finally, he spoke softly. "Ruth, I sense that you are struggling with some of our ways." His eyes rested upon her, burning into her very soul. "Tell me the truth, my child."

"I'm confused and don't know what to think anymore."

"It's understandable. You have been through a lot. But we must always remember that it is not what we want, but what God wants."

"But how do you know what God wants?" Ruth asked.

"Because he talks to me, just as he did in days past."

He smiled gently at her. "Do you believe that I am called of God?"

She hesitated then finally answered quietly, "Yes."

"And as such I am obligated to do what God reveals to me, am I not?"

"Yes, but why would God ask such a horrible thing?"

"Only God knows, my child." Peterson could see the doubt still in her eyes. Gently he took her by the hand.

"Did Abraham know why God asked him to sacrifice his only son? No, but he was obedient, wasn't he?"

"Yes."

"And did Saul know why when he was commanded to kill all living things among the Amalekites? No. But, unlike unlike Abraham, he was not obedient, was he."

Ruth shook her head in agreement.

"Who then did God destroy?"

Ruth looked at him, then lowering her eyes answered softly. "Saul."

"So we too must be obedient, even though we don't know all the reasons why. Only God knows the sin and darkness that is in the hearts of those who oppose us. Like Abraham, I have no choice but to be obedient, even when I find the revelations to be repulsive, as Abraham must have. Ruth, we must be obedient no matter what we are commanded to do. The Savior often said, not my will but thy will be done. So it must be with us." He smiled gently at her. "Do you understand?"

Ruth nodded.

Was she right? Why was it so hard for her to now understand something that she had know all her life? She had been told over and over how Satan wanted to destroy the church, their family, their way of life. She knew that he would use any tools available to him, friends, family, politicians, and neighbors. Had she unwittingly been a pawn in his hands?

She looked up but Rulon was not looking at her. His eyes were closed and his head was nodding ever so slightly. She had witnessed this before. He was receiving a revelation from God. When his eyes opened, he smiled at her and squeezed her hand gently.

"My child, the Almighty has smiled down upon you. He has commanded that I stop all that I am doing and comfort you with prophetic love."

David Sterago

Ruth's eyes immediately darted towards Joshua, who smiled down at her. He, too, was nodding his head.

Rulon Peterson stood and lifted Ruth to her feet. "Go, my daughter and prepare yourself for my gift to you. I shall be with you momentarily."

With a grandfatherly smile he ushered her out the side door of his office. As if in a trance, she shuffled down the hall to the special bedroom reserved for such blessings of love. She was to use the time to undress and to pray that she would be worthy for the blessing she was to receive.

She glanced around the spacious bedroom. How different she had felt when she had first entered this room over three years ago. Then she had been gleeful with religious anticipation.

Now she couldn't help but shudder.

Allen Peterson had been the leader of "The Eternal and True Church of Christ in the Last Days" when she was placed with Joshua.

He had been a kindly, old man, who seemed close to God in every way. He had prophesied that he would never die. He had let it be known that he had received revelation that when his time came, instead of dying he would become young again and be lifted up to heaven. He had also promised many of the young girls that if they remained sweet, sharing their youth with him, they would be taken with him to live with God forever.

Then to the shock and dismay of all, he died at the age of 86. That was when the seeds of doubt first began to spring up in Ruth's mind. If his revelation had been from God, then how was it possible that he could have died? And not one of the girls he had promised was taken. How could he have been so wrong? And if he had been wrong about that, what else had he been wrong about?

If you couldn't trust your chosen leader, who could you trust? It had taken effort, but, through counseling with Joshua, she had begun to understand that God's ways were not man's ways, that, sometimes, God would choose to go in a different direction, to test our faith and obedience. It wasn't important what God did, but how we responded to what he did. Obedience in all things was the key.

Her mind drifted back to the very first time she had waited in this bedroom. Rulon Peterson had just announced that he was to be the new prophet. He wasn't what you would call handsome, but that didn't matter. To his followers, he was God's chosen on the earth and she was sworn to obey him. He had called her to be blessed as only he could.

As she had stood in the living room, she couldn't help but smile at the thought of all the other women dying with jealousy because she had been called. Quickly, she forced herself to dismiss the evil sense of pride swelling up in her and causing her to place her own feelings above the others. She was there to serve, to allow the sweetness of her womanhood to be used to create children to be raised up in the ways of God, as had the mothers of Samuel and Samson in the Old Testament.

"Do you know why you have been called?"

Her thoughts interrupted, she quickly glanced to the gaunt man sitting at the desk in front of her. His smile was friendly and relaxing.

"Sometimes God wants to love his children. But because he is in Heaven he must depend on vicarious love. Do you understand?"

"No."

"Just as earthly parents often have favorites, so it is with God. To show his favoritism, he sometimes chooses to love his children in a very special way."

"How can he do that?"

"By using me to love his favored child."

He smiled at her as he gently took her hand. "Are you prepared to receive such special love?"

"I want to be."

I know you do, but you must prepare yourself, as I must. You must go into the bedroom, remove your clothes and pray until I am sent to you. Can you do that?"

She nodded enthusiastically. How had she been so lucky to be chosen? As she walked to the bedroom, she hoped she would be worthy.

Now, three years and six months months later, as she sat numbly on the bed, a thousand and one thoughts raced through her mind. Why was she being so rebellious? Why was she struggling to believe as she once had? How could she have allowed the things she had been taught by loving parents to be so distorted, to be used for such evil designs? This was not a church of love, but of lust and power. Had her love for Joshua, in the beginning, been so blinding that she had not been able to see clearly?

Ruth stood and began unbuttoning her dress.

It didn't matter how she felt. She had made Joshua a promise. He had taken Jeniffer to the hospital. She would keep her word. She would be as obedient as she could. Fighting back her tears, she sat on the bed. She couldn't keep them from taking her body, but from now on, her mind, her thoughts and her soul belonged to her.

In his study, Rulon Peterson ran his bony hand through his receding hair. He stood and moved towards Joshua. "You must get that diary," he ordered firmly. "If there is anything in it about us, it could bring condemnation upon our heads. You know how this state is just itching to find something on us."

"What if the private eye doesn't want to give it to me?"

Peterson's eyes turned dark, his smile vanished. "Then you must persuade him."

He placed his hands on Joshua's shoulder and stared directly into his eyes. "Never forget, Joshua, that God is on your side. Nothing done in his name is wrong. Nothing. Do you understand?"

"Yes.

The smile returned and he patted Joshua on the back.

"Now go and take care of your family. I will send Ruth to you when she has been blessed."

He turned and left Joshua standing in the middle of the room. When the side door of the office closed, Joshua turned and quietly left the house.

Fourteen

The next morning I awoke in my car, stiff and sore. I needed to exercise the kinks out but that would have to wait. I looked at my watch. It was 6:07 a.m. Maybe there was enough time to get to the nearest Maverick and get a large cup of coffee.

I was back at 6:30 a.m. with a large cup of "thank you, I really need this" and a half dozen glazed "I really shouldn't be eating these, but going to anyway."

I ate the doughnuts and sipped my coffee as I settled back to see who came and went from this curious community.

At 7:30 a.m. Ruth Mosley's brown Toyota pulled through the open gates and sped past me. I was tempted to follow, but I knew where she was going. What I didn't know was who else lived there and who needed no-neck goons, with attitude, standing guard in front of their house.

I decided to wait.

Two hours, and six doughnuts later, a sleek black Mercedes pulled through the gate. One of the no-necks was driving. The tinted windows made it impossible to see who was in the back seat. I quickly jotted down the license plate and dialed Jackson, who I knew would already be at his desk. He was always the first one in. As the phone rang, I flipped a U-turn and followed.

"I need you to run a plate for me," I said as soon as he answered.

"Good morning to you, too," Jackson replied.

"When does it get good?" I grumbled as I tried to move into a position that didn't ache.

"What's the plate?"

"462 Charlie, Edward, Tango."

"Where are you?"

"I spent a most uncomfortable night outside a very plush gated community that Ruth Mosley, an elementary school teacher, lives in. "

"Sounds pretty ritzy for a school teacher," Jackson commented.

"My thoughts exactly. And get this, directly across the street from her is an expensive mansion with large muscle-bound goons standing guard at the front door."

"What's your interest in this teacher?"

"I think she might have something to do with Jenny."

"Like what?"

"I don't know, that's why I'm here."

"Hang on."

I waited as he pulled up the owner and registration. I could hear him mumbling to himself in the background. When he came back he had my undivided attention.

"The car is registered to The Eternal and True Church of Christ in the Last Days."

"Isn't that Rulon Peterson's polygamist group?"

"One in the same."

"Well, that would explain why Ruth Mosely was so nervous. I'm pretty sure she's a polygamist."

"And if that got out, she could lose her job. I guess I'd want to keep that secret also," he remarked, before asking where I was.

"I'm headed down Little Cottonwood Canyon."

I glanced in my rear view mirror and noticed a large black truck moving around a blue Volkswagen Rabbit a few cars back.

"I'm going to get some breakfast at Katie Blues. Then I'll do some digging into her phone records and see if we can tie them together."

He was silent. "What are you thinking?"

"If Rulon Peterson is connected to Jennifer's beating in any way, we could be opening up a can of media hysteria of biblical proportions."

"Maybe I should get my hair cut so I'll look nice for the cameras."

"That might be the least of our worries. Be careful, these people are extremely touchy about prying eyes," Jackson cautioned.

"Yeah, I met two of them yesterday. Very helpful,"

"Keep me informed," he said. "Oh, that other thing we talked about yesterday."

"Franklin?"

"I have some interesting information on our boy."

An hour search on my office computer had revealed only four attorneys named Franklin in the Salt Lake area. All four were in their late fifties and sixties, happily married, and not the kind to be dating twenty-eight-year-old Jennifer. Though, I guess, never say never.

I had pulled up each of their legal websites and read about their histories, their families, and their successes. Nothing jumped out at me until I found a throwaway paragraph on the website of Franklin, Austin and Player. It seemed Kellen Franklin's youngest son, twenty-seven-year-old Thomas Franklin, who was about to graduate from the University of Utah law school, was serving as a clerk in their law firm and doing a bang-up job filing briefs and serving coffee. What father wouldn't be proud? When I told Jackson, he promised to check out young Mr. Franklin to see if he was passing himself off as a lawyer.

I waited as he flipped through his notes. "It seems our boy has a very violent temper. It also seems he can break the law and get away with it because of his daddy's political connections."

"What do you mean?"

"While he was attending Jordan High School he beat up two young girls."

"And he got away with it?" I asked incredulously.

"It seems his father was golfing buddies with the district attorney at the time. He agreed not to prosecute."

"Juvenile records are sealed. How did you find out?"

"CD is good friends with Brenton Salvesen, who was the the assistant district attorney at the time. He didn't have anything good to say about his former boss. He thought the kid should have been prosecuted and sent to jail. His boss chalked it up to overactive hormones and dropped the whole case."

I shook my head in disbelief. "Franklin beat two high school girls and the DA dropped it?"

"He interviewed the girls and came to the conclusion that they were simply bringing false accusations because Franklin had rejected both of them in favor of another girl whom they both hated."

"Any truth to that?"

"Not a shred."

"That type of anger doesn't just disappear."

"How right you are. It seems another accusation was

brought last year from a Utah coed. While on their date he got grabby and when she resisted, he got angry and slapped her around. She jumped out of the car and ran home and called the campus police."

"What happened?"

"He claimed it never happened. He said she got mad when he mentioned another girl he liked and made up the whole thing."

"Weren't there marks on her face from being slapped?"

"Her face was red but it was thirty degrees outside so the officer had no way of knowing if it was red from being hit or from the cold."

"Sounds like you need to talk to young Mr. Franklin," I suggested.

"My hands are tied," Jackson sighed. "If I go near him the full weight of Franklin, Austin and Player will come down on the department like ugly on a Utah coed."

"Ah, the joys of political influence."

Jackson was silent for a moment then said, "Nothing to stop you from digging around, though. I'll try to smooth all the feathers that you ruffle."

"I never ruffle feathers." I gave him hurt.

"David, the rich have very long tentacles, political, social and business wise, so be careful when you talk to him."

He hung up.

As if I didn't have enough to worry about. I tried to smile, but the realization of what I had just learned wouldn't let me. A highly volatile lawyer's son, with political connections, and a politically charged whacko polygamist group had just jumped to the head of the suspect list.

What had I stumbled into?

FIFTEEN

The large black truck moved slowly behind me like a giant leviathan prowling the roads for another victim. I had the distinct feeling that victim was me. Had I been paying attention, I would have waited to make sure no one else had left the gated community before I began following. Of course, at the time I didn't know who I was following. Or how dangerous it could be.

As we reached some of the narrow and winding stretches of Little Cottonwood Canyon, the large truck was getting dangerously close. In my rear view mirror I could make out the driver. He was a big man with short, cropped hair, a large oval face with narrow eyes, pug nose, and Jay Leno chin. He reminded me of the goons guarding Peterson's house. Whoever he was, I already knew two things about him. His truck was the one parked at the house Ruth Mosley disappeared into. And he was not happy that I was following Rulon Peterson.

I slowed down hoping he would go around me. He didn't.

There was a curve coming up that topped a thirty-foot ravine on the right. Even though there was a guard rail, it would not stop a powerful Dodge Ram truck from sending my Honda Accord over the ridge, an accident due to my careless driving, no doubt.

I accelerated. The truck did the same.

As we neared the treacherous spot, I thought about whipping around Peterson's car and racing ahead but the traffic driving the other direction was solid. Maybe I could slam on my breaks, forcing him to stop. Of course, why would he stop if he was planning on hitting me and sending me to hell anyway? I needed to come up with a plan. And fast.

Peterson's Mercedes began rolling into the curve with ease. The truck accelerated to within inches of my bumper. I couldn't stop and I couldn't go around the Mercedes. I was stuck. Looking in my rear view mirror, I could see a grin on his face. There was no doubt in my mind, that if I didn't come up with an exit strategy and fast, I would soon find myself crashing down the side of the canyon. It was not how I had planned to begin, or end, my day.

Then an idea popped into my head.

I floored my Honda.

As Peterson's car edged into the dangerous curve, I raced towards his car. The black Ram stayed on my bumper. As the Mercedes gracefully slid into the curve, I moved to within inches of his bumper. If the black Ram had any intentions of taking me out, the Mercedes was going with me. I saw the anger in the truck driver's eyes as he was forced to back off. As we rounded the curve, making our way out of the canyon, the black Ram peeled around me. Flipping me off, the driver roared ahead.

You gotta love Utah drivers.

I had been given a warning: stay away from Rulon Peterson, Ruth Mosley, or both. There was no doubt they were not above playing dirty. Did that include beating an innocent woman?

I drove to Katie Blues, my head swimming with questions, but no answers.

Was Ruth Mosley's nervousness connected to what happened to Jennifer, or had she just been terrified of the school finding out her secret? Was it just a coincidence that a black truck was at the motel and again at Ruth's house? There had to be thousands of black Dodge Ram trucks in Salt Lake City.

And what about Rulon Peterson? Did he and his polygamist family have anything to do with Jennifer's beating? Had she refused to join his group? That was a scenario I didn't want to think about. The political implications and bad publicity for the state would be epic. *Polygamist group terrorizing young women in Utah! Polygamy once again running rampant in Utah!* The national media, which was now little more than scandal sheets, would have a field day with a juicy story like that.

And how was Martin Parker connected to her? Why was he taking her to such an expensive and secluded hideaway for dinner? From everything I knew about her, Jenny wasn't the type to date older men. She didn't seem the kind to be impressed with money. So why was she with Parker?

Could Abigail Collingsworth shed some light on it? If she was Parker's mistress why had he gone out with Jennifer? Had Collingsworth resented the intrusion and taken things into her own hands?

Collingsworth was a well-known socialite, making appearances at all the state social and political events. She was also a well-known fund-raiser for the Democratic Party, though it was never clear just how she raised the money. Could she have called in a favor and hired someone to take out someone she considered a rival for Parker's attention? Okay–that was too far out there, even for me.

And then there was Thomas Franklin, an angry young man who had gotten away with beating women before. Had he wanted more from Jennifer and beat her when she refused? He had the history of violence against women and had taken her out on a blind date. Had things gone from bad to worse? The suspect list kept getting larger.

I plopped down into my favorite booth, hoping and praying that Katie would soon arrive with a gallon of hot coffee.

"You look like you spent the night in a cement mixer," she remarked.

"You should see what it looks like from this side."

She set my cup on the table and poured. I stirred some sugar and cream into it and gulped it down. It burned but it was a good burn. She placed my order of hot cakes, sausage, hash browns, well-done and soft scrambled eggs then returned with a hot towel.

"Here," she said, handing me the towel, which I placed over my face. I could feel some of the tension drain from my body.

"You know me so well," I replied, keeping the towel over my eyes.

She slid into the booth beside me. "That's what friends do. Want to talk about last night?"

"I'd rather go home and sleep for a day but that's not going to happen." I removed the towel and looked at her, smiling on the inside.

"I found Jennifer J."

"Alive?"

"Barely. Someone beat her nearly to death and left her at St. Mark's Hospital."

"Any leads?"

"Yeah, a big one, that will shake this town to its core if it turns out to be true."

"Is it true?"

"I don't know."

She remained silent.

"You don't want to know who?" I asked.

She kissed me on the cheek and stood. "Would you tell me if I asked?"

"No."

"Then why ask?" She sashayed away.

As I watched her walk away I noticed Beatle Brow sitting in the same spot I had seen him in a week ago.

"1956," Darlene said as she stood holding my breakfast.

I set the towel on the table. "Bring it on."

"You Belong to Me," she said without any fanfare.

I stared at her.

She smiled. "You looked like death warmed over so I thought I'd take it easy on you."

"Patience and Prudence, entered the top ten in September of 1956, stayed in the top ten for ten weeks, reaching number one by knocking Elvis's "Don't Be Cruel" out of the top spot until the following week when "Don't Be Cruel" returned the favor and again hit the number one spot until it was replaced by "Love Me Tender." How'd I do?"

"You won yourself a plate of eggs. Enjoy."

After my third cup of coffee, I was feeling like my old self. I dialed a friend of mine with AT&T.

"I haven't heard from you in over a month," the voice said after the second ring. "This is going to cost you, big time."

"Good to hear your voice too," I laughed.

Debra Rucker was a high school friend and someone whom I could always count on in a pinch, even if it did cost me. We dated briefly during our junior year, but she seemed more interested in one of the football players, so I backed off. We had lost touch until about three years ago. She had looked me up on Facebook and called me out of the blue. She was going through a messy divorce. Her husband, who liked to physically take out his frustrations on her, had done a great song and dance to the child protective services about how unfit she was and how he was the better parent. It took me about two days to blow his titanic charade out of the water.

Being a member of the Salt Lake City Police force, I may, or may not, have physically illustrated my point about how much I detest cowards who beat their wives and file frivolous law suits. He, not surprisingly, withdrew his suit and left her alone. She was able to retain custody of her two children. A year later she met a really great guy named Roger Conklin and remarried.

"How does dinner at Red Lobster and Jazz tickets for you and your husband sound?"

"What can I do for you?"

"You're so easy."

"Only for you, Crockett," she teased.

I gave her Jennifer Justice's name and phone number and asked if she could trace all of her outgoing and incoming calls for the past month with names of the second party and email me a copy.

"Give me a couple of hours and I'll scan it and send it to you."

"Thanks, babe." I hung up.

"Babe? Is that how you talk to women?" Katie slid back into the booth beside me.

"Only my mother."

She handed me a doggie bag.

"What's this?"

"Dessert for when you get back to your office. A growing boy can't drink his coffee without hot, homemade doughnuts."

"Someone ought to marry you."

"Someone did," she laughed. "It didn't work out."

Taking my doggie bag I left.

SIXTEEN

Sitting alone at a table in the corner, the man stared long after Crockett had left, his anger bubbling up inside him like an over-active volcano. Crockett had been the cause of all of his misery and anguish. He had put his nose where it didn't belong more than once. The day of reckoning, however, was just around the corner.

"Your hotcakes, sir." Darlene set the plate of hotcakes in front of him, then poured another glass of fresh squeezed orange juice. "Will there be anything else, sir?"

She smiled at him like they were old friends, which disgusted him. All she was after was money. She didn't know him. If she had any clue as to the pain he had been through she wouldn't have been laughing and joking with Crockett. She would be begging his forgiveness on behalf of all humanity. He had been wronged and humanity was going to pay, starting with David Crockett.

With his left hand partially covering the large scar

running from his left eye to his jaw bone, he shook his head. The hotcakes looked good, even if they were gluten free. Ignoring the butter, which he knew was bad for him, he poured fresh maple syrup over them and took a bite. They were, surprisingly, good. Rarely did he put such carbohydrates into his system. But today he was celebrating.

The image of Crockett's head exploding through his rifle scope made him smile for the first time that morning. It would be a joyous occasion, though now all he felt was anger.

Why wasn't Crockett afraid?

Why wasn't he worried about everyone he saw?

Why wasn't he wondering if this was the one who was about to kill him?

Why wasn't he nervously looking around, hoping the last person he glanced at wasn't the last person he ever saw?

Why wasn't he cowering in fear? That had been the purpose of the note. It hadn't been to warn him. It had been to terrify him. Instead Crockett was going about business as usual, eating breakfast and leaving with a doggie-bag. Not once in the days that he had been watching had Crockett shown any kind of apprehension or fear. How dare he take the fun out of it.

How dare he ruin all the enjoyment.

If nothing else Crockett deserved to die for that.

And die he would. And soon.

SEVENTEEN

Debra was true to her word. By the time I got back to my office she had emailed me Jennifer Justice's phone records for the past month. Four names stood out. Two calls were from Martin Parker, ten from either Rulon Peterson or Ruth Mosley, and one from Thomas Franklin.

Jennifer seemed to attract unsavory men.

It was fifteen minutes after I had called that Faith entered my office and took a seat. She looked anxious and concerned.

"Have you found anything?" she asked.

"Maybe."

I took out the picture of Jennifer and shoved it towards her. She looked surprised as she lifted the 8x10 photo. "That's Jennifer Marie. What has she got to do with my father?"

"I was hoping you could tell me."

"I don't understand. Jennifer is one of my dancers and the sweetest person you'd ever want to meet. She's also extremely good and has a chance to make it if she would just let herself go."

"What do you mean?"

"She's a rare talent, but will only take safe assignments, those that don't include anything she considers vulgar."

"She has morals, values. Nothing wrong with that?"

"Not at church, but in the dancing world, the two don't mix. The dancing world wants their dancers to be edgy, hard core. They believe that dancers with morals are like prima donnas in the sense that their morals won't let them be daring and bold. It holds them back. Dancing companies don't want to be held back by anything or anyone."

She set the picture back on the desk. "What does any of this have to do with my father?'

"A week ago Jennifer was beaten almost to death and left outside St. Mark's emergency door."

Her face registered real shock. "Is she all right?"

"She's in a coma."

She stared back at the picture as if looking at the smiling photo would erase the images of almost being beaten to death.

"Will she come out of it?"

"I wish I knew," I said, releasing a breath of frustration.

"I still don't understand what this had to do with my father."

"I found a credit card receipt signed by your father in her bloody jacket."

"Why would she have my father's credit card receipt?" "They had dinner together last month at La Caille. Maybe she kept it as a memento, or he dropped it and she picked it up. I don't know. The hostess recognized her and positively identified your father as her date."

"But how would he even meet her?"

"Has he been to your agency in the past month?"

"He would rather eat snakes. The only time he has been here was to tell me he was cutting me off financially."

"When was that?"

"Two weeks after Mother's death. That would be about a month ago. I remember it because it was two days after her will had been read. We were all shocked when we found out she had left everything to him."

"Why would she do that if she had planned to divorce him?"

This caught her off guard. "Divorce him? Are you sure?" she asked skeptically.

"I found a business card in one of your mother's coat pockets from Jakins, Jakins, and Schuster. They are a very expensive divorce attorneys. I paid them visit. It looks like she was in the process of divorcing your father."

"If that was true, he would have been financially cut off."

"What do you mean?"

"All the money was hers, not his. If she divorced him, he would have been left with nothing, except what he could have gotten in the settlement."

"Which would have been very little once Jakins, Jakins, and Schuster got through with him," I interjected.

"That could be a motive, couldn't it?"

"Money always is. So after he received your mother's money, he decided to cut you off?"

"I was in the middle of auditioning some talent when he barged past Bella and into my office. He pointed his finger at me and yelled 'the cash cow is as dead as your mother.' Then he stormed out."

"He could have seen her picture on the way out. She stands out among the rest," I pointed out.

"He wasn't here long enough for that." She paused and looked at the photo of the beautiful young dancer. Then her face went white.

"The parking lot," she whispered almost to herself.

"What?"

"Jennifer had a meeting scheduled with me about the

same time to go over her photos and talk about her career. When she showed up fifteen minutes late she said her car had overheated in the parking lot and a kind man had helped her. I didn't think anything about it."

"You think it could have been your father?"

"Where else could he have met her? You think he was having an affair with Jennifer?"

"No. He was having an affair with a local socialite named Abigail Collingsworth. According to the hostess at La Caille they have been meeting there at least twice a week for the past six months."

"I knew he was cheating on Mother."

"Did she know?"

"No." She paused. Sadness crept into her eyes.

"Mother was as hard as nails when it came to business, but when it came to Father she believed everything he told her. He was so convincing that I don't think she ever suspected."

"There's more. I found bits of sleeping pills near the baseboard. Someone killing themselves wouldn't spit out such a small fraction of pills."

"You think she was trying to spit them out?" she asked.

"Yes, and the only reason she didn't was because someone stopped her from doing so."

"How would they get on the floor by the baseboard?"

"Maybe she struggled and he hit her, or something causing them to spill out of her mouth. That's the only thing that makes sense to me," I said.

"If she refused to take them or struggled with him, that would have set him off. He may have finally hit her." Anger flared in her eyes.

"Was he abusive?" I asked.

"Not that I ever saw, but Father always controlled his feelings. He knew she would divorce him in a heartbeat if he ever laid a finger on her."

"That kind of rage and frustration usually results in murder. He could have finally snapped."

"Then you do believe me?"

She smiled at me like I was Magnum P.I. Now I just needed a red Ferrari.

I cautioned: "Everything we have is still speculation. I need some physical evidence."

"But the pills?"

"A good attorney will argue that maybe she panicked and tried to spit out what was left in her mouth but, by then, it was too late."

My phone rang. Seeing it was Jackson I answered.

"What's up?"

"I had tech take a look at Jennifer's computer. There was nothing unusual on it. Mostly school work."

"Any prints besides hers?"

"The motel manager who took it, but that's it."

"So we're back to square one."

"Maybe not," he said. "Her phone record indicates that she had been receiving calls from three very interesting people."

I interrupted. "Martin Parker, Rulon Peterson, and Thomas Franklin."

Jackson didn't miss a beat. "Debra isn't supposed to be giving you that information, you know."

"What can I say, I'm charming and persuasive."

"And modest. That's the part I admire most about you."

"I'm going to see if I can find out just what the relationship between those three and Jennifer entailed," I informed him.

"I'll lay odds one of them entailed violence," Jackson said.

"Which one?" I asked.

"When you find out, let me know." He hung up.

Faith sat staring at me, her fingers interlocked on her lap.

"Did that have anything to do with my father?" she asked.

"His name showed up in Jennifer's phone records. So far that's all I know about it."

As I glanced down at her interlocking fingers resting in her lap, a light bulb suddenly went off. Something had been perplexing me for some time. I hadn't been able to put my finger on it until now. Jumping up, I moved around the desk.

"Lie down." I blurted out, motioning towards the couch.

She stared at me like I had lost my mind as I grabbed her by the hand and ushered her towards the couch.

"Lie down on your back," I commanded.

"No foreplay?" Her grin took on a mischievous air.

"Something has bothered me about the photos of your mother's body. Now I think I know what it is."

"What are you talking about?"

"Lie down and I'll explain."

"I usually demand dinner and dancing first." She smiled as she lay on the couch.

"Now cross your arms over your stomach."

With a look of confusion, she obeyed.

"How does that feel?" I asked.

"Fine I guess. What's this all about?"

"Now cross your right wrist over your left wrist."

With a perplexed look, she did as I instructed.

"This doesn't feel as comfortable," she said.

"Why?"

"Because my arms want to slide off."

"Exactly."

"What does all of this mean?"

"You can sit back up." I reached down and helped her up to a sitting position.

"When someone lies down and crosses their arms over their chest, their elbows are usually touching whatever they are lying on. If not, they feel uncomfortable and their arms automatically want to slide back down to the most comfortable spot."

"What does this have to do with my mother's death?"

"Something about the way your mother was positioned on the bed bothered me. It didn't look natural but for the life of me I couldn't figure it out until you just folded your hands. In the crime scene photos your mother's wrists are crossed over each other."

"Why would she do that?"

"That's the point, she wouldn't. As you just illustrated, it's uncomfortable and her elbows would have naturally fallen back onto the bed. But they didn't."

"Are you saying she was posed after she died?"

"That's exactly what I'm saying."

She threw her arms around me, her body moving closer to me in the excitement. I found myself enjoying the moment.

"I knew you could prove it. Let's call the police and have him arrested."

Neither of us moved. Then like an idiot I untangled from the embrace.

"We can't," I said.

"But this is the physical evidence we've been looking for. Add that to the pills you found and we can prove she didn't kill herself."

"It's still not enough."

Her face dropped and the pain stretched across it as if she was ten years old and I had just shot her dog.

"I don't understand."

"As solid as it seems, it is not enough to break down his alibi. That's what we have to do before we can go to the police."

"How?"

"I need to go to South Jordan and visit the Wingates."

"I'm going with you."

"You have an agency to run."

"We have a killer to catch. Besides I could use a diversion."

The seriousness left her face and that mischievous grin returned, sitting there, teasing me, and tempting me.

Was I the diversion? Was she coming on to me?

If I was imagining it, things could really get awkward between us. Besides, she was my client. That old adage about mixing business with pleasure was there for a reason.

I smiled and got up. "I think maybe I should go alone."

Her jaw clinched stubbornly. "I know the Wingates and they are not going to want to say anything against Father to a complete stranger. The only way we are going to get anything out of them is to work together."

She was right, but the thought of spending time with her in a car, even the twenty or so minutes it would take to get to South Jordan, made my "bachelor forever" sign shake more than I cared to admit.

I yielded. "Set up an appointment for tomorrow and let me know."

She smiled like a cat that had just discovered the door to the canary cage door was wide open.

That sign really began shaking.

***

That evening I stood at the door of Room 236, wondering what to do.

It was a small room with a large window which made it seem much bigger as light poured in, filling the room with sunshine and hope. Everything seemed better with sunshine.

The large bouquet of flowers I had ordered stood in a clear vase on the desk across from the bed.

Daffodils.

The television was on as I had requested. I didn't want her to be alone.

The floor nurse took the multi-colored comforter I had taken from her apartment and spread it over her. I set the photo of her and her parents on the night stand near her bed. When she woke I wanted her to feel at home.

I leaned the large ballerina poster I had also retrieved from her apartment against the wall. I had bought some plastic strips in order to hang it without using nails and defacing the hospital wall. The hospital frowned on someone banging on the walls to hang a poster.

Quietly I moved to the chair beside the bed.

Setting the CD player and CDs of Elvis, The Beatles, Supremes, Weezer, Train, Donovan's greatest hits (I hoped she would get a kick out of that), and Mozart on the night stand, I sat down.

I didn't know if she liked music or what kind of music but Elvis and the Beatles had always made me feel better when I had been young and the world was crashing in on me. I wanted her to feel better too. Mozart made me think of genteel classical dancing. Weezer made me want to dance with wild abandon, in my mind of course, where I am one great dancer. She liked to dance so I hoped one of them would make her feel like waking up and dancing.

Or at least let her know she was cared about.

The swelling around her eyes had gone down and the bruises which covered her face were now yellowish purple. Soon they would be gone and the only visible sign of the beating someone had given her would be the fact that she was in a coma.

I had never encountered anyone in a coma. I had seen enough movies which all portrayed the comatose character as being able to hear and understand their loved ones speaking to them. Was that really true? I wasn't a Hollywood writer, so what did I know?

"If you need anything else, just let me know," the young nurse smiled as she left the room, the door closing behind her.

I was alone with a girl I had been looking for. I stood

silently by her bedside wondering what I was doing. She didn't know me. What if she awoke? Would my presence scare her? What could I possibly say to a girl in a coma?

I began to feel really foolish. Maybe I should just leave everything I had brought and make a run for it. But I didn't want her to be alone.

"Hi," I said, as if that made everything all right.

I was talking to someone who didn't know me and couldn't answer me if she did. The power of movies.

"My name is David. I found your diary."

I'm not sure telling a young woman that you found her diary was the smartest thing to say. It inevitably begged the question, did you read it? Answering a question like that was never a good idea.

"I'm a private detective. I am going to find out who did this to you and make sure they are punished."

I am not the greatest conversationalist as it is, ask my ex-wife—the first one—but talking to someone who didn't answer was sheer misery. I automatically turned towards the door to see if anyone was standing there. I guess I expected to see the entire nursing staff standing there laughing at me. No one was.

"I don't know what kind of music you like but music always make me feel better when I get down about something. Usually, it's a divorce, but that's a topic for another time.

"I brought you some daffodils. I know you like them. I had never paid much attention to them until you mentioned that you liked them. They really are pretty."

I had about hit my conversational limit.

There was a soft knock on the door jam.

"Mr. Crockett?"

I turned to see Roxanna Lewis standing in the doorway. She entered the room and looked around. "It looks comfortable."

"It beats the dungeon," I replied. "I appreciate you letting me bring all this in."

"Any luck on finding who did this?"

"Not yet, but I will. Any change in her at all?"

"Physically she's recovering, but mentally we just don't know."

"You think she will be a vegetable?" The thought struck me deeper than I would have thought as I stared down at a young woman who should be out dancing and enjoying life instead of lying still in a hospital bed.

"It's hard to say. It really is out of our hands."

"I brought some music. If you could have one of the nurses play it for her each day so that she has music in the room, I'd appreciate it."

"I'll arrange it. Anything else I can do?" she asked.

"Just keep me informed of any change."

"I will." She turned to go, then stopped. "What you're doing. It's a good thing. People don't care like that today."

She left the room.

Why did I care? Maybe because someone had to. Donovan had said that she didn't have anyone else. A long time ago a complete stranger had cared for me when I had no one else around. She had saved my life. It was the least I could do now.

I stayed for an hour talking about anything that popped into my head; music, dancing, a six-year-old being bullied by the school system, my eternal struggle to not get set up by my family. Funny, but by the time I left, talking to her didn't seem like such a chore.

Eighteen

Thomas Franklin was eating at the student center on the University of Utah campus. Trading on Lezanna's good nature, once again I had obtained his class schedule. I had pulled his picture off Facebook. In the old days it would have taken time to track him down, but with everyone falling all over themselves to put every bit of private information on Facebook and Twitter, tracking someone today was much easier.

By the time he sat down I knew everything about this creep that I needed to know. And most of it I didn't like. He was from privilege. He was used to getting his way because he had a father who was constantly bailing him out of trouble in order to protect the family name. I have never understood how any family name is helped by ignoring family members who run it into the ground.

Franklin was tall, manly looking with dark hair and dark eyes. He was dressed in tan slacks and a maroon polo shirt. I could see how girls might be attracted to him. But then again, girls had also been attracted to serial killer Ted Bundy.

I watched as he aggressively moved in on the young blonde sitting across from him. It was a safe bet she had no clue about the real Thomas Franklin. But that's why I was there, to fill in the blanks.

"Good morning, Thomas," I said as the girl pulled her hand back from his.

He looked up at me with a blank face. "Who are you?"

I smiled at them, focusing mostly on the girl. "I'm your new parole officer."

"I don't have a parole officer."

The girl looked concerned, her eyes darting over to him.

"Of course you do. You know, for the beatings you gave your two high school girlfriends."

The girl stood up, shoving her chair back from the table.

"It's all right, miss. He's getting much better. He's only beaten one college girlfriend."

I watched her race away.

Thomas glared at me, his temper flaring.

"Thinking about hitting me, Thomas, or do you just hit women?"

"Who are you?"

"I'm a private investigator, and I'm looking into the beating of Jennifer Justice."

"I don't know any Jennifer Justice," he snarled.

"Buzzz," I said doing my best game show announcer imitation. "Wrong answer."

"I don't, so leave me alone," he huffed.

I shoved her picture in front of him. "Does this ring a bell?"

He stared at the picture. "Her?" he said with contempt. "I went on a blind date with her, that's all."

I sat down across from him. "Didn't go so well, did it?"

"It was fine," he said defensively. "She just wasn't my type."

"According to Jennifer it was a miserable date." He looked surprised, but didn't say anything. "She said you were all ego and attitude, that everything was about you."

"That's not true. She enjoyed herself. All girls do when they go out with me." He puffed up like a blow fish, all ego and attitude.

"She said you stared at her like you had never seen a girl before. Is that right? Are you one of those momma's boy who spends his time in his parents basement playing video games and looking at Internet girls because that's the only kind you can get?"

His fists, resting on the table, clinched and his jaw tightened. I had hit a nerve.

"I'm a lawyer, not a geek."

"You're a law clerk in your daddy's firm. You haven't graduated from law school and you haven't taken the bar. That just makes you a lawyer wanna-be."

His eyes flashed pure hate. Leaping up, he leaned over the table and took a wild swing at me. Using his own inertia I grabbed his arm as it missed my head and yanked downward. His head hit the table, nose first, which split like a ripe cantaloupe.

"It hurts to be stupid, doesn't it?"

Standing, I grabbed him by the neck and lifted him back into his chair before anyone realized what was happening.

Pouring some water on my handkerchief, I handed it to him. He put it over his nose, whimpering in pain.

"Now tell me about you and Jennifer Justice. Someone beat the hell out of her and you better pray it wasn't you."

"Me?" He started moving back in the chair in protest, but the pain was too much. He winced, fighting the tears forming in his eyes. He was obviously only tough when it came to hitting girls.

"I only saw her the one time. Connie, a friend of hers, set us up. That's all. You can ask her."

"What's her name?" I leaned in closer to him.

He flinched as if I was about to strike him again. "Connie Wilkerson."

I wrote the name down.

"So where were you on the night of September 21?"

"I don't know, what day of the week was it?"

"It was a Friday."

He took out his iPhone and looked at his schedule.

"Oh that night." He looked relieved. "I was at our fraternity party. It was the night before the Utes played USC. We had a football party. I got drunk and passed out."

He tried to smile but the pressure on his nose halted it in mid smile. He winced again.

"You can check it out," he whimpered slightly.

"I'll do that."

I stood and looked down at the suffering kid.

"If I find out you had anything to do with Jennifer's injuries, or if I ever hear of you beating another girl, I'll come looking for you and you can take this to the bank, hot shot. Not even daddy will be able to protect you."

He smiled through the pain, past experience telling him there was no way I could ever reach him.

I leaned in close just so he could hear me. "Imagine what I could do to you if we weren't in a public place, kid? And Daddy won't always be around, will he?"

His eyes went wide.

"You hit another girl and I'll show you just how painful uncontrolled anger can be."

One unsavory date down and two more to go.

***

Two hours later, I watched as the second of those unsavory men left his office and made his way to his BMW.

Martin Parker walked like a man who knew he was more powerful and richer than everyone else. His head high, eyes straight ahead so as not to see the lower classes around him. There was an air of self-importance about him.

He was wearing a tailored, dark blue pin-striped suit over a light blue shirt and dark red tie. In his breast pocket was a red handkerchief. His tan was still as deep, a rich contrast to the thick wave of silver hair combed back from his wide forehead.

But I was more interested in his relationship to Jennifer Justice. Was their dinner at Le Callie an attempt to impress her into bed? Did she laugh at him, sending him into a fury and beating her nearly to death? Being Faith's father, did he have some spark of decency and regret enough to take her to the hospital in an attempt to save her?

"Mr. Parker, I'd like to talk to you if I could." I eased up beside him as he rushed towards his car. He turned, realized who I was and moved past me.

"I have nothing to say to you. If you desire to talk to me you can do it through my lawyer."

"And here I thought you were smart enough to talk without having to hide behind a gaggle of legal-beagles."

"You are surmising that I am afraid to talk to you?"

"When you find your courage let me know." I glared at him, daring him to challenge me. If Faith was right about her father, he detested someone getting the better of him, someone less intelligent challenging his superiority.

He stopped in his tracks. The man who turned to face me had fire in his eyes. His look towards me was like that of a CEO towards a lowly subordinate who had just dared question his business expertise.

"You think you are smarter than me?"

The smile on his face said it all. He really did think he was above the rest of us. "I am a member of Mensa. I have an IQ of over 183. Do you know what that means?"

"That you sucked at sports?"

"It means I eat simpletons like you for breakfast."

"Breakfast of champions," I quipped.

His face went white as the clever comeback he wanted failed him. High School - 1. Mensa - 0.

"Tell me about Jennifer Justice," I demanded.

"Who?" he asked coolly.

I removed her picture and shoved it towards him.

"Oh, her."

"Yes, the girl you conned into going out with you."

"I did no such thing. She was eager to go out with me."

"So you could help her with her dancing career? Is that the only way you can pick up girls, Martin?"

"I did not pick her up," he huffed, straightening his back. "She had car trouble and I stopped to give assistance."

"Where?"

"In the parking lot of my daughter's agency."

"The good Samaritan bit doesn't really suit you."

"You know nothing about me. The young lady was grateful and wanted to do something nice in return. I told her it was not necessary, but she insisted. I finally suggested that she allow me take her to dinner."

"And she agreed? Was that before or after you lied to her about helping with her career?"

"I did not lie."

He opened the back door of his 2015 Lexus and set his briefcase in the seat. When he turned back to me, his face was emotionless and calm.

"The young lady was studying dance, so I thought I could introduce her to Miles Copperton, the head of Utah Dance Studios."

"And did you?"

"When I phoned him he said he was not taking on any new clients at the time."

"So after dinner, when she was primed and ready for plucking, you made your move. What did she do, laugh at you? Throw a drink in your face? Did she make you mad enough to beat her nearly to death?"

"What are you going on about?"

"She is in a coma. Someone tried to kill her."

The color drained from his face.

"I escorted her home. She inquired about Miles. I told her the truth. She became upset, thought I had made up the story. She exited the car and rushed towards her apartment. That was the last I saw of her."

It was time to rattle the cage. "What did Abigail think of your excursion with Jennifer?"

He obviously didn't like having his cage rattled. A miffed look clouded his face but quickly faded, replaced by a plastic smile. "This conversation is terminated. From now on if you have anything you wish to say to me, you may say it in front of my lawyer."

"Just when we were getting so close."

"Mr. Crockett, you may think that you are smarter than everyone else, that you can go around poking your nose in where it does not belong. But make no mistake about this." His eyes narrowed in on me and his voice dropped an octave. "While you think you are important, I operate under no such false illusions. I do carry considerable weight in this town. I have golfing dates with the Mayor and the Chief of Police. I have their personal numbers in my IPhone."

He slammed the back door, then opened the driver's door. Before he climbed in he turned back to make sure I understood his power. "You have no idea who you are dealing with," he snapped. "You may rest assured that the Mayor and the Chief of Police will hear about this endless harassment. And if you continue, I will personally see to it that you lose your license and sue you for everything you have. Is that clear?"

Even to a non-Mensa member.

Nineteen

No one likes to be questioned but the w e a l t h y have a special resentment about it. Maybe they feel that because they are successful, no one below their pay grade should actually speak to them. Of course, when you're trying to get away with murder, the last thing you need is a hotshot private eye trying to prove you did it.

Parker had made it clear that I was to stay away from him. Any sane person would take his threat seriously. It made me more determined to find out just what he was hiding. No one ever accused me of being sane.

I took a beer from the refrigerator and looked around for Sam. He was nowhere to be found. He was spending more time outside than normal, which in the summer time would not be unusual, but in the middle of winter with the woods still covered in snow, there had to be more to it. Neither of us was much for traipsing through the snow, which led me to the most obvious conclusion. Sam had a girlfriend. "Sammie" Crockett was making the rounds. It was enough to make any parent proud.

I took my beer and walked out onto the balcony to see if Sam was close by. He wasn't. The sun was already down, but it was still light. The cold air felt good as I breathed it in. But not that good. Why stand in the cold looking at beautiful scenery, or waiting for an over-active cat, when you can do it from the comfort of a warm living room? With a shiver, I turned around to scoot back towards the kitchen.

Hearing some movement in the brush below the balcony, I turned my head slightly to see Sam high-stepping through the snow. I had just turned when it happened. Something whizzed past my head at tremendous speed and into the kitchen wall. I had been in enough fire fights to know the sound of a bullet. I leaped through the open door onto the kitchen floor. Two more bullets ripped into the pots hanging above my large prep table, knocking them onto the counter with a loud crash.

With everything going on with Jennifer and Martin Parker, I had forgotten about the note and threat on my life. Now I was paying for my carelessness. I was pinned down in my own kitchen by an unseen sniper who knew exactly where I was. I, on the other hand, had no idea where he was. The woods surrounding the back of my property were thick and led up the mountainside. He could be above me in a sniper perch staring at me through a telescope. I was strictly at a disadvantage. And angry. Someone had invaded the privacy of my home and I didn't like it.

I moved to the other side of the butcher block and slid behind it. Reaching for the broom leaning up against the wall near the pantry, I used it to turn off the lights. Even though it was still light outside without the light inside, he would have a somewhat more difficult shot. One of my carved-in-stone philosophies was, don't make it easy for anyone to kill you.

Removing my cell phone I dialed the police. My next

call was to Jackson. He and Marx were on another call, but he promised to let the patrol unit finish up and he and Marx would roll immediately.

Whoever this was had a clear view into my kitchen so I decided to wait him out. There was always the possibility that he had fled the scene, but I had no way of knowing and I wasn't about to stick my head out to see. Curiosity not only got the cat killed, it had been the last thought of many a man. I had seen it firsthand in the mountains of Afghanistan.

On my second tour our unit pinned down a small group of terrorists hiding behind rocks and trees. They dug in hoping to wait us out so they could head for the mountains once it was dark. We didn't move.

After fifteen minutes curiosity got the better of one of them. He peered around the tree to see if we were still there. Tommy Chambers, a trained sniper from Galveston, Texas put a bullet through his skull from two hundred yards. I didn't think Tommy Chambers was out there, but I wasn't about to stick my head around to see.

Within twenty minutes I could see the flashing lights moving up the road above my property.

It was a safe bet, or at least I was hoping it was, that whoever had been out there was now on the run at the sight of the red and blue blinking lights. It was also dark enough now to make a moving target somewhat difficult to hit, though not impossible, which bothered me, but it was a chance I had to take.

I leaped through the kitchen door and rolled into the living room. Nothing. The large thick drapes covering the picture window that looked out onto the mountain was closed, so I felt fairly safe. Still I wasn't taking any chances. I crawled behind my large leather couch and then raced down the dark hallway to my bedroom and my weapons cabinet. I removed my Helo Sniper SR25. It is fitted with a night scope and Harris bi-pod. I never went anywhere in Afghanistan without it slung over my back.

I made my way to my upstairs office, which faces the mountain, placed the night scope between the curtain and the edge of the window sill and surveyed the area. I could see the flashing lights and the deputy sheriffs combing an area about half a mile up the mountain. That was a long way for an average gunman. This one obviously had military training of some kind.

Officer Geoff Lamb and his partner were the first to arrive at the house. Then Jackson.

I spent an hour answering questions about what cases I had been working on, who might want me dead, and any suspicious people who might have been hanging around in the past few days. It was standard stuff but not a lot I could tell them. There were a lot of people I could think of but none that fit the parameters that would include a sniper. This smacked of ex-military and that sent the game in a completely different direction. Of course there was always the possibility of someone like Howard Duff, Bonnie Curtis, or some other angry spouse whom I had cost millions, hiring a professional hit.

After the circus left, I locked the sliding glass door and closed the kitchen drapes. Jackson found the last peach yogurt in my refrigerator hidden behind my last two beers.

"Looks like he used one of the unfinished houses about a mile up the road."

"Did he leave anything?"

"Nothing. No cigarettes butts, no soda cans, or beer bottles."

"You think he's ex-military?"

"It sure looks that way." He took a bite of yogurt; his face was grim. "The perch was meticulously clean. I'd guess military or a pro. Either way, watch your back."

"What about footprints?"

"Snowshoes."

"Snowshoes? Are you kidding me?"

"He made sure we couldn't track his footprints."

Now I was worried. This had professional written all over it.

"You pissed someone off, my friend."

"Surely he didn't walk up the mountain. Any tire tracks?"

"That was the only thing we did find."

"At least that's something," I sighed.

"Not really," he said as he finished the yogurt.

"What do you mean?"

"He used chains on all four tires to obscure the tire tread. The only thing we were able to tell is that, from the size of the tires, it looked like some kind of large pick-up truck or SUV."

Immediately an image of a large black Ram pick-up popped into my mind.

The next day I drove to the sniper's nest to see for myself. It wasn't that I didn't trust the boys in blue, but come on, no one is that careful.

He was.

There was nothing. No scraps of paper, food wrappers, empty drink can, foot prints, or cigarette butts. Nothing.

He had used one of the large houses under construction as a nest. It sat on the edge of a hill looking straight down to the few houses in my neighborhood, especially my backyard. It had a roof so the inside was dry, and enough walls framed to hide him from prying eyes.

I studied the area carefully. Judging from the angle of the shot and the place I would choose if I was looking down at my house, I was able to determine where he had waited. I placed myself in the same position. He had used one of the cross frames to steady his rifle. Using my Helo SR25 I found my kitchen door. I had left the curtains open so I could see what he had seen. Through my scope I could see every inch of my kitchen and balcony. Whoever he was, he had chosen well.

I sat there putting myself in his position.

How long had he waited?

Did he have to go to the bathroom?

Did he move around or touch anything?

I got up and scoured the area. About half a mile from the house I found the tire tracks. They were too big for a car, which left a large truck or SUV. There was only one person I knew who owned a large truck. But how did "Dodge Ram" know who I was? Yes, he had tried to run me off the road, but that seemed more of a spur of the moment opportunity to protect Peterson. Had Ruth Mosley told him who I was? Everything else he could get from public records. But what would be his motive?

I went back to the nest and sat back down. Placing my rifle on the cross frame, I studied my house. And then the juices started pumping. I started slowing down my breath and focusing just as I had done many times in another land. Nothing gets the heart pumping and the adrenalin flowing as waiting for the kill.

And then I saw it.

Lying nestled in the dirt near the house, in an area the blanket of snow hadn't covered, was a jagged rock. It was about two inches wide and covered with what looked like a brown stain. Maybe Tommy Chambers had been here. Slipping through the framing, I bent down to examine the rock. I had never been big on smoking and chewing tobacco was even more disgusting. In Afghanistan, it was something Tommy Chambers had enjoyed as he waited for his target. Many a time I would watch him stay perfectly still and suddenly like a frog snaking out its tongue to nab a fly, a stream of gross brown tobacco juice would flow from his mouth and land a few feet in front of him. It always made me shudder.

Going back to my car I pulled a plastic bag from the glove compartment and went back and gathered the rock.

Justin Boudreau wasn't going to like this one bit.

TWENTY

After dropping off the rock to a very unhappy Boudreau, I headed to a car specialty shop, run by a friend of mine who had a knack for customizing any kind of car. For price of course.

The next morning I went to the office to find out all I could about "Mr. Dodge Ram." After ten minutes on the phone with Lakeisha I found out that Ruth's husband's name was Joshua Mosley. A search on the Internet proved informative. He had been born in Delta, Utah, raised by solid Mormon parents. At twenty he had met Allen Peterson and had become a believer from the very first meeting.

While obtaining his teaching degree from Utah State he wrote long and tedious blogs expounding the virtues of The Eternal and True Church of Christ in the Last Days. He wrote blog after blog on the virtues of polygamy - socially, spiritually and economically. There was a lot of passion for his belief, but very few facts.

In 2009, he began teaching at Cottonwood Heights High School. Then all blogs on polygamy suddenly stopped. I guess he was more concerned about making a living than making converts. His ranting and raving suddenly slanted more towards love, marriage, education and family. According to his April 2011 blog on the "Joys of Love and the Eternal Family," he met Ruth when she began teaching there. He courted her for a year. They were married in 2012. There was no mention of any other wives.

I read everything I could find about him. In all the blogs and Google searches there was no mention of any military training.

Maybe he wasn't my sniper. All I had linking him to it was large tire tracks.

At three o'clock I shut off my computer and walked down the hall to the Parker Talent Agency. I still had a job to do and I wasn't about to let a whacked-out sniper scare me off.

Bella, short for Isabella, glanced up as I entered and immediately picked up the phone. No need to wait when you're a star detective.

"She will be right out Senor Crockett. Can I get you anything?"

"Just your undying love, my Bella," I said as I floated towards her. All great detectives know that the way to anyone important is through the secretary. More often than not they run the office. Make that connection and you'll always have a good chance of getting behind the closed doors.

She giggled like a school girl and shook her head. "My husband, he should take lessons from you, no?"

"No, he should take you on a romantic cruise and never leave the cabin."

"I'll tell him that," she said blushing.

The door opened and Faith stepped out. She looked radiant. Her shoulder-length hair was down with a rebellious strand hanging in her face. She brushed it aside and smiled at the same time. I started humming God Bless America.

She turned back to Bella. "I'll be gone for the rest of the day." With that she took my arm and escorted me out the door.

Salt Lake City is a sprawling metropolis with numerous municipalities surrounding it. Within ten miles in any direction, you will run into at least three different cities. Heading north on I-15 you will c o m e t o Bountiful and Ogden. South will take you to such cities as Midvale, Murray, Draper, Sandy, and South Jordan.

The Wingates lived in South Jordan. It was a twenty-minute drive on the freeway. During the ride I couldn't help but wonder how Faith would react to listening to the Wingates talk about her father. This whole sordid affair couldn't be easy for her, and yet she was determined to see it through.

As I pulled up to the house, Faith sat with a blank look on her face. I couldn't imagine what she must be feeling.

"Are you all right?" I asked.

She tried to smile but nothing came. She nodded her head.

"You don't have to come in if you aren't comfortable."

She turned to me, her eyes etched with pain. "I love my father but if he had anything to do with my mother's death he has to pay. I owe her that."

She unbuckled the seat belt and opened the door. I followed suit.

When the door opened, Bonnie Wingate smiled as bright as a light bulb the second she saw Faith.

"Faith, what a pleasant surprise."

It dimmed a few watts when she noticed me.

"Hi Bonnie, sorry to drop in on you like this but I need to speak to you and Don if you don't mind."

She looked hesitantly at me but swallowed the bullet. "Sure, come on in."

"This is my friend, David Crockett. He's a private investigator."

She moved and allowed us to pass. "Please come in."

She showed us into the large living room. "I'll go get Don."

She turned and left.

"She didn't look too happy to see me."

"It's early. She hasn't started her evening cocktails yet. She gets happier as the evening wears on."

The living room was celestial bright as the light from the wall to wall windows poured in from the north side. The walls were white and the ceiling was vaulted, giving the room a castle-like feeling. A large, expensive leather couch sat in the middle separated from two leather chairs opposite it by a glass coffee table. A small oak table sat between the two leather chairs. On the wall were various family photos, the centerpiece being a giant framed oil painting of Don, Bonnie, a young son and a younger daughter. A rock fireplace dug into one of the walls with two smaller chairs facing it for those cozy evenings during the winter.

"Faith, how good to see you," Wingate said as he entered the room.

Don Wingate was a powerfully built man with a Captain America jaw line, blue eyes and extremely short hair just this side of being completely shaved. He was wearing tan slacks and a green golf shirt. He didn't look very happy to see us.

Bonnie Wingate was just the opposite, small and slender with wide set brown eyes, a high forehead, sunken cheeks, and thin lips.

"I appreciate you seeing me. Don, this is David Crockett."

I extended my hand and he shook it. His grip was like a vise as he squeezed my hand until I thought I'd lose all circulation. He didn't say anything but just nodded his greeting. Mr. Tough Guy.

"Please have a seat," Bonnie instructed as she motioned to the couch. Don took one of the leather chairs opposite while Bonnie remained standing.

"May I get you something to drink?"

"Nothing for me," Faith answered quickly.

"Nothing for me either. But thank you," I added.

She looked disappointed as if our drinking would give her an excuse to start early. Then again, I guess she didn't really need us.

"Well, if you don't mind, I think I'll have a small glass of sherry. Don?"

"Get me a beer."

With a grateful smile, she turned and left.

"How's Chad doing at UCLA?"

"Fine," Don answered proudly. "He's got a 3.8 average and was on the dean's list this past month.

"What's he majoring in?" I asked hoping to relax him a bit as he didn't seem thrilled to have me sitting in his living room.

"Mechanical engineering."

"You have to be smart to pull a 3.8 in that field," I replied.

"Damn right you do. None of this liberal arts crap."

Suddenly realizing what he had said, he blushed as he glanced at Faith, who had received her liberal arts degree from the University of Utah.

"I mean nothing wrong with it but he wants to do more with his life."

Out of the frying pan into the fire. Again, he glanced at Faith.

"You know what I mean?"

"I do," Faith responded, her voice smooth and soft.

"So what brings you out to see us?" he asked gruffly, trying to change the subject, relieved when Bonnie handed him his beer.

"Don, I need to know about the weekend my father spent

with you and Bonnie. The weekend my mother died."

"I don't know what I can tell you that I haven't already told the police."

Don Wingate took a long swig of his Miller High Life, then set the long-neck bottle on the table between the two chairs.

"Sometimes going over it again will jog the memory," I answered politely.

Wingate took another long drink of his beer. Maybe it was important for him to finish it in two or three swigs. He wiped his mouth and his eyes bored into me. "I don't need to jog my memory. I remember exactly what happened, and Martin Parker did not kill his wife."

"We're not suggesting that he did, Mr. Wingate," I said, trying to reassure him. "We're just trying to reconstruct the days leading up to her death."

"It would mean a lot to me. For closure," Faith pleaded.

"Yes, of course, Don said. "This must be hard on you."

"Did my Father say why she didn't make the trip?"

Bonnie Wingate sat down, her sherry in hand. She looked at Faith, her eyes sad and downcast as if she was about to reveal bad news. "Why, the depression, of course."

"The depression?" Faith asked.

"Surely you knew about it? Martin was heartbroken about it. He just didn't know what to do," Bonnie continued.

Don jumped in to clarify his wife's meaning. "He didn't say it, but you could tell he was nervous that she might do something to herself."

"And did he say just how long Sylvia had been depressed?" I asked.

Don looked at his wife then back to us. "Couple of months I think. Like I said, he didn't really want to talk about it. I think that's why he was so anxious to call her."

"He called her from the boat?"

"He hadn't even been here a whole day and he had to call her. I accused him of being whipped. He just laughed and said thirty-two years of marriage would do that to you."

"Did either of you talk to her?"

"I did," Don Wingate answered immediately.

This caught my attention. If Wingate had actually talked to her, our whole theory was out the window. "You did?"

"Well, not personally, but through Martin. He was telling her how big the fish I caught that day was and I corrected him. Sylvia told me to quit exaggerating."

"So you didn't actually hear her voice?"

"Why would I have to hear her voice?" he asked irritability. "Martin called her and he talked to her, I heard him!" He took the last swig of beer and set the bottle on the table. "He was with us from early Saturday until he left Sunday morning after hearing the news about her death. According to the papers she died sometime late Saturday evening. There is no way he could have done it."

He glanced apologetically at Faith. "I'm sorry, Faith, but I just don't believe that your father could have or did commit such a horrendous crime. And I'll swear to that in a court of law if necessary."

His look was defiant, challenging me to contradict him. With nothing left to say, we thanked them and left. Faith was somber as we drove away. I let her get comfortable with her thoughts as we drove in silence. We hadn't gone very far before she turned to me. "What if I'm wrong? I'm accusing my father of murdering my mother!"

She shook her head as if her flowing locks would blow all the bad thoughts right out and everything would go back to being normal.

And then the tears came.

I pulled to the side of the street and reached for her.

She melted into my arms and sobbed.

She felt good. Her hair smelled of vanilla and coconut, her body firm in my arms. It had been a long time since I had held such a beautiful woman and I wanted more. But not like this. Not in such a fragile state.

I just held her.

Finally her body became still and the sobs subsided. When they did, she looked up embarrassed. "I'm sorry. I don't know what came over me."

She straightened up and immediately began fixing her make-up. "Do you think I'm wrong?"

Not knowing what to say or how to say it, I simply shook my head sympathetically.

"Am I subconsciously accusing my father because I am mad at him?"

"What do you think?"

"I don't know, David, I just don't know."

"You know your father better than anyone. You also know deep inside what your mother meant when she asked you not to let him get away with it. I think, if nothing else, you need to follow your instincts."

"What if I'm wrong?"

"Then you'll know for sure and it will be easier to mend fences if that is what you choose to do."

She thought about it for a moment then nodded her head.

"Thank you," she whispered. She leaned over and kissed me on the cheek.

The full-service private eye.

TWENTY ONE

The roar of sixty-five thousand rabid fans filled the air, causing Jackson to have to speak louder than normal.

"I dropped in on Boudreau yesterday afternoon to see if he had had a chance to get any DNA samples off the rock," Jackson said.

"And?"

"He growled at me and told me to come back when he wasn't up to his butt in dead people."

Jackson stuffed a giant bite of cougar dog in his mouth, washing it down with a swig of Seven-up. "Have you had a chance to visit Discreet Party Services?"

It was half time at a very entertaining BYU-Stanford game. The weather was sunny but cold as we sat bundled up in LaVell Edwards Stadium. It had snowed Friday night, laying a gentle blanket of beautiful, white powder across the area. By game time, however, the snow in the valley had melted leaving majestic snowcapped mountains under clear blue skies and a crisp chill in the air. It was a perfect afternoon for college football, huddling under blankets with Katie and Julie, eating hot dogs and drinking hot chocolate.

"Not yet," I answered after taking a drink of my hot chocolate. I would have preferred something a bit stronger but alcohol is not allowed in LaVell Edwards Stadium.

"I've been working on the Parker murder case," I went on.

"You mean suicide?" Jackson countered

"I mean murder," I said firmly, countering his counter.

Jackson remained silent.

His department had worked the case and ruled it a suicide. He wasn't just going to take my word for it, even if the lead detective on the case, Harry Reed, was a moron. I had to convince him, which wasn't going to be easy.

Katie and Julie stood. "We're going to the powder room, while you two discuss business," Julie said.

"Do they have powder rooms at football games?" I asked. "The only thing I have ever seen are smelly restrooms."

Katie glared at me. I suddenly became interested in the Cougar Band dancing onto the field.

Jackson laughed. "Why you are not married I'll never know."

"A mystery to me too," I replied, shrugging my shoulders. As the girls made their way down the bleachers, I turned back to Jackson. "Parker told his neighbor to call him as soon as he talked to her. Why wouldn't he just have him tell her to call him if he was so worried?"

"People say strange things under duress."

"Unless he knew she was already dead."

"That's a stretch, don't you think?"

"Not if you're setting up your perfect alibi. That's what I think he was doing."

He shook his head. "It doesn't matter unless you can prove it."

"According to his statement he told West he had been trying to call Sylvia all morning, but, the only call he made that morning was to West. He knew there was no reason to call her because she was already dead. The phone records prove he lied about calling her."

"Lying is not against the law. It's still all circumstantial," Jackson said insistently, before finishing the last bite of his cougar dog.

The crowd roared as the Cougars rushed back onto the field for the second half. I watched them warm up briefly then turned back to Jackson.

"He posed the body," I continued making my case. "There is no way anyone committing suicide would cross their hands that way. It's uncomfortable and unnatural."

"You may be right but you can't prove it. Parker was almost two hundred miles away when she died."

"He could have driven back, killed her, and then driven back before morning without anyone missing him."

"He has witnesses that placed him there all night. His alibi is solid, David."

"He killed her, I just know it."

"That's not scientific enough for me to re-open the case. You break his alibi and I might be more inclined to listen."

Katie and Julie sat back down, cuddling against us, trying to ward off the cold.

"Will you two stop discussing business? The second half is about to start," Julie chided good-naturedly.

The perfect wife. Julie was beautiful, kind, funny, a great cook, and loved football. What more could a man ask for?

Jackson wrapped his arm around her and kissed her.

"You two get a room."

"Don't be jealous, David," Julie teased, winking at Katie.

"I'm sure your sister will find someone perfect for you," Katie added with a laugh.

"You two are evil."

"By the way, I have some information on Discreet Party Services," Jackson said.

He opened his pocket notebook, which he always carries, and flipped a couple of pages until he found what he was looking for. "It's run out of a very expensive office in Sandy by an Abigail Collingsworth."

"Abigail Collingsworth? Are you sure?"

"According to the Documents of Incorporation. Why?"

"Because Abigail Collingsworth is Martin Parker's mistress."

This case had just gotten more interesting.

***

Monday was bright, sunny but cool. Perfect weather as far as I am concerned. I had the radio cranked full blast to an oldies station as I drove down I-15 South towards Sandy, a suburb of Salt Lake, and Discreet Party Services.

Abigail Collingsworth worked out of a ritzy, high-rise office building filled with banks and insurance companies. I would lay money that they had no knowledge what Discreet Party Services did.

Collingsworth passed herself off as a socialite, donating to all the right charities and political campaigns, attending all the high-profile political and social parties in the area. Though she had friends in high places, in reality she was nothing more than a very high-priced party girl.

The six-story building was located about three blocks from the large, red brick complex that housed all the local government offices, which made her location even more interesting.

I parked and waited. When I was sure no one had followed me, I hustled inside. It wasn't that I was being paranoid, but I was checking every car or person that I passed. I hated that, but being a target of an unknown hit man tends to do that to you.

I took the elevator up to the sixth floor.

The offices of Discreet Party Services were located at the end of the hall. Opening the large wooden door, I entered. The décor was professional but relaxing. The large room was painted a frosted green with art deco hanging on the walls. Four rich maroon leather chairs sat on each side of the room facing each other. Two small green ficus trees and a dark gray wall of rolling water behind the curved receptionist counter added to the relaxing nature theme.

A very attractive young woman, mid-twenties, light blonde hair, polished teeth, with a toothpaste commercial smile greeted me. She wore very little make-up but supported two diamond earrings in each ear. Her clothes said business chic, leading me to believe I was in a high-class law firm.

"May I help you?"

"I'd like to see Ms. Collingsworth, please."

"Do you have an appointment?"

"No, but this is important," I replied, trying to sound desperate.

"I'm so sorry, her schedule is booked solid. Without an appointment, I'm afraid I can't let you in."

I looked around the empty waiting room. She must have read my mind.

"Most appointments are made by phone," she smiled.

"Could I make an appointment?"

"And what would this be in regards to?"

"I'd like to use Ms. Collingsworth services."

"And what services would those be?" She asked as politely as if she were setting up a dentist appointment.

"I'm new in town and I have it on good authority that this is the place to come if I want to set up some unique activities." I smiled my best new-in-town smile and then produced the card I had found at the Baker crime scene.

"A friend gave me this card."

She glanced at the card.

"He said it was well worth the thousands I am willing to spend."

When in doubt throw down the money card.

"Your name?"

"Darrin Davis."

She found the appointment book in the computer. "How would tomorrow at three be?"

I took out my phone and pretended to look at my own schedule.

"I'm meeting with investors at 2:30, so could we make it 3:45?" Never appear too eager. She glanced back down at the schedule.

"How about 4:00?"

"That would be fine. See you tomorrow at four," I smiled.

I waited in my car for Collingsworth to emerge from her office building. An hour later a woman matching the image I had pulled off my computer screen rushed out the door towards her new Mercedes. She looked like she had just stepped from the pages of Vogue. She was tall, a porcelain face with large brown eyes hidden behind thick dark curly lashes. Her neck was swan-like, her legs long and firm. She was wearing a knit skirt that fell just above the knees, a light pink silk blouse, and matching scarf.

I intercepted her half way there.

"Miss Collingsworth?"

"Yes?"

She looked at me through cold, detached eyes.

"I'm David Crockett. I'm a private investigator and I'd like to ask you a few questions."

"About what?"

"Johnny Lee Baker."

Her eyes became frosty as she moved gracefully past me.

"I don't know anyone by that name."

"Well, he knows you. Your card was found in his apartment."

"I give out a lot of cards. I don't know everyone who gets them." She reached for the handle of her Silver Benz. "If he calls me I'll let you know."

"That might be difficult since he's dead."

She froze.

"He was murdered." I added to see her reaction.

"Murdered?" For a second I thought I saw fear in her eyes but it was instantly replaced by rock-hard granite.

"How unfortunate," she said coldly. "But I don't see how this concerns me." Her hand trembled slightly as she reached for the door handle. She glanced back at me then took a deep breath.

"Good day, Mr. Crockett. I trust you won't be bothering me again."

She got in her car and sped away.

I thought about following her but decided against it.

I went to see Jenny instead.

The room smelled like daffodils. I had placed a standing order with one of the local florist to put fresh daffodils in her room once a week.

She lay there so peaceful.

Donovan was there. I knew he would be. He spent as much time with her as he could. I had come to like this kid, even though we had nothing in common, except maybe loyalty.

"How is she?"

"She's doing great. She's going to be up and dancing in no time. I just know it." Mozart was playing softly in the background.

"How are you doing?"

He tried to smile, but there wasn't a lot of hope and joy left in him.

"You have fabulous taste in music. I know she's loving

it as much as I am."

"Thanks."

"She's looking better today," I observed.

"I put some make-up on her," he said proudly. "I know she would just die if she knew people could see her without make-up." There was a catch in his voice.

"No one's going to see her like this but you and me. Soon she will be awake and she'll be able to put her own make-up on."

He stood. "I hope so. I have a dance class. Can you stay with her?"

"For as long as it takes."

He stared at me as if I was from another planet. "You don't look the kind." He grabbed his back pack.

"What?"

"The kind of person who really cares. I mean you don't even know her and yet you've done all of this for her. Why?"

"Someone once took care of me," I answered reflectively. "I guess they didn't look the kind either."

The make-up helped hide some of the bruises and made her look almost normal. The swelling had gone down and the cuts were healing.

When Mozart ended I changed to Wheezer, then sat next to the bed. It's hard not to feel good while listening to Wheezer.

"How was your day?" I automatically asked before realizing how stupid it was. Why in the world would you ask a person in a coma how their day was? I felt like I was fifteen years old again and on my first date, awkward and out of place.

"Maybe I should just shut up and listen to the music."

"That's a good idea," a voice answered.

Shocked I looked at Jenny. Why that was my first instinct I don't know, maybe I was hoping for a miracle. She still lay there peaceful but mute.

Being the topnotch detective that I am, I turned to the door and was surprised to see Jackson standing there. He smiled and entered the room.

"How is she?"

"The nurses say physically she is healing, but they won't know if there is any permanent damage until she wakes up."

He moved close to the bed and stared down at her. I could see his jaw tighten and I knew exactly what he was thinking. God help the man who did this if we catch him.

"I got the lab results back on Baker," he said changing the subject. "His prints were the only ones found in the room or on the needle. It's being ruled a suicide."

"That seems to be going around. What about the bump on the back of his head?"

"As far as the big boys are concerned, that happened when he fell after passing out."

"I went to see Abigail Collingsworth this afternoon."

"What did she say?"

"She refused to talk to me. But when I mentioned that Baker was dead she seemed surprised and then scared. She covered her reaction well but it was there."

"She may know something."

"I'll follow her and see what and who she knows." He smiled down at Jenny. "Keep me posted," he said and left.

I began talking about anything I could think of. An hour later I said my good-bye. As I walked to the door, I heard a moan. I whipped back around to see if she was awake. Her eyes were closed but she seemed to be breathing heavier. Her hand twitched.

Or did it?

Did she move?

Was she finally coming out of the coma?

I rushed to the nurse's station.

"She's come out of the coma," I announced excitedly.

The head nurse smiled at me and casually got up.

Impatiently I led her back to the room, irritated that she wasn't more excited. No one had given her a chance and yet Jenny had beaten the odds. It was a miracle worth celebrating.

I burst through the door fully expecting to see Jenny's eyes open and her sitting up smiling.

She wasn't. She was exactly as I had left her.

"What you saw was most likely involuntary neurological responses. The nerves will sometime take over, causing the body to react. It's normal."

She took her pulse and then laid her arm back down. "Her pulse is still strong and her breathing is normal. Everything is fine."

But it wasn't. She was still lying there unconscious, the result of some bastard I was determined to find and make pay.

TWENTY TWO

Involuntary neurological responses.

I sat in my office devouring the Internet for anything I could find on it. Were such neurological responses any indications that the patient in a coma was getting better? Were there any incidents of patients having such responses and then coming out of their comas? I was hoping to find some sign that Jennifer was getting better, that she would soon wake up and be normal. She deserved it. I wanted it badly for her.

I had been at it for over an hour when my concentration was interrupted by a knock on my office door.

My eyes glanced at the Sig lying on the desk. I reached out and put it in my lap.

"Come in," I yelled, not wanting to get up.

The door opened.

I was shocked to see Martin Parker standing there. After our last meeting I was certain he was building a wall of lawyers to hide behind. After all, he had threatened to have my license revoked if I didn't leave him alone. Now he was standing in my office.

Why the change of heart?

Immediately the old adage of keep your friends close and your enemies closer popped into my head. Or was there more to it?

Was it a coincidence that the day after I had ambushed Abigail Collingsworth about Johnny Baker, he shows up at my office? I didn't believe in coincidences. I also didn't believe that people such as Martin Parker would put themselves out there for no reason. He was playing an angle. I just didn't know what it was.

"Mr. Parker. This is a surprise, to say the least."

"It seems we have gotten off on the wrong foot. I want to apologize for our two previous meetings. At my house I over reacted. However, in my defense, it is not every day I find a stranger going through my things."

He smiled like I should understand and move on.

"Except for the lump on my head, no harm done," I said, forcing a smile.

"And as for last week, I had just experienced a horrendous day and I am afraid I took it out on you. Sometimes I miss Sylvia more than I can bear and I strike out like a petulant child." He gave me sadness. "I hope you can understand that." He ended with sincerity.

I ignored both. "What can I do for you?"

His head moved back just a hair as if he was shocked that I was not reveling in his apology. He had given me sadness and sincerity all at the same time, how could I have ignored it?

He suddenly smiled. "May I?" He gestured towards one of the chairs in front of my desk.

"Please."

Sitting down, he calmly glanced around the office.

Obviously, it wasn't up to his decorating standards but he kept his decorating tips to himself. He stared at the John Wayne poster and smiled.

"John Wayne, a magnificent actor."

I would have pegged him for more of the Laurence Olivier type but I didn't say anything. I may have moaned. Pretentiousness does that to me.

"I hope you understand that the fact that Faith thinks I could do such a thing has unnerved me. I believe that is why I resented your presence the other day." Crossing his legs he leaned in towards me. I guess our small talk was over.

"That's perfectly understandable," I answered in my calm detective voice. His body relaxed, and he smiled at me like a professor talking to a troubled student.

"I am willing to answer any questions you might have about my wife and me."

I noticed he didn't say my wife's death.

"Does Faith know you are here talking to me?"

"No." He turned serious and glanced down at his cuticles as he fumbled with his fingers. "Faith and I are pretty much estranged."

"Because of what happened to your wife?"

He snorted and shook his head. "No. But I think the estrangement is the reason she is trying to frame me."

"Frame you? Why would she want to do that?"

He sighed as if it was painful to go into. "Mr. Crockett, this is troublesome for me to admit. My daughter has resented me for the past three years. I love her but she is not the kind of person you ever want to get on the bad side of, as they say. But I am afraid I did just that without meaning to."

I waited for him to continue. He leaned back in his chair looking tired and defeated. It didn't suit the narcissist I knew him to be.

"Three years ago her agency was having financial troubles. She came to me for a loan. I had been against her starting such an enterprise in the first place because I knew what a tough market this was. I feared that, in the long run, there was not enough work to keep her agency going."

"Some would disagree with you."

"Of course, that is what makes investing so difficult. I wanted to be supportive, but all the signs were against her succeeding. When she began having financial problems it validated what I had tried to tell her. Of course she refused to acknowledge it, and when I declined her plea for money, she became angry. She said she would never forgive me and stormed out."

He was painting himself as the victim, the caring father who not only had lost his loving wife, but also his only daughter through no fault of his own.

"Money does strange things to people. We have rarely spoken over the past three years." He sighed and ran his hand through his thick and wavy hair. "And now that Sylvia is no longer there to act as a buffer between us, I am ashamed to say, there is no longer even the pretense of a relationship."

Since he was in such a talkative mood, I remained silent, nodding sympathetically.

"I tried to speak to her a few weeks ago in her office but she wouldn't listen. The fact that Sylvia left everything to me in her will deteriorated our relationship even further. It broke my heart to see the hate in her eyes."

He looked down, staring at his hands. "Do you know what it is like to have your only daughter despise you?" His voice trembled and cracked as his emotions bubbled to the surface.

The emotions seemed real. Had I misjudged him? Was he that good of an actor, or simply a husband and father mourning the loss of his family?

"And you think the death of your wife was the excuse she had been waiting for to get even with you?" I asked.

"That and the will. She was extremely upset about that.

I tried to tell her I would help her with anything she needed but she refused, said she wanted nothing to do with me."

"You didn't go to her office and tell her the cash cow was as dead as your wife?" I asked.

He looked shocked. "She is my only daughter. I could never say something like that."

He glanced down and slightly shook his head, emphasizing the point he was about to make. "I should not be surprised at this, I suppose. When she was a child, Faith would accuse Sylvia and me of saying or doing things when she did not get her way."

"What do you mean?"

"When she was fifteen she desired to date a boy twenty-two years old. I refused, of course. When not getting her way, her retaliation can be intense."

I nodded sympathetically, allowing him to continue.

"She phoned the police and accused me of emotionally abusing her. It took us days to straighten it out with, not only the police but with child protective services. She used to drive her mother to distraction that way."

My wife's death was tragic. It hurt us both. But to go around and spread these vicious lies about me having anything to do with it is nonsense. It's beyond that, it is scatological."

"Scatological?" I asked, unable to contain my surprise.

His look made me feel like I had just asked if the moon was made of cheese, before he laughed uncomfortably.

"Obscene. I'm sorry I'm a member of Mensa and sometimes I forget my vocabulary is a little high-brow."

"Actually, it means more of a preoccupation with obscenity, not just the obscene," I replied calmly.

Mensa members don't like to be corrected. He stiffened then recovered with a forced smile.

"Yes, of course."

"Why do you think your wife changed her will?"

"She felt the same way I did when it came to Faith's business acumen. She mentioned numerous times that she was worried Faith would destroy the family business by chasing after this impractical dream of hers. She did not change her will because she wanted to, but because she had to."

He had just told me the same thing Faith had said about him destroying the family business. It was enough to make a confused private eye wonder. I decided to throw a curve ball and see if he could hit it.

"Did you know your wife was seeking a divorce?"

He stiffened again, but just as quickly relaxed. "Of course," he laughed. "She was always threatening to divorce me for one reason or another. It was Sylvia's way of keeping me in line."

"Did you have to be kept in line?"

"You know what I mean. It is simply an expression. Sylvia was somewhat of an invidious person if she did not know where I was or what I was doing."

"That must have irritated a successful businessman like yourself."

"On the contrary, I found it very endearing."

"Endearing?"

"Sylvia was not much for public expressions of love, but her actions always expressed how she really felt. You do not get jealous, detective, if you do not really care. Sylvia and I loved each other very much."

"So there wasn't any problem in your marriage?"

"Not beyond the everyday ups and downs."

"If she had divorced you, wouldn't she have taken the company, the house, the stocks, and left you with nothing?"

He smiled broadly at me. "You mean motive for killing her?"

I got the feeling we were playing a game and he was winning.

"Mr. Crockett, I have done well enough that I do not have to worry about money. I have my own personal stocks and bank accounts so that I can live comfortably for the rest of my life. But I am confident that you have already checked that out."

Okay, I hadn't yet, but first thing tomorrow, I would be all over that like Al Gore on global warming.

"I had no reason for wanting my wife dead. Once you finish doing Faith's bidding, I have no doubt you will come to the same conclusion." He stood and said, "And then maybe Faith and I can put all this pain behind us and try and resolve our differences."

The meeting was over.

"If I can be of any further assistance, please let me know." He marched to the door then quickly turned around.

"If it would help clear my name, I would be willing to take a polygraph test. You have my permission to set up an appointment." He left without shaking my hand or saying good-by. I affect some people that way.

Was he serious about taking a lie detector test? Was this his way of letting me know that he was telling the truth about Faith?

I quickly called Jackson and set up the test for Friday morning, then immediately began checking his financials. According to my research he had enough money to live on if they had divorced. There went the number one motive for murder out the window.

If it wasn't money, then what was the motive? And if there wasn't a motive, had he really killed his wife? Was it possible that Faith was setting him up because she hadn't gotten her way? Had I been conned by her looks and charm?

Three days later, Martin Parker waltzed into the Federal Courts building for the polygraph test. He appeared calm and collected, smiling at everyone like we were all his closest friends. He was wearing an expensive-looking suit that probably cost more than my yearly salary, with shoes to match. After introductions, he left Jackson and I in the outer room and entered the examining room where Brett Salinger, the police department's polygraph expert, waited.

In an adjoining room Jackson and I watched as Parker sat in the chair and smiled at Salinger.

"He looks confident doesn't he?" Jackson remarked.

"Mensa."

"Mensa?"

"He's let me know on numerous occasions that he is a member of Mensa and has an IQ of 183. He's either very proud of that or he thinks he's smarter than everyone else and can beat it."

"Maybe he is just innocent and wants to clear his name."

"Anything's possible, but my gut tells me this is just his way of showing us how average we are and putting us in our place. He really believes we can't touch him."

"If he passes, he may be right," Jackson said.

We watched silently as Salinger strapped Martin Parker to the machine and then put him through a series of questions. He answered every question immediately without hesitation or thought. Throughout the process Parker remained calm and even glanced at the mirror we were hiding behind as if to let us know he knew we were there and it didn't bother him one bit.

After it was over, Jackson and I, not really wanting to talk to him, took our time getting to the interrogation room. But Parker, it seemed, wanted to talk to us. He stood drinking his cup of coffee by the door. He smiled broadly as we approached.

"Thank you for setting this up."

"That's not the attitude we usually get," Jackson remarked.

"It seemed to be the only way I could convince you and my daughter that I did not kill my wife."

"You don't seem to be worried that you might have failed," I countered.

"Innocent men don't have to worry." He smiled and tossed his cup into the near-by trash can. "Or smart ones." He stared directly into my eyes as if challenging me to prove otherwise. With a confident nod, he turned and strolled calmly away.

After he left, Salinger walked us through the test. Parker had passed it with flying colors, even the question about killing his wife.

Maybe he was smarter than the rest of us.

TWENTY THREE

"You think I'm manipulating you?"

The anger blushed across her face as she got up and paced towards the wall.

"I didn't say that," I replied.

Faith whirled back to face me. "You said you didn't know who to believe."

"I said both stories are plausible. That's all."

"So you think that I am the type of person who uses lies and deceit to get what I want? You think I'm manipulative enough to call the cops and accuse my father of mental abuse because he wouldn't let me date someone?" Her face was red and the pulse on her neck was throbbing.

"I asked if the story was true, that's all."

My first instinct when someone gets that mad is that they are covering up the truth. Anger deflects someone from the subject sending it in a different direction. Was that what she was doing? She moved back to the chair and plopped down.

I remained silent as she sat staring at her hands.

"I'm sorry," she said, sounding defeated.

She looked up at me, moisture forming in the corner of those beautiful eyes. "I forget his convincing ways of twisting and turning the truth to his own advantage is not something that you are used to."

"So now I am the one being manipulated?"

"If there was an Olympic sport for manipulation, my father would win gold every four years. It's what he does."

"I'm just trying to find out the truth. That's why you hired me, isn't it?"

"You want to know about my father, talk to my Aunt Erin. Unlike Mother, she never fell for his pathological ways."

"You think she would meet with me?"

"She is old school when it comes to discussing family matters with others. According to her, family matters should always be kept within the family."

"I'll be as discreet as possible."

"Thursday the Huntsman Cancer Center is honoring Mother for her years of service and charitable donations. Aunt Erin will be in town for the ceremony."

"Do you think you can set up a meeting between us?"

"I'll try." She stared at me then grinned. "But only on one condition."

"And that would be?"

"That you'll be my date for the event. I hate these things and really don't want to go alone."

"Can I wear my boots and blue jeans?"

"No," she smiled and her eyes twinkled. "Surely I'm worth an hour or two in a tuxedo."

Damn that "bachelor forever" sign was shaking wilder than a desperate belly dancer.

TWENTY FOUR

When he finished his two hundredth push up, he stood. Grabbing a towel from across the couch, he wiped the sweat from his body. He glanced at himself in the full-length mirror. What he saw was a toned, lean and rock-hard body. He smiled. Most men his age were doing all kinds of reckless things, not at all concerned with their health or their body. They were too busy frittering away their time on useless pleasures. He wasn't that way. Being in shape was as important as being a crack shot. And he was both. Yes, he indulged in a chew of tobacco once in a while, but, he rationalized, that wasn't like smoking or drinking or filling his body with fast food.

David Crockett had been lucky the first time, but not the second time. And there would be a second time. Justice demanded that he should pay for his sins. The arm of justice was firmly anchored to his toned body, and justice would be his.

He took a drink of water and wiped his face and chest. One more proud glance in the mirror, then he set his water down and took a seat on the cold, hard floor. He had two hundred sit-ups to do before he could dine on fresh fish, a green salad, and steamed asparagus.

One.

Two.

There was no pain anymore, only the pleasure of accomplishment. And soon there would be even a greater accomplishment.

Soon David Crockett would be dead.

TWENTY FIVE

Erin Rosenstein Walker sat in a beautiful antique chair facing me.

Faith had decided that her aunt would be able to talk more openly without her in the room, so Friday morning I knocked on Mrs. Walker's suite door alone.

"Would you like some tea, Mr. Crockett?"

"I'm fine, thank you." It was ten in the morning and a bit early for tea. Actually any hour was too early for tea. If it didn't taste like coffee or Dr. Pepper, I usually stayed away from it. Tea tasted like neither.

"Nonsense, we shall have tea." She picked up the phone and ordered tea.

I guess I was having tea.

We were in her suite at the Grand America Hotel in downtown Salt Lake. One of the more upscale hotels, ten minutes from the Salt Lake Airport, it offered twenty-four hour room service, bathrobes, comfortable slippers, and polished marble bathrooms. It was luxurious to say the least. An elegant living room, a sitting room overlooking the balcony, and a large, closed off bedroom made it one of the premier places for wealthy tourists to stay.

The sitting room where we were was decorated in subtle yellow floral print wall paper with a rich red carpet with blue and yellow flowers. A heavy yellow curtain trimmed in soft brown accented the large glass doors that opened to the balcony. Mrs. Walker sat in a rich yellow chair trimmed in blue while I occupied the blue chair trimmed in yellow.

Last night, as we were introduced during the Huntsman Cancer Center gala honoring her sister, she was polite and cordial. But that was as far as it went, especially after I asked to meet with her to discuss her sister's untimely death. It was, obviously, something she didn't want to be reminded of. Even with Faith's insistence she had refused, saying she had no time as she needed to return to New York City the next day.

Then Martin Parker showed up. Attached to his arm was Abigail Collingsworth. By the evening's end, after watching Parker act as if nothing unusual had happened, Erin Rosenstein Walker was more than willing to open the family vault on Martin Parker.

Her voice was hard and brittle as she stared at Parker smiling and introducing Collingsworth to the assembled dignitaries. "My hotel suite tomorrow," she ordered. "Ten sharp. Do not be late."

Now she sat facing me, gracious but dignified.

She was in her sixties, stout with the rigidity that comes from old money and good breeding. Her pale face was covered by perfectly applied make-up, dark eyes with arching brows. Her posture was straight and she held her head high like the upper-crust society she had lived in all her pampered life. Her hair was short and graying blond.

"So you wish to know about the relationship between Martin Parker and my sister?"

She was direct to say the least.

"I realize this is a difficult time for your family, ma'am. Believe me I am sorry for your loss, but I would appreciate you answering a few questions."

"Do you think he killed her?" she asked.

"Do you think he did?"

"Do not be coy with me Mr. Crockett. If you believed she committed suicide as the local police, you would not be here asking questions."

The word *local* popped out of her mouth like a distasteful fruit.

"That's very astute of you, Mrs. Walker."

"Did he?" she repeated relentlessly.

Her eyes drilled into me and her tone was sharp. She had made up her mind, the local yokels were wrong, and she was waiting for me to validate her conclusion.

"I don't know. He has no motive and his alibi is rock solid." It wasn't what she wanted to hear.

"But you believe he might have?" she pressed.

"I was hired to investigate the possibility, ma'am." The tea came, and the porter rolled the serving set into the room. On the glass tray sat a porcelain teapot, china cups, a cup of sugar, a small pitcher of milk and a shiny silver serving tray.

"Please bring the box of cookies on the kitchen table in here." She ordered the porter like she had been ordering people around all her life. I would place money on the fact that she had. He left and returned with a box of cookies.

"Shall I place them on the serving tray?" he asked. When she nodded, he opened the box and laid them out on the small silver serving tray which had been brought for such a purpose.

"Shall I pour for you?"

"Yes, thank you. Cream and a spoon full of sugar." She directed *Helps the medicine go down,* I wanted to continue but my better judgment won out. He poured a cup of tea, added a small amount of sugar and cream, stirred it, then set it on the table beside her.

I was next.

"Cream?"

"No, thank you. I take my tea straight."

When he was finished, Walker gave him a five-dollar tip and somewhat disappointed, he left.

"Try one of these cookies," Mrs. Walker strongly suggested. "I have them imported from England. They are excellent."

She reached for one and I followed suit.

"They call them biscuits there. Heaven knows why."

I took a bite and tried not to spit it out. It tasted like soap. I smiled and took a quick sip of tea. She munched politely on the hard English biscuit then turned to me.

"My sister was a wonderful person and I loved her dearly, but her taste in men left a lot to be desired."

"How so?"

"She had this quaint idea that love was love and even someone from the lower classes could be taught to fit into polite society. One supposes it came from her love of the theater."

She noticed my quizzical look.

"My Fair Lady," she answered. "When she was young she loved that musical. She rather fancied herself as a female Henry Higgins."

"And Martin Parker was her Pygmalion?"

"We tried to warn her, but she was in love. He was a gold digger out to better himself at her expense."

"That couldn't have made for amicable dinner conversation."

"Do not be impertinent!" She took another sip of tea and set her cup down. "We may have not cared for him, but she loved him and we treated him with cautious respect. But that was before he showed his true colors."

"In what way?"

"He began manipulating her and worming his way into the family business. He was always bombarding Father with ways to make the company bigger and more profitable."

"That would seem to be a good thing, wouldn't it?"

"Except his ideas were impractical at best , and ridiculous at worst. He was always bragging about his high IQ. Believe me, I saw little of it, except for his throwing around big words."

"How were they able to stay married for so long, if it was so bad?"

"My sister was a romantic." She sighed as if that were the most useless thing in the world. "She believed that marriage was forever."

"Mrs. Walker, did he ever cheat on your sister?"

Her jaw tightened and her eyes narrowed. "Of that I have no doubt. Those kinds of men do that, you know." In her world, saying it made it so, and that was all there was to it. In my world I need more.

"Was there any proof that he did?"

"His arrogance was proof enough. The way he looked and carried himself. He was the kind of man who thought he was owed everything, that it was all his for the taking."

She snorted contemptuously and reached for her tea. Her hand shook a bit as she raised the cup to her mouth, but she quickly willed it to stop. As she lowered the cup back to the table, she stared at me like my third grade teacher about to prove me wrong in the believable lie I had spent five minutes weaving on the tragic loss of my book report.

"I am wealthy, Mr. Crockett, and I did not get that way by being gullible or naive. Martin Parker may have pulled the wool over my sister's eyes all these years, but not mine. As far as I am concerned, the man is a swine."

End of that subject. Her face became rigid and her manner businesslike.

"Did your sister ever talk to you about Faith?"

"She was so proud of her."

"Did she ever mention Faith calling the cops when she fifteen because Parker wouldn't let her have her way?"

"Heavens no. Faith was not like that."

"So she never caused Sylvia any problems in that way?"

Walker snickered as she raised her tea. "The only one she caused problems for was her father because he could not control or manipulate her. It seems she has more Rosenstein blood in her than Parker."

She took a sip of tea, set the cup back down, and smiled. "That was his game, control and manipulation. It drove him mad that Faith refused to let him do either with her. I have always loved her for that."

The smile disappeared and her eyes narrowed and her lips pursed. "Now, tell me what you have on that bastard. I would like nothing more than to send him to prison and be rid of him."

Her regal bearing slipped a bit. I tried not to smile.

"Unfortunately, as I said earlier, there seems to be no motive and his alibi is airtight."

"Then why are you here? Why continue with this investigation. I think you have more than you are letting on."

"Who's the detective here, Mrs. Walker?"

She smiled. It was a nice smile, a dangerous smile that could suck a man into her web of the rich and deadly. I had seen it before. Her niece had the same kind of smile.

"Money," she said flatly.

"That was my first instinct, but I have checked on his finances. If your sister had divorced him he would have still been financially secure."

"But for how long?"

"What do you mean?"

"You may have checked his bank accounts, but did you check his spending habits? Martin Parker spends money like he was the Obama Administration. No matter how much he put away it, would never be enough. If Sylvia had divorced him within a year he would have been broke. He knew that."

It was an angle I had overlooked. With the rich it was not just about money, but rather how much money. And the one thing they worried about was the supply drying up. Did Parker kill to keep the money from drying up?

"Mrs. Walker, you would have made a fine detective," I said with admiration.

She smiled, but just as quickly, her face became serious. She leaned towards me with the closest thing to humility I had seen, pleading in her eyes.

"Please find out the truth. I know my sister did not take her own life. She did not believe in giving up." Her eyes became moist and her lips trembled. It was just for a moment, then quickly masked by her aristocratic bearing. I guess the rich and powerful can love as strongly as the rest of us, if only for a moment.

As I walked to my car I pondered her last words concerning her sister. She did not believe in giving up. Staying in a loveless marriage for over thirty years was proof of her strength and determination. So why, after all that time, had she suddenly decided to kill herself? It didn't add up.

Crown Burger was a few blocks from the Grand America Hotel. I headed straight for it. I needed to get the taste of English biscuits out of my mouth, and Katie Blues was too far away. I ordered a large cheeseburger with pastrami, crispy fries, and a large Dr. Pepper.

As I ate, I stared out the large glass window at the

mountains off in the distance. I had an urge to call it a day, head up to Snowbird and go skiing. There was nothing like the fresh, crisp mountain air on your face as you are racing forty miles an hour down a mountain slope to get the adrenalin pumping and the mind focused. I have skied all over the country and Utah has some of the best powder in the country.

I got in my car, but instead of the mountain, it ended up at St. Mark's Hospital. As I came to the door of Jennifer's room I was surprised to see someone sitting beside the bed talking to her. Instinctively, I stopped. The woman was about Jennifer's age, thick, reddish hair. Elvis was singing "Devil in Disguise" softly in the background.

"Do you remember this?" The woman animatedly asked. "We took my niece Pam to see *Lilo and Stitch* when she was seven."

She smiled and took Jennifer's hand. "After the movie we had to buy her the record, and for two weeks straight all she did was sing this song over and over. I have never been so tired of a song in all my life."

I knocked softly on the door so as not to startle her.

She turned to me. Her face was long, lean, and very attractive. Her skin was flawless, her eyes bright green with long lashes, her hair was a thick shag of shiny, auburn.

"Hi. May I come in?" I asked.

She jumped up to greet me. "Please."

She immediately offered her hand. "I'm Connie Wilkerson. You must be Mr. Crockett."

The look on my face must have been one of surprise. She laughed. "Donovan told me all about you."

I walked over to the bed and stared down at Jennifer.

"I can't believe someone would do this to her," Connie said sadly. "Do you have any leads or anything?"

I shook my head. "A lot of roads leading nowhere."

"Something will turn up. It just has to."

"What can you tell me about Thomas Franklin?"

"Who?"

"Thomas Franklin. You set her up on a blind date with him."

"Oh, him," she laughed nervously as she turned the music down. "Do you mind?"

"No," I answered. "You're the one who set her up with him, aren't you?"

"Yes. I'm sorry I didn't recognize the name. He was a friend of a friend I met at a party. He seemed nice and was very good-looking. I thought she might have fun with him."

"And did she?"

"Jennifer is not what you call a serial dater. In fact, she rarely goes out at all. It wasn't so much about him as it was getting her out of her apartment to do something fun. But no, she didn't really enjoy herself."

"Did she say why?"

"He wasn't her type. She's so down to earth, and he was all about impressing people."

"Did she ever talk to you about someone named Martin Parker?"

"The rich guy?" She shook her head as if she couldn't believe him. "She met him at her agency and he asked her out."

"She didn't initiate the date?"

"No, she only went out with him because he seemed nice. She said he insisted, said he could to introduce her to the people who ran the Utah Dance Studio."

"What happened?"

"He wines and dines her, then tells her the company's full and is not seeing any new dancers."

"How did she take that?"

"She was disappointed, but she said she understood. And then he kept coming around."

"He saw her after their date?"

"He tried. He'd call or just show up saying he had convinced the Utah Dance Studio to see her. But by then she wasn't buying it anymore. And she told him so."

"How did he react to that?"

"He got furious. He told her she'd be sorry for leading him on."

Martin Parker had lied to me. Surprise, surprise.

Twenty Six

I called Justin Boudreau for the third time.

"Justin Boudreau, please," I said as polite and businesslike as I could. My last two calls had been answered by his annoying assistant, Wesley Wyler, who had been his normal, patronizing self.

"Who's calling?"

"David Crockett."

"What's this about?" he asked like I hadn't spoken to him twice today already.

"The same thing it was about the last two times I called," I said trying hard to keep the irritation out of my voice.

Wyler was a Harvard graduate, thus the attitude. He had graduated first in his class at medical school and had come to Salt Lake City with every intention of showing the local yokels how things were done in the big city. Imagine his surprise when he found someone as renowned as Boudreau. Imagine his disappointment when he wasn't treated like the golden boy of the Ivy League and given the key to the city. Like most progressives, he tried my patience. He was a miserable little troll who made everyone else miserable.

"Sorry, Mr. Crockett, but as I informed you the last two times you called, Mr. Boudreau is extremely busy and can't be bothered. I'll tell him you called again." He stretched out the word again as if it was the most bothersome thing in the world to have to keep answering my calls when he obviously had much more important things to do.

"Wesley?" I said as politely as I could. "One more thing."

I hoped he could see my fake smile through the phone.

"Please tell Justin I am on the line before I come down there and rip your tongue out of your mouth, tie it tightly around your skinny white throat, and stuff you into one of the meat lockers."

I paused to let it sink in. "Thank you."

Sometimes polite and businesslike only gets you so far.

There was a long pause then Justin picked up the phone.

"David, you don't have to scare my assistant," Boudreau said when he came on the phone.

"I said please and thank you."

This brought a gruff grunt which is about all one gets out of Boudreau.

"I don't have anything for you yet," he said.

"I need to know who this guy is."

"I realize that, David, but I'm up to my eyeballs in cases, including the ones you keep throwing at me."

"And someone is trying to kill me, Justin!" I yelled into the phone. I hated to admit it, but the waiting and wondering when this clown would take his next shot was getting to me.

"I'll get to it as soon as I can. I promise."

He hung up. I felt even more frustrated. I felt like hurling my phone at the wall, going down to the medical examiner's office and putting a gun to Boudreau's head until he told me what I needed to know.

I ended up sorting through Martin Parker's trash instead.

An hour later I had been rewarded for my self-restraint and diligence with absolutely nothing. There were no prescription receipts for sleeping pills, no gags, no chloroform or financial statements indicating he was in trouble, no note saying, 'I am tired of being married so I think I will kill my wife and make it look like a suicide'. There was nothing that could connect him to murder. Parker was a very careful man. The only thing that he had thrown away that might be of use was his gloves. And I still wasn't sure how they fit into the murder.

I took everything I didn't need, put it back into the trash bag, and started out the side door towards the dumpster. I was so frustrated and angry at this point I didn't care if I got shot.

Until I saw him.

Near the front of the office was a tall, athletic-looking man peering around the large tree next to the sidewalk. He was powerfully built, with light-colored hair cut in a military-type buzz. Hiding behind the dumpster, I watched him as he stared at the building. I didn't see any rifle, but it could be hidden under the long dark trench coat he was wearing. There wasn't anything threatening about him except his military bearing and the fact that he was staring at the building where I worked.

He nervously put his hand under his jacket, felt something then removed it. My danger meter suddenly moved from observation to action. I didn't know if he was hiding a rifle under his coat, but I wasn't going to wait to find out.

I tossed my latex gloves into the dumpster and plastered myself next to it. Inching my way to the small wooden fence separating my complex from the dentist offices behind me, I leaped over.

Moving quickly through Doctor Harding and Doctor

Bott's parking lot, I circled around the Willow Creek
Dental Care building, coming out the far side and up the
street from where the raw-boned man waited.

Swiftly and silently, I moved towards him, hoping he
wouldn't turn around. Luck was on my side as he intently
stared at the building's front door. He wasn't aware of my
presence until the barrel of my Sig pressed up against the
back of his head.

"Hands on the tree."

He immediately placed his hands on the tree. Now he
didn't look so dangerous or so cunning. I quickly patted him
down and was surprised not to find a rifle beneath his coat.
But something in his inner coat pocket felt hard. I removed
it. It wasn't a pistol but a small ring box. I glared at him and
he smiled weakly.

My first instinct was to talk him out of it, but I had
other things on my mind. I removed his wallet from his
pants and glanced at his driver's license. Mike
Richardson, age 20, from South Jordan.

"Please don't hurt me. You can have my wallet and
whatever else you want, just don't take the ring."

"I don't want your wallet. Why would I want your
wallet?"

"Aren't you robbing me?"

"Robbing you? No. What are you doing lurking outside
my office?"

"Your office? Are you David Crockett?"

"I'm asking the questions. What are you doing out here?"

"Trying to get the nerve to come see you."

I lowered my Sig.

"Turn around."

He turned around and the fear on his face was evident.
Up close he was nothing more than a large, frightened kid.

"Relax, I'm not going to hurt you."

He relaxed a bit, but not much.

"Let's get out of the street before someone calls the cops," I suggested. I motioned towards the door. He moved in that direction.

Once in my office he glanced around in awe. "I've never been in a private eye's office before."

"Have a seat and tell me what I can do for you, Mr. Richardson."

He plopped down in one of the director's chairs in front of my desk. Glancing down at his hands, he quickly looked back up at me. "My girlfriend wants to talk to you."

"The one the ring is for?"

"Please don't say anything to her. I want to surprise her."

"Can I talk you out of it?" I said, half joking.

He looked at me with innocent eyes. Poor sap. He was already a goner.

"Why does your girlfriend want to talk to me? Is she having trouble at home?"

"Nothing more than normal family problems."

"Is someone following her?"

"No."

"Is she being threatened?"

"Nothing like that," he shrugged.

I waited for him to continue.

"She heard something that has been bothering her for the past two months."

"What did she hear?"

"Ringing."

"Ringing?"

"I mean there was nothing when there was supposed to be something," he stammered.

So far he wasn't making much sense. "So why does she think she needs to talk to me?"

Because her father told her not to."

"Her father told her not to talk to me? Why would he do that? Who's her father?"

"Don Wingate."

Don Wingate? Now I really was curious. "Is she downstairs?" I asked.

"I left her in my car in front of the coffee shop.

"Maybe she'll be more comfortable there. Why don't you take her and get her something to drink. I'll meet you there."

"Okay." He got up and hurried out of the office.

I had no clue what was going on, or why Don Wingate had told his daughter not to talk to me, but my curiosity was sufficiently piqued. I locked my door and headed for the coffee shop.

Mike Richardson was sitting in a back booth facing the door. When he saw me he half stood and waved me over. As I approached I took notice of the young blonde girl beside him. She was very pretty, with delicate features, long eyelashes above huge brown eyes. When I stopped at the table, her eyes narrowed and her long lashes fluttered like hummingbirds.

"Mr. Crockett, this is my girlfriend, Chelsea Wingate."

"Ms. Wingate," I smiled, hoping to put her at ease. "It's nice to meet you."

"Likewise, sir," she smiled. "I hope you don't mind meeting here."

Her voice was soft but strong. She appeared frail but I soon sensed she was anything but.

"Mike says you wanted to talk to me."

She nodded and took a sip of her soda.

"My dad said you came to visit, that you were looking into Mrs. Parker's death."

"I am."

"She was a nice lady. My dad said I shouldn't talk to you because you are trying to frame Mr. Parker for killing her."

"I'm trying to find out what happened. Why does your dad think I am trying to frame him?"

"He thinks all cops are that way. He says there's no way Mr. Parker could have killed Mrs. Parker and you know it. He thinks you're just trying to stir up trouble because you've got the hots for Faith. Is that true?"

"No, I'm not trying to stir up trouble. I'm trying to find out if Sylvia Parker really did kill herself. And if she didn't, I want to find out who did."

She shook her head. "No, I mean about Faith. Do you have the hots for her?"

"That's not relevant to this meeting," I replied firmly.

She glanced knowingly at Mike and smiled.

I ordered a Dr. Pepper from the waitress, then turned to Chelsea. "Did you know the Parkers well?"

"They were good friends of my mom and dad. We would all meet at Lake Powell each year to fish and hang out."

"But Mrs. Parker didn't come this last time?"

The girl stared at me, her brow wrinkling. "No. Mr. Parker said she wasn't feeling well enough to make the trip."

"He was a strange dude," Richardson interjected. "Go ahead, Chels, tell him about the phone call."

"What phone call?" I asked.

"Saturday afternoon he called his wife," Chelsea said.

Wingate had told Faith and I that Parker had called his wife Saturday afternoon and was certain that he had talked to her. He had been insistent on it.

"What about the call?"

She straightened up and glanced at Mike. She seemed to draw strength from him. He smiled at her and she continued.

"He pretended to talk to his wife."

"Pretended? What do you mean?" I said somewhat confused.

"About five till four, I go to call Mike."

"I leave for work at the Maverick at four. Chels always calls me before I leave," Mike explained.

"Anyway, I pick up the phone in my room and I hear Mr.

Parker talking to someone. As I start to hang up I noticed the phone on the other end is ringing.

"So he was waiting to talk?"

"No, he was already talking, that's why I decided to listen."

"Are you saying he was talking while the phone was ringing?"

"Yes, I thought it was really strange so I kept listening."

"Could he have been talking to someone in the kitchen?"

"Not unless he is gay," she answered quickly then blushed.

"Gay?"

"I mean he was saying something like 'hey sweetheart, how are you?' Then he said, 'I miss you too.' But I didn't hear anyone say anything to him. He then talked about fishing and told my dad that Sylvia told him to quit making up stories or something like that."

"And you didn't hear anyone on the other end?"

"Just the ringing phone." She paused and took a drink, then looked at me with her big, brown eyes. "Then he said something like 'Sylvia this has gone too far.'"

"What did he mean by that?"

"I don't know, I quit listening for a moment because I just wanted him to hang up so I could call Mike. When I started listening again he was saying good-bye."

"Was the phone still ringing?"

"Yes. He asked her to promise him that she would go see some doctor first thing Monday and then hung up."

"Are you sure about this?"

"Positive."

The smoking gun? Maybe, maybe not but it was another bullet in the barrel against Martin Parker. "Did you tell anyone else?"

"I told Mom and Dad."

"What did they say?"

"Dad said I was just imagining it and not to say anything to anyone."

"He told you to keep quiet?"

"Like I already told you, he thinks the police are trying to frame Mr. Parker. He said we were not about to help them do it."

"Did Parker say anything else that you can remember?"

"Not on the phone, but when I came to the kitchen to tell Dad I was going to go shopping, I heard him say that Mrs. Parker sounded depressed. He said that was one of the reasons she hadn't come with him. I thought that was strange since she wasn't on the line."

She reached over and laid her hand on top of Mike's. "Anyway that's what I remember. I hope it helps."

"And you're positive about this?"

"Why would I lie?"

"I don't think you would, but I need to know if you're positive enough to swear in court to what you heard," I explained.

"My dad would never let me testify in court, but truth is truth."

"Is there anything else you can tell me that might help me get a better understanding of why Mrs. Parker might have committed suicide?"

She thought for a moment then shook her head. "No, I didn't know her as well as my parents did. Sorry."

She stood and reached out for Richardson's hand. "You might want to talk to her best friend. She could probably tell you a lot more than me."

"Her best friend?"

"Yeah. Some rich lady she was always talking about, you know, doing all this party stuff together."

"Social events," Richardson clarified.

"You remember her name?"

"No, I usually tuned out when she started talking about

it. I just remember thinking it was strange for old people to be talking about BFF and stuff."

I watched them walk out of the coffee shop, holding hands, smiles etched on their faces like they had been planted there by a benevolent fairy godmother, never to be removed. There was nothing more exciting than young love. It was like the thrill of going down a water slide at fifty miles per hour. This was when love was new, exciting, full of hope and promise. Of course there was always the big splash at the bottom. Talk about a lot to learn.

I made the short walk back to my office, thoughts of Chelsea Wingate's comments buzzing around in my head. Like a thousand-piece puzzle, the pieces were falling into place. Martin Parker's rock-solid alibi was beginning to crumble.

Being the topnotch detective that I am, it took me about five minutes to find out the name of this best friend. I looked up the Huntsman Cancer Center gala honoring Sylvia. It had been organized by Melanie Skoff. *The Desert News* had covered the event and had displayed a photo of Skoff and Sylvia.

I called her office. I told them of our meeting at the Sylvia Parker gala (which was almost true since I had seen her there) and that I was following up on her invitation to discuss ways I could contribute to the cancer charity. (Another almost truth since she had given an open invite for the guests to contribute to Huntsman Cancer Charity). They joyfully gave me the information I needed.

The Ranches country club was filled with the rich and the famous. It was also guarded by a large maitre d' who wasn't about to let just anyone into the area where the rich were enjoying a dining experience free of those less fortunate than themselves. I, of course, was one of those less fortunate.

I could see Melanie Skoff sitting alone at her table. I

recognized her from her picture with Sylvia in the society page. Her hair was a light chestnut, accented with pewter streaks that made her look high-class.

She was older, but there was no diminution of beauty. Her face was oval, fine-boned like Christy Brinkley in her prime. Her hair was brushed back from a smooth, high forehead and spilling over slender shoulders. Her eyes were ocean blue, her smile wide, her lips full like everyone's favorite Pretty Woman. It was enough to make me gasp.

"May I help you, sir?" The maitre d' looked at me with measured contempt. I guess my attire wasn't up to their standards. I wasn't wearing an expensive golf or tennis outfit, nor did I have that look that sets the rich and famous apart from the rest of us.

"I'm here to see Mrs. Skoff."

"Is she expecting you?"

"Let's just say yes," I nodded enthusiastically.

He saw my nod, and countered with a shake of his head.

"Let's just say we check and see."

He turned to go.

"Give her this," I added quickly.

I removed one of my cards and quickly scribbled on the back that I was looking into Sylvia's murder and I needed her help. He glanced at the car, reacting as if it was day old caviar, then turned and strolled to her table.

I waited as he handed her the card. She read the back and glanced my direction. I gave her my best poor-people-are-people-too-smile. She stared at me for a beat, then waived me back.

With some sense of satisfaction at being let into the inner sanctum, I imitated the maitre d's chin in the air as I passed him. He ignored me.

"Mrs. Skoff, thank you for seeing me."

"Have a seat, young man."

I promptly sat down.

"Would you like something to eat?"

"No thank you, ma'am."

"Nonsense." She waved over the waiter. "Bring this young man a roast beef sandwich." She stopped and turned to me. "You do eat meat, don't you?"

"Like a pro," I smiled.

"Ignore the roast beef," she demanded. "Bring him a Monte Cristo instead, and a beer."

With a nod the waiter shuffled away.

She flashed a finishing school smile that, most likely, could be turned on with the flip of a switch.

"You look like a beer man. My late husband was a beer man."

"I appreciate the lunch."

She picked at her food then turned a steel-like gaze on me. "Do you know why I agreed to see you?"

"No ma'am."

"Because you, young man, are the first person with sense enough to contemplate the possibility that Sylvia didn't commit suicide. I like smart people. Ignorant people give me a rash."

"You don't believe she did?"

"There is no way she would have committed suicide."

"What makes you say that?"

"I knew Sylvia better than most people. She told me things she wouldn't tell her own family. She was happy and looking forward to a new life."

This caught me by surprise. "A new life?"

The waiter returned with my food. It was the most elaborate Monte Cristo I had ever seen. The deep-fried sandwich, cut in half, was filled with enough meat and cheeses to feed a small village. It was sitting on a bed of crisp green lettuce surrounded by sliced cucumbers, olives, and spoon full of strawberry Jam.

Skoff waited until the waiter poured her more wine, then waved him away. Once he was out of earshot she continued.

"She was determined to divorce Martin. She had given it her best and nothing had changed. All he cared about was running the business and proving he was smarter than everyone else."

That seemed to be a continual theme where Parker was concerned.

"She didn't care about the business anymore?"

"She wanted to retire. After divorcing Martin she planned to move to Park City and open up a flower shop."

"A flower shop?"

"That's what she really enjoyed." A wistful look clouded her eyes. "She loved flowers. Her backyard was full of colorful flowers. She was good at growing and nurturing them. I used to tell her that it wasn't something a lady of prominence should be doing. That's what gardeners were for. She just laughed and said if she had it to do over, she would have refused her fathers offer of the business, married a florist, and lived happily ever after."

"But she married Martin Parker."

"He was all charm and starch in those days. And she was headstrong and in love."

"But lately?"

"She wanted Martin out of their lives. She had a Realtor looking for the right place in Park City."

"If she was planning to open a flower shop, who would have run the family business? According to her will, she left everything to Martin, including the business."

"Not in the will I saw. She left everything to Faith. She knew Faith did not want to run the business so she planned to retire and appoint her nephew, Jarad Walker as CEO. He is an extremely sharp businessman. She was confident in his abilities to keep the company profitable."

"Could she have changed her will without telling you?"

"No, she would have talked to me about it."

"Did she tell Parker her plans to make Walker CEO?"

"Yes."

"Do you remember when?"

"Around July. That's when she told me about the place in Park City. When I asked her about the business, she said she was in discussions with the Board of Directors to make Jared CEO. I warned her not to let Martin know until it was finalized. She said she had already told him.

"And she committed suicide in September."

She arched a perfectly shaped eyebrow. "Rather convenient wouldn't you say?"

"How did Parker take the news?"

"He went ballistic. He said the company was his, and he would stop her anyway he could. He swore he would sue her and her family for everything they owned."

"Did he threaten her?"

"You mean physically?" She shook her head. "That wasn't his style. He was more of a manipulator. When he could not manipulate someone, he was not above seeking revenge."

"I don't mean to beat a dead horse, Mrs. Skoff but are you sure she was planning to appoint Walker CEO?"

"She said she had her attorney already working on the contract. She was so proud of Jared."

"Who was her attorney? Do you remember?"

"Richard Harvey, poor man."

"Poor man?"

"He was in a serious auto accident about six months ago. Since then he has had serious lapses in his memory. I don't think the man is all there anymore."

"Which would make it difficult to dispute the changing of the will, if it occurred?"

"And impossible for the family to challenge it," she pointed out.

"What about Faith?"

"She loved Faith more than life itself." She took another drink of wine and delicately wiped her lips with her satin napkin. "She would have never left Faith. Not like that."

"Nor cut her out of her will?"

"No. Never."

"Yet, according to Faith, her father got everything."

Setting her fork down, she planted that steel-like gaze again on me. I could see how this woman was so successful.

"Mr. Crockett, I don't know how he did it, but I have no doubt that Martin Parker killed my dear friend."

"Faith thinks so too. That's why she hired me to look into the matter."

"If you need anything to help you prove it, call me."

She removed a business card and wrote her private number on the back. "You prove that snake killed her and I'll make sure your agency never lacks for anything."

"I appreciate your very kind offer, but I'm doing fine."

She smiled, but in a no-nonsense manner. There was an elegance and grace about her, but also a touch of mischievousness.

"You remind me a lot of my late husband. He was a man's man. He worked hard and didn't ask for anything. But I still managed to help him when he wasn't looking."

There was a twinkle in her blue eyes as she dismissed me.

"Good day, Mr. Crockett. I'll be watching you."

I stood and smiled down at her. "Thanks for lunch."

Twenty Seven

I stopped at the Spicy Thai for dinner and ordered chicken massaman to go. I needed time to figure out what to do about Thomas Franklin and Martin Parker. Both of them were hiding something. But what?

Parker had lied about seeing Jennifer more than once. I had no doubt he had something to do with his wife's death, but was he also responsible for what happened to Jennifer? Had it not been for Thomas Franklin, I would have said absolutely, but Franklin also fit the bill. He was a hot head use to getting his way, especially with his father running legal interference for him. Had Jennifer refused his advances, sending him over the edge?

I fed Sam, then took my food into the living room and sat down behind closed curtains. Sam finished liver and chicken chunks before joining me on the couch. He looked at me, stretched, then plopped on the sofa and closed his eyes. It was bonding time.

I tasted the massaman and was not disappointed. I kicked up my feet and enjoyed the solitude. Maybe too much? Was I getting where I enjoyed being alone? My line of work was well known as one of the "divorce professions," and for a good reason. Maybe I should let Tonja set me up. That thought sent me bolting upward, almost knocking over the massaman.

No pot roast, no setups, and no more solitude.

I got up and put on some classic rock and roll. It was time for fast cars, beaches, holding hands, and teenage breakups.

The good vibrations of youth filled the room. I danced back to the couch and finished my massaman curry.

As the food and the music helped clear my head, I removed a yellow legal pad from my briefcase and began looking at my notes from the two cases I was working on. There were such large gaps in them that I felt like I was doing a giant puzzle with critical pieces missing.

I jotted down the name, Thomas Franklin. I needed solid evidence against him, and that meant digging into his past. I wrote the names, Greta Delancy and Sharon Siggard. Both of them had been attacked by Franklin in high school, but, because of Keller Franklin's long political reach, neither had been taken serious by the district attorney. Maybe they would be more inclined to have their say now.

And Martin Parker. His name kept coming up in both cases. Usually when that happens you can stop looking at everyone else. So many things just didn't add up. Did Sylvia Parker change her will? What happened to the contract naming Jared Walker CEO?

My interview with Chelsea Wingate may have unlocked an interesting part of the puzzle. I was hoping Rick West could do the same, but I wasn't too optimistic. West had found Sylvia Parker's body, and, from what I could see concerning his statements to the police, he wasn't a fountain of information.

As I scanned my notes on the various interviews I had already conducted, my phone rang. I didn't recognize the number.

"Crockett Investigations."

"Mr. Crockett? This is Ruth Mosley."

I sat up straighter. "Yes?"

"I need to talk to you about Jennifer."

"Why the change of heart?"

"Can you meet me at the park on Seventh East and Ninth South by the oak trees at eleven tonight?"

"Why so late?" I inquired suspiciously.

"My husband goes to bed by ten-thirty. I can't let him know I'm meeting with you. See you then." She hung up.

I glanced at my watch. It was seven-thirty. I finished going over my notes, hoping something new would jump out at me. It didn't. Two beers later, I gathered all my notes and set them on the table. My brain was spent.

Turning on the television, I sat in front of it like a zombie. Ruth Mosley's call bothered me. There was no doubt she was hiding something, but her participation in Jennifer's beating didn't make sense. What was her motivation? If it was nothing more than trying to hide her lifestyle, why had the mention of Jennifer's diary sent her into panic mode? And why, all of a sudden, was she willing to tell me what had happened?

At ten-fifty I parked in one of the parking areas and studied the park. It was empty. A good place for an ambush, I thought, my mind drifting back to my childhood days of watching John Wayne movies on television. Of course in my line of work, it was always a good place for an ambush.

Instinctively placing my hand on the Sig under my coat,

I got out the car. Cautiously I made my way to the clump of oak trees that were cut off from the rest of the park by a high grassy area that curved around the north side of the park. As I drew closer I noticed Ruth Mosley standing in front of one of the tall trees. Even in the dark she looked tense, nervous as she wrung her hands back and forth. That should have been my first red flag, but a nervous woman alone in the park seemed normal. It wasn't.

"Ruth."

"Mr. Crockett. Thanks for coming."

"What would you like to tell me?"

She glanced behind her then began backing up towards one of the large trees. I followed, but before I could reach her, three of my old no-neck friends stepped from around the trees, blocking my way. Another man stood in the shadows with Ruth. I couldn't see his face clearly, but I could see his short hair and broad shoulders. He looked like a mammoth linebacker from the Fifties. He also looked like the driver of the black Dodge Ram truck, Joshua Mosley.

"We want the diary," the muscle-bound Arnold sound-a-like said menacingly.

These were the no-neck goons standing guard at the house of polygamist Rulon Peterson. The Arnold-sound-alike was the one with the pastrami and pickle breath. He also had bad teeth.

Why would these goons be after the diary?

"And I'd like world peace and a date with Kate Upton."

"Who's Kate Upton?" bad teeth asked.

I guess being in a cult. he didn't get the *Sports Illustrated* swimsuit issue. Or professional dental work.

"We don't want to hurt you," the goon in the middle said. He was tall with an angular head, buzz cut and tiny ears for such a large man. "Just give us the diary and we'll leave you alone."

A goon with a heart. I liked that.

"What diary?"

"So you want to play it that way?" the third goon asked. He was bald with short stubby legs, which made him look like a bowling ball with feet.

"Why would a polygamist cult want a young woman's diary?"

Tiny Ears looked at me like a little boy caught by his mother with his pocket full of unpaid candy. I guess I wasn't supposed to know about their little group of believers.

"We don't know what you're talking about," he finally mumbled. "We just want the diary because it belongs to one of our sisters."

"And which sister would that be?" I asked casually, hoping they would realize I knew their game and go on their merry way. They obviously didn't feel like going anywhere, merry or otherwise. "Tell me the name of the sister it belongs to and you can have it."

Confusion clouded their faces as they turned to look at each other. Sometimes soldiers do the only thing soldiers can do. They fight. Tiny Ears swung. How sad. I was just beginning to like him.

He was big, but slow and ponderous. I leaned back just enough to dodge his powerful punch, grabbed his arm and kicked him in the solar plexus with all my weight. The air gushed out in a mighty whooshing sound and he hit the ground.

The two remaining goons rushed me, knocking me down. Bad Teeth grabbed me and lifted me into the air like I was a rag doll. He was extremely strong and held me in a vise-like grip. Bowling Ball began tenderizing my face with his huge fists. Using all my strength, I brought my knee up as hard as I could into his groin. I knew I had struck gold when his eyes bulged and he immediately leaned over clutching himself like Madonna in concert. With Bad Teeth still holding me like a fish caught in octopus tentacles, I began backing up.

Once I had him moving to keep up with me, I suddenly stopped and shifted all my weight forward. Bending at the waist, I sent him flying over my head.

Tiny Ears, back on his feet, rushed at me like the proverbial bull in the china shop. I stepped aside and using his forward momentum, drove him headfirst into the tree. He bounced off like a butterball turkey hitting the side of a wall; not much bounce but a lot of thud. He landed on the ground, clutching his head.

Bad Teeth came at me with his fist high, circling me like he knew what he was doing. He didn't. He charged, throwing a lot of overhand rights and lefts like he must have seen in all those bad fight movies. I guess he forgot the part where the other fighter took advantage of the slow and high punches. I ducked under his molasses right and, spinning around, grabbed his arm with my left hand and hit him in the face with my right. As his head snapped back I reversed my position and hurled him over me onto the hard ground. He bounced once on the ground until his head found the one immovable rock sticking out. He made a coughing sound, then was quiet.

Bowling Ball hobbled towards me, arms swinging wildly. I caught his right arm with my right hand and, using my left hand, shoved it forcefully into his extended elbow. It snapped like a twig. He went down writhing in pain.

From the shadows I caught of glimpse of the linebacker rushing at me with a club in his hand. I turned to meet him but was too late. As I turned, he brought the wooden club crashing down on the side of my head. I fell to the ground, my head throbbing like a blue whale's massive heart. He began kicking me in the ribs, back, and kidneys, over and over. All I could do was curl up in a fetal position and hope for the best. Suddenly it stopped. A large meaty hand reached into my coat pocket and removed the diary.

Once the diary was secured, the kicking resumed.

Through my pain I heard Ruth cry out. "Stop! Please, Joshua, I've done everything you asked. Please stop."

One more painful kick for good measure and it stopped. I heard the no-neck goons groaning as they were helped to their feet. As the footsteps retreated, there was the sound of a slap and Ruth's painful cry.

"Don't ever tell me what to do!"

Moments later, a loud engine started up then drove away.

I lay there for a moment, letting my body relax, hoping the pain would go away. It didn't. Realizing I couldn't lay there forever, I pushed myself into a sitting position. I stayed that way until I could get breath enough to pull myself the rest of the way up. The pain shot through my body with every move. Using the tree for support, I tested my balance. When I could stand without my head spinning like the tea cup ride at Disneyland, I slowly, and painfully, dragged my body to my car.

The drive home seemed to take forever. No matter how I sat, the pain was ever present with every turn of the steering wheel, every bend, curve, and bump.

As I stumbled into the house, Sam rushed to his empty bowl. He was not happy when I ignored him, but he'd have to deal with it. I took my coat off, laid it over the sofa, and headed upstairs to the bedroom. Removing my shoulder holster, I laid my Sig on the dresser, unbuttoned my shirt and stumbled into the bathroom. Holding onto the sink, I opened the medicine cabinet, removed a bottle of Aleve and popped four tablets into my mouth.

Painfully, I removed my clothes so I could inspect my aching body. My lower back ached enough to make me wonder about my kidneys. Getting kicked repeatedly in the kidneys could cause blood in your urine.

Holding on to the towel rack, I stretched my body as far to the left as I could, then to the right. It was painful but not the kind of pain brought on by broken bones. I raised my arms above my head and stretched again. Fortunately I had escaped any broken bones.

I urinated. There was no blood.

Relieved, I crawled into the shower. The water felt good. I let it wash over me, relaxing my aching muscles. After what seemed like an hour, I cut the water off and carefully and painfully stepped out of the shower. As I dried off I noticed my face in the mirror. It wasn't pretty. My left eye was swollen and quickly turning a really great shade of black, my lip split and swollen.

I inched my way into the kitchen, where I fed Sam then dumped a tray of ice into a kitchen towel and held it to my face. Sam looked at me for a moment as if trying to decide if I was all right. He came and brushed against my leg.

"Yeah I know, I'm still handsome."

He left and stuck his face into his food.

I was in bad shape and should have gone to the hospital, but I wasn't in any mood to drive myself there or to answer questions once I got there. I hadn't been hit on the head hard enough to give me a concussion, but I also knew I shouldn't be alone, just in case. Slowly, I reached for my phone and called the only person I wanted to see.

TWENTY EIGHT

I awoke the next morning. My eyes were blurry and my head felt like a big bass drum. I tried to sit up but hands gently held me back.

"Not so fast cowboy." Katie laid me back on the pillow. "You're not getting up until I tell you to," she snapped.

She wrung the water out of a wash cloth and laid it on my aching head. It felt good. I closed my eyes and tried not to think of Ruth Mosley and goons with no-necks.

"You could have been killed, do you know that?"

"I wasn't though. I'm fine, Katie."

Her anger burst forth and rained down on me. "You're not fine, and if anything ever happened to you I don't know what I would do, and I'm mad at you for even putting me through this."

I reached for her and brought her down to me. She laid her head on my chest and cried. Even though it was painful I held on to her. I couldn't help but think of Donovan and Jennifer. Some bonds were just naturally strong for all the right reasons.

For four days Katie took care of me. It seemed natural for her to be there. For as long as I can remember we have talked about anything and everything: work, hobbies, relationships, religion, politics, and even sex. The only thing we have never talked about is our relationship. It just is, always has been, and always will be, no matter what or who comes into our lives. There's a strange sense of comfort in that.

"Something smells good," I announced as I wobbled into the kitchen the afternoon of the fourth day. While my face still looked like it had been sent through a meat press, my body was almost back to normal. Three days of painful stretching, karate routines, and Katie's healthy food had me feeling much better.

Katie glanced suspiciously at me as I laid my holstered gun on the kitchen counter. I don't know why I felt the need for it, but I did. I guess getting shot at and beaten up by large ugly goons makes you a bit more cautious.

"A special treat since you have been so good at following instructions. Sit down."

I obeyed.

She sat a bowl of rice in front of me. I waited as she returned with a steaming pan of chicken massaman. She gently poured it over the rice and sat opposite me.

"What are you going to do now?" She grabbed her own spoon and helped herself.

I could see the concern in her eyes, but she knew me too well for me to lie to her. That was something else we never did—we never lied to each other. There had been painful moments because of it, but we had always worked through them. Being shot at by a professional hit man had been one of those painful moments. She had not taken that well, and even now would not open any of the curtains in the house. I didn't object.

I stared at her, then answered plainly.

"I'm going to get the diary back."

"I called Jackson," she said matter-of-factly.

I felt the anger rising in me. This was my problem and as much as I appreciated my friendship with Jackson, I didn't feel right asking him for help. I was the one they had beaten. I was the one they had stolen it from. I was the one who would get it back.

"I can't stop you from being you, but I don't have to let you go in there by yourself."

"Jackson is a Salt Lake City detective. He can't help me. He'd lose his job."

She took another bite of massaman, a bit of sauce running down her chin. "Then maybe you need to think about that before you go charging in there," she said wiping her chin. "I have to get back to work." Standing, she kissed me on the forehead. "Don't forget to clean up this mess."

One last look and she was gone.

I took another bite of food, enjoying the first pain-free day in a while. With a mouth full of food, my cell phone rang.

Chewing furiously, I had most of it gone when I grabbed the phone and answered.

"Hello."

"David?" So much for a pain-free day.

"Mother."

"Are you coming to dinner Sunday? You missed last Sunday's you know."

I was bruised and broken, I started to say, but didn't.

"We're having your favorite, pot roast."

"Mother, I haven't liked pot roast for the past twenty years."

"Nonsense. It used to be your favorite. Tonja called to say she was sorry about the way she reacted to you helping Joseph. She has invited a very nice woman for you to meet."

"Mother, I'm not at my best at this moment. Maybe next week."

"David, I won't take no for an answer."

I was about to argue with her when I caught a glimpse of my reflection in the mirror. If my battered face wouldn't scare off the latest of the matronly women my sister had set me up with, nothing would. If I was lucky, this would put an end to this find-lonely-David-a-wife-game.

"What time?"

"Be here at six."

"It'll be my pleasure, Mother. See you then." I hung up and smiled. Even that hurt.

I heard the front door open. Moving as fast as I could, I reached for my Sig. I was feeling much better, but, even so, I was not in any condition to take on a no-neck goon. I listened, but didn't hear anything.

"David, put the gun up, it's only me." Jackson's voice floated into the kitchen.

I quickly holstered my Sig and reached for the coffee pot as if nothing was wrong. "I don't have my gun out," I lied. "I'm not that paranoid." Two lies in four seconds. It was probably a record, but who was counting?

Jackson entered the kitchen and headed for the stove.

"How are you feeling?" he said as he pulled down a bowl from the cabinet and helped himself to the rice and massaman.

"A lot better than four days ago," I replied truthfully.

He found a spoon in the drawer and took a bite as he walked to the counter.

"You ready to fill out a complaint against Joshua Mosley?"

"No, I don't want him to know I'm on to him just yet."

Jackson sat on one of the kitchen stools, took another spoonful of massaman and stared at me. "You're going after the diary, aren't you?"

Thinking about it made my head hurt.

"Why would Mosley attack me for the diary? Why not just try shooting me again?"

"We don't know yet if it was Mosley."

"That's where my money is. Also, if he had anything to do with Jennifer, surely he had to know going after me like that puts him squarely in the crosshairs as the number one suspect."

"Maybe he thinks there is something in there that implicates him."

"But there isn't," I shot back.

"He doesn't know that."

"Maybe it just got out of hand and he couldn't pull them back."

"Then why attack you at the end?"

"I don't know," I sighed. "Either he doesn't care that I suspect him or he is just dumber than dirt."

"If he's the sniper, he probably doesn't care if you know. A successful shot and his identity is a moot point," Jackson said.

"Comforting thought. Thanks."

"Which is why you are going after the diary, aren't you?"

"Why would I do something stupid like that?"

"When?"

I knew he was concerned, but I also knew as a detective his duty would be to stop me. I remained silent.

"You can't do it alone, you know," Jackson said.

"Not doing anything."

"Monday wouldn't be good for me. I have Family Home Evening that night."

"Not doing anything," I repeated.

"Tuesday I have tickets to the Jazz game and Thursday I'm filling in for Dick Allen again." He scooped a large spoonful of Massaman into his mouth and swallowed it.

"Not doing anything."

"Friday is my date night with Julie." He took the last bite and moved to the sink where he set his bowl. "Wednesday night I'm free.

"Not doing anything," I said as firmly as I could.

"Wednesday it is." He rinsed the bowl and left it in the sink. "Try to stay out of trouble until then."

With that pearl of wisdom, he left.

I stayed in bed most of the day, watched television, read and decided upon my plan of attack. After their visit I knew Peterson and his guards would be on the alert. I couldn't just knock on the door and say hi. Breaking in was impossible since they would be guarding the house like it was a terrorist safe house. Trying to come up with a feasible battle plan made my head hurt.

At six, I went into the kitchen, made myself a bowl of chicken noodle soup, toasted a slice of bread and grabbed a beer.

Sam was nowhere to be found. He was not used to having me around so much and had decided on a day in the great outdoors playing Sammie Crockett—king of the wild neighborhood. I watched television until my mind was finally numb enough for me to sleep.

The next morning I showered and dressed in my most comfortable blue jeans, a black t-shirt to match the black rings under my eyes and a brown corduroy sports coat. After a bowl of oatmeal and a piece of toast, I headed towards Sandy to keep my appointment with Rick West.

By ten I was sitting in the parking lot of ReQuest Computer Services. It had taken me an hour more than normal as I circled back and forth at least six times to make sure no one was following me. I hated feeling this way, but then again I hated the thought of being shot even more.

ReQuest Computers was a large complex just south of Rio Tinto Stadium where the Real Salt Lake Soccer team plays.

Laboring to get out of my car, I slowly made my way to the three-story building of gray polished granite and glass. Inside, I took the elevator to the third floor.

The secretary w a s   i n   h e r   late   twenties   with   short blonde hair, slender face with large blue eyes. She had arching eye brows, and gold dragon earrings dangling from her ears.

She looked up from her *People* magazine as I entered. She j u s t   s t a r e d ,   u n t i l   s h e   finally   forced   out   her inquiry. "Can I help you?"

"I'm here to see Mr. West."

She continued to stare at my bruises and black eye before glancing down at her appointment book.

"Are you Mr. Crockett?"

"Yes. And it's not as bad as it looks."

She blushed, embarrassed. "I'm sorry, I didn't mean to stare. Are you all right?"

"I'm fine, thank you. Disagreement with my butcher."

"What?"

"He insisted on selling me the round chuck and I wanted the London broil."

"Butcher?"

"You let them dictate your meat order one time and it never ends," I said with a straight face. "You have to draw a line in the sand sometimes."

She stared at me as if I was crazy. "Please have a seat and I'll let him know you're here."

As I took a seat in one of the chairs that lined the room, she picked up the phone and talked briefly with West.

"He'll be just a moment," she said as she hung up. "Can I get you something to drink?"

"No thanks, I'm fine."

With a nod she went back to her magazine, glancing covertly at me every few minutes.

Five minutes later the phone rang and the secretary

showed me into the office. West was a large man at least six-four, 210 pounds, and not a lot of body fat. He appeared to be in his early thirties, with sandy brown hair and a full beard to match.

"Mr. Crockett." He greeted me with a Texas-size smile and handshake. "Please sit down."

I took a seat in one of the plush chairs in front of his desk. He walked around and sat down, rolled his chair closer to his desk and turned his attention towards me. I could tell he was wondering about the bruises and black eyes. I tried my best to smile.

"It looks worse than it is. Occupational hazard, I'm afraid."

"On the phone you said you wanted to talk about Sylvia Parker." He stopped and glanced at me. "Are you sure you don't want something to drink?"

"I'm fine, thank you."

He leaned back. I wondered how the chair could hold his large frame.

"I don't know what I can tell you that I haven't already told the police."

"Sometimes after a certain amount of time has elapsed, the memory recalls things you may have forgotten."

"I remember everything about that morning. It's not every day one finds a dead body."

"Could you walk me through that morning?"

"It was Sunday about eight-thirty. My wife and I were rushing to get the kids ready for church. As I was chasing down our five-year-old, the phone rang. It was Martin calling to ask me to check on Sylvia."

"Were you close neighbors?" I asked.

"No, that's what was so strange about the call. We were never on the best of terms. Anyway, he asked me to check on Sylvia. He said he had tried to reach her all night, but she hadn't answered. He said he was worried about her.

When I told him I was about to leave for church he sounded desperate. He said he had called her twice that morning and she still hadn't answered. Finally, I agreed. He seemed relieved and then asked me to call him as soon as I talked to her."

"He didn't say to have her call him?" I asked.

West immediately shook his head. "No, I remember because I thought I didn't have time to be a go-between, so I would just have her call him direct."

"That's odd, don't you think?"

"Now that you mention it, it does seem strange."

"So you went over to the house?"

"I rang the bell at least twice . When no one answered, I used the key Martin had told me where to find. I called for Sylvia and when I got no answer I went upstairs to the bedroom. That's when I saw her laying on the bed."

"Did you touch anything?"

"No, of course not."

He looked resentful, as if I thought he was a novice when it came to crime scenes. "I've seen enough crime shows on television to know you are not to touch anything."

The power of make-believe crime shows.

"So you found the body and called the police?"

"Yes."

"Then what did you do?"

"What do you mean?"

"It must have taken the police at least twenty minutes to get there. What did you do in the meantime? Did you sit in the bedroom and read a magazine? Go downstairs and wait, or go outside the house?"

"I cut the air conditioner off, closed the door and went downstairs to wait in the entry hall for the police."

"I'm sorry, what?"

"I went downstairs to wait for the police. It was too cold to wait outside."

"What air conditioner?"

He looked at me like a confused three-year old. "The air conditioner in the bedroom, of course."

"You're saying it was too cold to wait outside but the air conditioner was on in the bedroom?"

"It was on full blast. That's the first thing I noticed as I opened the door, how cold it was in there. It was like a meat locker."

"And you didn't tell the police that?"

His eyes dropped to the desk and he shrugged his shoulders like a little boy trying to explain why he had hit the baseball through the window. "I forgot about it. I mean, it was so cold in there that I just automatically turned it off as I left the room. I guess I wasn't thinking."

As I drove away I realized that Richard West may have just handed me the key to unlock the whole case against Martin Parker. I immediately called Boudreau. Wyler answered and without any hesitation put me through to Justin.

"To what do I owe this irritating call?"

"I need some information."

"What's wrong with the library?"

"It doesn't have you," I said. I knew he was smiling because I heard part of his stern face crack.

"What do you want?"

"If someone is killed in their bedroom and the air conditioner is cranked up full blast, would that throw off the ETD?"

He thought for a moment, before replying. "How long?"

"A weekend maybe?"

"No doubt the cold would affect the decomposition of the body, which might throw off the estimated time of death."

"Enough to fool a coroner into thinking that death had occurred much earlier than it had?"

"Possibly. Is this something I need to know about?"

"When I get more information, I'll get back to you. I'm

bringing some gloves over for you to look at."

"I guess I could just close the office and simply work on your cases." His sarcasm was biting at times, but funny.

"I'd appreciate that, thanks, Justin."

"What do you mean thanks, you postulating sack of sewage. Who are we talking about?"

I hung up and could still hear all his swear words.

An hour later when I walked into the office with the gloves, Wyler saw me and immediately left the room. And I had been nothing but nice to him.

TWENTY NINE

By Sunday my aches were gone but my left eye was still swollen. The bruising remained around my eyes and face and my lip still showed signs of being busted. I was looking forward to seeing my mother and sister and the matronly aunt that Tonja had lined up for me.

"Oh my lord, what happened to you?" Mother said as soon as she opened the door. Noticing the concern on her face, I suddenly felt bad for my deception. Concern was suddenly replaced by anger. "Who hurt you?" she demanded. She was like a riled bear when someone hurt one of her cubs.

"I'm fine, Mother," I said, concerned at her concern. "It looks much worse than it is."

"What happened?" She pulled me inside.

"I had a disagreement with three no-neck goons."

"Over what?"

"Their looks."

"I'm calling the doctor."

"Mother, I have already been to the doctor," I lied. "Really, I'm fine. The bruises will be gone in a couple more days and you'll never even know I was hit."

She stared at me with all the concern and love a mother has for a wayward son. She also knew that she wasn't going to get much more out of me about the incident, so she did what she always does in a crisis.

"You need some food in you."

As she led me to the dining room I began to feel like maybe this wasn't such a good idea. Stopping the eternal wife search was one thing, but worrying my family needlessly, was another. When we entered the dining room, I was rewarded for my stupidity.

Sitting beside Tonja was a very attractive woman who looked to be in her mid-thirties. She was the athletic type, strong but not masculine, more toned than muscles, like a tennis player. Her blonde hair hung down to her neck, her eyes deep blue and dimples highlighted her knockout smile. She was wearing a simple cotton blouse, which made her sports tan stand out. There was only one word for her: stunning.

"David, this is Renee Ewing," Tonja said, hoping to relieve the tension that had fallen over the room.

Maybe she wouldn't notice. I gave her my best boyish grin.

It wasn't enough. She noticed.

She swallowed that dazzling smile as soon as she saw me.

Of all the times for Tonja to get it right.

***

The next night, feeding all the pent-up anger in me, I decided to take matters into my own hands and get Jennifer's diary back. If I had to beat the living snot out of Joshua Mosley, so be it. Okay, I was actually looking forward to that part.

The street paralleling the gated community of The Eternal and True Church of Christ in the Last Days was deserted, with the exception of a few empty cars.

The front gate was guarded by two no-neck members of the prophet squad, as I liked to refer to them, but the rest of the area seemed to be clear.

I found the most likely place to scale the large stone wall that separated the community from the outside world and parked.

It was about nine o'clock Monday evening, so I knew most Mormons, like Jackson and Julie, would be finishing up their "Family Home Evening" and either be settling in for the night, playing games, or were already out enjoying, ice cream, pizza, or the movies.

As I had hoped, I had the street to myself. I climbed out of my car and took in the area as quickly as possible. I was wearing all black. If anyone saw me their first call would be to the police, so I could ill afford to spend much time standing around. Before I could move away from my car, I noticed headlights turning the corner and headed my way. As the driver's side of my car was next to the sidewalk, I ducked down behind my car and waited.

I had no doubt the car would move past.

It didn't.

To my dismay, it stopped across the street from me. I heard the engine shut down. The lights went off. As the door opened and footsteps began echoing off the pavement, I silently slid under my car and out of sight.

Did this person live nearby? Then why were they moving around the back of my car instead of towards their house? Had someone spotted me? Has someone called the cops? Had one of the no-neck guards recognized me as I turned around down the street from the front gate?

I had been very careful. No one could have spotted me. So who was standing by my car?

My hand slid under my coat to my gun.

"Are you going to stay under there all night?" a familiar voice asked, then laughed softly.

I scooted out and stood up, anger in my eyes. "What are you doing here? You should be at Family Home Evening."

"Do you really think I don't know your tricks by now?"

"What tricks?"

"I tell you Wednesday night and you show up on Monday night because you know I won't be here."

"Jackson, I can't let you do this. You're a police officer. A stunt like this could get you fired. I can't do that to you."

"And if the roles were reversed?"

"That's different."

"Yeah I know." He stared at me then smiled. "I left my badge and gun at home. This is just me helping a friend. Now do you want to talk all night or get over the wall?"

Using all of our professional training we were over the wall in seconds, landing in a small park neatly tucked in between the large houses. Giant trees lined the wall, adding to the security of keeping unwelcome and potentially prying eyes out.

We silently made our way through the park. Bright street lights could be seen along the wide streets, but none lined the park, giving it a somewhat ominous look in the dark.

Our eyes alert to every possible sound or movement, we glided between empty slides, sand boxes, merry-go-round, jungle gym, and swings gently swaying in the night breeze.

Once we left the park we stayed in the shadows of the trees lining the street or pasted ourselves to the darkness provided by the side of the houses.

Leading the way, I guided us carefully down the various streets until we came to the back side of the house next door to the one owned by Rulon Peterson.

From our vantage point in the shadows, we could see two large goons standing near the back door. Both were carrying rifles and wearing side arms. One, who must have thought he was Indiana Jones, was wearing a fedora and chain-smoking. The other was playing something on his iPhone. As they were otherwise occupied, Jackson and I had no trouble scooting to Peterson's house and flattening ourselves within the shadows of the back side. Edging our way to the front of the house, we peered around the corner. Two more large and well-armed n o - n e c k g o o n s were stationed in front of the lighted door. How in the world was this guy able to attract so many goons? What happened to small, squirrelly accountant-type guys who were there because no one else wanted them?

"How do you want to play this?" Jackson nodded towards the two guys standing by the door. "We can't just rush them. They'll alert the whole place before we can get there.

"Then we give them what they expect," I replied.

"Which is?"

"An intruder. Since they have all these guards to keep out reporters and the paparazzi, we'll give them what they fear most."

"A situation where they'll react instead of think," Jackson mused. "Not bad. Who gets to be the reporter?"

"Neither, but I get to be the guard rallying the troops. You get to be the Ninja who sneaks up on the other guard and knocks him out."

"How come I don't get to be the guard rallying the troops?"

"Because they won't be able to see you in the dark."

He looked at me and deadpanned. "Really, black jokes?"

"Ninja jokes. There's a difference." I looked at him and smiled. "Be the dark."

"You're not funny, you know."

"I'm very funny."

"No, funny would be one of the idiots shooting first and asking questions later when you show your face."

"Really, dead jokes now?"

"Bullet humor. There's a difference," he smiled.

"Since the gate is over there," I said pointing south, "I'll work my way to the other side of the house and signal you when I'm in position."

"And then what?"

"Like you said, these goons are conditioned to react at the first threat of a breach. Hopefully, when I sound the alarm of reporters at the front gate, one of these clowns will rush to help me. When he does you take care of the remaining one."

"And if they both rush to help you?"

"I shoot them."

"Funny."

"Let's hope they aren't that stupid," I sighed.

He shrugged. My confidence soared like a chicken trying to fly.

Hoping I knew what I was doing, I rushed across the street and behind one of the large trees that guarded Ruth Mosley's house. Moving from one tree to the other, I prayed that no one was actually looking out their window. I rushed across the street to the house on the other side of Peterson's. Pausing to catch my breath, I waited, listening for any sound that might indicate someone had seen or heard me. There was nothing.

I watched to make sure the no-necks at the back were not on a routine patrol. When no one showed their face around the back corner, I dashed to the near side of the house. After a moment I crept my way to the front and peered around. I could see the two guards at the front door. They looked bored and ready to fall asleep. That was a good sign. If they had been rigid and staring straight ahead, my ill-conceived plan would have no chance. Trained guards don't allow distractions to interrupt their duty. I was betting my life that these were not trained guards. Of course part of that not thinking and just reacting could be shooting first and asking questions later. I didn't relish the thought of bullet holes in me.

As I peered around the corner once more, I noticed Jackson. I nodded and moved back behind the house to prepare myself for my Academy Award-winning performance. A moment later I felt the cold, hard steel against my neck. So much for my award-winning performance.

Thirty

I stood motionless as the distinctive shape of a gun pressed harder into my neck.

"What are you doing here?" Fedora asked.

"Looking for an extra wife?" I quipped.

The gun barrel lowered from my neck to my back. He shoved it with extreme force into my kidney, causing pain to shoot up my back.

"Another word and I'll drop you right here."

No sense of humor.

"Start walking," he commanded.

If I whipped around to my left maybe I could catch him off guard and hit him upside the head with my extended elbow. Maybe I could disarm him. Maybe I could get shot too. I chose door number three and began walking instead.

He spoke into the microphone on his shoulder. "Intruders," he said softly. "Check the grounds immediately."

As we moved down the side of the house, the area was

immediately swarmed with bodyguards. These boys were serious with their security. Who knew?

Rounding the corner, we were met by Jackson being escorted by two other no-neck brutes. So much for plan A, B or C.

Within minutes we were ushered into the presence of Rulon Peterson. He was sitting behind his large desk his nose buried in the diary. Joshua stood near-by. They looked up with surprise as we were shoved into the room.

"We found them sneaking around outside," Fedora said.

"Check around for anyone else," Joshua immediately ordered.

Peterson's eyes narrowed as he quickly closed the diary and stared at us. "Who are you?"

"Professional diary hunters," I quipped.

"You're dumber than you look, Crockett," Joshua smiled with as much sincerity as a politician with his hand in your pocket.

"I work at it."

"To what do we owe this surprise visit?" Peterson asked.

"I guess the angels didn't tell you we were coming, huh?" I responded.

"Please do not make light of spiritual things," Peterson said. A pained look crossed his face.

"Spiritual men don't use God for their own carnal desires," Jackson remarked matter-of-factly.

Peterson stared at us, then, as if he was talking to his followers, spoke in a quiet voice. "It is hard for sinners to understand the ways of God. Jesus said in order to understand and know if his ways were true, we had to live them."

Jackson's rebuff was sharp and to the point. "Jesus didn't marry off young girls to his apostles."

The old man kneaded his chin between his thumb and index finger, staring at us as if we just didn't understand. With a sad shake of his head, he reached for his cell phone.

"You are trespassing."

"Go ahead and call the police," I challenged. "I am sure they will be interested in hearing about how the owner of that diary is lying in a coma in a hospital after being beaten nearly to death and how you came to have it."

"I have no idea what you are talking about," Peterson answered calmly.

"I'm talking about your muscle boys, including this moron, beating the crap out of me and stealing the diary," I responded angrily.

His eyebrows shot skyward, then fell back to earth. He put the phone down on the desk. Glancing toward Mosley he asked. "Is that true?"

Mosley glared at me, then turned meekly towards Peterson. "I went to ask him for the diary and things just got out of hand."

"Joshua, violence is never our way. You know that."

Mosley looked like a puppy hit with a rolled up newspaper as he lowered his head and stood silently.

I said. "Give us the diary and we'll walk out of here."

Peterson picked up the diary and laid it near the edge of the large walnut desk.

"Joshua was wrong taking it from you." He blinked, his lips tightened as he struggled to regain his grandfatherly veneer. "I'm afraid it was my fault. I wanted to read it and I said we needed to get it. I'm afraid Joshua misunderstood my meaning."

"A failure to communicate, huh?" I asked in my best *Cool Hand Luke* voice.

He ignored it, or had never seen the movie.

"I'm sure you understand how fragile our standing in the community is. When it comes to polygamy, a young woman speaking ill of us, especially in such a hypersensitive community, could have dangerous repercussions for our families. It was my hope to avoid such a problem."

Jackson brushed by Mosley, moving closer to the desk. "What reason would she have to talk ill of you?"

He stared as if we would never understand. Then, with the patience of a kindergarten teacher, he continued. "We are an easy target. For those filled with political agendas, it is easy to take something as innocent as a request to join our family and turn it into a failed seduction in order to stir up emotions against us. Surely you can understand that?"

"Was it a failed seduction?" I asked bitterly.

"It was no seduction at all, only a few phone calls and visits to allow her to get to know us better. When she decided against joining us, we parted on friendly terms."

"Then why steal the diary?"

"As I have explained that was not my intention. I don't expect you to believe me, but I can only offer you my most sincere apology for what was done to you. I can assure you those responsible have been dealt with."

I looked at Mosley. He didn't look like he had been dealt with. Jackson ambled to the desk where Peterson was sitting and motioned towards the box of tissues sitting there.

Peterson nodded. "By all means."

Taking a tissue from the box, Jackson used it to pick up the diary. "Then we'll take this and be on our way."

Peterson's passive face suddenly looked concerned, but just as quickly the grandfatherly mask was back. Mosley wasn't as subtle. His eyes closed to slits. He glanced to Peterson, who remained calm.

Jackson handed me the diary, which I dropped in a plastic bag I removed from my pocket. "Fingerprints," I smiled. "Just in case we need them."

Peterson's face went ashen as it dawned on him. His mellifluousness quickly disappeared and his voice became harsh and brittle. "You obtained them illegally."

"You just handed it to us," I corrected. "There is nothing illegal about that."

"Sir, I'm not sure this is a good idea," Mosley said to Peterson, his eyes never leaving me.

"Joshua, I believe you have things that need to be taken care of. You may go prepare."

Mosley didn't like being dismissed, especially in front of us. He continued to stare at me, then, finally, like a petulant child, stormed out of the room. It wasn't long before the front door slammed.

"I must again apologize for Joshua. He is very loyal and sometimes gets carried away."

"If you call assault and battery getting carried away," I reminded him.

"Please do not judge him too harshly. He has a good heart, but sometimes he takes protecting this church a little too seriously."

He rose and came around the desk. "I hope there are no hard feelings." He took my hand in his. "You have my word that Joshua will be punished for his transgressions." He smiled his best plastic smile as he let go of my hand.

I returned his plastic smile with my best running-for-office smile. "If I find out you had anything to do with the beating of Jennifer Justice, you won't have to worry about the police or reporters bothering you, because when I'm finished there won't be enough of you or this place left to bother with."

We left him standing in the middle of the room, the smile still frozen on his face.

The night air felt good as we stepped out of the house. The street was well lit and the houses seemed like giant soldiers standing in a row guarding the beautiful manicured yards.

No longer having to hide our presence, we strolled down the sidewalk toward the park and the wall we had climbed over.

It was strangely quiet, which added to the beauty of the

cool night.

"He should have been an actor," Jackson said as we moved down the empty sidewalk.

"Why do you say that?"

"When you told him about being beaten, he acted genuinely surprised."

"So?"

"So, then he told you that those responsible had already been dealt with? He already knew about it," Jackson continued.

"You think he was just performing for our benefit?"

We came to the small park, passing swings and other toys as we reached the wall we had climbed over.

"I think he is knee deep in this, and Joshua is his enforcer," Jackson replied.

"Which means everything that has happened probably has Peterson's fingerprints all over it."

"Including the diary, which we now have back in our possession."

"But not for long," a voice sounded out of the dark.

Both Jackson and I turned as Mosley and two other members of the goon squad stepped from behind the large trees. I glanced at Jackson, then faced Mosley as he moved closer to us, a gun in his hand.

"No sniper rifle this time?"

He looked at me quizzically. "What are you talking about?"

"A week ago at my house, taking a shot at me?"

"You're crazy. I don't hide like a cowardly sniper. I like to see who I'm teaching a lesson to."

"Lesson?" I sneered. "And just what lesson could you possibly teach us?"

"That after all your deceitful efforts, you are still going to crawl out of here empty-handed."

I moved closer to him, my eyes never leaving his. "That's

not going to happen, but if you want a beating, I'm more than willing to give it to you."

"I guess the lesson we gave you before wasn't good enough."

"I've always been a slow learner," I grinned. "How about another lesson? I motioned towards the gun. "That is if you are man enough to face me one-on-one."

"Why don't I just shoot you and take what I want?"

He had a point, one I wasn't fond of, but a point nonetheless.

"That's what most cowards would do," I snorted disgustedly, hoping to get under his thin skin.

"You think I'm afraid of you? You think I'm a coward?"

"You're the one with the gun and the two bodyguards to hide behind."

"I don't need them or anyone else."

"And yet here they are."

He stared at me as if trying to decide if he really could take me. He must have decided I was no threat. He tossed the gun to one of his no-neck friends and grinned like I was a piece of meat he was about to devour.

"I have God on my side."

He also had about fifty pounds and three inches on me.

Without warning, he charged, like a deadly bull charging a matador.

Unlike our last meeting, I was ready. I sidestepped him and brought down both of my fisted hands in the middle of his back. He crashed to the ground. But, to, my surprise, he rolled and jumped up. He swung at me with his right, but I blocked it and countered with my own right, which landed on his jaw. His head snapped as he weaved sideways. Not wanting him to get any momentum, I stepped forward, twisted sideways, and landed a kick to his stomach. As he backed up, I leaped into the air and slammed my foot into the side of his head. He dropped.

As he tried to get up, I grabbed him by his loose shirt and began pounding him with my fist. He fell to the ground. I waited as he rolled onto his knees and tried to get to his feet.

"Maybe God is busy doing something else," I chided.

Groggily, he climbed to his feet. Jackson shook his head at me. It was over. But the anger was still seething in me. Anger from being shot at. Anger from being jumped and beaten by cowards. Anger from seeing a beautiful young woman lying in a coma. Anger from having to deal with morons, and every other anger festering in my soul.

I grabbed him by the shirt and slammed him up against the tree, our faces inches from each other. The blood pouring from his nose spilled onto my hands and all over my jacket. I didn't care.

"You better pray you personally didn't have anything to do with Jennifer's beating. If I find out you did, you are going down. You got that?" He tried to resist, but my grip on him was so tight he couldn't.

"And just so you understand, God won't be on your side next time either. He hates wife beaters as much as I do."

I let him fall. He hit the ground with a thud and remained still.

The other guards stood there looking confused. Should they interfere or let us go? They decided on the latter.

"Here."

Jackson handed me a handkerchief. I wiped Joshua's blood from my hand and handed it back to him.

He shook his head. "Consider it a gift," he smiled.

I balled it up and stuffed it in my inside jacket pocket.

With one last look at Mosley, Jackson and I climbed over the wall and disappeared on the other side.

THIRTY ONE

I stared at the diary sitting on my counter. It seemed like years ago since Jackson had dropped it on my office desk and challenged me to read it. Since then I had found Jenny J, but not who had hurt her.

Sam finished his food and made his way to the couch. It was his evening nap time. I followed with my Chinese takeout.

Opening the boxes of fried rice, sweet and sour chicken and walnut shrimp, I dumped them onto a plate and picked up my fork. I know, suave and intellectual guys always eat with chopstick and never spill a drop. I spill like a two-year-old and hate chopsticks.

I took a bite of my sweet and sour chicken. At that moment the phone rang. Why is it always when your mouth is full of food that the phone rings? I glanced at the number and didn't recognize it. I answered anyway. Maybe it would be a cute sounding telemarketer who would spend hours trying to sell me something I didn't want or need. I needed a date and soon.

"Crockett Investigations."

"Hi, Mr. Crockett?" The voice on the other end sounded young, excited. Hello, cute telemarketer.

"This is Regina, from La Caille."

I sat up and pressed the phone closer to my ear. I didn't need anything anyway.

"Yes, Regina."

Her voice became a little more than a whisper. "You asked me to call you when Mr. Parker and Ms. Collingsworth came in. They have just been seated."

"Thanks, Regina. I owe you."

La Caille was about thirty minutes from my house, which meant I would have to hurry in order to get there before they left. One last bite of sweet and sour chicken and I was out the door.

I arrived at La Caille and gave my dirty Honda Accord to the valet parking. He didn't seem excited to take the keys.

I rushed inside the turret door. Regina had reserved a table hidden from their view for me. I ordered coffee and a dessert. Even that was more than I could afford.

Abigail Collingsworth looked like a supermodel. She was wearing a dark, low-cut dress that hugged her ample figure. I could swear she had been poured into it.

Score one for Martin Parker.

They seemed comfortable together as they sipped wine, waiting for their meal. Every so often she would laugh and reach over and take his hand. His eyes never left her. He seemed to be completely mesmerized. I wondered if Parker had been similarly mesmerized with Sylvia in the beginning, or had it always been about business and climbing the corporate ladder?

An hour and a half later, after dining on shrimp cocktail, beet salad, lamb piled high on fluffy mashed potatoes, and finishing it off with a decadent looking dessert and

Irish coffee, Parker paid the bill and they left. I followed them down Little Cottonwood Canyon to Thirteenth East, where they turned left, meandering through various neighborhoods until they came to a large gated community in the hills of Draper. After showing the bored looking guard something, they were buzzed through the locked gates.

I waited until they had disappeared before I approached the gate. The guard slid his window open.

"Hi," I said in my friendliest voice. He didn't seem impressed.

"I'm with Martin and Abigail. Have they arrived yet?"

"You have a pass?"

"Martin said I didn't need one. He said just tell you I was with him."

"No one is allowed in without a pass from one of the residences."

He glanced from me to the small television on in his booth. The Jazz and the Sacramento Kings.

"How are the Jazz doing?"

"Getting beat," he replied despondently.

"By the Kings," I asked surprised, hoping to build a Jazz rapport with him.

"They can't stop the three pointers," he replied disgustedly.

"When have they ever?"

"You got that right," he agreed nodding his head.

I pulled two Jazz tickets from my glove compartment. In sports-crazy, Salt Lake City, Jazz, Utes, or BYU tickets have opened more doors than keys.

"Look, I can see you'd much rather be watching the game than having to deal with guys like me, so if you could just let me through, I won't bother you anymore."

"I wish I could but without a pass I can't."

"Will this do?" I held out the Jazz tickets. "Upper bowl, but still great seats for Thursday's game against the Lakers."

He stared at the tickets and then at the list of names on his clipboard. "I am off on Thursday. I really would like to see that game."

"And I'd really like to give them to you. It's a win-win for both of us. What do you say?"

"Hell with it." He stepped out of the booth and quickly wrote down my license number. "If you do something stupid, I've got your number."

"Nothing stupid planned, just a friendly visit with friends who forgot to give me a pass."

He opened the gate. "By the way, what's the address Martin and Abigail were going to?" I held the tickets out for him.

"2235 Panga Circle," he said quickly before ripping the tickets out of my hand.

I drove through the gate.

2235 Panga Circle was a large Southern-styled house with a circled driveway. I parked across the street and watched. Within minutes, four cars drove up and parked. Expensively dressed single men emerged from their BMW, Lexus, Mercedes, and Jaguar, respectively. At the door, each man checked in with two large security guards, who checked their names off on a list after being shown a card. Only then were they were allowed into the house. Whatever was going on was for exclusive members only and no one without an invitation.

From the number of cars parked out front, it seemed too small for a political fund raiser, which Collingsworth was known for throwing. And social events were not usually held at private residences. Whatever it was, I was not about to get in, which made me even more curious. Lifting my camera from the passenger's seat, I settled in to see just who came out of this private event.

Three hours later the door opened and the first man came out. I began snapping shots. I didn't know him or the next four men, but the fifth gentleman was State Senator Tom Holden. What was he doing there without his wife?

I continued snapping photos. Whoever these men were, they were successful. Their suits were tailor-made, their cars expensive, and each one had spent the evening in a large expensive house without their wives. What kind of social or political event was this without wives? That didn't make sense. Or did it?

I got out of the car and made my way towards the side of the house. A tall locked iron gate was my only obstacle. Looking around for cameras, I noticed one moving back and forth covering this gate. I figured I had about ten seconds before it came back. I was up and over in six. The curtains on each side window were closed tight. I moved around towards the back. The backyard was enormous, filled with trees and flower beds. A beautiful rock waterfall sat at the edge of one of the rock paths that led through the immaculately landscaped yard. On the polished wooden deck was a large hot tub. Inside, four stunning young girls were lounging in the warm water, laughing and enjoying themselves, All were early twenties. And naked.

This had all the ear markings of a high-class sex party. I was beginning to understand how Abigail Collingsworth had risen so fast in the local social and political scenes.

Using a large, perfectly trimmed Lime-Lite Hydrangea bush with its full white blooms to protect me from the camera, I snapped photos of the yard, the back of the house and the girls in the hot tub (for research of course) then rushed back to my car.

***

The next evening I called, Boudreau. It was 6:30 p.m., but I knew he would still be working. He spent more time at his office than he did at his home.

I was praying that he had the information I needed. I was counting on the fact that the brownish stain was indeed tobacco juice and that Boudreau had been able to pull DNA from it. Of course, if it was just dirt I was up the creek.

Wyler left at 6:00 p.m., which meant Justin would answer the phone. I was wrong.

"Medical office, Wesley Wyler speaking."

"Bucking for overtime, Wyler."

"One moment please."

He was growing on me.

"David Crockett, what a surprise." The voice was low and gruff.

"Justin, please tell me you have good news."

"You want the good news first, or the great news?"

I couldn't help but smile. "Let's go great and work our way back to good."

"The rock you brought in was covered with tobacco juice. I was able to pull DNA off of it."

"Anybody we have in the system?"

"Yes." He paused and I could hear papers being shuffled as if looking up the name. "Do you know a Karl Stallings?"

"Stallings?" I asked in disbelief. "Are you sure?"

"One hundred percent."

"I'll be damned." He had actually tried to make good on his wild threat. As I thought back to the trial, I suddenly remembered that he had been in the Army and served a tour in Vietnam. He was also an expert marksman and had been a sniper there. Now it was beginning to make sense. I shivered at the thought of how lucky I was to be alive.

"Thanks, Justin. I really appreciate that. What's the good news?"

"I'm sending you a copy of my findings now."

I took out my cell phone.

"The pills were from the same batch that killed Sylvia Parker."

"Then the only way they could have gotten on the floor by her bed was if she had been trying to spit them out."

"Her DNA was found on the pills. There is no doubt they came from her mouth."

I raised my fist in a victorious fist pump. "What about the bruise on her face?"

"I would say the gloves you brought me match the slight ridge I found, but it is only an educated guess. Without digging up the body, there is really no way to conclusively match the gloves to the slight discoloration on the face."

"But the possibility exists?"

"Yes. Now answer me a question. The air conditioner. Are we talking about Sylvia Parker?"

"Yes."

"When I got there the room was colder than the rest of the house. My first inclination was that the air conditioner had been on, but there was no way I could substantiate it." He paused and I could hear his deep breath. "You have proof that the air conditioner had been on?"

"I spoke to the man who turned it off about twenty minutes before the police arrived."

"That could have thrown my estimated time of death off for sure."

"By how much?"

"As much as a day."

"Are you saying it's possible he could have killed her Friday night, turned the air conditioner up full blast so that it would look like she had been killed no later than Saturday night?"

"It's possible, yes."

"Thanks, Justin, I owe you."

"That you do, my boy. One of those heavenly hamburgers

from your friend's restaurant should suffice nicely."

"I'll bring it by personally for lunch tomorrow." I hung up.

I checked to make sure Justin's medical report concerning the pills, the bruise, and the revised time of death had been sent to my IPhone. It had. Having talked to Jackson an hour ago, I knew he was still at the Federal Building. He had wanted proof and I now had it. Martin Parker was going to jail.

I grabbed a piece of cold chicken on the way out the door. I should have grabbed my Helo SR25.

Thirty Two

Karl Stallings sat waiting.

He had monitored the house for the past week. He knew the construction crews left at three. He waited until five and always had the place to himself. It was a perfect spot. The only drawback was the fact that, in the evening, he never knew if or when Crockett might leave his house. But it had to be evening so as not to come face to face with the daily crews working on the house. It was inconvenient, but that was okay. He had waited in far worse conditions in Nam. When Crockett did leave his house, he wouldn't get far.

Seeing all the curtains closed had made him smile. He knew Crockett was afraid. That was good. He wanted him to be afraid. Actually, he wanted him dead. And the time had come.

When he pulled out of his garage and backed out onto the street he would stop the car before pulling forward. When he did he would be in the cross hairs. A fraction of a second was all he needed. In that moment, Crockett would be as dead as his name-sake. "Remember the Alamo," he chuckled, then spit his chew into the dirt outside the house.

Resting his rifle on a small crossbeam of the living room framing, he glanced around at the area. There was nothing that could ever identify him as the shooter. Once the shot was fired, he would pick up the cartridge, break down his gun, put it in his empty tool box and casually walk to his car. He had left his car one block over on a crowded street so he would be able to blend in. Even if someone did see him, he was dressed like all the other construction workers, so no one would give him a second look. He would be just a dedicated worker staying late to finish the job. His lifestyle had always forced him to blend in, to be like everyone else so as to hide his real intent. He had become very good at it. Today was no exception.

The thought of killing Crockett and then casually walking away made him chuckle. It was indeed a great day to die—at least for Crockett.

Next he would take care of his inept defense lawyer, and the prosecutor, and the incompetent judge who didn't have the courage to throw the case out like he should have. All of them would pay for the misery and pain they had caused him.

Two blocks to the west, he saw the garage door go up. He spit his tobacco juice into the outside dirt again. He was careful about that. The dirt would swallow it up. And even if it didn't, with all the workers coming and going, it would be quickly trampled into oblivion.

Smoothly he readied his rifle. It was show time.

***

I pulled my Honda out of the garage. I was so pumped about Martin Parker going to jail that I backed into the street faster than I anticipated. I immediately slammed on my brakes harder than I had intended, sending me forward like a crash test dummy.

That's when something jolted my driver's side window.

I had been expecting this and I was ready. A day after the first attempt on my life, I had paid a friend of mine to install bulletproof windows on my car. I had kept all the drapes in my house closed so the only way he could get to me was the exact way it was happening. I had spent two days combing the area above the front side of my house and had found the place that, from my experience, offered the clearest shot as I pulled into the street. It was an empty house two blocks east and directly above my house. It sat in a cul-a-sac with four other homes, all under construction. It was private and the only one facing my house. He had already tried from the back. Now the only other logical spot was from the front.

On sheer instinct, I hit the gas, sliding towards the side of the street and the protection of a cluster of large oak trees that lined the sidewalk. I knew where he was. I also knew, I hoped, just how he would be making his getaway.

I raced to the cross street, turned left and sped to the street where the houses under construction sat. Speeding past it, I continued until I was a block on the other side. The only escape he had was to have parked his car east of where he had fired. It was the only completed development in the area that was full of parked cars and people inside their houses. After thoroughly checking it out, I had come to the conclusion that it was the best escape route, since he could blend in without anyone noticing. As illogical as it sounded, it was much safer than trying to run through people's backyards making his escape. That would merit a call to the police if anyone saw him. While I wasn't a hundred percent sure this was the case, I was sure enough to race towards it.

I reached the street and yanked the car to the left, sliding into the middle of the street and braking hard. My Honda screeched to a halt in the middle of the road.

I reached into the glove compartment and removed a small, powerful set of binoculars. Training it on the end of the long street, I waited. I felt like a gunfighter waiting at one end of the street for his enemy to walk into the dusty street to face him. I was going to end this in the only way I knew how, with deadly force.

Karl Stallings had gone to prison because he was a scumbag preying on innocent people. He had made a living bilking hundreds of hardworking people out of hundreds of thousands of dollars. The expiration date for sympathy for him had expired. He deserved the prison time he had received, and he was deserving of what he was about to get.

My wait was short. Down the street came a non-descript, beat up red Ford, doing the speed limit so as not to attract any attention. Or maybe it wasn't capable of going any faster.

The driver was Karl Stallings. His three-year prison stay hadn't changed him much. His silver hair was still wavy and his skin still tanned. But his handsome face now had an added feature. Across his cheek I noticed an ugly scar. It was most likely a souvenir from his prison stay. Maybe that was what fueled his thirst for revenge.

Removing my Sig, I jumped out of my car and stood in the middle of the road. Instantly the car took on speed. It raced towards me with one intention, to kill me. I raised my gun and waited. When he was within fifty-yard, I fired four of the thirteen rounds in rapid succession. His right tire exploded and the car jerked sideways. He tried to brake but lost control, sending the car directly into the path of a large oak tree.

There was no need to hurry. The force with which the car had slammed into the tree left little doubt as to the end result. Still holding my Sig, I called Jackson.

"1236 East Olympic Parkway. You might want to notify the coroner."

"Stallings?"

"He had an accident." I hung up.

A man was dead. I felt numb, then, as callous as it sounds, relief.

THIRTY THREE

For the first time in months I felt relaxed as I sauntered into the bull pen of the Salt Lake Police Department. Not only was Stallings in hell but soon Martin Parker would be in jail. Life was good.

I was back again after having spent most of yesterday filling out paper work on the Stallings accident. The rifle found on him was a perfect match for the bullets that Geoff Lamb had pulled from my kitchen wall. There was no doubt that Karl Stallings had been my sniper.

Harry Reed and his brain-dead partner, Jeremiah Cummings, were assigned the case. They found my photos marked with "death" on Stallings bulletin board, also my address, and a detailed map to my house. They found a schedule for one of the near-by shooting ranges, and had interviewed witnesses who placed Stallings there day after day for a month.

A quick call to the Utah State Prison had told them that

Stallings had been raped while in prison. The scar across his face was a constant visual reminder of his stay there. His hatred for me, and everyone else he blamed for his situation, had burned white hot.

Even with all the evidence, motive and means, Reed and Cummings still made me sit through two hours of questioning, just to annoy me. How did I know I was shooting at the right guy? Had I used deadly force without just cause? Why hadn't I called the police instead of taking matters into my own hands? Did I have a permit for my Sig? Would it have bothered me if I had shot the wrong guy? I answered all of their hare-brained questions until they finally got tired of busting my chops. I was eventually cleared of any wrong doing.

I took the rest of the day off, got some Mexican food for me, some chicken and liver for Sam, and rented a movie. Somehow, *Die Hard* seemed appropriate.

The next day I sat down beside Jackson's immaculately clean desk and began pleading my case concerning Martin Parker. He listened quietly, stirred some honey into his herb tea then leaned back.

"They don't arrest like everyone else."

"What does that mean?" I shot back as Jackson casually took a sip of his tea.

"It means they have an army of lawyers and friends that play golf with the police commissioner and the mayor. The rich don't play by the same rules as we do. You know that."

"Dammit, Jackson, we can't just let him get away with murder." My voice was much louder than I wanted. I looked around the bull pen at the other detectives. No one was paying any attention to us.

Well, almost no one.

Harry Reed was glaring daggers at me. As lead detective on the Parker case, he had ruled it a suicide, and, as far as he was concerned, that was the end of it. I tried to talk to him about the case when Faith first approached me, but he completely shut me down. "The case is closed and I don't need some two-bit private eye sticking his nose where it doesn't belong. You got that, Crockett?" he had yelled at me.

Obviously, I didn't.

Needless to say, he had been less than helpful. His unwillingness to help me went much deeper than this case. We genuinely disliked each other, which was why he had made me sit for hours answering question about Stallings.

I watched as he ambled over to us.

"Still putting your nose where it doesn't belong, Crockett?"

"Still got brown on yours, I see."

He moved towards me, but Jackson stood. "We're talking here Harry. It doesn't concern you."

"The hell it doesn't. It's my case this asshole is messing with and I don't like it."

"I said, it doesn't concern you. Now get back to your desk before you say something you'll regret."

Reed stared at Jackson, trying to out man him. He didn't have a chance. Jackson was as tough as they came. I had never seen him back down from anyone. Well – except Julie.

Reed broke eye contact first. He shifted his gaze from Jackson to the clean desk, then to the floor. "I don't like him trying to make me look bad," he mumbled.

"You don't need me for that, Reed," I shot back.

"Stop it, David." Jackson said sharply.

"Come on, Paine," Reed whined. "If it was one of your cases you'd bitch and moan too."

I gave him my most innocent and sincere look. "But not as good as you, Harry. When it comes to bitching and moaning, no one does it better."

Who said I couldn't say nice things?

"I said enough, David," Jackson snapped.

Reed clinched his jaw. His hands balled up into fists as he glared at me. Finally, he turned and stormed back to his desk.

Jackson sat back down. "Why do you antagonize him so much?"

"I hate blowhards who think they know it all."

"What about you?"

"I *do* know it all. There's a difference."

He shook his head and looked down at his immaculately clean desk. "I can't arrest Parker, David. I just can't"

"But the evidence suggests that he killed his wife."

"That's the problem."

"What?"

"It suggests, it doesn't prove. You have to bring me something so concrete that a good defense lawyer won't shoot holes in."

"How about an eyewitness or a confession?"

"Bingo."

"I hate bingo."

"That's what I thought. Until then, quit wasting my time on this. And stay away from Harry. He's a pain in the butt without you antagonizing him."

Thirty Four

A week after I had snapped pictures of those coming and going from the social party hosted by Parker and Collingsworth, I discovered I wasn't the only one snapping secret pictures.

In my usual spot at Katie Blues, I noticed "Beatle Brow" sitting uncomfortably at the counter. I also noticed him staring overtly at me every few minutes.

"1966." Darlene interrupted my train of thought. "Stop, Stop, Stop."

I waited for the information to pop into my brain but nothing came. Now, to add to my troubles, Darlene was about to be victorious. I hated that.

"I'm waiting."

"So am I," I confessed. "I'm drawing a blank.

She sat my food down. "Don't feel too bad," she laughed. It wasn't one of their bigger hits anyway. The Hollies. It entered the top ten in December of 1966 at number ten, jumped to number 6 the following week, then disappeared." She turned to go.

"Hey?"

She stopped.

"Do you know that guy in the plaid shirt sitting at the counter?"

"Not really." She glanced at him then back to me. "He's been in here a few times but that's all." She paused. "Come to think about it, the first time he was in here he asked about you."

"Me?"

"Yeah. He wanted to know if you were a stand up kind of guy. I told him no, but that we all still loved you. He looked disappointed, like he had no idea I was joking, and went back to his food."

"Thanks." She drifted back to work.

Ten minutes later, Beatle Brow finally got up the nerve to approach me.

"Mr. Crockett?" He stood nervously at my booth.

"Please call me David. Have a seat, Mister—?

"Bobalow. Robert Bobalow."

Bob Bobalow? Suddenly I didn't feel so bad about David Crockett.

He slid into the seat across from me.

"What can I do for you, Mr. Bobalow?"

"What we say..." he paused and glanced nervously around as if cops were sitting at every table listening. Satisfied he continued. "What we say, is just between me and you, right?"

"No." I took a drink. "If you hire me, I keep everything we say between us. If, however, the cops subpoena me, I am obligated to tell them everything I know.

"But you don't talk unless you have to, right?"

"What's this all about, Mr. Bobalow?" I reached for my hamburger to take a bite.

"Murder."

Once again I set my hamburger down. He had my attention.

"Who?"

"Let's just say an acquaintance of mine."

"Is this acquaintance of yours someone you met on the inside?"

He again, glanced around the room, his eyes darting all around under his heavy dark brows.

"I can't help you unless you tell me everything."

He looked around once more then leaned across the table.

"Two months ago me and a friend got invited to this party." He shoved a large envelope towards me, nodding for me to open it. I did. Inside were 8x10 black and white photos of various people in various stages of undress. The men were older looking. The women were all young and hot.

"A sex party?"

"Yeah. We were surprised too because we didn't know the people that invited us. Turns out they needed our services."

"What kind of services?"

"Breaking and entering. My friend was one of the best."

"What about you?"

"I keep a low profile."

I thought back to the night I had followed Martin Parker and Abigail Collingsworth to the ritzy neighborhood.

"Let me guess, your friend was Johnny Lee Baker."

"How'd you know?"

"Just an educated guess."

"He's dead ,and I'm afraid I'm next."

"Has anyone contacted you personally?"

"No. I mean, I don't know nothing anyway. The night Johnny hit the place I was laid up with the flu."

"Then why send you photos?"

"That's the strange part. Look at me, you think I'm going to take my clothes off and do that kind of stuff?"

He removed a note from his pocket. "This came with the photos." It was a plain sheet of copy paper with the words: *Silence is Golden and ensures a life outside of Prison.*

"So they're trying to ensure your silence concerning his crime. What did he steal?"

"Nothing. He just replaced one will with another one. And some legal papers, contracts or something.

"A will? Are you sure?"

"Yeah, that's what he told me. Said it was easy money, some big law firm downtown."

Richard Harvey's office. Suddenly it was starting to make sense. Richard Harvey with his memory lapses, due to his accident, would not be able to say with any degree of certainty that he hadn't negotiated the changes. Martin Parker had, indeed, thought of everything.

"Look, I need protection. Can you do that sort of thing?"

"I'm not a bodyguard."

"Please, you gotta help me."

"Why not go to the police?"

"And tell them what? That I'm on parole and almost got involved in a B&E operation with someone who is now dead?"

Putting it that way, I could see his point. "Given your particular skill set, maybe you should return the favor. It's been my experience that people like these have egos too big not to take part in at least one party."

"What good would that do?"

"Depends on what you do with them. You know what they say, fresh air and nightly exercise is good for the soul."

He didn't seemed convinced. He left disappointed.

Lately I tended to affect people that way.

Thirty Five

I watched as Ruth walked to her car. She looked tired and worn out. Maybe the strain of keeping secrets was getting to her.

Mosley stealing the diary, and his actions the night we took it back, had shifted all my energy to him. As much as I hated to admit it, I had been wrong about Franklin. Not about him being a sniveling, cowardly abuser of women, but of having beaten Jennifer. His drunken alibi for the night Jennifer had been beaten and left at St. Mark's Hospital had proved to be correct. His frat buddies verified it with embarrassing pictures they had posted on Facebook. Some friends.

Joshua Mosley was the protector of The Eternal and True Church of Christ in the Last Days. And his actions towards me proved just how far he was willing to go. But as much as I felt it in my gut, I still had no concrete proof. I was hoping Ruth Mosley would be the answer. She had refused to talk. It was time to press her.

Shifting her book bag to her left shoulder, she put the key into her car door.

"Your husband is going to prison."

Ruth whirled around at the sound of my voice. Upon seeing me, I thought I saw relief on her face. It instantly disappeared as she gained control once more.

"If it's the last thing I do, that predator is going to prison where he belongs,"

She flinched, then quickly opened her door and threw her book bag inside.

"But don't worry, you can write to him from your own cell.

"I didn't do anything."

"A woman you know is lying in a coma because of you."

"I had nothing to do with that. I swear," she replied, desperation in her voice.

"Your word doesn't mean very much these days."

"Please, just leave me alone. You don't understand."

I removed my cell phone and pulled up a picture I had taken of Jennifer. "This is your fellow teacher. Have a good look." I held it up for her to see. She turned her head. I forced it back.

"This is what you did."

"I didn't," she whimpered and her eyes closed tightly.

"You know what I think? I think you tried to convince her to join your cult, to be your sister wife."

Her face shot up in surprise. "No!"

"What happened? Did she threaten to go to the police? Did she laugh at you and your husband? I bet that made your husband mad, a woman laughing at him. How could she laugh at such a serious proposal? After all, he must have been told by God to take another wife. Now, she was laughing at him, and at your beliefs. Is that what happened?"

Ruth shook her head and the tears started. I was making this up as fast as I could, but knew I had hit a nerve.

"He got mad, didn't he? He hit her and couldn't stop. How dare she defy him? So he kept beating her until she lay still on the ground. She was beaten to a pulp and you left her there to die."

The tears turned to sobs as she buried her face in her hands.

"It was my fault!" she whimpered. "I hurt her!" She turned to me with the pain of a thousand deaths on her face.

"She was my friend."

"What happened?"

"Joshua caught us together."

"Together? You mean at the High Class motel?"

She lowered her head and nodded, ashamed to look me in the eyes.

"You mean this was all about an affair?"

This shocked her. She looked at me with startled eyes.

"No," she said shaking her head violently from side to side. "I wasn't trying to get her into the family. She was trying to help me escape. She got hurt because of me."

The tears burst forth again as she leaned against her car.

I handed her a handkerchief. She wiped her eyes.

"She was trying to help me leave Joshua and the church. All I wanted was to get my life back. I just wanted out."

I stood there staring at her. I hadn't seen that coming.

A half hour later, we sat in a booth at Katie Blues. After all she had been through, Ruth wanted someone to know the truth.

"Jennifer seemed so happy. At school she smiled all the time and seemed to love life, even though I knew she didn't have much." She stopped talking as Darlene brought our drinks.

When Darlene left, Ruth glanced up at Katie sitting beside me. She had been very nervous at first, but having another woman sitting there seemed to calm her. Katie smiled and reached across the table and took her hand.

"Even though she wasn't married, she didn't worry about it," Ruth said wistfully. "I had always been taught that unless you were married at the sweet age—"

"Sweet age?" I asked curiously.

"We were taught that a young girl must be sweet and innocent when she is given to her husband. That shows obedience to God, and to the Prophet who gives you to your husband. Unless you are lucky enough to be presented to a man who can guide you and mold you to be obedient, you have no chance of going to heaven."

She looked up with hope in her face. "But Jennifer taught me so much. She told me the real truth about God's plan for us. She gave me hope that maybe I could get my life back. I was so excited that I made plans to leave Joshua. But she didn't want me to do it alone."

"So she tried to help you?"

Ruth nodded and lowered her head. Katie and I waited as she took a deep breath, forcing up painful memories. I moved her drink of hot herbal tea closer. She took a sip. Setting the cup back on the table, she interlocked her hands and began telling her story.

They had decided that the evening of the school's parent-teacher meeting was the best time to leave. It would give her an excuse to be late without alerting Joshua.

That night at nine she met Jenny in the parking lot.

Opening the door to Jenny's black 2002 Honda Civic, she jumped inside the passenger's seat.

"I don't know if I can do this, Jenny. What if Joshua finds out?"

"He won't. He has no reason to come here, and no one else knows about this. By the time he finds out, you will be safe in the local women's shelter.

"What if I don't fit in? What if no on accepts me?"

"You will. And I'll be here to help you."

Ruth struggled to fight back her tears. And fears.

"Ruth, it's going to be all right."

She looked up at the calm and smiling face of the friend who believed in her, who had accepted her for who she was. Jenny's courage was contagious.

"What do we do first?"

"The women's shelter is closed for the night so we will have to find a motel to stay in. Tomorrow morning we'll go to the shelter and ask for protection for you. It's all going to work out, Ruth. I promise."

Ruth nodded and tried to smile. "I hope so."

Jenny put the car in gear and pulled out of the parking lot. Neither of them noticed the large black pick-up truck that pulled out onto the street immediately after them.

Fifteen minutes later Jennifer pulled into the parking lot of the High Class Motel. It wasn't much of a motel, but they hoped its shabby appearance would prevent anyone from looking for them there.

Hiding her car near the back, Jennifer and Ruth made their way to the office. The room was empty and Jennifer pressed the bell.

Like the great and powerful OZ, a craggy-faced, middle-aged man with bad complexion and thinning hair quickly emerged from behind the curtain. Seeing two girls standing there, his eyes lit up. He smiled a crooked smile. "What can I do for you lovely ladies?"

"We'd like a room, please," Jennifer announced.

He gave them the once-over, lingering longer on Jennifer.

"Would you like a room with two single beds or a large double?"

Jenny glanced at Ruth who shrugged. "A double will be fine, thank you."

"That will be forty-two dollars."

Jennifer reached into her purse and removed the money.

"Will you be staying just for the one night?" he asked.

"Yes."

"Well, you two have a pleasant stay." He handed them the key. "Room 12, all the way to the back. Do you need any help with your luggage?"

"No thank you."

Jenny unlocked the door and Ruth entered first. They took in the dingy room. It was not much, but then again they would only be there for the night. Tomorrow they would be safely at the Utah Women's Shelter.

"Thank you, Jenny."

"For what?"

"For believing in me and for helping me find the the courage to seek the truth and follow it."

"Everything is going to be fine from now on," she smiled.

Then the door crashed open.

Joshua Mosley stood in the door way. A wicked smile crossed his face as he stepped into the room. Two of Rulon Peterson's guards followed him, shutting the door behind.

"You've been disobedient, Ruth."

"I want out, Joshua. I don't love you anymore."

"God doesn't like it when you are disobedient."

Jenny stepped in front of Ruth.

"God has nothing to do with this, and you know it. This is all about your own lust and power."

"Whores should keep their mouths shut." Quicker than she would have thought, Joshua's powerful hand slammed against her face. Jenny went tumbling to the floor.

"I don't blame you, Ruth. You were deceived by this whore of Babylon who wanted to lure you from God's happiness to her sinful world and eternal damnation.

"What happiness, Joshua? Where is the happiness?"

"You're happy because I say you are happy."

"She's not your slave. She's a human being with rights and agency," Jennifer screamed from the floor.

"What do you know?" He reached down and yanked

Jenny to her feet. Holding her arm tightly, he hit her with his free hand. Her head snapped back. His eyes grew dark and contemptuous as he held her tight.

"All this talk of freedom, yet you're more of a slave than she is."

He hit her again and again until the blood began pouring from her lips and nose. His words spat out like a machine gun. "You're a slave to immodesty, rampant sex, lying, cheating, and killing the souls of all those around you."

He continued hitting Jenny until she went limp. Reaching down, he lifted her up and hit her in the stomach. The air rushed out of her as she crashed upon the bed. He nodded to one of the goons, who lifted her up. With the goon holding her tightly, Joshua began beating the unconscious woman, hitting her again and again. Blood poured from her lips, mouth and nose, spattering against the walls, the floor and the bed.

Ruth grabbed his arm. "Joshua, stop! Please."

"She needs to be cleansed!" he yelled. "It is the only way to save her soul. She must be taught the price of disobedience."

He paused, his breathing ragged, his hands bloody.

Using all her strength, Ruth grabbed Joshua and pried him away from the battered girl. "Please, Joshua, stop it. I'll be good, I promise."

Joshua turned to her, his eyes ablaze with fury. "You did this. You forced me to do this. I didn't want to, but you forced me to protect the church and our family."

"I'm so sorry. I don't know what I was thinking." Ruth stared at the bloody body of her friend hanging helplessly in the arms of Rulon Peterson's body guard. With a nod, the goon moved and let the girl fall onto the bed, her blood soaking though the covers.

"Our work here is done."

He motioned to the two goons. "Clean this place up and

take the bedding and throw it in the trunk. We'll destroy it later. Make sure you wipe this place down. I mean good."

"What about her?" one of the goons asked.

Joshua stared at the limp body on the bed. "Dump her in the garbage bin. It's where she belongs."

He turned towards the door. Ruth jumped in front of him. "No." Her voice was strong and forceful. "We have to help her."

"We have helped her," he sneered. "She is no longer possessed with evil. God sent us to rid her of sin."

He reached for the door.

"I'll keep running away then. Every day if I have to until you kill me."

Joshua stopped and turned to face his rebellious wife.

Ruth forced herself to stare at him, locking her eyes onto his. She pushed the fear back inside her and stood her ground. Then, as calmly as she could, she spoke. "If you get help for her I won't try to escape. I'll be obedient to whatever you ask of me. I promise. Just help her."

For what seemed like hours, Joshua remained quiet. Finally he turned to the other two men who had stripped the bed and wiped down the walls.

"Get her in the car," he barked.

The guards lifted the limp woman, dragged her to the truck, and tossed her onto the floor between the seats. They crawled in, resting their feet on the unconscious girl.

When the car stopped a few miles later at St. Mark's Hospital, the two guards jumped out, yanked Jennifer's unconscious body out of the car, and dropped it onto the walkway in front of the emergency room door.

As they sped away, Ruth glanced back at the bloody body lying on the hard concrete.

Katie handed Ruth a napkin. Dabbing at her eyes, Ruth sat silently, her head lowered, her eyes down. For a while no one spoke.

"David, she can't go back there. She can stay with me until you throw that sorry wife-beating pig in jail."

"Will you testify to what you just told us?" I asked.

"No."

"No?"

"I mean yes, but no, I can't stay with you."

This caught us both by surprise.

"Why not?" Katie asked.

"Because if I don't show up, Joshua will know something is up, and he will take the family and flee. The church has safe houses all over the state for just this kind of emergency. You'll never find him, and he'll never pay for what he did to Jennifer."

"She's right," I reluctantly agreed. "If he rabbits, we may never find him."

"I have to go back until you are ready to arrest him. When he is in jail, I will testify against him and Rulon Peterson."

"Peterson? You mean he was involved in this?"

"He said God had told him that Jennifer was to be his wife. When she refused, it made all my old doubts resurface. She laughed at him, saying he was a crazy old man that God would punish one day for his sins. Later, he told me that God had told him that in order to save her soul, she had to be punished for her sins. I have no doubt he ordered the punishment Joshua gave her."

Rulon Peterson. That was one sorry old charlatan I wanted to bust.

Ruth looked at me with tears in her eyes. "I'm so sorry."

"For what?"

"For luring you to the park to be beaten. That too was Peterson's doing."

Now I really wanted the son-of-a-bitch.

I walked Ruth to her car. She opened the door, then stopped and turned to face me.

"May I ask you something?"

"Sure."

"The night you took the diary back and gave Joshua the beating he deserved, did it feel good?"

I tried not to laugh, but I failed. "It felt great."

She got into her car and closed the door. With a sad smile, she spoke through the open window. "I'm glad."

I watched her drive off, feeling a good deal of respect for her. But mostly concern.

Thirty Six

For two days I had been waiting anxiously for Randolph K. Birdwell, District Attorney of Salt Lake County, to make up his mind and find a judge who would issue arrest warrants for Joshua Mosley and Rulon Peterson. I had called twice a day, and each time the answer was the same - they were working on it. As far as I was concerned, they weren't working hard enough on it. He had Ruth's affidavit and my assault complaint. What more did he need? Ruth could very well be in danger, and the longer she stayed the more concerned I became.

Sometimes as a private eye you get so caught up in your thoughts that you fail to take in your surroundings. Sometimes that can be fatal.

Today wasn't one of them.

I spotted the dark blue Kia following me as I turned off West Temple onto State Street. He was four cars back, one lane over. Was this person simply headed to the other side of the valley like me? Was he only a tourist visiting

Temple Square or the Conference Center and now cruising down State Street looking for a good place to eat?

Maybe it was my imagination. Maybe I was getting paranoid again.

I stayed on State Street all the way to Twenty-First South then turned left towards the mountains. If he was going to the freeway, he would turn right. If he was going anyplace else, he would continue on State Street. There was only one reason he would turn left.

He turned left.

Karl Stallings was dead. Joshua Mosley didn't drive a blue Kia. So who was he? And why was he following me? Laying my Sig beside me, I weaved my way through a residential area and then back to Twenty-First South towards State Street. He stayed back but continued following me. I decided to find out why.

Making sure he was still with me, I pulled into the local Burger King parking lot and quickly went inside. As he pulled into the parking lot and drove to the far side of the building, I exited the building on the other side and rushed behind the line of cars waiting in the drive through lane.

He parked by the dumpster in the back. I circled around and came up behind him. Before he could react, I opened the back passenger's side door and jumped in. He whipped around and saw me. He also noticed the large Sig pointed at his head.

"Welcome to Burger King," I said politely. "May I take your order?"

His mouth opened but nothing came out as he fixated on the gun.

"Put your hands on the steering wheel where I can see them," I demanded. He immediately obeyed.

He was a large guy in his mid to late forties, with squinty eyes and jowls that sagged. His frightened eyes told me being held at gun point was all new to him. He was anything but cool and professional.

"There's no need for that," he quickly pleaded. "I'm not armed."

"Take out your wallet. Slowly. I get really nervous with sudden moves."

His eyes never leaving my gun, he reached into his coat and removed his wallet. "Really, you can put the gun away. I'm a private detective from California."

"I hate California. It's filled with a bunch of overpaid looney-toons with inflated egos. I may shoot you just for that."

He inhaled quickly. Scare tactics 101.

Trying to keep his hand from shaking, he handed me his wallet. His driver's license listed him as Garret Russell, 35 from Los Angeles, California. He was five nine, one hundred and eighty-three pounds, brown hair, and eyes. No driving restrictions.

"You're a long way from home, Mr. Russell."

"I came to hear the Mormon Tabernacle Choir." He tried to look calm and poised. He wasn't succeeding. His left eye lash fluttered nervously. His voice quivered ever so slightly as he stared at the gun. Most likely, he was a bored California accountant who had made a career change after watching too much television.

"I hate to be the bearer of bad news, but I don't hang with the Mo Tab Choir. So why are you following me?"

"When did you spot me?"

"West Temple and State."

"I underestimated you. You're good."

"Pride cometh before the fall."

"I'll remember that. Now what?"

I tossed back his wallet. "Give me your phone, and start singing like the choir you said you came to hear."

"You can't take my phone."

"I'm the one holding the gun. I can take whatever I want."

He reached into his pocket and turned over his phone.

"Now put your hands back on the steering wheel and keep them there." Turning back around, he obeyed.

Once I had all his incoming and outgoing calls, I selected 'share contact' and downloaded all the information to my phone. When that was done, I tossed his phone into the passenger's seat.

"Who hired you?"

"I don't know."

"Don't like the song. Try again."

"It's the truth."

He turned back around and stared at the gun again. "Look, put that away and I'll tell you what I know."

"Let's pretend I put it away and you tell me anyway."

He sighed and tried to relax. "I got an email hiring me to tail you."

"Someone hired you to come to Utah to tail me, and you didn't think that was weird?"

"Look, I'm new in this business and a job's a job. And they were offering good money."

"Did they say why they wanted me tailed?"

"They suspected you of trying to frame them for something. They didn't say what. They wanted to know where you went and with whom you talked. I picked you up yesterday and have been following you ever since."

My mind raced back to where I'd gone yesterday and with whom I had talked. What had he learned? And how come I hadn't spotted him before today? I had broken one of my own cardinal rules. Never get so wrapped up in a case that you fail to notices your surroundings. I had failed to notice him. It was a mistake I would be extremely cognizant of from now on.

In the rear view mirror, I noticed him smiling a

cheesy grin like he had pulled a fast one over on me and was proud of himself. Actually, he had, but I wasn't about to let him know it.

"I know."

His confidence wavered for a moment. "Then how come you waited to rush me?" he said as confidently as he could.

"Information," I lied.

"What do you mean?" The unsuspecting detective becomes the teacher.

"By waiting, it gave me more opportunity to lead you around by the nose while you were busy calling in my every move."

He nervously glanced at his phone.

"And you did call, didn't you?" Now it was my turn to smile. "Every place I went, you reported in like a good detective, making sure they knew how much progress you were making. Typical rookie mistake."

"I'm not that naive." He tried to sound tough, but it came out petulant.

I held up my phone. "We'll see, won't we?'

His shoulders slouched and he sighed.

"Your work here is done. I suggest you go back to Los Angeles."

"What's the point?" He glanced at me in the mirror. He was defeated and he knew it. "I might as well go back to being a Von's Supermarket manager for all the good I am at playing detective."

An accountant, a supermarket manager, they were pretty much the same thing. I opened the door. He didn't move.

"I wouldn't give up just yet if I were you. You've got potential." The professor encouraging the shaky student. "Just be more observant of everything around you. Don't take anything for granted. You'll be fine."

I got out of the car and closed the door.

Why hire an inexperienced detective out of L.A.

when there were plenty of excellent private eyes in Salt Lake? It didn't make sense. Did they really think I wouldn't spot him? Were they really that careless? The thought kept nagging at me for the next two days.

"I ran your L.A. detective," Jackson said as our hamburgers arrived. He had suggested we grab lunch at Katie Blues, and I was all up for it. I needed a sounding board and he was one of the best.

"1967," I said as Darlene set his meal in front of him and stood holding mine.

After perusing through the various books I had bought including *Billboards Number One Hits* and *The Top Forty, Hits of the Rock-and-Roll Era* I had found one of those popular songs that make you go 'oh yeah,' I remember that, but can never, for the life of you, remember who sang it. It was so simple, which made it difficult. I had her, and I knew it.

"Apples, Peaches Pumpkin Pie," I smiled my confidence sky high.

She stared at me, set my food on the table, turned and walked away. Victory is such an excellent side dish served with a great hamburger. I was starving. I picked up my bacon and avocado burger and took a large bite.

Darlene returned. "I forgot this." She sat my Dr. Pepper on the table. "Jay and the Techniques. It entered the charts in October at number 8 and stayed on the chart six weeks, peaking at number three."

She turned and strolled away. Suddenly I wasn't hungry.

"You're never going to stump her, you know?"

"If I have to spend the rest of my life looking through every book ever written on rock-and-roll, I will find the song that will have her stumbling all over herself."

Jackson took a bite of his pastrami burger and wiped his mouth. "You were right about Russell. He only received his private detective license six months ago. He's as green as they come."

"Why hire someone so inexperienced? Surely they aren't that stupid."

"There is another possibility," Jackson dipped his french fry in Katie's fry sauce and took a bite.

"What's that?"

"Maybe they wanted you to catch him," he said, dipping his french fry again.

"Why would they want me to catch him? That would put me onto them."

"Maybe we are looking at this backwards."

"What do you mean?"

"Think about it." He dipped two more fries into the fry sauce and gobbled them up as if it were a magic elixir fueling his genius. "What if whoever hired Russell isn't one of our suspects? What if they are an interested party trying to lead us to the truth?"

Maybe it was a magic elixir.

I needed to get those phone numbers. Right after I started covering my fries with fry sauce.

Back at the office, I called Debra Rucker.

"You do know that I work for AT&T, not David Crockett Private Investigations?" she asked.

"That hurts. I've always looked at you as a loyal employee."

"Someone you can boss around and take advantage of, you mean."

"Deb, I would never take advantage of you."

"Don't I know it," she laughed. "I tried everything in my power to get you to all those many years ago."

"I never was very bright, you know. What have you got for me?"

"I'm sending it to your phone now. Roger and I have wanted to spend a night at the Grand America. You know, kindle some of that old magic." I could hear her smiling through the phone.

"You're expensive, you know that?"

"But I'm worth it."

I watched as the information appeared on my phone. One of the numbers jumped out at me. Now it was my turn to smile.

"How's Friday night for you and Roger to turn that smoke into a full fledged, five-alarm fire?"

"Perfect. Who knows, if all goes as planned maybe we'll name our next child after you. Crockett Conklin. Has a nice ring to it, don't you think?"

I had to laugh. "The kid would hate you forever. Thanks, babe."

I hung up and stared at the numbers. If what I was seeing was correct, I was way off base. It didn't make sense. Why would she do it?

THIRTY SEVEN

I didn't wait for an invitation. I barged past the protesting secretary and burst through the door.

I had been played and I didn't like it. I wanted answers, and I wanted them now.

She looked up with a start, then smiled.

"You are good."

"I don't like someone following me. And I don't like being played."

She smiled and crossed her legs under the glass table top, allowing me a view of her long, toned legs visible in her tight, short cream-colored knit dress.

"Now what can I do for you?"

"Stop playing games."

"Playing games is what I do for a living, David." Her smile was pure sex. "And I'm very good at it."

"Playtime's over. You wanted me here, so out with it."

Abigail Collingsworth smiled up at me, uncrossed and

David Sterago

crossed her legs again, this time wider and slower. If I were one of her clients, I would already be pulling out my Gold Platinum card and signing on any dotted line she wanted me to. She was gorgeous, sensual, and deadly. She knew how to manipulate men.

My credit card stayed where it was.

Her lips pouted, and she looked at me with those beautiful greenish brown eyes. Even with too much make-up around them they were still dangerous. "I really don't know what you are talking about, David."

"Something scared you enough to stage this whole charade. Is it Parker? Out with it."

"I can't break confidence, you know. Professional-client privilege."

"You're not a lawyer, and there is no such thing as hooker-client privilege."

"That's such a distasteful word." She locked onto me with that unwavering, penetrating gaze. "I prefer professional game show hostess." Her voice tightened.

"And I prefer lying on the beach sipping Pina Colada with super models, but that's not going to happen either, so let's dispense with the cat-and-mouse game. Either tell me what's on your mind or quit wasting my time."

I waited for her to say something, but she just sat there like a ten-year-old trying to figure out a difficult math problem.

"Fine, have it your way." I turned to leave.

"Wait!" She jumped out of her chair.

I stopped and turned to face her. Her coy attitude had vanished. What I saw on her face was fear.

"I need your help."

"Then start talking."

She leaned back, her eyes glancing at anything and everything on the desk, moving back and forth like a pin ball. Her hands were shaking. She wet her lips. "I think Martin is going to kill me."

Now she had my full attention.

"What makes you think that?"

She stared at me for a moment, then stood up. I watched as she removed her jacket. I don't know what I was expecting, but it wasn't a long slender arm covered in large black bruises.

"Parker do that?"

She pulled a tissue from the box on the desk and dabbed it softly under her eye. Once the heavily applied make-up was gone, another black and bluish bruise became visible under her right eye.

"When did this happen?"

"The day after your visit. I made the mistake of asking him about Johnny Baker. When I asked if he killed him, he flew into a rage. He grabbed my arm and began hitting me. I thought he was going to kill me."

"And you didn't call the police?"

"And tell them what?" she asked incredulously. "A friend of the police commissioner beat me up? Who do you think they would believe?"

She sat back down and removed a pack of cigarettes from her desk. With trembling hands, she pulled one from the pack, only to shove it back inside and drop it on the desk. "I hate these things."

"Why didn't you just call me instead of this elaborate ruse?"

"Because Martin has been watching me like a hawk since that night. I thought about calling you from here, but he pays the bills. I couldn't take the chance of your number popping up on the bill."

She again nervously reached for the pack, this time successfully lit one. Taking a deep drag, she blew the smoke towards the ceiling. "Besides, I didn't think you'd help me after the way I treated you at our last meeting." She looked up at me through frightened, pleading eyes. "I was desperate," she cried. "I needed to find a way to get you here on your own, and the only way I could think of to do that was to make you mad."

She was right, but I remained silent on that secret.

"Tell me about Baker?"

She took another drag then crushed the cigarette out in the near-by ash tray. "Martin hired him to break into Richard Harvey's law offices and replace his wife's will with one he had forged."

"What about the contract making Jared Walker CEO of the company?"

"He took that also. With his wife dead, there would be no way to prove that she ever intended to leave the company to Walker."

"Sounds like motive for murder to me. Will you testify to what you've just told me?"

"That depends."

After what she had been through, her reluctance surprised me. "On what?"

"On whether you will protect me."

"I'm not a bodyguard."

"What about police protection? You're friends with the cops. Can't you get someone there to protect me?"

Her voice rang with desperation. Even if I wanted to help, her situation didn't rise to the level of police protection. "Being a witness to forging a will doesn't merit protective custody."

All the bluster had dissipated, leaving a scared, and desperate little girl.

"How about killing one's wife?" she asked softly.

I was all ears.

THIRTY EIGHT

"I don't see it," he said firmly.

Jackson and I sat in stunned silence as District Attorney Birdwell shook his head. He was a tall, skinny man of fifty-three with small beady eyes, overly rosy cheeks that were, either the results of too much booze, or he was secretly Santa Claus's skinny younger brother. My money was on the booze. He pasted on his plastic smile and interlocked his hands on his desk.

"Mr. Crockett, Martin Parker is a successful and well-respected business man in this community. I cannot issue an arrest warrant on the flimsy and circumstantial evidence you've presented.

"Circumstantial?" Jackson leaned forward in the leather oak chair he was sitting in. "We have an eyewitness who has signed an affidavit stating that Parker admitted to her that he killed his wife."

"Detective, you and I both know that just because

someone swears something is true doesn't make it so. I can't go around arresting everyone who is accused by someone else."

"How about those who commit murder?" I said, trying to keep the contempt out of my voice.

"You're a guest in this office, Mr. Crockett. Please remember that." He flashed me his best political smile. "I appreciate your convictions in this matter, Detective Paine, but from what you've presented to me, I just don't see it rising to the level of an arrest. Will there be anything else?"

"Some justice might be nice," I said bitterly.

He glared at me, then lowered his eyes to the make-believe paper work on his clean desk. We were officially being dismissed.

Jackson had been right. The rich don't arrest like the rest of us. There was no doubt Martin Parker had friends in high places. There was a slim possibility we might go over his head to the State Attorney General, but that was a long shot. It would also bring the entire chain of command down on Jackson's head. Martin Parker had proven to be Teflon after all.

That evening in my office, I broke the news to Faith over a fifth of Johnny Walker Red. With each successive drink, she took the news better and better. We both did. An hour later all common sense and logic was out the window. And so were our clothes. Deep in the back of my alcohol-fogged brain, I knew I would regret it in the morning, but I didn't care.

I was tired of being logical.

I was tired of being outsmarted.

And I was sure as hell tired of being alone.

She felt good in my arms, soft and supple. Our kisses took on an urgency of their own, and soon we were entwined in a heated and passionate love-making that only two lonely people could understand. It was the right place, the right time, and the right people. But mostly it was the booze.

The next I awoke alone on the couch. When had she left?

I got up and stumbled into the bathroom. Running cold water in the sink, I drenched my aching head. It didn't help. I needed coffee. Drying my hair with a towel, I headed for the front door. The Elvis clock, his legs swinging back and forth said it was nine a.m. Had I really slept that long?

John Wayne stared disapprovingly at me from *The Alamo* poster, his torch raised like he was ready to beat some sense into me. I needed it, but not until I had my coffee.

As I opened the door I was surprised to find a tall, well-built man standing there. He was wearing a chauffeur's hat and coat.

"Mr. Crockett?"

"I'm not sure," I grumbled, my head pounding like Motley Crue's bass drum.

He handed me a folded piece of paper and then turned and walked back down the hall.

Leaning against the wall for support, I opened the letter, hoping my eyes would be able to focus.

When the words of the letter came into focus, I was even more confused. There were only two lines written on the paper. It read: *Mr. Birdwell has changed his mind. Go see him again. Thanks for not giving up. I'm still watching you.*

I don't know what pull Melanie Skoff had over Birdwell, but she was correct. That afternoon, he reluctantly sanctioned the arrest warrant we had been waiting for. But there was a catch. Birdwell was sending us to Judge John Gordon Reno. Reno was a tough old bird who took civil rights and privacy issues very seriously. I had to believe that was why Birdwell had chosen him. Was he hoping that Reno would turn him down? The joke was on him. Reno was also hard on those who broke the law. After reading the Collingsworth affidavit, he issued the arrest warrant without batting an eye.

One arrest warrant down and one more to go, I thought as Jackson and I drove to the offices of Martin Parker. Though I had no jurisdiction in the process, Jackson allowed me to tag along, if I behaved myself. I would try.

Abigail Collingsworth had made a statement implicating Martin Parker in the death of his wife. With her testimony, I had no doubt Martin Parker would be going to prison for a long time. He had been so smug, so sure of himself. I couldn't wait for Jackson to put the cuffs on him.

With me tagging along like a hungry puppy, Jackson strolled to the receptionist and showed his badge.

"Martin Parker, please."

After checking, the receptionist informed us that he was in the conference room on the second floor. We took the stairs two at a time.

As we moved down the hallway, Parker's personal assistant met us before we got to the conference room.

"What's this about?"

"Its official police business, ma'am."

"Even so, I must insist you not disturb Mr. Parker. He is in a very important business meeting."

"More important than murder?"

She gave Jackson a blank stare.

"More important than truth or justice?" I said before I could stop myself. But I wasn't done. As a child in the late Fifties, my father had avidly watched *Superman* starring George Reeves, on his black and white television. This was for him. "And the American way?" I finished as patriotic as I could. Dad would be so proud, I'm sure.

Jackson rolled his eyes, probably wondering why he had brought me along.

She continued to boldly block our way into the conference

room.

Jackson moved to within an inch of her nervous face. "If you don't turn around and get out of my way, I'm going to arrest you for obstruction of justice. How's that for important?"

With a gasp, she turned and rushed down the hall. Loyalty only goes so far, I guess.

Parker was standing in the middle of the conference room holding court with his employees as we entered the room. He looked at us with a start. When he recognized me, he smiled.

"Gentlemen."

"Martin Parker, you are under arrest for the murder of Sylvia Parker. Please turn around and put your hands behind your back."

The room filled with audible gasps. With a shocked look on his face, Parker hesitantly obeyed. Jackson slapped the cuffs on him.

As we led him into the hallway, his rock solid composure crumbled slightly. He yelled to his secretary who had wandered back down the hall. "Janice, call my lawyer and have him meet me downtown."

"I bet that Mensa IQ is really going to impress them in prison," I quipped.

Regaining a measure of confidence, he fought to not look worried. I had no doubt he was reminding himself of all his political connections and how they could help him beat this wrap. I wanted to deflate his arrogance by telling him his mistress had turned on him and she would be sending him to prison for a long time. I decided to let him find out the old fashion way—on the six o'clock news.

That evening it hit the media like a hurricane ripping through Florida. The next afternoon all the local television stations converged on the police station. It was a juicy murder case with everything the media could want: an important local business man accused of murdering his rich wife. A beautiful socialite mistress scorned and turning against him. His daughter, fighting for justice for her dead mother at the expense of her father; a rich and powerful family torn apart by greed, power, and murder. It was the stuff of television movies. Maybe Vince Vaughn would play me in the made-for-television movie.

It was also the stuff politicians couldn't leave alone. A news conference had, hastily, been called for noon.

I decided to go down for the sideshow and applaud when Jackson was introduced to the media as the arresting officer, and hero of the day. Since he hated publicity, I was going to enjoy his misery.

I grabbed a couple of tacos from the taco truck, parked a half a block from the station, and strolled toward the steps of the Salt Lake City Police Department.

It was like the circus had hit town. All three major networks were there. State and city politicians were promising not to take advantage of the situation while taking advantage of the situation by grabbing as much camera time as they could.

Chase Rangel, the Police Commissioner, was dressed in his finest blues. He had a round, gelatinous face that seemed to dissolve in the folds of skin. Images of Jabba the Hut popped into my mind.

Captain Sokolowski flanked Rangel on one side and, to my surprise, Detective Harry Reed stood silently on the other side. He was wearing his finest suit, which was only ten years old. His hair had been slicked back with enough gel to lube every car in the city.

The only person not there was Jackson.

I left the circus and wandered into the building. Even Tom Clayson was caught up in it. He buzzed me through without any hassle.

A television was on in the area but Jackson wasn't watching it. I sat down facing it.

"Rangel take over the case?"

"He gave it back to Reed," Jackson grunted.

"It's important to have someone to kiss his butt, and do it his way."

I turned my attention to the television in time to hear Rangel heap so much praise on Reed that I automatically glanced around the squad room for a shovel.

"Detective Reed was the officer on the case when it was ruled a suicide. But, as with all of our outstanding detectives, something didn't set well with him." He nodded his head, agreeing with himself before turning and smiling at a rim-rod straight Reed.

"He kept digging until Martin Parker's alibi began to crumble, and Detective Reed was there to see that justice was done."

"Really?" I laughed. "When we arrested Parker, Reed was at South Town Mall attending a scrapbooking convention with his wife," I said incredulously.

"He must have seen it on the news, so in a way he was there to see it," Jackson said without looking up from his work.

Rangel paused, letting his words sink in to the crowded media, making them wait and hang on his every word. When all eyes were glued to him he nodded. "We'll take a few questions now."

I watched as Rangel began fielding questions. The man would hold a press conference to announce the arrest of an eighty-year-old jaywalker if he could. His political aspiration outweighed his common sense.

I glanced at Jackson. "You have to love an outstanding detective like Reed."

"The man's a pit bull when it comes to dedication," he deadpanned.

A Ken doll-looking reporter from KSL, Channel 5, pushed forward to ask the first question. "Detective Reed, what led you to believe that Mrs. Parker's death wasn't a suicide as originally thought?"

Reed looked stumped. Maybe the outstanding detective hadn't realized the press would ask such tough questions.

He paused, glanced around then took a deep breath. "I really can't discuss that. It's evidence for the trial."

"I thought Mr. Parker was at Lake Powell when his wife was killed?" asked a bubbly blonde reporter from the Fox Network, who looked more like a college sorority sister than a news person. She wrinkled her brow in an attempt to look serious.

Reed glanced at Rangel, who smiled and jumped in to cover his incompetence. "Since this investigation is now on going, I am sorry to say we can't answer any more questions about it."

An audible sigh rang out from the disappointed media looking for any juicy tidbit to turn into a hard-hitting news story. Rangel smiled and held up his hand for quiet, waiting until all the media attention was focused back on him. "While we can't say anything more about this case, I can tell you, that after months of good old-fashioned police work from Detective Reed and others in the Salt Lake City Police Department, District Attorney Birdwell has granted my request for an arrest warrant for—" He paused to take a drink of water as if he was so thirsty he just couldn't continue without it.

The media sat waiting.

He sat the glass down and smiled at the attentive audience. "As I was saying our courageous District Attorney, Randolph K. Birdwell, has issued an arrest warrant for one Rulon Peterson, leader of the Eternal and True Church of Christ in the Last Days."

A loud gasp shot through the shocked crowd. Martin Parker and Harry Reed were immediately forgotten.

I bolted up in my chair and stared at the television as Rangel continued.

"Captain Sokolowski and his fine department have been investigating the operations of this shadowy cult for some time. And now, thanks to the courage of a cult insider, we have what we need to proceed against this dangerous group."

I turned to Jackson in disbelief. "Did that political peacock just out Ruth?" I slammed my fist down on his desk. "We've been trying to get an arrest warrant issued for a week and now it suddenly becomes a priority?"

Jackson looked at me, his voice calm but urgent. "We need to get to Ruth. We have to pull her out of there."

THIRTY NINE

Ruth sat in silence reading her scriptures. For the first time she began to understand them, not the way Joshua and Rulon Peterson had explained them, but the way they were meant to be understood. God didn't expect women to be slaves to their husbands. He didn't take away their agency just so they could be chattel bought and sold to unrighteous men.

She glanced up. Carol was staring at her.

"Tonight is your night to be with Joshua," she smiled.

Ruth wanted to be obedient. She had promised Joshua. But she couldn't. She wouldn't. How could she lay with someone who was capable of doing what he had done? She shivered.

"Carol, I have so much homework to do. Maybe you could take my night."

"Nonsense. It is a privilege to show Joshua your devotion."

"I don't feel up to it tonight. I have so much to do."

Carol stepped back, her eyes squinting in amazement. "Ruth, perfect faith only comes through perfect obedience. It is not important what you want or feel, only that you serve your husband and obey our Prophet. Is that clear?"

Ruth knew she couldn't win the argument no matter how hard she tried. There were no words to defy Rulon Peterson. While she no longer believed his views on salvation, Carol did and to argue with her would be like trying to explain common sense to a roomful of university academics.

She had to be obedient. Joshua had kept his promise and had taken Jennifer to the hospital. Now she must keep hers.

The door opened and Joshua entered. He nodded to Ruth, then turned and strolled into the bedroom.

The other wives smiled as they gently pulled Ruth to her feet and ushered her forward. Tonight was her night. They all envied her.

Slowly, Ruth moved towards the bedroom. "Your duty is to your husband, to serve his every need," she began whispering to herself. Maybe if she said it enough she would believe it again.

As she entered the room, she knew she didn't. And never would again. She had found the truth, and this counterfeit gospel of evil men made her sick.

This would be the last time. Soon the police would come for Joshua and she would be free. With a small smile of victory, she closed the door behind her.

Joshua gazed at her as she entered the room. There was no smile of affection, just a cold stare. Ruth stood in the doorway until he waved her over to the bed. Obediently she took a seat on the bed next to him.

"You were always my favorite," he whispered. "Did you know that?"

She shook her head. He kissed her forehead, then reached up and brushed the hair out of her eyes. "I really believed we were destined to be together for all eternity."

"And now?"

"And now God has revealed another plan for us." He smiled as he put his large hands gently on her shoulders, caressing, massaging.

"God has a very special purpose for you, my love."

With one hand he reached behind him and produced a neatly folded letter. She knew what it was without even looking. It was the good-by letter she had written when she believed that she was leaving with Jennifer. She had written it, but then realized she could never show it to him for fear he would have come after her. She had shoved it into her glove compartment and forgotten about it.

"I'm going to miss you."

His hands moved from her shoulders to her neck. As they quickly tightened, Ruth realized what was happening. She tried to move away, but his grip was too tight. His face contorted into an evil demon as he began squeezing tighter and tighter. Instinctively, she fought him but it was no use. He was too strong.

Then her body went limp. She closed her eyes and gave in to the darkness surrounding her. It didn't matter anymore. Maybe this was the only way she could be truly free of him.

That was her last thought as the darkness engulfed her.

FORTY

Rangel had made it clear an arrest warrant was being issued on Peterson. He didn't care about Mosley. He wasn't high enough in the organization to cause a media frenzy. Peterson was.

While it put Ruth in danger, it did open the door for Jackson to try and get an arrest warrant on Mosley.

While he was tilting at the political windmills, I went back to my office. I removed the 8x10 black and white photos I had taken outside the house on Panga Circle. While the powers that be could prevent Jackson from working on the Parker case, they couldn't stop me, or at least I hoped they couldn't.

It had taken time, but I now had the names of the local rich and famous cavorting at the sex party thrown by Parker and Collingsworth. Besides Democratic State Senator, Tom Shelly smiling, his arm around his beautiful and very young companion, there was high-priced divorce attorney, Watson Cartridge and Draper city councilman,

Republican, Hollis Waxman, a purveyor of family values, except when it came to his own, obviously. Businessman Robert Warren, one of the largest financial contributors to the Democratic Party, was smiling also as he held his young companion close to his sixty-two-year old body. And last, but not least, was Judge John Ginsberg, a federal judge who gave stern lectures from the bench covering every digression known to man. A few had even been hurled my way. Even with a beautiful young companion next to him, his face still looked like he had sucked on a lemon. Some people are just never happy.

As I stared at the photos, I couldn't help but wonder in what way these prominent people had been asked to help Parker or Collingsworth in exchange for their discretion.

The door slammed opened and Harry Reed and his partner Jeremiah Cummings stormed into the office.

"I want everything you have on Martin Parker," Reed announced without any fanfare.

"And I'd like world peace," I smiled. "For the children, of course."

"I have orders to remove all evidence you have collected," he declared as he moved towards my filing cabinet.

I picked up my Sig. "You're not that stupid are you, Harry?"

He stopped and turned to Cummings for help.

"You have to give them to us," Reed said as if saying it I would just automatically comply.

"No, I don't. My files are private and unless you have a warrant, get the hell out of my office."

"Commissioner Rangel ordered you to give them to us," Cummings said.

"I don't work for the police department anymore, so Rangel has no jurisdiction here."

"We're the police. You have to give them to us." The look

of frustration on his face made me want to laugh.

"Not without a warrant," I reminded him. "And I don't see one."

I though Reed was going to cry. He was Rangel's lap dog, and like all trained lap dogs he just couldn't understand me not jumping to following their orders.

"I'll tell you what I'll do."

They both jumped to attention.

"I'll give you everything I have in that filing cabinet on the Parker case if you stay completely away from me for the rest of your natural-born life. Deal?"

I gritted my teeth trying not to burst out laughing as they both looked at each and moved back to discuss it like it was the most important offer they had ever had.

"Deal," Reed finally said triumphantly.

I opened my filing cabinet and removed the folder on Martin Parker. "Here you go."

Reed grabbed the file like it was a cream-filled doughnut. Turning, they strutted out of the office, giant smiles of satisfaction across their faces.

A few minutes later Jackson sauntered in.

"What were Dumb and Dumber doing here?"

"Trying to get everything on the Martin Case."

"You gave it to them?"

"No. I told them if they stayed away from me I'd give them everything I had in my filing cabinet on Martin Parker."

I removed the manila folder out from under the pictures spread across my desk and held it up.

"So what did you give them?"

"All the press clipping from the original story."

"They saw you coming, didn't they?"

"Hey," I said feigning hurt. "Who can hold their own against such ruthless negotiators?"

He held up the arrest warrant, waving it proudly in the air.

"Judge Reno was in a very good mood. Let's go get Ruth and arrest that low life."

"After that stunt Rangel pulled on television, Mosley may have already rabbited. Ruth said they have safe houses all over the state."

"Let's hope he wasn't watching television that day," he sighed. "I have someone from the local women's shelter meeting us there. This time she's got a place to go and someone to help her."

Fifteen minutes later we passed the two black and white units and pulled up to the locked gate. A large man with short hair, dressed in a black suit and tie, stepped out of the guard shack and walked slowly to the gate.

"This is private property."

Jackson got out of his car waving the warrant. "And this is an arrest warrant, so if you don't want to be arrested for obstruction of justice, open the gate."

"Who's it for?"

"You have ten seconds to open the gate or we're going to break it down." Jackson turned to Officer Lamb, who jumped out of his car with a small battering ram used to smash in doors during drug raids.

The guard stared at us, then back down the street towards the houses where Peterson and Mosley lived. He seemed confused.

Jackson nodded at Lamb. "Break it down."

As Lamb moved to the gate, the guard raised his hands in a defensive motion. "No, wait, I'll open it."

He quickly stepped back into the guard shack and pushed the button. The gate swung open.

Immediately, we sped into the exclusive community, stopping in front of Joshua Mosley's house. I was somewhat surprised that nothing out of the ordinary was happening. No one was rushing items out of the house and packing their cars for a hurried escape. Then again, maybe they didn't watch television.

As we pulled up, Mosley opened the door and walked out to greet us. He stood there waiting, a confident smile plastered across his smug face, taunting us.

His wives followed him out of the house, standing in a group behind him. They stared at us with suspicious eyes. I shouldn't have stared but I had never seen polygamist wives. Two of the women stood in front of three children, who were trying to peek around their mothers. The third one, the youngest and the prettiest, glanced nervously at her husband. Maybe it was my imagination but I thought I saw a sense of relief in her eyes as we came towards Mosley. When I looked again her face was as cold as the other two. They didn't trust us and were not afraid to show it.

Mosley was calm and unfazed. "Can I help you?"

"Joshua Mosley, you're under arrest for the attempted murder of Jennifer Justice," Jackson announced.

"I know nothing about that."

As I stared at the wives I suddenly realized that one was missing. I stepped around Jackson. "Where's Ruth?"

Mosley shook his head sadly. "I wish I knew. It seems your constant harassment turned her against me. She left."

"What do you mean, left? Where did she go?"

"I wish I knew. She wrote me a note saying she wasn't happy anymore and she wanted out."

"You're lying," I shot back.

He stared at me then calmly turned to one of the woman standing behind him, "Carol."

The oldest looking of his wives stepped forward with a folded piece of paper. "I found this after she had gone," he said, handing me the note. It was in Ruth's handwriting and it said what he claimed. I stared at it, then handed it to Jackson. "It's from Ruth, but it was written the day she planned to leave with Jennifer."

"Can you prove that?" Mosley smiled, challenging me.

"She told me about it the day she said that you had caught her and Jennifer together. The day you beat Jennifer within an inch of her life."

"I guess we just have your word on that. Which all here will agree is extremely prejudiced because of your hate for our religion."

Jackson glanced at me. We both knew without Ruth we had no case against him. And he knew it too.

"It seems without your witness you have no case," a voice from behind us said gleefully.

I turned to see, Rulon Peterson standing there. "If you persist in this personal vendetta against my flock, I will see to it that you are brought up on charges of harassment."

"That may be the least of your worries," Jackson said.

"Oh, you mean the arrest warrant?" His smile was confident. "My attorneys assure me it is nothing more than a political witch hunt."

Jackson glanced at the letter, then to Peterson. He knew he couldn't proceed without just cause, and our just cause was now missing.

"This isn't over," he said directly to Peterson.
"You can't let him walk away. We both know he's guilty," I vehemently protested.

"We don't have any proof now."

"I don't need proof, I know he did it."

Jackson turned to the others. "Let's go." He walked towards his car. Officer Lamb and the others followed.

"If you've hurt her, I'll make you pay."

"Now that would be breaking the law, wouldn't it?" I clinched my fists tight. I wanted to hit him, to make him tell me what had happened to Ruth. She had not just left and I knew it. The self-righteous smirk on his face told me all I needed to know.

As I turned to go, Mosley leaned in close to me and

whispered just loud enough for me to hear him. "You'll never find her," he smiled. "The bitch got what she deserved."

Like a bomb, I exploded. I grabbed a handful of shirt, forcing him backwards until he slammed against the door frame with a violent thud. He winced as the breath was knocked out of him.

"I'll kill you, I swear I will," I shouted.

He fought to breath. I held him tight, my rage blocking out the screaming of the women and the crying of the children.

"Where is she?"

Through his pain I saw that self-righteous smirk again. Before I could hit him, I felt strong hands grab me and yank me backwards.

"Stop it, David!"

I whirled around to face Jackson, my face twisted in guilt and anger. I had allowed her to go back to him, and now she was gone.

My eyes never left Mosley's as I was pulled away from him. He gasped and rushed towards me, his eyes bulging out of his head.

"Everyone heard you threaten me! They all saw you attack me!"he screamed. "I'll sue you for every dime you have, and the city too!" Spit drooled down the corner of his mouth as he raged on. "Everyone here is a witness to your unprovoked attack on me and my family! I'm going to own you, Crockett, you hear me?"

"Are you crazy? You can't attack a private citizen in his own yard," Jackson scolded as he pulled me to his patrol car.

I stood, letting the anger wash over me. As I glanced back at Mosley, he smiled and slightly nodded his head. He had just played me. And I let him. My anger had gotten the best of me and now, no matter what I said, it would be chalked up to a personal vendetta.

"We'll get him," Jackson said. "Just not now."

I hoped he was right, but now, because of my rookie

mistake, his capture had just become a much steeper hill to climb, if at all.

FORTY ONE

Captain Jensen Sokolowski is never a very happy camper. Today he was especially unhappy; the object of that misery was Jackson and me.

Like two lambs about to be slaughtered, we sat waiting as Sokolowski listened to the voice in the phone stuck to his ear. He glanced at me, his eyes narrowed. If he had a cigar in his mouth, it would have shifted from one side to the other before being clenched angrily in his teeth.

"I'll take care of it, sir. Thank you, sir."

He hung up the phone.

"Do you know who that was?" His voice was low and menacing.

"The producers of *Dancing with the Stars*," popped out of my mouth before I could stop it. It could have been.

"That was Commissioner Rangel. He wants your head on a platter, Crockett, and I would like nothing better than to give it to him. He has an army of Peterson's lawyers crawling up his backside, and he is not very happy about it.

After that stunt of yours, Judge Reno revoked Peterson's arrest warrant. What were you thinking, Crockett?"

"Mosley killed one of his wives."

"And you know that how?"

"He told me," I replied. "He whispered that I'd never find her, and that she got what she deserved."

"Did anyone other than you hear it?" he asked.

"No," I admitted.

"Then you have nothing."

"I think he's right, Captain," Jackson interjected. "Mosley is a very hostile person, capable of anything."

"What were you thinking, taking a civilian along with you on an arrest? Do you know that makes the city liable for his screw-up?"

"He was part of the effort to solve the case."

"I don't care if he's the Angel Gabriel, you don't take an unauthorized civilian along on an arrest. I should suspend you for a month without pay."

"It wasn't his fault, Captain. I talked him into it. I'll take the blame and the consequences."

"You're damn right you will," he said, his eyes boring into me. I had seen that look too many times not to know he was wondering if he should throw the book at us. He took a deep breath.

"Do you have anything solid on Peterson?"

"We have the testimony of an eye-witness who says Peterson ordered the beating of a young school teacher who wouldn't join their cult," Jackson explained.

"Will this eye-witness come forward?"

"Thanks to Rangel, who never met a microphone he didn't love, that eye-witness maybe dead," I said hotly.

He glanced up at us with surprise.

"David was building a case against him. He had an inside eye-witness who was willing to come forward. That's why

I had been trying to get an arrest warrant," Jackson continued.

"And since the Parker case wasn't big enough for him, Rangel stuck his political nose into this case and outed my witness on television," I pointed out angrily.

"That's the Police Commissioner, Crockett. Show some respect."

"I'm not that good of an actor, sir."

Sokolowski bit his lower lip as if he were stifling a smile. In spite of his faults, Sokolowski was a hard core police officer. He had worked his way up the ranks the old-fashioned way, hard work and excellent detective skills. Though part of his job as captain was to endure political fools, he didn't always endure them well. He hated publicity-seeking political appointees as much as we did. To him, justice always came before politics. I thought back to his sour expression as he stood beside Commissioner Rangel as he ripped the Parker case out from under all of us.

With a deep sigh, he leaned back in his chair. "If you've got something on him, you can't prove it from jail."

"Are you saying you want to be kept in the loop, sir?" I ventured.

His face got red and he exploded. "What are you, brain dead? I strictly forbid my officers to have any contact with Peterson or any of his followers. Do I make myself clear?" His voice rose, and heads in the detective bull pen turned towards the glass partition separating us.

"Now get out of my office!" he barked even louder.

We got up.

"Crockett?"

I turned back to face my former captain. His voice was soft and low, and I could swear I saw camaraderie twinkling in his dark eyes. "Do what you have to do, only do it quietly until you have something concrete. The last thing I need is the Commissioner giving another press conference."

Two days later I had absolutely nothing on Rulon Peterson or Joshua Mosley, except the memory of Mosley's smiling face as he as much as admitted to killing Ruth. I couldn't get it out of my mind, no matter how hard I tried.

Jackson and I had been going through all the possibilities and bouncing ideas off of each other for over an hour, and still nothing. I knew I could get Mosley on assault and battery but that wouldn't get us Peterson. We had to tie them together to Jennifer's beating and to Ruth's death. But how?

Jackson sat up and tossed the file he was reading on to his desk.

"We need hard evidence, David. And there just isn't any."

Joshua Mosley was a blood-sucking predator who preyed on innocent girls, but he was also part of the Peterson religious machine that had enough lawyers on retainer to ruin our careers if we accused him of anything without proof. We had foolishly made our move, and he had out-played us. Now anything we did, without absolute proof, would land us in legal hot water.

"With Ruth Mosley disappearing—"

"He killed her," I cut him off. "I know he did." The anger and guilt boiled up inside me.

"You're probably right, but without her testimony we have nothing to go on."

"Maybe we can turn one of the other wives?" I said, throwing out suggestions even though I knew they were meaningless.

"You saw the look of devotion on their faces," Jackson replied.

"Then maybe I'll just go and beat the crap out of him again," I said just to make myself feel better.

Something stirred deep inside my brain as a memory was

pushed to the front. It was something I should have thought of weeks ago. It was basic forensics 101.

"Jenny's jacket."

"What about it?"

"It was covered with blood."

Jackson bolted up in his chair. "And if your hands were aching because of the quick beating you gave Mosley, imagine what his hand must have looked like after the beating he gave Jennifer."

"DNA. Her clothes have to have his DNA on them."

Jackson quickly pushed the pause button on the excitement train.

"Even if they do, we don't have enough evidence against him to merit a search warrant to obtain a DNA sample from him to compare it to."

He was right.

"And after what you just pulled, there won't be a judge in the state that will let us get near him."

He was right again.

We were out of cards to play. I had run out of ideas. I glanced up to see Jackson staring at me like I was his long lost brother.

"What?" I asked feeling a little uncomfortable.

"Your jacket!" he exclaimed excitedly. "Mosley bled on it. Remember?"

I remembered. I also remembered I had taken it to the cleaners yesterday. My heart sank. "I took it to the cleaners."

"Go get it."

"Why?"

"Because if we are lucky, and I mean really lucky, the stain didn't come out completely."

"You think Boudreau might be able to pull some DNA off the coat?"

"It's the only chance we have."

"We'll need something to match it to."

"Can you get her clothes, or do you think the hospital will require a search warrant?" he asked.

I immediately picked up the phone and called Roxanna Lewis. After listening to my plea, she explained that hospital policy provided that only family members could claim victims' belonging. That left me out.

I thanked her and was about to hang up when she threw me a life line. "Of course since she has no immediate family and since you are paying for her room and providing for her care, that technically makes you family, doesn't it?"

I grinned a King of the Wild Frontier size grin. "It sure does." I knew legally it didn't, but who was I to correct her?

I hung up the phone. "I'll get everything and meet you at Boudreau's office in an hour."

I drove like NASCAR greats, Richard Petty, Kyle Petty, and every other Petty as I raced to the small cleaners three blocks from my place. Unlike the movies, there was no parking place right out front, so I had to park two blocks away and run.

I hate running.

I burst through the door, praying they had not gotten to my jacket.

The Last Stain is a small mom-and-pop, family operated cleaners. Because they do excellent work, they have more business than they can handle. If there was a god above and if he had missed all of my grievous sins over the years, they would not have had the time to get to my insignificant pile of clothes.

The bright smile on the face of Mrs. Chilton told me otherwise.

"David," she grinned. "We were not expecting you until tomorrow."

"I know and I apologize, but I need my coat now."

The smile faded. "Is everything all right?"

"Yes. It's just that an emergency came up and I really need my coat."

"Of course. I'll go get it."

I crossed my fingers as I waited for her to return. If she came back with the coat over her arm, I would kiss her.

She didn't.

It was pressed and in a plastic bag with my other two dress shirts. She must have noticed the disappointment on my face.

She announced proudly, hoping to cheer me up. "I'll have you know we got all the blood stains out. It looks good as new."

She hung the clothes on the rack and rang up my bill. I paid and left feeling miserable that they had done their usual excellent job. Talk about an upside-down world.

An hour later I walked into Boudreau's autopsy lab. He frowned at me when he noticed the two evidence bags with Jenny's jacket and pants. "Of course this is a top priority, like everything else you two bring in here," he sneered.

"If you are not up to the challenge, we could always let Wyler take the lead on this one," I said.

"Get out of my lab," Boudreau snapped as he yanked the evidence bags out of my hand and turned his back on us. "That little turd couldn't find any evidence if the body sat up and pointed it out to him. Let him take the lead. Morons."

I handed him the jacket.

"You picking up my cleaning now, Crockett?"

"This jacket had blood stains on it."

He shook his head in disgust. "And like an idiot you had it cleaned, didn't you?"

"Guilty as charged," I answered sheepishly.

"And now you want me to see if I can pull trace DNA off it?"

"That's why you are the best."

"And you two are a pain in my ass." He grabbed the jacket and muttered to himself.

"We wouldn't ask you, Justin, if it wasn't important,"

Jackson said hoping to sooth him.

"It's always important with you two."

"A young girl was beaten nearly to death. She's in a coma. We need to put the person who did this in jail. And fast."

He removed the plastic wrap and held the jacket up. His eyes narrowed as he stared at it.

"This is going to cost you, Crockett."

"Anything you want, Justin," I said, regretting it as soon as the words came out of my mouth. With Boudreau you never could tell. I might be cleaning his lab for a month or worse, cleaning dead bodies.

"As soon as you find anything, let us know," Jackson called over his shoulder to the muttering Boudreau as we started for the doors. He was still muttering to himself when the large doors closed behind us.

Four days later Jackson and I were having lunch at Katie Blues when Boudreau phoned, telling us to meet him in his office. I ordered his favorite burger as a reward and we rushed over.

He was sitting in his chair eating a large hoagie sandwich. When he saw me hold up the burger from Katie Blues, he instantly tossed the hoagie into the trash and yanked the doggie bag out of my hand. We watched as he breathed in the aroma of the blue cheese burger and then, with a satisfied sigh, took a giant bite. With grease and sauce running down his chin, he closed his eyes and smiled.

We waited for him to say something. He didn't.

"What did you find on the jacket?"

He shook his head as he continued to chew. Finally.

"There was no DNA on it. Whoever your cleaners are, they do excellent work."

My heart sank.

"Are you sure?" I pleaded. "There was nothing useful on it?"

"Do you have wax for brains?" Boudreau snapped. "I said there was no DNA on the jacket and I meant it."

I plopped down into one of the chairs, defeated. Joshua Mosley was not only going to get away with killing Ruth, he was also going to get away with beating Jennifer.

"Thanks for trying, Justin," Jackson said softly. "Anything useful on the clothes?"

"A whole store full of DNA," he grinned. "Most of it was the girls, but there was plenty that belonged to Joshua Mosley."

My head snapped up in time to see a wide grin cross his ugly face. "How do you know that? You said there wasn't anything on the coat," I stuttered.

"There wasn't, Nimrod, but there was plenty on the handkerchief I found stuffed in your pocket."

He held up the blood-stained handkerchief in a plastic evidence bag. "The blood is a perfect match to the DNA on her clothes."

"We have him!" Jackson yelled. "I'll get a warrant for his arrest and, we can go tell him the good news."

"What about Peterson?"

"Nothing like a double feature. I'll get one for him too."

"On what grounds?" I asked.

"We can tie him to the diary through his prints. The diary and the blood samples tie him to Mosley. We'll simply connect the dots for the judge."

This was the kind of dots I liked.

District Attorney, Birdwell, who had been throwing up road blocks for the past two weeks, was all smiles and more than willing to give us everything we needed. He sent us to Judge Reno with the request. I didn't know what had suddenly come over him, but I wasn't about to look a gift horse in the mouth. Reno listened and signed his name to the arrest warrant.

We entered the community with sirens blasting. Jackson wanted them to know we were here. It worked. Families came out of their houses as the line of cars screeched to a halt in front of Mosley and Peterson's houses. Jackson and Officer Chumley went to Peterson's house. Under strict orders to not cause any trouble, I was allowed to follow Officer Lamb and his partner, towards Mosley's residence.

Mosley met us at the front door with the same cocky smirk on his face. And a baseball bat in his hands.

"You've hassled me for the last time, Crockett." He brushed past the unsuspecting officers, and came at me with the bat. I quickly side stepped him. As the bat slammed into the ground, I brought my elbow down hard between his prone shoulder blades. He hit the ground hard. Straddling his body, I grabbed his hair and raised his head. I slammed it into the ground. His nose busted open like a ripe melon. Before I could smash his face again, Lamb tossed me off of the bleeding man. With his knee in his back, Lamb forced Mosley's left arm back. Painfully, he clamped the cuffs on one hand, then the other.

"You're going to prison for life, you son-of-a-bitch," I snarled as Officer Lamb lifted him to his feet.

"What for?"

"Because I don't like you," I answered.

"You can't arrest me for that."

"Then how about for murder?"

"You can't prove I murdered anyone." He sneered at me, confident in his alibi.

Maybe I couldn't prove he had killed Ruth, but I sure as hell had him on the assault and attempted murder of Jennifer.

"Yes, he can."

The voice startled me. I turned to see the youngest of his wives, tears in her eyes. "I believed you were inspired, but God doesn't instruct His people to kill those obedient to Him; especially someone as kind as Ruth."

"Shut up, Sarah. This is none of your business."

"Ruth was your wife, and you killed her. And we're just as guilty because we have remained silent."

His eyes locked in on her. "Shut up, you whore or you'll go to jail."

"I don't care. I'm so ashamed of what we did."

"What happened to Ruth?" I asked as I stepped between him and Sarah.

"He killed her. Then he forced us to help him bury her in the mountains."

"Can you show me where?"

Her eyes glanced nervously at Mosley and then back at me. "Yes, even if it means I must spend time in jail."

She moved to face him, tears in her eyes.

"Sarah, baby, don't do this," he pleaded. Tell them you're lying. God wants us to be together. I love you so much."

She gently wiped away the tears, transfixed by his words.

My breath caught in my throat. How many times, as a policeman, had I seen this same scenario play out? After a heated fight and a call to the police, the wife suddenly cools down, and, after pleading from the husband, she suddenly changes her mind, and all is love and apple pie again – until the next time. It was standard operating procedure in domestic violence cases.

As she rushed towards him, her face stained with tears, his smile increased. Until she knocked his smug smile right off his face. With more power and force than I would have thought possible, she slapped him so hard his head snapped back. Then whirling around, she stormed towards the waiting police car.

"You fool," Mosley screamed. "I did it for us. She betrayed us. She was going to tear apart this family. I had to silence her!"

"And now you are going to prison for the rest of your life."

"Wait, what if I cut a deal?" He asked frantically.

"What if I spread it around the prison yard that you like it rough?"

"I'm serious," he said.

"So am I," I grinned.

The panic was evident on his face as Officer Lamb pushed him towards the patrol car. Across the street Jackson had Peterson.

"I was just following orders. I didn't want to do it." His bravado was crumbling as the reality of prison settled on him. "He ordered me to do it." He motioned towards Rulon Peterson, who was being placed into the squad car by Jackson.

The hyenas were quickly turning on the lions. I would have good news to share with Jenny. This group of religious pedophiles and murderers were going away for a long time.

Now there was only one thing bothering me about Jenny's beating, but that would have to wait.

FORTY TWO

The arrest of Rulon Peterson caused a major media feeding frenzy. It was so frantic that it knocked Martin Parker right off the front pages.

Rangel held several press conferences praising Detective Jackson and the dedication of the police department under Captain Sokolowski. He even threw my name in there once—or was that the day he ordered me to get him three tacos from the taco truck?

But for some strange reason, one that Jackson and I couldn't figure out, he didn't swoop in and become the focus of the case. He didn't take it over or give it to his butt-kissing detectives. Surprisingly, he let Jackson, and by extension, me, continue working it, tying up all the loose ends.

He even gave Jackson back jurisdiction on the Parker case. Something was wrong in the political wonderland that was the Salt Lake City Police Department, but neither Jackson, nor I, had the time to climb down the rabbit hole to see how things had suddenly been turned right side up.

Jackson was besieged by the press who hounded him for any comments on Peterson and the Eternal and True Church of Christ in the Last Days. The media tried to do profiles on him, the handsome, young detective who brought down a murderous polygamist cult. The story even went national as Fox News, ABC, NBC and CBS sent reporters to Salt Lake to cover it.

Jackson hated every minute of the spotlight, especially having to stand with Commissioner Rangel and listen to the lavish amount of praise heaped upon, 'his brilliant, young detective.' Once the cameras were off, however, Rangel, and the other political operatives, would barely give Jackson, or myself the time of day - not that most of them actually knew the time of day.

As was his custom, Jackson spent a lot of his 'fifteen minutes of fame,' trying to direct the hordes of press to me. Like the excellent tennis player that I will never be, I volleyed everything back to him. I did, however, yield to one interview. It was with a national women's magazine. I told of the friendship of Jenny and Ruth, how both had fought to bring the polygamist cult down. Donations poured in from across the country for Ruth's family and for Jenny's care.

With help from Sara Mosley, the police were able to recover Ruth's body from a shallow grave in the mountains. Two weeks later, her grief stricken parents gave her a beautiful, but simple funeral.

I told Jennifer everything. Everything, that is, except about Ruth's death. I didn't know if she could hear or understand me, but I didn't want to chance it. She had enough to deal with, wherever her mind was.

Sarah Mosley agreed to testify against her husband. When he realized he was going to prison for a long, long time, he begged to make a deal. He rolled over on Peterson

like a monster truck over a smart car. There was no doubt
that both of them would spend the rest of their lives in prison.

FORTY THREE

It was late May before Martin Parker finally went to trial. The circus started all over again. With all the circumstantial evidence, combined with Collingsworth's testimony, I was confident of a conviction.

The day of the trial, as I was walking down one of the long hallways leading to the courtroom, the door to the witness room opened and Abigail Collingsworth stepped out. She was getting a drink of water from the fountain when she noticed me. Wiping her mouth, she smiled and waited for me to catch up.

She looked nervous.

"Are you all right?" I asked.

"I'm scared to death. What if they don't believe me?"

"They will."

"I hope so."

An awkward moment ensued as the conversation simply died.

With nothing left to say, I gave her an encouraging smile and moved towards the courtroom.

"David?"

I turned back to her.

"Thank you." Her eyes begin to mist up. "I really believe he would have killed me if you hadn't helped me."

With nothing to say, I nodded and walked away.

The courtroom was packed with media whores and spectators. As far as I was concerned most of the media, who had been hounding me for weeks for any juicy tidbits on the case, were like cockroaches, nothing useful about them; simply a blight on humanity, their purpose long forgotten.

Martin Parker leaned over and spoke softly to his attorney. Dressed in his finest suit, he looked hopeful, if not confident. I had no doubt he believed he could beat the wrap. I hoped his arrogance would be his downfall.

I was sitting two rows behind and one row over from the defense table. I had a clear view of Parker. His confidence irritated me. I wanted to yank him out of his chair and slap him across his well-groomed face.

Faith entered. Ignoring the press, she made her way to me. Her smiled seemed confident, but I sensed the vulnerability hiding behind it.

As she slid in beside me, Parker turned. He gave her a self-righteous smirk, then went back to talking as if nothing was wrong. She grabbed my hand and locked onto it. I tried to reassure her, but today my charm had little effect.

"What if he beats this?" she whispered.

"He won't."

What if we don't have enough evidence?"

"We do."

"What if he charms the jury and they believe his story?"

"He won't."

"What—"

"Faith," I cut her off. "Relax. It's going to be all right. The prosecutor has done his homework. This is a solid case."

I wished I believed it myself.

While Prosecutor Percy Wright had compiled a strong case against Parker, it was still nothing more than circumstantial evidence. A really competent defense attorney, with a flair for hyperbole, could argue it away. Steven Bains Daniels was one of the best. With his round face, green eyes hidden behind gold rimmed spectacles, shock of dark hair with ample streaks of silver blended in and a reassuring smile that could lull you into a false sense of confidence, he looked like the absent-minded professor instead of a tenacious ambulance chaser. It was an advantage he often used to the regret of those taken in by his boyish charm.

He had once defended an unlikable, spoiled rich kid, who, in a drunken stupor, had run down an innocent family standing by their car while the father was changing a flat tire. To the shock of all, he was found innocent by reason of 'traumatic wealth syndrome.' Daniels successfully argued that it wasn't the kid who had caused the problem, but the fact that he had grown up spoiled and rich; he had not been properly taught the difference between right and wrong. By the time Daniels had finished turning this kid's wealth into the Darth Vader of lifestyles, the jury bought it, hook, line and sinker. Instead of being guilty of murder in the death of four innocent people, the kid was found guilty of involuntary manslaughter and given five years' probation.

And now Steven Bains Daniels sat reassuring Martin Parker.

The bailiff stood ram rod straight. "All rise. The court of Salt Lake City, District 3 is now in session. Judge Michael Clark Neilson presiding."

We all stood as Judge Neilson entered the courtroom and took his place on the bench.

"You may be seated," Neilson instructed.

I felt some sense of comfort since I knew Neilson to be a no-nonsense judge not easily swayed by hyperbole from flashy attorneys. He was in his sixties, with a shock of fluffy white hair, penetrating eyes, and forty years of experience etched in his round face.

Lowering his silver glasses onto his nose, he eyed the courtroom, then nodded to the prosecutor. "The prosecution may make its opening remarks."

Wright stood and moved towards the jury box. Wright was tall and debonair. He looked like a prosecutor should. Smiling his flashy smile at the jury, he looked them in the eye as if they were the best of friends.

"Nothing like jury duty, huh?"

This brought laughter from the box and a quick pounding of the gavel from Neilson. The laughter quickly died and Wright continued.

"I say that because it is an important civic duty each of us are asked to perform. You have the responsibility to right wrongs and to help dispense justice for those who can't do it for themselves. Think about that for a moment. When someone's life, like Sylvia Parker, is diabolically taken, that person has no say in justice. Her voice is silent in this courtroom." He paused to let his words sink in. "But not totally, because you, ladies and gentlemen of the jury have her back. You are her voice in this courtroom. You, and you alone, can make sure that there is justice for Sylvia Parker. We will prove beyond a shadow of a doubt that Martin Parker murdered his wife because he didn't want to be cut off from her money, after she divorced him. He methodically planned and executed her murder with such precision that it boggles the mind. His disdain for the law was such that he believed that he was too smart to get caught. And even if he did, he believed that he could beat the rap because a 'jury of his peers' were not, according to him, actually his peers. Martin Parker is a cold blooded killer. I know that after all the evidence is presented, you will find him guilty of murder, that you will be the voice of justice for Sylvia Parker."

With a confident smile, he strode back to his chair.

Daniels stood. Like everyone's kindly uncle he smiled and strolled to the jury box. Leaning against the railing he nodded at the twelve people sitting there. He grinned. "Justice for Sylvia Parker is why we are here. Believe me no one wants that more than I do."

He paused as he looked at each juror. "But justice isn't justice if you convict the wrong person. Martin Parker loved his wife. They had an unbreakable bond. Thirty-two years of marriage. The prosecution is going to put on a brilliant dog-and-pony-show, with flashing lights and toe tapping music, to divert you from the truth. And the truth is, Martin Parker did not kill his wife. I know it, the prosecution knows it, and, by the end of this trial, you will know it. We will prove that not one shred of concrete evidence ties my client to his wife's death. All I ask is that you keep an open mind and listen to the evidence and not to the circus meant to distract you. Thank you."

Daniels strode back to his seat and sat down.

Judge Neilson glanced down at the prosecutor. "Mr. Wright you may call your first witness."

Wright stood and glanced down at his notes. "The prosecution calls Richard West to the stand."

One of the guards opened the courtroom door and called for the witness.

After being sworn in, West sat down. He looked nervous as he turned towards the jury, then back at Wright standing before him.

"Mr. West, according to your sworn affidavit, you found the body of Sylvia Parker on her bed on the morning in question, after being contacted by her husband, is that correct?"

"Yes sir."

"What was the first thing you noticed when you entered the bedroom?"

"How cold it was. It felt like a meat lockers."

"And why was that?"

"Because the air conditioner was on full blast."

"According to the weather report for that weekend, a cold front had moved in. Temperatures were in the low forties. Are you certain that the air conditioner was on?"

"I'm positive, because I turned it off right before I went downstairs to call the police."

"Why would Sylvia Parker have the air conditioner on when it was so cold outside?"

Daniels jumped to his feet. "Objection. Calls for speculation. The witness has no way of knowing why, or what, Mrs. Parker would do."

"Sustained."

Wright looked at the jury, then turned back to West.

"Mr. West, was your air conditioner on that morning?"

"No, of course not."

"Why not?"

"Because it was cold outside. No one would have had their air conditioner on that morning."

"No one that wasn't already dead," Wright said.

Seeing Daniels leap to his feet, Wright turned. "No more questions." He walked back to his table and sat down.

Daniels stared at his notes, then strolled to the center of the room. He held up the police report of the incident.

"Exhibit one, your honor," he said showing the report to Neilson. Once Neilson had returned the report, he moved to the witness box in front of West.

"Mr. West, there is no mention of the air conditioner being on in this police report. Can you explain that?"

"I didn't tell them about it."

"Why was that?

"I forgot."

"You forgot." Daniels smiled. "How convenient."

"Objection," Wright protested. "There's no need to badger the witness."

Neilson paused then sustained the objection.

"The room felt like a meat locker, as you stated, and you didn't tell the police?"

"Once I got downstairs, I forgot about it. I guess it didn't seem important."

"Or it never happened," Daniel said directly to the jury. "It wasn't in the official police report. It wasn't in the coroner's report. No one, anywhere, made any mention of it. It's like it never happened, which is the case. No more questions." Daniels turned and ambled back to his chair.

I stared at the jury, trying to get a fix on their reactions but no one revealed anything.

Wright called Chelsea Wingate.

She looked like the perfect school girl as she took the stand. I listened as she related her story concerning the phone call Parker had made to his wife that day. The jury hung on her every word, some even leaning towards her as they listened, glancing back and forth between her and Parker. She made a terrific witness. I could see her immediate impact on the jury.

As Daniels approached her, I felt a chill run through my body. If she could just hold her own against him we might have a chance. The jury liked and wanted to believe her.

"Miss Wingate, why were you listening to Mr. Parker's phone conversation?"

"I wasn't at first. I was just trying to call my boyfriend."

"But you didn't get the chance, did you?"

"No."

"And why not?"

"Because Mr. Parker was on the line."

"Did that make you mad?"

"Sort of."

"You had waited all afternoon to talk to your boyfriend, and when the time came, someone else was hogging the phone. I don't know about you, but when my daughters were teenagers, if I was hogging our only phone, and they couldn't talk to their boyfriends at the time, they would become furious."

"I'm not your daughter."

This brought a ripple of laughter from the spectators. Neilson pounded his gavel. Levity was not something he permitted in his courtroom. Still, score one for Chelsea.

Daniels waited until quiet had been restored, then moved over to the jury box. "Still, as you just admitted, you were angry. And isn't the real reason you concocted this specious lie is because you were mad at Mr. Parker?"

"I'm not lying. I would never do that."

"Isn't it true that when you were fifteen, you told your parents that you were studying at a friend's house when in reality you had gone to a party where you met a boy you thought you were in love with?"

Wright leaped to his feet. "Objection. Relevance, your honor?"

"It establishes a pattern of lies, your honor."

"I'll allow it, but tread lightly, Mr. Daniels. The witness will answer the question."

"So, Miss Wingate, did you not lie to your parents?"

"Yes, but I was fifteen."

"Obviously the lies didn't stop at fifteen." Seeing Wright jump to his feet, Daniels whirled about. "No more questions for this witness," he said softly with a grandfatherly smile.

Wright stood. "Redirect, your honor?"

Neilson nodded.

"Chelsea, why are you testifying today?"

"Because I was told I had to tell the truth."

"And have you told the truth?"

"Yes, sir."

"I think you have to. No more questions."

Chelsea had held her own even though Daniels had tried to make her out to be a habitual liar.

Faith moved closer, eyes heavy with concern. "How can he twist everything around like that?"

"That's what defense attorneys do."

As she glanced towards Daniels, her eyes locked with her father. He smiled at her as if everything was normal. She immediately lowered her eyes, unable to meet his gaze. Even though she believed he was guilty, it was still hard to realize that she was trying to convict her father of murder.

"The prosecution calls Justin Boudreau to the stand." Wright's voice snapped us out of our reverie.

We watched as Boudreau took the stand. His testimony, concerning the pills I had found, and the way the time of death had been altered by the cold from the air conditioner, was crucial. It was his testimony, along with the collaborating testimony of Abigail Collingsworth, that could break Parker's previously air tight alibi.

"Mr. Boudreau, what is your occupation?"

"I am the chief Medical Examiner for the State of Utah and the City of Salt Lake."

"And as such, did you perform the autopsy on Sylvia Parker?"

"I did."

"And were your original findings correct?"

"No."

"Why not?"

"My initial finding set the time of death sometime Saturday night."

"And now?"

"With the new information, concerning the air conditioner, I believe it's now possible that she could have been killed as early as Friday night.

"Could you explain this to the court?

"After death, the body goes stiff for the first twelve to

twenty-four hours as rigor mortis sets in. When I first looked at Mrs. Parker's body, it was in the early stages of rigor mortis. That led me to conclude that she had been killed somewhere within the prior twelve hours, which would put the death at early Saturday night."

"How would learning that the air conditioner was on full blast change that?"

"Because an air conditioner on high slows down the progress of rigor mortis and the decomposition of the body, making it appear more recent than it actually was."

"So, again, you are saying that Sylvia Parker could have been killed as early as Friday night?"

"Yes."

"Which would give the defendant ample time to kill her and get to Lake Powell to help cement his alibi."

"Objection! Counselor is testifying, your honor."

"No more questions." Wright made eye contact with the jury and smiled as he took his chair.

Daniels moved in like a lion on an injured gazelle.

"Mr. Boudreau, you are considered one of the finest pathologists in the country, are you not?"

"Damn straight."

This brought a burst of laughter from the spectators, which Neilson quickly quelled.

"You expect us to believe that someone with your renown reputation could make such a rookie mistake?"

"It's not a mistake when you don't have all the information. "

"About that so-called *new* information." He spit out the word new like it was a rotten piece of pork. "There is no mention in the police report of the air conditioner being on and there is no mention of it in your report."

Daniels ambled towards the jury box, looking kind and trustworthy. "I've never been one to believe in magic, but this sudden *magical* appearance of new information is pretty amazing, wouldn't you say?"

Boudreau frowned. He hated lawyers more than most people.

"It only affirmed my original suspicion," he said tightly as he glared at Daniels. "Because the bedroom was so much colder than the rest of the house, I thought the air conditioner must have been on."

"Why didn't you include this 'suspicion' in your original findings?"

"Because it was just speculation at that point. I can 't make medical decisions on speculation."

"Isn't that what you're doing now. Speculating in order to convict my client of something he didn't do?"

"Objections," Wright yelled. "Counselor is testifying."

"Sustained. Stick to the facts, Counselor" Neilson said. Daniels paused, then moved closer to Boudreau. "The fact is, that your original findings concluded that she died sometimes Saturday night. Can you say with absolute certainty that is no longer the case?"

Boudreau stared at him, then quietly answered. "No."

"No more questions."

The trial was in its third day before the witness everyone had been waiting for took the stand. Abigail Collingsworth walked through the crowed courtroom like she was taking a stroll through a jewelry story. Her head high, her oval face highlighted, with just a touch of make-up, light green eye shadow setting off her sparkling greenish brown eyes. She wore a conservative pale blue skirt with a soft yellow cotton blouse, topped off by a matching blue coat.

As she walked to the stand, all eyes moved with her, especially the men. Even Judge Neilson couldn't help but glance at the extremely attractive Ms. Collingsworth before forcing his eyes back onto the bench. She had that kind of effect. I was hoping the men in the jury would pay more to her testimony than her legs. Wright rose and approached the stand. "Good morning, Ms. Collingsworth. Thank you for being here."

She smiled and nodded.

"Ms. Collingsworth, do you remember telling Mr. Crockett that you were afraid that Martin Parker was trying to kill you?"

"Yes."

Wright allowed a smile of relief to cross his face.

"But I lied when I said it," she quickly added.

Wright stepped back, his face contorted in shock.

The courtroom broke out into pandemonium. This was the prosecutor's star witness who had just confessed to lying. iPhones came out and reporters began texting the news.

Shocked doesn't even come close to what I felt at that moment. I turned towards Faith as if I had just crossed over into the Twilight Zone. Collingsworth had told me that she was afraid for her life, and that she thought Martin Parker was trying to kill her.

"You asked for protective custody. Do you remember that?"

"Yes, but I was afraid at the time."

"Of Martin Parker," Wright said reminding her of her original statement.

"No." She slowly raised her eyes and turned her head in my direction. "I was afraid of Mr. Crockett."

Wright looked around, not sure how to proceed. Collingsworth continued as if nothing unusual was happening.

"He burst into my office and threatened me. You can ask my receptionist. She was so taken aback by his violent behavior that she had to take the rest of the day off.

"That's a lie." I found myself standing in protest.

Neilson pounded his gavel trying to restore order.

"Sit down, Mr. Crockett, before I have you removed."

I sat.

Wright turned to Neilson. "Permission to treat this witness as a hostile witness, your honor."

"So ordered."

"Ms. Collingsworth you told the police that you were afraid of Martin Parker. Was that also a lie?"

"Yes. I wanted protection from Mr. Crockett who seemed determined to make me say whatever he wanted me to say."

I started to jump up but stopped myself. This has suddenly turned to a hunting expedition and I was the one in the cross-hairs.

"You are aware that you can be prosecuted for filing a false police report?"

"Yes. But at least I'm not dead."

"Objection!" Wright yelled. "Your honor, the witness has no proof that Mr. Crockett wanted to harm her in any way.

"Sustained. Ms. Collingsworth please stick to what you know to be facts, not speculation."

Wright rushed to his desk and retrieved an affidavit. Moving quickly he handed it to her. "Ms. Collingsworth, this is an affidavit in which you state that Martin Parker told you that he had killed his wife?"

"I was only telling them what they wanted to hear."

"You signed it, saying that he told you he had killed his wife."

"No." She stared at Wright then a slight smile creased her delicate features. "All I told the police was that his wife had been murdered. That's what he told me."

Her eyes never left Wright. "If you look at it closely, I didn't say by whom, just that he told me his wife had been murdered."

"Ms. Collingsworth you inferred that Martin Parker

had killed his wife and was trying to kill you. I have two witnesses who will testify to that."

"I can't help what your witnesses inferred from my statements. All I can tell you is what Martin Parker told me. He said that she murdered herself because she was so depressed."

She paused, turning to the jury, her head high, her eyes pleading for understanding through the film of moisture covering them. I wanted to give her an Academy Award on the spot. "He called it 'murder by suicide.' I remember because it struck me as an odd thing to say."

"Your honor," Wright countered. "She signed a sworn affidavits saying that Martin Parker murdered his wife. Nowhere in the document is any mention made of depression or this preposterous murder by suicide theory."

Collingsworth shook her head as if fending off invisible tears. Shifting in the chair, she removed a tissue from her purse and wiped her eyes. "I'm so sorry for all of this, your honor, but I was afraid for my life." She shifted to face the jury box. "I know what I did was wrong, but who wouldn't do the same thing in my position."

An impatient Neilson glared at Wright. "Counselor, can your witness verify the things you have said or not?"

"Your honor, I need time to discuss this with my witness."

Before Neilson could answer, Daniels jumped to his feet.

"Your honor, due to this turn of events, I believe you have no choice but to declare a mistrial."

"Objection." Wright responded vigorously.

If the judge declared a mistrial it was over. Everything we had worked so hard for over the past six months would be flushed down the drain. Like everyone else in the courtroom, I held my breath as Neilson pondered the possibility. Glancing at his watch, he finally turned back to the two eagerly awaiting lawyers.

"I'll take that under advisement. It's 11:36. Let's break for lunch. This court will reconvene at 1:30."

With a slam of his gavel, court was dismissed.

Forty Four

I slumped back into the booth. Even my cheese burger couldn't relieve the anxiety I felt all the way down into the depths of my soul.

I looked up as Wright slid into the booth next to Faith.

"I hope you have good news."

He shook his head. That wasn't good. Percy was one of the most upbeat and positive persons you'd ever want to know. If he was down in the dumps, we were screwed.

"If Neilson declares a mistrial, it's over."

"What do you mean over?"

"I talked to District Attorney Birdwell. He said if this ends in a mistrial, he is not going to re-file the charges."

"He's going to let him walk on a murder rap?"

"He said he wasn't about to waste any more of the tax payers money on a trial that shouldn't have gone forward in the first place."

"He's the one who brought the charges."

"And he's the one who doesn't think our case is strong enough anymore, especially with Collingsworth claiming that her testimony was all a lie."

"He could bring charges against her to force her to tell the truth, couldn't he?" Faith said, pleading in her voice.

"I'm afraid not."

"Why?" she asked.

"Because he said it would be a waste of time and money."

I didn't say it, but I had a pretty good suspicion that Birdwell may have had in his possession a manila envelope with some very clear, and damaging, photos.

Martin Parker and Abigail Collingsworth had played us, and they had played us well. Her whole desire to testify wasn't to put Parker in prison because she was afraid of him, but to cause a mistrial and free him. They had been three steps ahead of us the whole time. Parker had made no bones about being smarter than us all. As much as it pained me, I had to admit he was right.

"So, Martin Parker is going to get away with murder," I sighed.

Wright stood his face tight, his eyes tired. "It looks that way."

"Maybe Neilson won't declare a mistrial," Katie said hopefully.

"And maybe I'll win the Publishers Clearing House Sweepstakes and be set for life. But don't count on it," Wright sighed.

"But there is a chance, isn't there?" Faith pleaded.

Wright shook his head. "Three times Judge Neilson has been faced with the possibilities of declaring a mistrial. All three times he's pulled the trigger. If the evidence isn't rock solid to get a conviction, and if he believes that to continue would be a waste of taxpayer's money, he's always shut it down."

Wright turned to Faith, his face like a depressed ostrich.

"So yes, there is always a chance, just don't bet your money on it."

He left the three of us sitting in our misery. I guess misery doesn't really love company.

I had underestimated Martin Parker. He had always been so sure of himself that I had just assumed that he would slip up. But he hadn't, and now he was about to get away with murder, and with all his wife's money.

I needed a strong drink.

"Maybe we missed something," Faith suggested.

Maybe, but for the life of me, I didn't know what.

I took out the thick file and laid it on the table between us. I knew every picture, every article and every piece of evidence in it, but still I opened it up and spread everything out on the table. I had seen it all a hundred times. There wasn't anything else to find.

"Come on, David, you're missing something," Katie said. "What? I've been through every bit of information twice."

"Then go through it again."

"Hey, I don't tell you how to cook, do I?" I snapped.

"Yes, almost every time you come in here," she replied with equal vigor. She got up, stopped, then picked up the photo Faith had laid on top of the stack.

"That must be one expensive house," Katie said shaking her head.

"What do you mean?" Faith asked

"To have two security companies, that must be one expensive house."

"We don't have two security companies," Faith replied.

Katie reached down and picked up the photo of the Vivint receipt and the photo of the front of the house with the Allied Security sign clearly visible.

"Allied and Vivint," she said.

Something stirred in the back of my mind. I looked

at the picture Katie dropped on the table. "You have an Allied Security sign in your yard," I said to Faith.

"Yes, that's our home security company."

"Allied Security?" I repeated for clarification.

Faith looked at me like I had lost my mind. "What's the matter?"

"I need to get back into the house."

"Why?"

Faith followed me out of Katie Blues almost running to keep up.

I drove like a man possessed. "Look up the address for Vivint Security, the Sandy office."

I grabbed my cell phone. "But first, call Jackson."

With a dumbfounded look on her face, she took my phone, found Jackson Paine's number, and dialed. She handed the phone back to me, before returning to her task.

"Jackson. I need you to meet me at Martin Parker's house."

I gave him the address. He asked if he needed to get a warrant.

"No. I have Faith with me. She has a key so it's all legal. I think I can prove exactly what happened that night. See you there."

I handed my phone back to her.

"Do you still want Vivint's address and number?"

"Dial it," I commanded.

FORTY FIVE

Judge Neilson entered the courtroom, his robes fluttering like a giant black phoenix. He took his seat and waited until the courtroom was also seated. His demeanor was solemn. If I was a betting man, I would bet he was about to declare a mistrial. With the District Attorney refusing to retry the case, and, with the jury tainted by the testimony of Collingsworth, it was really his only option.

I glanced at the twelve men and women occupying the jury box. They sat in as much anticipation as the rest of us.

Before Neilson could speak, Wright jumped to his feet."

"Your Honor, before you make your decision, there is some new evidence to present."

Daniels also leaped to his feet. "Objection! I'm not aware of any new evidence."

Wright ignored Daniels. "It just came to light, your honor, and it will have a great bearing on this trial."

"I was under the impression all evidence had been

presented, Counselor. I believe it is too late for anything new."

"You are going to want to see this, your honor," Wright persisted.

Neilson stared down at Wright. "Why should I interrupt this proceeding to look at any new evidence?"

Wright's eyebrows shot up and he sighed. "Because you will be able to see firsthand your honor, the truth, the whole truth and nothing but the truth concerning this case. I'd say that's worth interrupting these proceedings for."

"With all due respect counselor, every attorney thinks they have all the truth. I can't delay the inevitable for perceived truth."

"I understand, your honor, but I also know that if you fail to take a look at this evidence and declare a mistrial, your decision could be overturned on appeal."

Neilson glanced around the courtroom, then glared down at the two attorneys, angry at the position he was in.

"Court is in recess for thirty minutes," he barked gruffly.

With a pound of his gavel, he stormed away.

Ten minutes later, after some powerful discussion, Judge Neilson reluctantly allowed me to set up the video equipment I had brought, and sit in on the viewing. Once the lights had been dimmed, Wright, Daniels, Neilson, Parker and I began watching the death of Sylvia Parker play out on the small screen.

After years of being told her husband was cheating on her, Sylvia had decided to find out. Using Vivint Security, she had a small security camera installed behind the large oil painting of her family. Her father's red tie was the lens. While she never caught her husband cheating, she did capture her own murder.

Neilson stared at the flickering images in utter disbelief. He glanced at Martin Parker, who was sitting ashen faced beside Daniels.

"I said I don't need anything else," Sylvia Parker said as she readjusted her reading glasses and picked up the magazine.

"I am afraid you have no choice in the matter, my dear."

We watched as Parker grabbed his wife by the hair and forced the pills down her throat.

Neilson stared intently as Parker slapped her hard with his gloved hand, snapping her head to the side, forcing wine and small bits of crushed sleeping pills out of her mouth. We all winced.

I turned to Parker. His composure crumbled, his face went pale. and he looked queasy as he watched himself set the wine glass down and hold his wife's nose, forcing her to swallow the pills.

"Relax, Sylvia, it will soon be over," his screen voice said.

We watched as she glanced franticly into the camera.

"Your old man can not help you now." Parker laughed." But look on the positive side. You will be back together soon."

"You won't get away with this."

"On the contrary my dear, I have every intention of getting away with this. When they find your body, I will be miles away."

Neilson got up and turned on the lights.

"I've seen enough."

"Your honor, you can't show this to the jury." Daniels pleaded. "It would be highly inflammatory and prejudicial."

"You think?" I said before I could stop myself.

Neilson glanced my direction. I thought I saw his stern face crack into a slight smile at the corners of his mouth.

Maybe not.

"If you're thinking it would get your client the death penalty, you're right." He sat back down, leaned back in his chair and closed his eyes. We all waited.

After a few minutes he opened his eyes and leaned

forward.

"While there is no doubt this evidence is highly prejudicial, it has a direct bearing on the case. The jury has every right to see it."

He turned to Wright. "I will allow this to be shown but only to the jury. The rest of the courtroom will be cleared."

"Thank you your honor."

"Now let's get back to court."

As Neilson stood, I noticed Parker franticly whispering to Daniels. As we left the judges chambers their frantic conversation continued unabated.

FORTY SIX

The jury never got to see the video. Parker pleaded guilty. He was sentenced to life in prison without the possibility of parole.

Two days after the trial, I found a plain envelope slid under my office door. There was no post mark or return address. Inside were nine explicit 8x10 black and white photos of Police commissioner Chase Rangel, District Attorney Birdwell, among others, in very compromising positions with beautiful young women, none of whom were their wives.

A note pasted together from clipped magazine read: *Decided I needed fresh air and nightly "exercise" after all. Politics shouldn't get in the way anymore of the excellent work you or your police friend do. Jillian Michaels*

Since Jillian Michaels was a well-known female fitness instructor, and looked nothing like "Beatle Brow," I had to laugh.

Clever.

Now I understood why Rangel had kept his nose out of the Peterson case and had given the Parker case back to Jackson. It also cleared up the sudden, and baffling retirements of Rangel and District Attorney Birdwell.

Exercise was indeed good for the body.

***

The next day Jackson and I were waiting when Connie came out of the school.

When she saw us she tried to smile. It died on her face.

Since the day Ruth had told me what had happen the night Jennifer had been beaten, one thing had weighed heavily on my mind. How had Mosley known that Jennifer and Ruth were planning to leave that particular night?

"How did you know?"

"I didn't until I found Joshua Mosley's high school year book on line. And even then I wasn't sure, because the girl on his arm who wrote, 'forever and ever' under her picture was Madeline Connie Albright, not Connie Wilkerson."

She rubbed her arms and looked past me, somewhere in the distance.

"But it wasn't 'forever and ever' was it, Connie?"

"It could have been if it hadn't been for her."

"Two years later he dumped you for Ruth Carson. You and Mosley were both teaching at Cottonwood Heights. You thought he was still in love with you and were furious when you found out he had replaced you with someone else."

"I should have been his wife, not her," she said hotly. "She didn't know him like I did. She didn't believe in him like I did."

"And so you started planning to get even with her. As fate would have it, a year later you became friends with Jennifer Justice. You both were substitute teachers at East High School at the time. Imagine your surprise when you both started subbing at Daniel John Clinton Elementary and found Ruth teaching there. So you bid your time. Then one day you over heard Ruth plotting to leave Joshua. That was the chance you had been waiting for."

She started to deny it but instead the dam of frustration broke sending a roaring soliloquy of anger our direction.

"She didn't deserve him, I did! I thought he would be grateful and come back to me, but he didn't. Do you know what he did? He said 'thanks, see you later,' like I had just given him the directions to McDonalds. He was mine! He promised me forever and ever."

She pinched her lower lip then burst into loud, racking sobs.

For Jennifer?

Her failed attempt at love?

Or the fact that she was going to prison?

***

Rulon Peterson was convicted of conspiracy to commit murder, theft, assault, child endangerment and child rape for arranging marriages for under aged girls in his cult. He was sentenced to twenty five years to life.

Joshua Mosley pleaded guilty to anything and everything, co-operating like a twelve year old boy scout, in a desperate attempt to avoid the death penalty for killing Ruth and beating Jennifer. He received life in prison without parole. As far as I was concerned, it still wasn't punishment enough.

Connie Wilkerson pleaded no contest to actions leading to the death of Ruth and was sentenced to five years in prison.

Abigail Collingsworth was shocked when the Assistant District Attorney charged her with perjury. Betting on her ability to sway men, she demanded a trial. Her jury ended up being mostly women. She lost and was sentenced to two years in jail. The ironic thing is, had she pleaded guilty to lying under oath, she would have received no more than a year, most likely with time already served.

Even so, she will still look good in prison orange.

Once Sylvia's original will had been recovered, and adjudicated, Faith received what was left of her mother's inheritance. With the large infusion of cash, she moved her offices into a ritzy business complex down town. With a new movie studio being built in Park City, she had more clients than ever.

We went out to celebrate, but somehow the magic was over. Maybe I was nothing more than a hired gun. I suppose I should have been hurt, but I wasn't. I got a hefty pay check, and all the publicity I could want.

I also received, as she had said I would, a check from Melanie Skoff for fifty thousand dollars. Her note simply said 'thank you.' I sent the money back with my own note.

Two days later I received an invitation to lunch at the country club and another note which read: Just like my late husband would have done. I'll still be watching.

As Shakespeare once wrote, "all is well that ends well."

Only it wasn't.

Ruth was dead.

Jennifer was still in a coma.

And I still had to spend Sunday nights at dinner with my mother, my sisters and the matronly lady behind door number three.

The End

David Sterago spent ten years in Hollywood as an actor before deciding he would much rather be behind the scenes. Having always been interested in writing. "Murder by Suicide" is his first novel. Mr. Sterago grew up in Texas, but now calls the mountains of Utah home.